PRAISE FOR SEELEY JAMES

Jacob and his sidekick god, Mercury are two of the best characters ever created

—Secret World Book Club

It wasn't only the story that kept me riveted. It was characters that I loved or detested with a passion.

—DreamBeast, Vine Voice

Plenty of edge of the seat suspense, a splash of well-timed humor, and adventures that leave you wanting more

—Susan Gainoutdinov

An excellent fast-moving action thriller

—Eric Crown, Founder of F500 company, Insight Enterprises

I fell in love with the characters and can't get enough of them. I felt every ounce of rage and desperation.

—CarolAnn Review

SEE THE SEELEY JAMES COLLECTION

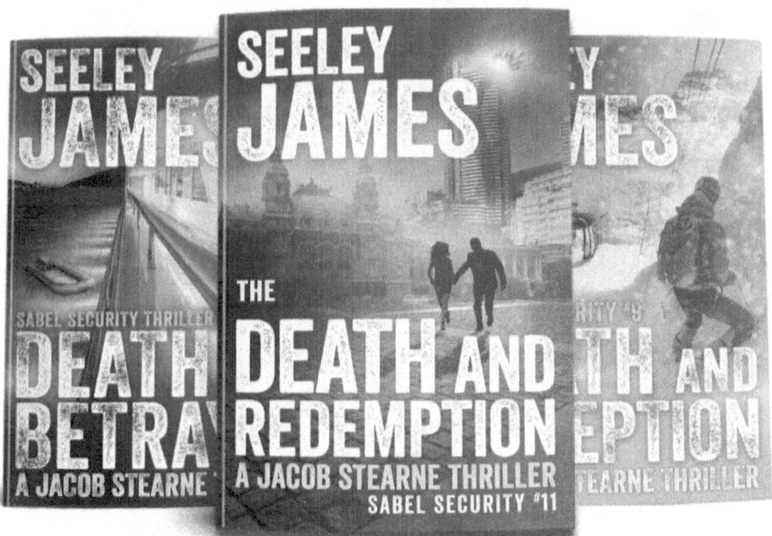

SEELEYJAMES.COM/BOOKS

THE MORPHEUS DECISION

A PIA SABEL MYSTERY

SABEL SECURITY #10

SEELEY JAMES

Published by
Machined Media
12402 N 68th St
Scottsdale, AZ 85254

THE MORPHEUS DECISION: A Pia Sabel Mystery
First Edition, released January 21st, 2021
Print ISBN: 978-1-7333467-8-8
ePub ISBN: 978-1-7333467-7-1
Distribution Print ISBN: 978-1-7333467-9-5
Sabel Security #10 version 2.32

Formatting: BB eBooks
Cover Design: Jeroen ten Berge

For my granddaughter
Sasha

CHAPTER 1

Blood drifted over the curb on its way to the gutter as Chloe England tried to shift her gaze for a better look. Her eyes wouldn't respond. Not even a blink. Her vision was fixed on the chemist's across the narrow lane. Closed. And for a long time judging by the dirty windows.

Her arms and legs wouldn't move either. The blood felt warm on her cheek. Chloe had the strangest feeling it was her blood. After all, she was lying on her side with her face pressed to the cement, but she wasn't sure why. When she tried to think, all that came to mind was TS Eliot from a boring literature class long ago:

> *I have seen the moment of my greatness flicker,*
> *And I have seen the eternal Footman hold my coat, and snicker;*
> *And in short, I was afraid.*

She'd rather have been on the pitch playing football than stuck in a classroom reading that drivel.

Chloe sensed a presence lean down over her. Maybe it was a good Samaritan who could help her up. Her muscles weren't responding. Someone reached over her shoulder and plucked the phone out of her hand. The person disconnected her call.

So, not a good Samaritan.

Chloe felt embarrassed. The stalker just cutoff the voicemail to Pia Sabel before she'd finished. What would Sabel think of the poorly worded message? Rambled on like a fool, she did. To top it off, she'd blanked before telling Sabel what she wanted. Such bad form.

A throbbing pain came from the back of her head. Along with the throb came a dim memory of the previous few seconds. She'd been chattering on about the woman in the hospital and her ridiculous story about people who could kill your enemies through their dreams. For a fee. Had she told Sabel that part? It's what she'd intended to say. Now that she thought about it, she'd prattled on about their rivalry on the soccer pitch. Was that all the further she'd got?

Hardly a rivalry, though. Chloe did her best to defend for England in every game—but who could stop Sabel? Chloe remembered their first encounter. The young phenom was sixteen and out to prove herself in a friendly. Chloe had twenty-five caps by then. She'd considered the teenager a trifle. Young Sabel came straight at her, no fear. Charging in like a freight train. But she was ready. She herded the kid to the sidelines, making the only option to go out of bounds. Sabel played into it, dribbling into a rapidly narrowing lane with nowhere to go. Rookie mistake. Then Sabel popped the ball between them, waist high, smacked it with her knee, sending it over Chloe's head. Using her height advantage, Sabel jumped in the air like a rocket and headed a perfect cross to the American forward flying up the middle. It happened so fast Chloe could only laugh. *What the hell was that?* Thank god the game didn't count for anything.

Sabel was a thorn in her side for the next four years. The Mexicans called her *La Tigresa*—the tigress—for good reason. And the international press adopted the nickname. But in the privacy of England's locker room, especially among the defenders, she was known as *that cunt*. When Chloe retired, she rejoiced that her endless nightmares of Sabel hurtling toward her would finally end.

Now they were both out of the beautiful game. Chloe had bounced around until she found her calling: police constable. Who would've thought? All those years leaving your blood, sweat, and tears on the pitch for your country and what career options await you? Sportscaster? A crowded field. Coach? Underpaid profession. Talent scout? Too many rows with desperate parents—whose children didn't know the difference between a football and a cheese loaf—kept Chloe out of that one. Then Dad suggested she follow him into the Greater Manchester Police, the illustrious GMP. It wasn't the bright lights and big stage she'd hoped for.

It had even caused her some embarrassment when dialing Sabel. *How you doing, old frenemy? Running a huge company these days, I hear. Chilling with presidents and prime ministers, are we? Me? Oh, you know, constable. Still. Working on becoming a DI like Dad, though. So, what's new?*

Yeah. That was a tough call.

She hoped she hadn't botched it. It was important. Sabel's name was on the nutter's list. Even if *La Tigresa* had been hell to defend, she did deserve to know someone had her on a list. It might be nothing, but some of the names on the list were dead. And Chloe hoped Sabel would help her figure it out. Reconnect for some laughs. Maybe.

A warm hand touched Chloe's neck. Not in a kind way. The person who'd taken her phone feeling for a pulse? She tried to check her heartbeat, too. She wasn't feeling it. Or was she? Not strong, anyway. Was she dying?

Once, she'd run to the scene of a man hit by a car. It was obvious to everyone around him that he was a dead man with a few seconds of life left, yet he had no idea. He kept apologizing for being a bother.

That's when Chloe remembered the loud crack. The sound of metal connecting with bone. Big bone. Hollow. Like her skull. Is that where the blood was coming from?

She felt it now. Sliding down the back of her head, into her hair, onto the sidewalk. Someone had smacked her a good one with a baton. They could fix that in casualty, right?

The hand withdrew. Chloe heard someone walk away. The street was empty. Thick dark clouds obscured the remnants of twilight. The heavy sky closed in on her. It would rain soon.

It was her own fault, Chloe realized. She'd been so preoccupied with the call to Sabel—trying not to sound like one of those barking-mad fans—that she hadn't noticed where she was going. It was a mistake. She'd taken the shortcut. A short, dark lane lined with defunct businesses. Now she wouldn't have a chance to save Pia Sabel's life. She wouldn't be the heroic constable who solved the dreamland-assassins mystery.

Worst of all, there would be no security video of who killed Chloe England.

CHAPTER 2

PIA SABEL NOTICED DR. HARRISON had gone silent while she covertly—she thought—read her messages on the phone hidden in her open purse. Swiveling her eyes to Harrison without moving her canted head, she said, "I heard you."

Dr. Harrison waited patiently, as he often did, for her to elaborate.

"But an overwhelming desire to win is what drives all successful people," she said and tossed up her hands. "Ask anyone who's gone after something big. I didn't win the World Cup by going around thinking, 'oh well, whatever.' It's something most people around me just deal with."

When he didn't say anything, she blew out a breath and did what he wanted. "Fine, I'll turn it off for the session."

She clicked her phone and dropped it back in her purse. He still wasn't satisfied. Under his withering glare, she set the bag on the floor. While he continued to scowl, she pushed it out of reach with her foot.

"Thank you," he said. "Pia, you've been seeking a good night's sleep for years. That's what we're trying to do here. We're not going to make progress if you're not going to participate. Fully."

"I get that. Go ahead."

"So, once again, we must go over events from your childhood—"

"We plowed that field."

"Those are issues we need to address. They have a bearing on why you're so driven." He sighed. "We will come back to that when you're ready. Like always."

While he scribbled a note on his pad, he absently asked, "And you're keeping in shape?"

She didn't answer. Conditioning was automatic, like breathing. She completed an Olympic triathlon every morning before bakers heated their ovens. She could try out for the National Team in the morning and be a starter by lunchtime.

He wordlessly withdrew the question and tapped his pen on the pad. "All right, update me on your sex life."

"Pass."

"Answer enough." He jotted a short note this time. "Pia, these things are interrelated. Your obsession with winning, your traumatic childhood, your romantic relationships, all drive a debilitating form of paranoia—"

"Only the paranoid survive."

"Yes." Dr. Harrison steepled his fingers. "You quote Andrew Grove a lot. Young women like you needn't spend time reading the corporate philosophies of Intel's long-dead CEO."

This was where Dr. Harrison remained disconnected from Pia's reality. She'd tried to explain it before but, like so many others, he lived in the safe world. A world where a few locks on the door gave people worry-free lives. For people with Pia's wealth, paranoia was hardly abstract. When you have something, there is always someone who wants it. When you have a lot of something, there are a lot of people who want it—and will stop at nothing to take it. Where Roman emperors had the Praetorian Guard, today's wealthy use bodyguards. The same reason ancient kings had food tasters. Not that it helped. Emperor Claudius was poisoned by Halotus, his food taster. The wealthier you are, the more sensible paranoia becomes. Do the people around you care about you or your money? When you date a guy, what is he really after? People always assume massive quantities of material goods will free them from worrying. It doesn't. While she didn't worry about the cost of calling a plumber, she worried about other things. Lots of other things.

"Pia, a woman of your youth and vitality should be out having fun, romance, adventure, not reading dry treatises—"

"What do you expect me to do when I wake up at three in the morning?"

"That's what we're working on," he said, letting his exasperation heat his words. He inhaled sharply, recovering his calm. "Do you want to dial it back just enough to get a good night's sleep?"

"Yes." She felt her molars grinding.

"Then let's discuss the things that are driving your problem."

They stared at each other while the old-fashioned pocket watch he kept on his desk ticked. Pia wondered how many times he'd delivered the same prognosis and how many times she'd ignored his recommendations. And how many times she'd come back out of desperation. How many times had she heard, *Insight doesn't change behavior.* Some days, she felt like Plankton trying to steal the recipe for Krabby Patties from Mr. Krabs.

Or Sisyphus.

"OK, fine." She rolled her hand.

"As I was saying, your overwhelming desire to win is driven by your need for endorphins. Your need to stand before a stadium filled with screaming fans grew out of your mother's tragic death—"

"Murder."

"—and your subsequent lack of her affection. At an early developmental age, you replaced your mother's love with mass adoration. Since leaving the game, you've replaced those fanatic followers with the adrenaline rush of surviving deadly confrontations. As an example, you are the sole owner of a conglomerate with many divisions: Sabel Capital, Sabel Technologies, Satellites, Weapons—and yet you spend all your time with the most dangerous division, Sabel Security. Your headlong pursuit of this unhealthy desire ratchets your paranoid social cognition into the realm of full-blown—"

"Remind me," Pia said. "Social cognition?"

"Paranoid social cognition is the everyday concern people have that others are trying to undermine them. Whispering behind your back, for example, or suspecting someone of damaging your career, or believing people are spreading rumors. These mild forms can be exacerbated by your perceived social distinctiveness, perceived evaluative scrutiny, or uncertain social standing. When this—"

"I don't worry about those things."

"You told me you do."

"What? When?"

"Social distinctiveness takes many forms. For some it's gender, ethnicity, or age. Your height and fitness make you stand out in ways you'd rather not. Several times you've told me some men are intimidated by your—"

"Fuck 'em."

His eyes closed deliberately and reopened quickly.

"Moving on," Dr. Harrison said. "Evaluative scrutiny for most people is when an asymmetrical relationship, such as teacher and student, becomes pressurized before a big test. In your case, it used to be when coaches critiqued post-game videos of your performance. Today, that would be the company's performance compared to how well it did before your father's untimely—"

"Murder. I get it. Go on."

"Patience, Pia." He paused to make his point. "That leaves uncertain social standing. Everyone, especially those most successful in their field, feel uncertain about their social standing. Even Maya Angelou suffered from imposter syndrome. You let certain people's assessments, whether warranted or not, affect—"

"Wrap it up, Doc. They need me in a meeting at nine."

Dr. Harrison closed his eyes and breathed in slowly. She sensed he was counting to ten.

Finally, he said, "Some people consider it a virtue, Pia."

"Not the people who have 60,000 employees expecting them to keep the company profitable so they can keep their jobs and get year-end bonuses."

He leaned forward and met her gaze. "Uncertainty about social standing, right there. You're worried people think you lucked into owning the company and that you're not qualified to—"

"They'll get over it. What's the bottom line?"

"You're not dealing with these issues, Pia. You're glossing over them. 'They'll get over it' is a prime example. It is you who needs to get over them and what they think of you."

"Great. How do I do that?"

"These minor things, when not dealt with, grow into true paranoia, the mistaken belief that everyone wants to destroy you. And it is that misguided thinking that keeps you worried all night. It is the source of your insomnia."

They stared at each other for a long time. Pia thought about *Stearne's Law*, the axiom her best friend and longtime bodyguard told her: *Paranoia is the result of acute situational awareness—everyone really is trying to kill you.* His maxim had saved her life several times. She considered telling the good doctor. But then he would argue that a philosophy of that nature led to deepening her crisis, not helping it, so she skipped it and waited for him to finish.

He said, "From the endorphins of winning, you've turned to adrenaline. You keep putting yourself in these dangerous situations because—like an addict—you need it. You ignore your personal problems by trying to solve those of others. That leads you to dangerous situations. You can't save everyone. You must relax. Learn that trusting people will not lead to an early grave. Find pleasure in simple things that don't involve life-and-death decisions. To yourself, you must renounce the need for danger. You must repeat it like a mantra, 'I no longer need to risk my life to save others.'"

That sentiment nearly made her choke. She wondered what he would've been like on the *Titanic*.

"You know where that leaves me? In boring corporate boardrooms. We spend all day buying companies and integrating them. It takes five years to figure out if it's going to work. Can you imagine kicking a ball and waiting five freaking years to see if it went in the net? Who would watch that? And when we're not doing that, we're 'energizing' the employees. Don't get me wrong, I love motivating people, but the Major is better at it than I am. She knows their metrics and can say, 'Great job hitting your goals for return on assets.' I still don't know what *return on assets* means—and they're *my* assets!"

"Yes, yes, Pia," he said. "Take a deep breath. No need to get worked up."

"How about skydiving? I'm working on my 30,000-foot certification. Can I keep up on my skydiving lessons?"

His mouth dropped open before his face formed a perplexed frown. "For now, yes. First, let's focus on the dangers involving firearms. You needn't compete with Bruce Wayne. There's no need for a young lady—

just because she owns a security firm—to carry a semi-automatic pistol in her purse. It practically invites a violent response when a perfectly passive solution would be—"

"Great theory, Doc. When you find yourself surrounded by a militia on an abandoned pier in Mumbai ..." She blew out a breath. "Yeah, I hear you. I shouldn't have been on that pier in Mumbai."

The appointment alarm on the phone—the one she hadn't actually turned off—buzzed in her purse a few feet away. She glanced at the purse. Dr. Harrison glanced at the purse. Their gazes met in the middle.

Pia said, "Thanks. Great session. I'll work on it. Um. Gotta go. See ya."

CHAPTER 3

THE ELEVATOR PINGED AND THE doors folded back. Pia hurried out onto the top floor of Sabel Towers in downtown Bethesda, Maryland. George, her executive assistant, met her and trotted alongside. A thousand people a day wanted to contact her. Most pinned their hopes and dreams on her answer. Buy my company, fund my charity, marry my son, fix my roof. Some blamed her for their problems. You fired my husband, your employee assaulted my wife, your satellite gave me cancer. George filtered those calls and messages.

Instead of dealing with it, she could sell it all. There had been plenty of offers. Take it public or sell off one division at a time. But that would leave the fate of her employees to an uncertain future. Too many would be laid off. They had worked hard and made her a wealthy young woman. So, on her CEO's advice, she'd started an employee investment program that would see the company transform from privately held to employee-owned over time. It was the most exciting announcement they'd made since her father died. The employees were counting on it for their retirement, and by extension, counting on her to make it worthwhile.

Which meant she had to get things done. Now. Like dig through the 121 messages that George sent to her inbox during the session. Something Dr. Harrison failed to appreciate. Perceived social distinctiveness, evaluative scrutiny, and uncertain social standing be damned.

She took a deep breath and did what Dad used to do: charge ahead like a locomotive plowing snow.

As they crossed the executive lobby, George said, "There's a man named Jeff Benton who's been calling every ten minutes for over an hour now."

She gave him a smile and kept walking while waiting for an explanation.

"He won't say what it's about," George said. "Just says it's urgent and he can only discuss it with you. Sounds English. He's insistent."

George didn't often push unknown callers up the list. She said, "Send him over."

George pressed a few buttons on his tablet and walked away. Pia's earbud buzzed. She looked around the lobby, still twenty feet from her office where a desk and chair waited for her. She clicked on and announced herself with a simple, "Sabel here."

"About bloody time. I am Detective Inspector Jeff Benton of the Greater Manchester Police. I've questions for you. When was the last time you spoke to Chloe England?"

She stopped and tried to get a grip on the caller and to place the name he asked about. It rang a bell, but it had been years. "I'm sorry. Do you mean Chloe England, who played for England?"

"Right." It sounded more like *royit*.

She heard no humor in the man's voice. No hesitation either. She liked that he wasn't wasting time with small talk. That saved her time as well.

"No idea," Pia said. "Years ago. What's this about?"

"What was the last thing she said to you?"

That Pia remembered like it was yesterday. It was classic Chloe England. "She said, 'I'm going to kill you, you fucking cunt.'"

Benton was silent a moment before he spluttered, "Why would she say that?"

"She clotheslined me and got red-carded for it. She had to blame somebody." Pia laughed at the memory. She hadn't thought about that incident in a long time. "I talked like a frog for a week."

"She rang you last night, Ms. Sabel. Records show you chatted for more than five minutes. I'm giving you one chance to tell me the truth. What did you talk about last night?"

"I don't care for your tone of voice, Brandon. I said I've not spoken to her in years. What is this about?"

"It's Benton, B-E-N-T-O-N, detective inspector." He hurled his words as if they would intimidate her. "I ask the questions here. Where were you last night around eight?"

"OK, either this is a prank call or you're trying to pull something. I'll have my attorney call you back."

Benton yelled something, but she'd clicked off in the middle of the first syllable. She marched forward, plowing snow off the tracks.

People waited in her office. Jacob Stearne faced her from a loveseat at the far end. Tania Cooper sat opposite him, her back to Pia. Her two most trusted bodyguards, the co-heads of her personal security team. Vice presidents, she reminded herself. Their new ranks were hard-earned, even if neither of them cared for titles.

Absent-mindedly, Tania massaged her leg. Pia winced at the sight and instantly contemplated the sacrifices Tania had made for her country. An Army MP in the war, her Humvee hit an IED and burst into flames. As the fates would have it, Jacob was first on the scene and pulled her from the burning wreckage. They became good friends and came to Sabel Security together. But Tania's burns never healed completely. The extensive skin grafts kept her out of bathing suits in public. Only her closest friends knew what was under her long pants. And those weren't the only unhealed wounds for these two decorated ex-soldiers.

Tania was in mid-sentence. "—is why she needs to get laid worse than any white girl in DC. Stefan's platonic relationship will never work. When he looks at her, all he sees is the night he blew his dad's brains out to save her life. And when she looks at him … what? Why you staring over my shoulder? Shit. She's standing right behind me, isn't she?"

"Yes," Pia said. "Don't apologize."

"I wasn't going to." Tania tossed her hands in the air without craning around to face the boss.

"Fine."

Pia went to her office closet and traded her running shoes for a pair of flats. One perk about owning the company: she could wear flats and not worry about what people said about her behind her back. Which made her wonder for a moment … what did they say behind her back?

"Don't gimme that passive-aggressive bullshit, girl. I ain't gonna apologize because it's true. You keep spending time with Stefan Devoor so you won't be spending time looking for a real man. You keep your eyes open. You'll see. They're everywhere. And with your money, you—"

"Hoo boy," Jacob said. "I'm outta here." He slapped his hands to his knees and pushed up.

"—could have any man you want. Buy him a Rolex, let him drive your Lamborghini, and he'll be going downtown on you like there's no tomorrow. Sheeyit, you could have threesomes whenever … what?"

"Stop," Pia and Jacob said in unison.

"Well, somebody's gotta say it." Tania stood, tossed a bushel of wild hair over her shoulder with a flick, and crossed her arms.

Pia shook her head and wondered if Dr. Harrison had been talking behind her back about her sex life. Or was that perceived social distinctiveness? Evaluative scrutiny? She could never remember that stuff. But she didn't have time to think about it.

What she really wanted was to change the subject. "Have you ever had that dream about falling? Do you ever hit the ground?"

"Basophobia? The primate's fear of falling?" Jacob asked. When both Pia and Tania tilted their heads in question at him, he continued. "When primates evolved, they were sleeping in trees. We have a primeval fear of falling out of the branches. Basophobia. It's a dream common to just about everyone."

"Where the hell does an Army boy with only one year of college get a word like basophobia?" Tania asked.

Jacob said, "I read."

"So, anyway, if you hit the ground, do you die in your sleep?" Tania asked. "That's what we used to ask each other in grade school. I never found out the answer."

All three shrugged.

Mission accomplished: Tania was no longer talking about her love life. Or lack thereof. Who has time?

"We found the Freedom Stone," Jacob said. "Mislabeled and shoved in the back of the Ops Center behind the Ark of the Covenant. Should I call Rafael Tum?"

"We don't owe him anything. I think—"

"Ma'am, sorry to interrupt," George said from the doorway. "There's a different detective from Manchester calling. He says it's about his daughter. His name is Dominick England." George dropped his gaze. "Uhm. Ma'am, I think he's crying."

Pia frowned and checked her message log. Thirty minutes before the next meeting and now 154 messages to plow through. She did the math in her head: eleven seconds each.

Two calls about Chloe England in a few minutes was odd enough. But her dad was crying? That moved the call to the top of the list. She said, "Put him through."

She clicked on and greeted him warmly.

"Thank you for taking my call," he said. "I'm sorry to interrupt your busy day. Jeff, I mean, DI Benton is handling the case and … it didn't go well, I gather. He doesn't know you … and how you knew Chloe." The man choked up, then gathered himself with a sniffle. "I've straightened him out. Would you please give him another chance?"

"If you'd like," Pia said. "But I've not spoken to Chloe in a long time."

He broke into sobs but managed to get out, "She was murdered last night."

CHAPTER 4

IT FELT LIKE A GUT-PUNCH. Pia dropped her purse on her desk and steadied herself against it. No matter how many times she'd experienced it, unexpected death still shocked her. No chance for goodbyes, no chance for reconciliation, just an empty hole in the heart that rapidly fills with regrets. Regret for not calling, for not apologizing, for a lack of appreciation—for a thousand things that swirl in the minds of survivors when they try to sleep.

"Murdered? I … I'm so sorry. What happened?"

"I've calls to make, family to notify yet." Dominick England took a deep breath. "I'd appreciate it if you'd talk to Benton."

"Sure, anything," she said. "My dad was murdered a couple years ago. I know there's nothing anyone can say to ease your pain. But I want you to know on the pitch, I was scared to death of Chloe."

"Nice of you to say so." He dropped to a whisper. "Here's Benton."

She heard a shuffling of the phone as the men handed it off. "Ma'am, this is Benton again. I apologize for being a bit daft earlier. I'm desperate to catch Chloe's killer. Based on your phone number, I thought you were local and being difficult—as some of our locals are known to be. Dominick's explained your connection. I've not followed women's sports, or sports in general, so I've not heard your name."

"Apology accepted. One of my companies owns a classified satellite phone service. Our caller ID always looks local no matter where we are. It's part of how we keep MI6 and our own NSA from listening in. How can I help?"

"She rang this number last night. Did she speak to you, then?"

"Only fifteen people can dial this number and get straight through to me. How long was she on?"

"Five minutes roughly," Benton said. "She was sent round to interview a dying woman who'd been making some wild claims. Someone killed her right after, so we're keen to know what happened that motivated her to call you."

"My people screen calls in no more than two minutes." Pia rounded her desk and fell into her chair. "That means my assistant sent her to voicemail. I'll check."

She brought up her message logs. Tania and Jacob approached. Knowing it was serious, they waited in case she needed them.

"Found it, Mr. Benton," she said. "Three in the afternoon our time, yesterday. I'm in Bethesda, a suburb of Washington, DC."

"I'll need that recording."

"To save time, I think I can play it for you right now. Hang on."

Pia merged the call in with their messaging system, put it on speaker phone, and pressed play.

With a little street noise in the background, Chloe England's voice came on sounding chipper and happy. "Hi, Sabel, Chloe England calling. You probably don't remember me, but I played for England when you were coming up. I retired several years ago and … um." Chloe gave a self-conscious snicker. "I heard you left the game what, three, four years ago, too, yeah? I miss it. Those were the days. Hard work and all that. I gotta tell you though, I don't mind having what I want to eat now and again. Still keeping on the fitness track as best I can, though. Oh, listen to me going on about the good old days. Not even forty. Well, if you're going to Dame Millie's fête, maybe we can catch up then. That's a hoot, innit? Old Millie's a dame now."

The background noise diminished as if she'd turned off a street and into an alley.

"Right. What I'm calling about. I'm a constable these days and they sent me round to a lady who's dying in the hospital. Doctor said she's gone a bit balmy in the end. Some kind of neurological disorder they can't pin down. He says she's mostly lucid but has these hallucinations. When I talked to her, he said she was in right good shape, so it might be real.

"Bella Davis, her name was, gave me a list. Said there was a place called the Morpheus Institute that killed people in their dreams. She gave me three names. I googled 'em while I interviewed her, and sure enough, two of the three I checked are dead. Died in their sleep with a generic cause of death, medical examiner says. You know, when the doc doesn't have a clue, he puts down cardiac arrest. Well, we all die when the old ticker stops ticking, but what caused that to happen, eh? These two, David Breach and Jiali Yang, had neurological problems. But Yang died in Hong Kong and Breach died in New York City. When I asked Davis how this Morpheus bunch pulled off that one, she got right mad and grabbed at me. I tell you; she was serious.

"Then she coded, and they pushed me out. I waited around for an hour to get more out of her, but she died. Doctor thinks she could've been talking bobbins, but I tell you, Sabel, when she grabbed me, it was real to her. I kinda feel like I owe it to her to figure this out. Especially since your name is on it. Yeah, I might've said I'd kill you once, but that was just trash talk on the pitch, right? Sure you got that. Could be a different Sabel for that matter. I only got first names for the three when I was checking.

"Anyway, here's the list. Oh, hang on." It sounded as if Chloe were fumbling the phone for a moment. "Gotta put you on speaker so's I can read my notes while I'm talking. Here it is, then: Yang and Breach (like I mentioned earlier), Anton Petrova (he's the only other one I got a first name for, and he's alive as far as I can tell), Sabel (might be you, didn't get a chance to ask), Kusumawati, Wilson, Vermeer, Nhung, Duval, Eden-Sonnet, Krueger, and Santos.

"Think that's you, then? I looked it up and you Sabels aren't exactly Smiths or Joneses, but there are a few scattered about. Norway, Poland, the like. Yeah. So, come to think of it—"

The sound of rushing steps behind her was followed by a loud whoosh and a sickening crack. A thud on the pavement, then quiet. Chloe let out an exhausted breath.

It was an exhale Pia knew all too well. The last breath of the dead.

CHAPTER 5

BENTON ASKED HER TO KEEP the contents of the voicemail confidential and she agreed. She clicked off, sent him a digital copy, then looked at her friends. She needed air and space.

Jacob accompanied her to the coffee shop across the street from Sabel Tower. She wanted companionship and Tania had talked herself out of favor for the day, thus Jacob. Tania was wrong; Pia didn't need a boyfriend. Sure, the touch, intimacy, sex, and elation of a relationship were exciting. But with her workload, she didn't need the downside: the trifecta of perceived social distinctiveness, evaluative scrutiny, and uncertain social standing. Or whatever. She would forgive Tania later.

In the meantime, Jacob's friendship was perfect. He was a big man, as tall as Pia, and strong and dangerous to boot, and they shared a bond as if they were family. Like the brother she never had. She told him everything. They even thought alike. They didn't finish each other's sentences; they finished each other's actions. He cared about her. She cared about him.

And so it was on her mind. Why did people care about their friends? Why care about anyone, for that matter? Why did she care about Chloe England? They hadn't been teammates. They had been rivals at the rarified level of international competition. Sure, they'd partied a few times after the dust of the match settled, but it wasn't like they called each other on birthdays. Why had her murder hurt so much?

"Because she was in your safe zone," Jacob said.

Pia wondered how many of her thoughts were spilling into spoken words as they got off the elevator. They crossed the lobby to the swirling glass doors in silence. Then she asked, "What do you mean *safe zone*?"

"We have circles, zones of people. On one of my tours, I pulled a new guy out of the line of fire. Then we got hit from the opposite direction. The rounds hit my armor, but one hit him in the face. Instant death. It bothered me. He was one of us. But he'd signed up for a dangerous job. We knew the risks."

Jacob checked several directions and sniffed the air of early May like a hunter as they stepped out of the revolving door. Always the bodyguard. Always vigilant. Always paranoid.

And still alive.

"But the next day," he continued, "a guy from my high school track team was killed in a car accident back in Iowa. Regular people aren't supposed to die. Especially in Iowa, center of the country. It should be the safest zone. It hit me hard. Same thing happened to Tania with her little brother. Like you and me, she's seen too much death. And what sticks with her to this day? Little Dwayne pulling away from Daddy's hand on the subway platform and falling in front of the train. When you're ten, little bro's supposed to be in your safe zone."

He was right. Soccer had been her safe zone. They were competitors in athletics. They were young and fit and healthy. Few careers lasted beyond a player's early thirties. People aren't supposed to die that young. Pia had been the youngest throughout her career and retired early at her father's insistence. If she recalled correctly, Chloe had left the game after a second torn ACL. She should've been fine to walk or run, but never again at the speed of international play. Still, her murder felt close. Like a family member. Maybe they were family. The tough, fast, hard-playing women of World Cup football. She missed them. Even the nasty ones. They worked hard for days to win a game. With a result that week—not the next decade.

The coffee shop was crowded and noisy. The espresso machine hissed like a cornered wildcat. The scent of brewing coffee came thick and comfortable like a blanket in winter. Baristas called out customer names. Jacob grabbed a juice, Pia ordered black coffee. They looked around for chairs and snagged a table along the wall when a group of three left.

Jacob got a text. "Someone tried to break into the Ops Center. Must be after the Freedom Stone."

He made a call to check in.

Pia's mind wandered back to that rarified family of players. Chloe was right; those were the good old days. Playing until you dropped from exhaustion. Vacationing with a select few after the big tournaments. Clubbing with teammates and rivals after the Olympics. Watching the gay girls pair off and finding herself alone with a leftover Serbian too drunk to make his move. Good old days, indeed. And what was Chloe talking about, not-yet-forty? Pia wasn't even thirty.

That's when he walked in. Not accompanied by a chorus of angels, just the hiss of that wildcat in the espresso machine. It made her think *bad boy* even if he was dressed to look good. Tall and lanky with waves of caramel hair she'd like to run her fingers through. Green eyes— greener than hers—and electric as lightning bolts. A solid jaw and strong chin. Shoulders. She'd read about love at first sight in books but never believed in it. Before. Suddenly, she began to believe in many things, like past lives and reincarnated lovers. Centuries of lasting love. Then she shook her head.

Silliness.

Did she see green eyes? Is that what they were? He'd turned away. He carried a laptop bag and wore an Italian suit. A fashion that wouldn't hit American shores for another season. His gaze swept the room. As it swung toward her, she found herself turning away like a schoolgirl.

OK. Maybe Tania was right. It had been too long. Way.

Jacob clicked off his call. He tried to follow her wandering gaze, missed the hunk in the suit, and settled back on her. "Serious damage out there. Might be the Knights of Mithras back for that stupid stone."

"What do you think we should do with it?" she asked and sipped her coffee.

"Throw it back in the ocean where we found it."

She sensed the tension in his face. He hadn't liked being around women lately. Nothing sexist, nothing personal in his distance. For Jacob, being around women made him think of Jenny. Only time would heal that pain. She said, "I want you to go out there and check it out. If those guys are back, we need to take precautions. Make your best decision. I trust you."

He looked at her thoughtfully. Then he concurred with a dip of his head. "OK. As soon as Tania can get here to take over."

"I can get back to the office without getting kidnapped. Go."

He gave a tight smile and another nod. He downed the rest of his juice in a single swallow and tossed the bottle in the recycling on his way out.

The handsome guy held a cup in one hand and scanned the room again. There were only two empty chairs. Both at Pia's table.

Pia kept her head down, reading the messages on her phone. George had forwarded a group of texts from players, friends of Chloe's, old teammates of Pia's, and others less familiar. Everyone shocked to hear the news.

"D'you mind?" Handsome-man had a Scottish accent. "I just need a wee bit of table space."

"Not at all." Pia waved a hand at the table. She couldn't look at him. An odd sensation came over her.

He opened his laptop and started typing and squinting at the screen. He glanced over the top at her.

Caught.

So what? Who could blame her? She turned to the side and kept reading without facing him. Just as she turned, she noticed a sticker on the corner of his computer: McKenna Engineering. It sounded familiar. She thumbed through and disposed of half her emails.

The group-chat of Chloe's teammates and rivals kept distracting her. Everyone wanted to know who killed Chloe England. Realizing she couldn't say anything because DI Benton had asked for her discretion, she resisted the urge to tell them about the voicemail. She sent instructions to George to put the players' group chat straight through.

One last check of her schedule showed her next meeting was in fifteen minutes—with McKenna Engineering. She glanced back at the sticker on the Scot's laptop. Hmm.

But time was up. Preparing to leave, she gathered her purse and drained her coffee.

"Begging your pardon, ma'am," the Scot said. "Are ye a local lass?"

Savoring his accent, she craned over her shoulder at him. "Yes."

"This might sound a bit, what do you Americans say, creepy? But I'm nae trying to be." He hesitated and blushed. "Oh. Pardon me. Name's Liam Pickford."

He extended a hand. She shook it lightly. He nodded, inviting her to give her name. She ignored it.

He pointed at his laptop. "I've been working here and couldn't help but see you over the screen. I felt a connection. Like our meeting was a bit of destiny. I couldnae let you leave without asking a favor."

She squinted at him without making any commitment.

He bit his lip as if he hoped she would smile or something. "You see, I'm working on the biggest presentation of my life. I'm going to sell my dad's company to Pia Sabel. At the moment, I've got to focus on getting it right. But I'll be done in ninety minutes. Would you do me the favor of having a cheeky pint to celebrate with me after?"

He was bold. She had to give him that. If he hadn't blushed, she would've blown him off as an overconfident womanizer. But he had blushed. And he had no idea who he was talking to. Which was fun in a slightly mean way. She managed to keep herself from laughing. At the same time, her heart raced. She tried to make it slow down. She didn't want to give anything away. Unfortunately, her schedule didn't have another ten minutes in it. She'd already blown through what extra time she had for the day. The message count had ballooned to 241.

"Destiny?" she said with a smirk.

"Aye." He held her gaze. "I noticed you sneaking a peek now and again. You know I'm right."

"What makes you think Pia Sabel's going to buy your dad's company?"

"She's got to." He sighed with exhaustion and gazed at the floor. "My other options are shite." He looked up quickly. "Pardon my language, miss."

Pia rose. His eyes followed her expectantly, waiting for an answer. But he also showed some surprise, as men often did when seeing how tall she stood.

As if the words accidentally escaped his lips, he said, "Well, you're a strapping lass, aren't you?"

A pain shot into her head like an ice pick. In grade school, when she grew above the other girls, they called her *the Sabel Monster* or *Godzilla.* Girls are mean, and she became the lightning rod for their meanness. Perceived social distinctiveness was not just mild paranoia; they really were talking about her. Some phrases she didn't mind, like the awkward and persistent jokes about "the weather up there." And, to be fair, she didn't know what the Scot meant by "strapping lass." Is that good or bad? The same went for "cheeky pint." For some Brits, cheeky meant casual. The way he'd said it sounded salacious.

For some reason, she'd hoped for something more from Liam Pickford. Was that evaluative scrutiny? Whatever it was, she didn't like it. Which meant she didn't see a future with Liam Pickford, in any life past, present, or future. That's what she didn't like about relationships. So many disappointments.

"If it's destiny," she said, "I'm sure we'll meet again."

She walked out.

CHAPTER 6

HEADING BACK TO THE OFFICE, Pia decided to research things from Chloe's message. She found plenty of Morpheus references online, mostly about software. She realized she had just let her expert in mythology leave. Jacob Stearne had been diagnosed by the finest doctors she could find as having PTSD-induced schizophrenia due to his excessive number of combat tours. While they considered his delusions benign, none of them could explain why Jacob's imaginary friend Mercury—the currently unemployed winged messenger of the Roman gods—filled him with otherwise impossible insights.

She didn't judge the man. Was Mercury real? Or a manifestation of mental illness in his shell-shocked head? It didn't matter. How many times had he saved her life listening to that voice? And that voice filled him with inexplicable wisdom and knowledge. Sometimes.

Other times, it drove him to strange behavior.

She dialed him as she waited to cross the street.

Before she could say anything, Jacob said, "Did he ask you out?"

"Who?"

"Tall, pale, and handsome. I'm not agreeing with Tania, but you deserve a good man. You're working too much. You text me a business question at 2300 hours and send me the answer at 0200. You could use a snuggle-buddy."

Tania's opinions had infected Jacob. Were they discussing her behind her back? If things went the way they had in the past, there would be a secret company-wide betting pool on when the boss-lady would fall into bone city. Maybe she allowed too much transparency.

"Look who's talking," she snapped. As soon as the words fell out of her mouth, she regretted them. In her head the words seemed like a fun retort to a good friend. When she heard them out loud, she instantly remembered Jenny.

Jacob didn't speak.

"Sorry," she said. She waited for the light to cross. Other pedestrians gathered. "That was out of line. It's too soon since Jenny—"

"Why did you call?" he asked.

"Could you ask Mercury about Morpheus? I know he was a Greek god, and associated with sleep, but that's all I know."

Whenever doctors advised her to put Jacob on heavy medications, she would challenge them to ask him about obscure Roman history, literature, or art. His immediate and accurate answers silenced his critics. No one could memorize that many books. Not that it didn't backfire from time to time. Sometimes he would evangelize for the one true path to glory: following the way of the Dii Consentes, the twelve ruling gods of the Roman pantheon. That got awkward fast. Especially at formal dinners.

The light changed and she started out at a pace to ensure she reached the other side first.

Jacob said, "People think Morpheus is Greek. The only reference we have to him is from the Roman poet, Ovid. He wrote something about the guy."

"OK, what?"

"Juno sent orders to Somnus, god of sleep, to fake a dream for the queen, Alcyone." Jacob pronounced it ALL-sigh-own-ee. "Somnus sent his son, Morpheus, who made himself look like King Ceyx." Jacob pronounced it SIGH-ex. "Ovid wrote, 'Morpheus flew on silent wings through the dark / Came to her city and took off his wings / and took the face and body of Ceyx, the color / of a deadman and stood naked before / Alcyone's bed, his beard was soaked and water / dripped off his sodden hair and tears ran down—'"

"Not to rush you," Pia said in her most soothing voice, "but my next meeting starts in five minutes. Could I get the highlights?"

"You know the gods don't like the way they're ignored these days. There was a time, long before hip hop, when the poets would stand on the temple steps and hold epic rap battles.”

“Uh.” Pia thought quickly as she strode through the revolving doors. “I’m sorry to have missed those days. But I do watch Kendrick Lamar and Megan Thee Stallion on YouTube. Does that count?”

There was a long silence.

Then Jacob said, “So, anyway, Morpheus, posing as King Ceyx, tells Alcyone that a storm wrecked his ship and he drowned. She broke down and cried in her sleep, begging him to take her with him to the underworld. Then she woke up in the middle of the night, screaming and crying and tearing her hair. She told the servants what she’d seen. They thought she’d gone nuts. No one could comfort her. Falling back to sleep, she dreamed she ran to the coast and found her husband’s corpse floating in on the waves. She turned into a bird and flew out to him. He turned into a bird and they flew off together.”

She pressed the elevator button and glanced around to make sure she would be first on.

Pia thought for a moment, then asked, “What does that mean?”

“She had a premonition of her husband’s death and died in her sleep.”

“And the servants thought she’d gone crazy before she died?”

“Guess so. Helluva love story, no matter how you slice it.”

Pia didn’t see a love story. She saw a patriarchy telling a story of gender dependence. She blurted out, “You mean because she couldn’t live without a man?”

“Because they wanted to be together, in this world or the next.”

That caught her by surprise on several planes. On the face of it, he was right. The ancients often considered true love to transcend the Earthly plane. The subtext was different. Jenny was in the next world and Jacob, never a suicidal thought in his head, had been volunteering for suicide missions lately. Too many.

Pia considered ways to tell him she needed him in this world. As did his family and friends. She thought of ways to tell him she couldn’t imagine a world without him, how valuable he was to everyone around him, how many lives he’d saved, and how many more he was bound to save. Instead, she heard herself say, “I see what you mean.”

He made no reply.

Again, she wanted to say a million things about his indispensable presence. And again she fell short. She said, "Thanks."

He inhaled sharply. "Uh, Ms. Sabel, before you go. I just got a text message. It reads, 'We have kidnapped Professor Rafael Tum.'"

CHAPTER 7

PIA EXITED THE ELEVATOR AND strode toward her office. A direct-text buzzed the phone in her hand as Jonelle Jackson, known throughout the company as the Major, crossed the executive lobby toward her. She glanced at the text at the same time the Major stopped in front of her.

"McKenna Engineering is in the boardroom," the Major said with a nod in the opposite direction of Pia's office.

Pia's CEO had reclaimed her old hair style. Her afro was gelled back into a tight bun at the nape of her neck. Pia's urging to let loose hadn't stuck. The Major took comfort in the fashions that had forged her Army career. She liked things buttoned down and squared away. So be it.

While the Major waited for a response, the text Pia had noticed registered in her mind. It was an invitation from Millie Tindall, former star of the English Women's National Team. It said something about Chloe England. She wanted to read it along with the other 207 messages on her ever-growing list. She said, "I'm going to be few minutes late. Something came up."

"They have a promising bit of software the Satellites division wants. If it lives up to the hype, it could extend our lead in that industry."

The Major gave her a critical nod that spoke volumes and walked away. Pia understood that nod as a rebuke of her organizational skills. Pia did not have everything buttoned down and squared away. Not that her CEO judged her harshly. The Major reminded Pia of coaches who had impossibly high standards. At least they felt impossibly high at first. She'd stepped up to those standards in soccer just as she would in the Major's corporate world. Someday.

Was that evaluative scrutiny? She'd figure it out later. She headed for her office.

The text from Millie read, "Perhaps you've not gotten my invitation of week before last. Not that we expected you. We thought you might reconsider since Chloe's met her tragic end. Her funeral is Friday and the fair is still on for Saturday. You're welcome to stay at Padley House with us. The Peak District is charming this time of year. Cheers."

Pia called George and asked him to dig up the invitation from Millie. Then she sat in her chair, put her elbows on the desk, and sank her head in her hands. Her fingers ran through her hair. Why would anyone want to kill a retired athlete? Chloe England had been an ass-kicking competitor in the game but a lot of fun after. Who was that friend who'd tagged along with Chloe? Abby Stokes, the team joker. Abby once posed as a reporter—complete with a mic, respectable suit, camera girl, and lights—and asked questions of Pia. When the questions turned overtly sexual, Pia recognized the prank. They had a good laugh. Then there was Millie herself. Was she fifteen years older than Pia? Twenty? They'd only crossed paths a couple times. What was it Chloe said about her in the message? She was a dame? That meant something to the English, but Pia didn't know what exactly. She'd love to step back in time for the weekend.

George forwarded her Millie's invite. It was a request to participate in a fundraiser benefitting sports for underprivileged girls. Some famous soccer stars from various parts of the world would attend to give autographs and take selfies. George had not put it in front of her because she locked down her charitable engagements. She preferred to concentrate her time and energy on a few causes rather than spread herself thin. George sent the standard donation along with her regrets only hours earlier. Millie hadn't seen it yet.

Pia looked up Padley House. There were a few places named Padley. One was a halfway house in Derby. Another was a historic ruin. The next was a new country house in the Peak District outside of Manchester, England. A mansion built in the 17th century tradition, it sat like a stone monolith on the landscape. Several acres of lawn stretched behind it. Retired soccer players needed smooth, flat spreads of grass. Millie had done well for herself. Outside of tennis, few women in sports retired to that kind of estate.

Jacob called.

"I want to make the exchange," he said. His voice brought her back from her thoughts of idyllic rural England. "They want the Freedom Stone. Should be simple enough."

"Who does?"

"The people who kidnapped Rafael Tum. They're demanding the Freedom Stone as ransom."

She took a deep breath and remembered. It made no sense. Few people in the world knew she had come into possession of the ancient meteorite fragment called the "Freedom Stone." And neither she nor Jacob had any connection to Rafael Tum, former Guatemalan-revolutionary-turned-college-professor, other than an adventure in which Tum had been a constant problem for them.

"Why?" Pia couldn't hide her surprise. "We don't know the professor and have no intel on the kidnappers. It would be a—"

She stopped herself from saying *suicide mission*. Jacob knew as well as she that kidnappers almost always killed their hostages. Saving the victim was next to impossible. Which made Pia stop to consider his motives. It had been over a month since his fiancé, Jenny Jenkins, had died while saving his life. He'd fallen into an existential depression since then. Survivor's guilt. His behavior had become increasingly risky and out of character. Six weeks earlier, he would've insisted on tons of recon and intel before weighing the risks of a ransom exchange. Now, he was ready to mount a mission against hopeless odds.

"No," she said. "Call their bluff. We have no interest in, nor responsibility for, the good professor."

"That doesn't sound like you, Ms. Sabel. You're always the humanitarian."

"We can't solve every problem in the world," she said. "We haven't the time or resources to chase this when you know the outcome will be the same no matter what. Refer it to the FBI."

"As you wish," he said. His tone indicated his displeasure.

Did he know she was trying to keep him alive? Did that make him angry?

Jacob said, "OK if I ask them for proof-of-life before I get the feds involved?"

A meeting reminder popped on her desktop screen. Her phone buzzed with a call from Bianca Dominguez, head of Sabel Technologies.

"Do what you think best, Jacob. I've another call."

Harsh, but she couldn't live without her soul-brother. He was the only person who kept her sane. He had to stay alive.

She clicked over to Bianca and exchanged pleasantries as she stole a glance at her meeting reminder. While she talked, she went to her office closet and chose a pair of heels that would give her authority and matched her outfit.

"The team working on your list found something," Bianca said. "No conclusions yet, but I thought you'd like to hear the first correlation we found. David Breach and Jiali Yang died a week apart and a world away from each other. They were both founders of successful companies. But this is the strange part: Both companies were up for sale before their deaths. The heirs sold the companies at fire sale prices, a tenth of their assessed value."

"Same buyer?" Pia asked.

"No. Not related at all. One was a private equity fund and the other was a law firm that turned around and sold it to someone else the same day. Yang's company sold for 10 percent of the asking price. My people are still sorting through tons of data on the others. Without first names there's not much to go on. Those two were an odd coincidence. I thought you'd like to know."

Pia thanked her and clicked off.

Her eyes fell back on the meeting reminder without processing it. After the call ended, she wondered how she kept sane when, in the space of ten minutes, she'd gone from ancient Roman poetry, to being late for a business meeting, to evaluating ransom demands, to weekend invitations, to insights into Chloe's message. And now, the McKenna Engineering meeting. At the top of the attendees list: Liam Pickford. The man who just knew he was going to sell his company to Pia Sabel waited for her in the boardroom. Her smile spread as she remembered making her exit. How would he react now? Destiny?

Then she glanced at her phone. 281 unread messages.

Still on her screen: Padley House. A charity weekend. The lush expanse of grass stretched behind Millie Tindall's country house. Pia could feel her cleats digging in as she spun from a defender in an exhibition game made up of former players. Chloe's chipper voice, her last spoken words, came back to her. *Well, if you're going to Dame Millie's fête, maybe we can catch up then.* Chloe's funeral. Innocent, vibrant Chloe with a bright future ahead of her—and someone chose to brutally murder her. That was something she'd like to chase down. Who the hell killed Chloe?

Her meeting reminder pinged again.

Reluctantly, she rose and marched across the building to the boardroom.

CHAPTER 8

PIA HEARD THEIR VOICES AS she approached the boardroom's glass wall. All eyes were glued to an older gentleman who pointed to a flat screen filled with diagrams at the front of the room. People from Sabel Satellites sat on the window side of a massive, polished cherry table. They faced McKenna's people, whose backs were to her. Liam—like Pia, a head taller than everyone else—sat in the center of the group, facing the Major. There was one empty chair directly across from Liam.

Pia opened the door and strode in.

The man at the front, his gray hair swept straight back, kept talking before noticing everyone's attention turning to the new arrival. He stopped with one hand gesturing toward a flow chart that meant nothing to Pia.

"My apologies," Pia said, her gaze engaging each of the McKenna people, as she swept around to the empty chair. She left Liam for last. "An emergency came up. I meant no disrespect."

She lingered on Liam's face. His mouth was falling open like a slow-motion waterfall. A blush rose from his collar. Not a coloring produced by humility like before; this time it was embarrassment. Pia realized her odd pleasure at seeing him squirm was both unfair and slightly sadistic, but she relished it anyway.

She reached a hand across the broad expanse of wood to him. She said, "Pia Sabel. I should've introduced myself when we met earlier."

"Would've been nice." He rose and reached to meet her halfway. His expression turned cold, almost angry.

"We did discuss destiny," she added.

"Aye, that we did."

The man at the head of the table fumbled a phone out of his pocket as they shook. He raised it to take a picture as they broke off. He said, "D'ya mind holding that?"

Pia smiled and extended her hand again. Liam's expression softened and his eyes resumed their sparkle. He reached out and held her hand warmly.

"Your dad?" she asked, tossing a glance toward the man.

"No," Liam broke off the gaze. "He couldnae make the trip."

"There, thank you," the cameraman said.

"Go ahead." Pia nodded to the presenter. "Pick up where you left off, I'll catch up."

He resumed his presentation with a recap of the slide on the screen.

Pia stole a glance at Liam. She'd bothered him. His boldness was gone. A little humility sat well on him.

The Major pushed a yellow pad between them for Pia to read. On the right side, she'd jotted the important numbers: top line revenue, debt, assets, shareholders, expenses. Below was a double line and the final number: negative fifty million. The negative meant Liam had been right when he said he had to sell. He was out of cash.

To her left, Pia's Satellite division president asked the old guy questions. Complicated questions about software engineering. Answers came from both the old guy and another engineer. They may as well have been speaking Greek. She tuned out and stole a glance at her phone. The message count ticked higher, but one was from Bianca. She tapped it surreptitiously.

Liam noticed her move.

Bianca wrote, "Several companies with Morpheus in the name. The most prominent is a New Age approach to sleep disorders in the UK, twenty-five miles outside of Manchester. No connection to the names on this list, though."

The boardroom discussion turned politely argumentative. They'd come to the numbers, a contentious point in any negotiation. Voices became sharp and snapped. Numbers were thrown back and forth. The McKenna people floated future earnings. Her people cited the current state, the negative.

Pia thought the Peak District and Millie Tindall were a few miles or so outside Manchester. She didn't recall ever going there but vaguely recalled it was an area filled with quaint Elizabethan villages and open, rolling hills. Millie's invitation could give her an excuse to offer DI Benton Sabel Security's help on his investigation.

Voices rose again. Her team was not happy with Liam's answers. Her gaze fell to the yellow pad. Negative millions. After the last question and answer, a long silence stretched between them. No one made eye contact. Her people jotted notes and added up numbers. The Major added a note to her pad: ROI = 10 yrs, then shook her head sadly. If it went through, it wouldn't pay dividends for an eternity.

Pia drifted back to Chloe and the police investigation. Millie's invitation listed a whole lot of women Pia knew from her days in the game. Abby Stokes, Lena Schuller, Debinha Alves, Susan Walker, Kika van der Gagt, and others would be there. Maybe Pia could prank Stokes back. That would be fun. And the result would take less than ten years.

The silence around her grew. She felt eyes on her. Liam had asked her a question. Rolling back time in her head, she realized he wanted her thoughts on the deal. With a glance at the Major's notes, she thought through her answer.

Pia looked each of the McKenna people in the eye and said, "Full disclosure. Liam and I spoke briefly in the coffeeshop across the street. Liam, you said then you had to sell the company. You emphasized *had to*. Why?"

The McKenna team turned to Liam like a school of fish, a sense of betrayal on their faces. He hadn't told them he'd met Pia Sabel ahead of time. But then, he didn't know. Or so he'd claimed.

Liam bit the inside of his cheek and worked his jaw for a moment. He swiveled glances at his people then sucked in a deep breath. He said, "It's gone a bit Baltic in here, hasn't it? Aye, I'm off my nut when a good-looking woman's about. Cannae deny that."

The boldness returned to his smile. His eyes were indeed green. Deep green.

"M'dad built this company. His life's work it is. A year ago, he took on venture capital for this software. Kept his plans all in his head. Nearly done last month, then he gets sick. Pancreatic cancer. He's not got long to live and doesn't get around much anymore. The investors, nasty lot, offered a buyout for pennies. They aim to sell the assets for scrap and fold the rest." He waved his hands at his people. "We can finish it. It's going to take more time than they've given us. We're looking for an angel investor to give us breathing room."

An honest answer, no bullshit, no hyperbole, just raw facts and desperation. She liked that. It saved time.

Still moving like a school of fish, his people turned their expectant faces to her. All their hopes for their families, their jobs, their futures waited on her answer.

A wave of understanding came over her. During the discussions, he answered the financial questions, leaving the technical things to the others. He wasn't an engineer like his father. Just as she wasn't an executive like hers. He walked the same tightrope as she. The one stretched above the dark abyss of failure—one wrong step and thousands could lose their livelihoods. And he had stepped onto it the same way as she, because of his father's imminent death. Neither of them wanted to be in their positions. Both worked day and night to avoid disaster.

To save everyone's jobs, the only thing Liam Pickford could think of was to sell it. Why sell it to Pia Sabel? Because her name was on the building. She could make the decision in an instant, if she were so inclined.

The way his employees held their collective breath, they considered the investors to be flesh-eating demons. They would be out of jobs by morning. He was selling his inheritance not to save himself but to get the best deal he could for his people. A noble pursuit.

The hard glare coming from the Major reminded her that she had employees to think of as well. Ten years was a long time for an investment to pay off. Decisions like this weren't about being nice. They were about numbers.

"I'm sorry to hear about your father," she said. "Your offer sounds promising. I hope we can come to terms. A friend of mine was killed yesterday, and it has me distracted. So, I'm leaving the details to my executive team. Again, I apologize for my late arrival, and I apologize for my early departure. I must be going."

She rose and took a last look at Liam. He looked like an intestinal bug had roiled his digestive tract. Nonetheless, he rose out of respect for her.

"I'm glad," she said, "that destiny brought us together again."

She crossed the executive lobby to her office and sat at her desk to start in on the message pile. She replied and forwarded and deleted and filed a hundred without absorbing their content. What bothered her: Across the pond, the killer of an innocent athlete ran free.

The Major stepped in, three other executives behind her, for the post-meeting wrap-up.

Decision time.

She motioned to the couches and joined them.

CHAPTER 9

THE ANALYSIS WAS QUICK. MCKENNA Engineering's asking price was too high. Sabel's programmers had a similar software project in the works and McKenna's version would accelerate their program by only six months to a year. She could fast-track her own program for half what it would cost to buy Liam's company. If they cut their offer in half, it would still take five years to pay off. All four of her executives agreed: it wasn't worth his asking price.

Pia wanted to try harder, for the employees' sake. "Could we help them through their cash shortage?"

"That option's not on the table," the Major said. "His investors want to cash out now."

"But he's trying to save jobs."

"If you bail out every problematic company, we will all be out of jobs." The Major gave her a sympathetic look. "It's tough, I feel for them, but it's not our problem. Buying McKenna would be like inviting contagious people over for dinner."

"OK," Pia sighed. She pictured Liam's confidence in the coffeeshop. "Tell them we're out."

The execs rose and filed out. The Major hung back. She stopped at the office door.

"You still want to help him?" the Major asked. "I know he's a hottie, but don't let him tug on your sympathies. Keep focused on the sixty thousand employees who expect you to make rational decisions that directly affect their futures."

"It's not that. His dad's dying and he's trying to do the right thing: save jobs. You run this company and you're damn good at it, but he doesn't have a Jonelle Jackson to guide him through this mess. Couldn't we help him somehow?"

"Sell him to our competitors. Let them sink under the negative cashflow."

"Hey, that's a good idea." Pia tapped a finger to her lips while she thought. "Dave Krueger wanted to buy Sabel Satellites. He might need this software."

"A fate worse than death," the Major said. "If McKenna wants to pursue a deal with the biggest asshole in business, let them."

"I'll call Dave," Pia said. "See if he's interested."

"You didn't meet Dave when he made the offer, did you?" The Major gave her a knowing nod. "That's right, you were attending the G20 Summit. Well, don't take anything he says personally. Good luck."

When the Major left, Pia didn't bother sitting down. She stood at the front of her desk, looked up the man's number, and called him at McDowell Aerospace. While she dialed, she remembered Chloe's voice mail. There was a Krueger on the list of twelve. A fairly common name, though.

When he came on the line, she explained the value of McKenna Engineering in a pleasant voice.

He cut her off. "You really are a dumb jock, aren't you? You never worked a day in your life, then get a major company handed to you and you think you have a clue? You're nothing but an overprivileged brat who had the finest coaches money could buy. If you hadn't won all the trophies, that would've been the shocker. Then you step into the helm of an international conglomerate like you belong there? Bullshit. We made a solid offer for your satellite division and you treated it like it was an heirloom. It's not. It's a business. And you'll run it into the ground because you don't care about your customers or your employees. All you care about is the big shiny bauble daddy left you when you got him killed. You should've sold out while you had—"

Pia had been berated by the finest coaches in international sports. All coaches had two kinds of speeches: 1) you lost because you suck; and 2) they lost because they suck worse. It went with the territory. Sometimes there were nuggets of truth. Early on, she learned to tune out the volume and aggression in a rant. She shrugged off Krueger with ease.

"—the chance. Now, we'll pick up what's left of your assets in Chapter 7 bankruptcy. Where did you get the stupid idea that you could manage a company the size of American Express? You've never had any training. You're nobody. You're nothing. You live with that same smug 'Sabel exceptionalism' attitude Alan had. But you're not him. If it weren't for that black woman you have running the show, the whole thing would've fallen apart last year. You aren't running that company—you're just a figurehead. And the people around you are undermining you so they can pick up the pieces when you fail."

She waited a beat while he collected his breath. Then she asked, "Have you ever heard of a place called the Morpheus Institute?"

He inhaled sharply and blubbered a couple incoherent syllables. He paused, then said, "Here's why you're so stupid, Sabel: If you didn't want McKenna, why the fuck would I want them?"

He clicked off.

She stared at her phone for a moment, then remembered the Major's knowing nod, and reminded herself, *the biggest asshole in business.* Understatement. At least Krueger left no uncertainty about her social standing.

But every rant carried some truth. And the truth she heard from Krueger seared into her. It had been her constant insecurity since she first went to work in Dad's company. No one close to her dared mention it. She had enough self-confidence to never let it show.

She turned her laptop around to face her. The aerial picture of Millie Tindall's Padley House remained open.

She pulled up the email app on her phone and thumbed a quick note to Krueger. "Thanks for the chat. The black woman has a name, Jonelle Jackson. Your company is publicly held, so everyone knows how much your board values your services by how much you get paid. Because Sabel Industries is private, our executive pay is not released. I thought you should know that I value Ms. Jackson three times more than your board values you. Good luck in your next compensation negotiation."

She looked at it. Then changed the signature block to read, "Your favorite figurehead, Pia Sabel."

While it felt good to press send, it hadn't saved Liam's employees.

The Major stood in her doorway and knocked on the frame.

"Am I a figurehead?" Pia asked.

CHAPTER 10

"YOU DIDN'T TAKE MY ADVICE." The Major crossed the room and took Pia's hand. Her gaze dropped to Padley House still showing on Pia's laptop screen then back to Pia. "Dave Krueger is involved in a thousand lawsuits. He never pays a bill, he waits until you sue him, then settles the lawsuits for pennies on the dollar. It's why we didn't sell. He offered too little, and we'd never see half of that. He loves it when people hate him. He thrives on conflict."

"Nice dodge."

The Major gave Pia a long look as if she were back in the Army inspecting one of her troops. Jonelle Jackson ran a ship as tight as her bun. She barked orders and told people in no uncertain terms how well or poorly they'd executed those orders. She sugar-coated things for Pia, but never dialed down the honesty. Sometimes her assessments landed like a barbed wire lash and other times like someone lifting her up. They'd always had a strong bond.

"The Queen of England is a figurehead." The Major backed up a step and crossed her arms. "Notice the English haven't gotten rid of her? When there's a war, a plague, a national calamity, they rally around their symbol of unity.

"You've always been our symbol of unity your whole life. We don't pay any better than anyone else. Our workplace has the same intrigues and politics as any other company. You make Sabel Industries different. Back in the day, the employees watched your games and felt every loss and victory. When you were involved in that shooting in Mumbai, they prayed for you at their desks. When you were dragged in front of the Senate committee, every employee watched those hearings. Yes, you're a figurehead. But you're a damn good one."

Pia deflated like a popped balloon. Her gaze fell to the floor.

"You're twenty-nine," the Major said, squeezing her arm. "No one so young can take over and run a big company."

"Gates, Zuckerberg—"

"Not without mistakes. Remember, Steve Jobs was fired from Apple—the company he built—when he was thirty. It could be argued Gates and Zuckerberg should've been. Jobs came back to Apple when he was forty-two and was a much better executive. Those people knew their industries because they created them. You didn't build this company. You have decades of catching up to do. There's time for that. None of us expect you to be Alan Sabel reincarnated. And we hope you're not Steve Jobs. We don't expect you to make decisions guiding the future of the company. We expect you to be a good example. Someone we can respect. Someone who makes us proud."

The Major nodded at the picture on her laptop.

Pia took the hint and explained about Chloe England's brutal murder, her voicemail, the list of twelve, and the Morpheus Institute. She explained Millie's invitation and Padley House. The Major listened intently. When Pia finished, neither said anything for a long moment.

"What did you come in for?" Pia asked.

The Major tapped a finger to her lips while she thought.

"Your competitive nature drives a lot of what we do," the Major said. "Sometimes you get so wrapped up in winning, Pia, you lose sight of the cost. Like that time you played with a broken ankle. This time—"

"It wasn't that broken. It hardly hurt at all."

"Yes, well. Ordinary people don't go to the same extremes. It occurred to me that you want to help Liam's employees with the same passion you applied to winning games. Sometimes your headlong pursuit of something has adverse consequences. And sometimes advantageous consequences."

Pia sensed something coming. She waited patiently. Patiently for her, anyway. Her foot was tapping.

"Your idea about Krueger was a good one," the Major said. "Except, we shouldn't sell it to him. We should buy it to keep it out of his hands.

When we were leaving, the Satellite execs pointed out we'd suspected Krueger wanted our company because his satellites were too far behind in technology. If Krueger bought McKenna, he could pull even or possibly get ahead of us."

Pia's brows shot up. "You said they'd drag down our company."

"It's not a done deal," the Major said. "We think the underlying technology Liam's father was working on has merit. If we can figure out where he was going; if we can use AI to get the time frame down; if we can get Liam's investors to stand down; if, if, if … then we might make it work."

"That's a great idea."

The Major kept her gaze locked on Pia. "I have the annual dinner with Sabel Capital scheduled in London on Monday. Since McKenna's HQ is there, I'll move the negotiations there."

The Major's eyes moved to the image of Padley House on Pia's screen. She said, "Figurehead or not, a smart leader also knows her employees would rather see her honor the dead because that means they work for an empathetic human being. You should go to Chloe's funeral. And meet us in London afterwards."

Pia felt a great weight lifted from her shoulders. She pursed her lips and nodded.

"And since you're a smart leader," the Major said, "I thought you'd want to tell Liam the good news yourself. Before you leave."

CHAPTER 11

Pia summoned the McKenna crew to her office. Liam looked like a condemned man waiting for the noose to be tightened around his neck. Pia gave him a smile that lifted him from the bottom of his canyon for a moment before his confidence waned again.

"We're looking for a way to say yes," she said. "My people have a lot of questions about the timeline. If our AI can help, and we can deliver the software significantly ahead of your schedule, we might—and let me stress might—come to terms."

While Liam and his crew brightened, Pia waved in the Major, who led a team of engineers from Satellites. Immediately, her people buttonholed their counterparts at McKenna. Serious conversations— those involving programming terms unknown to Pia—swirled around the room.

Liam asked the Major to wait for a moment and took Pia to the side. He said, "I feel I've gone and offended you in some way when we first met. I apologize, for I meant no harm in offering you a pint after."

"You didn't recognize me?"

"The photos online don't do you justice. You're much more the bonnie lass in person, no doubt about that."

Pia hadn't googled herself in a while. Last time she checked, there were many shots of her in a game, muscles flexed and sweat flying. Then there were the corporate mug shots, staged with curled hair she rarely wore and drab backgrounds. Today she wore a business skirt suit with her trademark ponytail. His mistake was plausible. But the fact that he'd tried flattery conflicted her. What woman wouldn't feel a tingle at being called a bonnie lass? Or was it a lothario's way of getting in her pants?

Or selling her a company for too high a price?

"If destiny is what we feel," she said with a smile, "I'm sure we'll get that cheeky pint someday. But not today, I'm leaving town shortly."

"Oh aye?" Liam's smile grew enthusiastic. "Ms. Jackson said we'd move the proceedings to London tomorrow. Would that be your destination as well?"

"No." She walked away.

Immediately she chastised herself for giving too much away. Did she have to say *if destiny is what* we *feel?*

Pia led Tania and George away from the small convention of her people and McKenna's to the other end of her office.

Jacob appeared at the door and approached. He stopped an arm's length behind Tania and waited his turn.

She filled George in on her new travel plans, wrapping up by saying, "Refer the business messages to the Major and the personals to Tania."

George nodded and left.

Tania didn't miss a beat, "What do you mean, 'personals?' No way I'm handling your Tinder for you."

Pia ignored her while thumbing out a message to Dame Millie accepting the invitation. When she finished, she looked up at Tania. "I'm going to Chloe's funeral in Manchester and—"

"When do we leave?"

"You're not going," Pia said. "I'm taking Jacob."

Jacob started to say something.

"You what?" Tania screeched. "You're taking Jacob 'Eeyore' Stearne? Sister, you're making a big mistake. He's in a mood, and I don't mean a good one. He'll take you to that smoldering trash heap of heartache and sorrow he lives in. Being around him is like getting sucked into a black hole."

Pia glanced over Tania's shoulder at him while answering. "I hope it'll cheer him up a little."

"Cheer him up? Only thing's going to keep him out of the abyss is sex. That's all men think about. Why do they build rocket ships to the moon? So they can brag about it and get women into bed. To them, it's all sex, sex, sex. They don't think about anything else."

Still behind her back, Jacob raised a finger as if he were going to make a point. Then he thought better of it.

"So you won't be in town this weekend, huh?" Tania's gaze rolled to the ceiling. "Then Ima find me a little bed and breakfast in the Shenandoah and cuddle up with my man for a couple days."

Tania spun on her heel and plowed right into Jacob. "How long you been standing there, Mr. Nosy?"

"I don't keep track of time," he said. "All I think about is sex."

Tania hmphed, "Smartass." She pushed him out of her way and stalked out.

Pia turned to Jacob and said, "I wonder what's on her mind?"

She chuckled awkwardly. He didn't.

"The attempt on the Ops Center didn't damage the building," he said. He pulled up a photo on his phone. It showed a hole at the edge of the property. "Your dad had sensors put around the edge—that's what alerted us. Somebody dug a tunnel from half a mile away. They did a lot of damage, but they didn't get near the building."

She squinted her curiosity. "What makes you think they were after the Freedom Stone and not the armory? We keep thousands of weapons in there."

"There are ten federal armories easier to break into than Sabel Security. What makes this attempt stand out is the tunnel. They used a boring machine, high tech and expensive. They had highly sophisticated tracking involved. Of all the bizarre secret societies we've encountered, only the Knights of Mithras could finance that kind of operation." He paused. "If they're back, they won't stop at kidnapping Rafael. I want to go after them. We take them down, free the professor, and tick off a good deed for the week."

"We could do that," she said. "But the FBI should handle this. That's what we pay taxes for. You called them, right?"

Jacob turned to his right as if listening to someone else. He did that an annoying number of times in a day.

Pia searched his eyes. "Right?"

"Yeah. I called them. They're tracing the message."

"Good, because we're going to England." She stepped around him and started for the Satellites gang by her desk. Over her shoulder, she said, "Wheels up in an hour."

Jacob looked stunned at her decision. Leaving Rafael Tum to his fate was out of character for her and they both knew it. Written in his expression were the arguments he was preparing in his mind.

"We have a good deed in front of us," she said. "We're going to figure out who killed Chloe England."

CHAPTER 12

PIA WATCHED THE GENTLE RAIN falling across Manchester, England from the large oval window of Sabel One. She glanced at her watch. Dame Millie and her husband, Albert Tindall, were fifteen minutes late. At this point, would it be rude to take a limo to her meeting with Detective Inspector Benton? He'd been reluctant to meet with her to begin with. Now she would be late. Just as she was about to call a limo, a ten-year-old deep-blue Bentley pulled alongside.

Pia felt a surge of excitement at seeing someone from the old days, even someone she didn't know well. A middle-aged woman with the poise and elegance of an actress crossing a stage stepped from the passenger seat and waved back.

When the pilot dropped the airstair, Pia found herself bounding down it into the drizzle.

They collided with hugs and laughter and so-good-to-see-you-agains. When she pulled back to look at her one-time adversary, she saw a woman whose skin was Botox-smooth and tanning-bed bronze. Each strand of her hair looked individually polished, and her brown eyes sparkled with joy. She wore a tasteful navy dress with a diamond pendant that sparkled in the late afternoon slate gray.

Suddenly, Pia felt underdressed in her skin-tight athletic wear.

Pia's hostess tugged her toward the car. She said, "Quick, before we're drenched. Your bodyguard can ride with Albert."

They slid into the back. Jacob took the front.

Pia felt a lump under her. Reaching behind her, she pulled out a medicine bottle. The label listed the liquid drug as Anectine. As soon as her hostess clicked her seatbelt, Pia handed her the bottle. "Sorry, hope I didn't crush it."

Dame Millie snatched the bottle and dropped it in her purse without looking at it.

The balding fiftyish gentleman at the wheel turned to greet them in a patrician baritone. "Albert Tindall, charmed."

He and Jacob shook hands. Pia touched the hand Albert offered between the seats. And they were off.

"Congratulations on your damehood," Pia said. "I'm not sure what to call you now."

"No worries," her hostess said, patting her knee. "You can call me Dame Millie."

"Oh, before I forget," Pia said. "I need to stop at a place called Manchester Town Hall."

"Bloody hell," Albert scoffed. "Downtown at this hour?"

"We offered our services to the investigators."

"Perhaps you could call him," Dame Millie said. "Our dinner reservation is for half seven."

"Did you know Chloe's last call was to me?" Pia asked.

"You don't say. And she was murdered just after?"

Pia considered how much she should talk about the message. Benton had asked her not to reveal its contents to anyone. Yet it didn't seem right to leave one of Chloe's former teammates in complete darkness. She said, "She'd just come from interviewing a woman named Bella Davis, who told her—"

Albert gasped or coughed from the driver's seat. She couldn't tell which. Pia went on and sketched a brief version of Chloe's message explaining about the twelve names without naming them.

"I'd like to hear that message," Dame Millie said. "Could you play it for me?"

"The police haven't released it to the public yet."

Dame Millie leaned back. "Surely, people at our level don't need a policeman's permission."

"Whose names did she rattle off?" Albert asked. "Anyone we know?"

Uneasy about what she'd already revealed, Pia said, "She mentioned an outfit near here called the Morpheus Institute. She said they kill people in their dreams."

"The Morpheus?" Albert sneered. "What rubbish."

Pia glanced his way, then returned her gaze to Dame Millie. "You're familiar with it?"

Her hostess looked angry. "I can't believe Chloe would trade in useless village gossip. She shouldn't have done."

"Sorry, what gossip?"

"Kill people in their dreams?" Dame Millie was incredulous. "Has to be gossip. Sounds like the idle chatter of schoolgirls. You really shouldn't show up in our corner of the world spouting bizarre conspiracy theories. That's so American. Did you and Chloe talk often?"

Pia found the sharp response out of synch with the old Millie Tindall. "Haven't seen or heard from her since a party after her last game, years ago."

"Why on Earth would you take her seriously then?" Dame Millie looked out the window. "One should never speak ill of the dead, but Albert's right. Pure rubbish. Really. May as well tell me they practice voodoo or some such."

"What do they do?"

"I would think you were a client of theirs." Dame Millie touched her arm and said in a conspiratorial whisper. "I know all about your insomnia. Waking up half the Olympic Village with your nightmares, I heard."

Pia had long since ignored people who tried to devalue her over her sleep disorder, but for some reason it hurt coming from someone with a title in front of her name. "You've been to them?"

"Not I, certainly." Dame Millie leaned back. "Lots of important people have been to them, though. We would never know for certain, but one could imagine the royals going there. Albert struggled with his sleep as the demands of his business weighed on him. There's a good deal of pressure to perform in the corporate world. I dare say it's loads more than we had to deal with in football." She let out a laugh.

Pia recalled England's team had reached the World Cup Semi-Finals after Dame Millie had retired. She'd missed the mounting stress that went with those games.

Pia turned to Albert, "They helped you?"

"Indeed." He inhaled and glanced at the traffic. They were boxed in on all sides. "Brilliant methodology, that lot."

"How does it work?"

"Tell, me," he said, craning around the headrest, "what keeps you up at night?"

"At the moment," she said, "I'm trying to buy an engineering firm before vulture capitalists sell off their assets."

He squinted in disbelief. "You're involved in all that, are you? I'd heard you had managers handling the business."

Pia sat still. *You're just a figurehead.* Apparently, everyone had gotten together and agreed. Or was that what Dr. Harrison called uncertain social standing?

Traffic started moving again.

"Yes, to both," she said. "I'm involved, and I have the best executives."

Albert hid his surprise as he faced front. "I'm in M&A myself. We've a bit of a private equity fund on the side. Perhaps we should talk later. As it is, if that robs you of a good night's sleep, you should certainly see the Drs. Rohan at the Morpheus."

Pia thought it odd for someone in mergers and acquisitions to have an equity fund *on the side*. But the English did things differently. Maybe they didn't mind the inherent conflict of interest a setup like that suggested. Or perhaps she was overthinking it.

Dame Millie touched her arm and leaned in with a whisper again. "He doesn't know about your childhood."

Pia wondered what her hostess knew about it.

"They can work with that kind of thing too," Dame Millie continued. "They've worked wonders for several murderers already."

"Excuse me?" Pia couldn't keep the sharpness out of her voice.

"Oh." Dame Millie cast a glance at Jacob. "Did I say something out of turn?"

Pia didn't move.

"Well, it was all well-known in the game," Dame Millie said. "I heard all about it. You killed a man and Alan Sabel kept it quiet. That's all fine by me. People at our level simply must keep certain things out of the press."

She'd heard many odd rumors of her childhood over the years. Her dad burying a murder was such a cynical interpretation of actual events, she didn't know how to respond. For some odd reason, she felt no urge to explain any of it to Dame Millie.

Albert stopped across a plaza from a large Victorian building with a clock tower not unlike Big Ben. An unruly crowd streamed across the expansive city square toward the front door.

"Here you are," Albert said. "Didn't know the GMP were in this relic anymore. Thought it was just weddings and that."

"DI Benton said they're working off-campus to keep focused." Pia started to open the door.

"Tell you what," Dame Millie said. "I'll arrange a tour of the Morpheus for us. You'll see firsthand what a marvelous operation Edward and Sybil Rohan run. Let's see, Chloe's funeral is tomorrow, the fête the next day. Hmm. I'll make it work. Right. Run along now and don't let that DI slack on the job. Damned Labor Party runs this city like a trades hall. We have to keep after their kind."

Pia hesitated with the door open. She weighed her hostess's attitude against the invitation to the Morpheus. She would rather visit the place alone or with Benton. Manners prevailed. She said, "Thank you. I can't wait to meet them."

Jacob held the door for her. Together they started across the plaza.

Jacob said, "Interesting friends *at your level.*"

"Thank you for not snickering."

CHAPTER 13

A CROWD OF PROTESTORS GATHERED on the plaza near the grand entrance. Pia guessed there were a couple hundred. Signs were raised. As she and Jacob came closer, they heard chants and angry shouts. The crowd was growing, stretching across the front of the building. Pia looked for side entrances but didn't see any. There was one main door up five steps under a church-like arch. People surged in from all directions. Many carried signs reading, *Kill Corruption* and *Ethical Living Now.* By far, the most common were mass-produced with a logo of an outstretched hand sideways bearing the words *Manifest Morals* across it.

Jacob tried to push their way through but made little progress with the gathering throng holding them in check. Jacob disappeared for a moment, then reappeared when he roughly pushed a few people aside. The crowd stopped moving. They found themselves facing a bearded young man in a plaid flannel shirt who stepped onto a makeshift platform on the Town Hall steps. Pia thought he was young to be the leader, barely out of college. The crowd shouted their slogans, then quieted.

The bearded man held up a bullhorn and spoke. "Once we idolized gods, then we idolized science. Now, we idolize corrupt billionaires."

The crowd echoed his words as if it were a mantra. He repeated the phrase, growing in volume and the crowd responded. He went for a third round, shouting this time. The crowd responded at full volume. Then an eerie silence fell over them.

Sounding distinctly American, the bearded man said, "There was a time when people pleaded with their gods for safety and sustenance. They did their best to adhere to the Ten Commandments, Sharia, the Path of Asha. In the Age of Enlightenment, we pivoted from our religious roots to idolize knowledge, reason, and logic. Humanity exploded when we chose the pursuit of science to better our global community."

Around Pia, people nodded and added affirmations. They were people from all walks of life. Some wore business suits, others work clothes, most were more casual.

The bearded man said, "Over the last forty years, a great cultural change has rippled through the world. Today, we cast aside evidence-based science. We belittle researchers and experts. We disparage edited journalists in favor of inflammatory entertainment parading as news. No longer do we care about the rules. No longer do we stop to help our neighbors. No longer do we rise up against injustice. Today, we idolize the ultra-rich who abuse the law and build their wealth on the backs of taxpayers."

Several voices around Pia shouted, "Manifest Morals!"

The bearded man smiled and nodded modestly, then continued, "We idolize those who game the system, not for pennies to feed their children, but for billions in government contracts. They have become so bold they feel entitled to murder anyone who stands in their way."

The people agreed loudly. Pia found herself liking what the bearded man said. Having survived the brutal murders of her parents, she knew injustice firsthand. She had dedicated her post-soccer life to finding justice for the innocent. Like Chloe England.

He went on, "If you steal a little, they throw you in jail. If you steal a lot, they name a building after you."

The people laughed.

He continued. "The net worth of the billionaire class has exploded to proportions not seen since the French Revolution. The top ten billionaires have more money than the nation of Saudi Arabia. The only way they could accumulate such affluence is through corruption. Out of nearly eight billion people on this planet, a hundred and sixty thousand own over half the property and assets. That's zero-point-zero-zero-zero-zero-two of the total population. They have a private assassination service that can kill the founder of a rival business while he sleeps, allowing them to buy the company cheap. A man named Charles Eden-Sonnet has—"

His gaze fell on Pia.

She felt a shiver and looked around for Jacob. Pushed to one side, he was trying politely to wedge between three or four people.

"There's one of them now," Bearded-man said. He pointed directly at Pia. "Pia Sabel, a billionaire who made her money the old-fashioned way—she killed her father for the inheritance!"

The crowd turned to face her.

"That's not true!" she shouted back. "He was murdered in—"

"Her company, Sabel Weapons Systems, has rained death and destruction on unstable countries around the globe. Another of her companies, Sabel Technologies, powers the NSA and MI6 systems that spy on every word we say. She runs a cabal that kills for the rich. Her name is on a list of other billionaires and their victims. She's had a lifetime of experience murdering and using her wealth to cover it up. The only way—"

"That's not true!"

"—she could amass a fortune like hers was through bribery and corruption!"

Someone yanked her ponytail, forcing her head back. A Manifest Morals sign swung overhead. She pushed back off her heels as the sign, stapled to a heavy 2x2 slammed into the cement at her feet. A burly man threw a haymaker punch.

When she was fifteen, her boxing coach told her she'd never survive a fight with a man unless she was quick. Since then, she had practiced speed and reflexes daily. She twisted to her right. The fist skimmed her cheek. It landed in the face of a young man behind her.

Jacob appeared on her left, both his hands shoving someone away. Several hands began grabbing at his shoulders from behind. He fell backwards, swallowed by the crowd.

Pia turned back to face the man who'd thrown the punch. Next to her stood a teenager holding a bloody nose. People held phones high over their heads, recording the fight. Pia heard Bearded-man barking over the megaphone. She couldn't tell if he were encouraging them to beat her up or urging them to calm down. It didn't matter. The crowd's bloodlust was up. The man who'd thrown the punch shoved the teenager aside and tried a right cross.

Pia buckled her knees, lowering her body as his second punch sailed over the top of her head. She rose back up, using her legs to power an uppercut that sent her brawny attacker sprawling backwards. Behind her, she could hear Jacob embroiled in a fistfight of his own. A woman shoved her sign at Pia, catching her in the ribs. It scraped and tore her top as it pushed her unzipped jacket backwards—exposing the pistol she kept holstered at her lower back.

"She's got a gun!" someone yelled. Contagious screams of fear came from several people behind her.

She couldn't let someone take that from her in a crowd like this. She ripped the stick from the lady's hands, tossed it aside, and pulled her jacket down. Which allowed a grizzly older man to pound a fist into her left eye.

She reeled backward, unable to keep her balance. She fell against someone's back and toppled to the ground. An opening in the crowd formed around her. She heard Bearded-man shouting over the bullhorn for everyone to calm down. In the gap before her, she saw a man pry the lid off a can of yellow paint.

Two hands grabbed under her shoulders and lifted her to her feet. Jacob. She knew him by his musky scent.

Bearded-man stepped between Pia and the paint can as its owner swung it back.

Pissed beyond words, Pia grabbed Bearded-man's shoulder, spun him to face her, and slammed the heel of her hand into his nose. He flew backwards into the paint can. Both men went down.

She yelled, "You son-of-a-bitch!"

Curses flew and men and women on all sides grabbed her. She'd decked their leader and they weren't happy about it.

From the outside edge of the crowd, whistles were followed by the loud cracks of batons hitting people's shoulders and sides. The crowd thinned quickly. Uniformed police constables, PCs, spilled out of the building, tossing people like rag dolls, and whacking those who took too long to flee.

Bearded-man scrambled from the ground, his shoulders covered in yellow and his face dripping blood. The paint can owner dropped the can and ran. The teenager holding his bloody nose gave Pia a dirty look and followed the crowd.

A mid-thirties, square-jawed man in a blue blazer and open-collared white shirt stepped around the PCs.

The man in the blazer gave Bearded-man a once-over glance, then turned to Pia and said, "Right, what's all this, then?"

CHAPTER 14

"I WANT HER ARRESTED FOR assault and battery," Bearded-man said while holding his nose.

"Shut up," the man in the blazer said while staring at Pia. "Detective Inspector Benton. You must be Ms. Sabel."

"I am." She extended a hand. She figured him for a swimmer based on his thick shoulders and thin waist.

Benton shook lightly, then thumbed at Bearded-man's bloody nose. "You do that?"

"Hard to tell." She pointed at her swelling cheek. "He whipped the crowd into a frenzy and sent them after me. Lots of people were taking swings at me. I defended myself."

"Corruption and lies!" Bearded-man yelled. "She yanked my shoulder and punched me in the face! You can't let her game the system—"

"Shut up," Pia and Benton said in unison.

Benton looked at Bearded-man, then back at Pia. He nodded at her swelling cheek. "You'll want ice for that."

He headed for the big door, waving for her to follow.

Bearded-man shouted, "Blatant corruption! You offer the rich girl an ice pack and I get nothing."

"We'll put you up on charges for inciting a riot," Benton said over his shoulder. He gave a nod to a PC, who marched straight for Pia's victim.

Pia watched three uniformed officers herd Bearded-man away. She couldn't help but notice there was some truth in his complaint. Although she had little compassion. A broken nose was hardly worth whining about. Or whinging, as the Brits said.

"Thanks for the rescue," she said as he held the door for her.

"I don't hold with his way of thinking," Benton said, "but I've a lot more sympathy for him than the rich."

Inside, Pia unstrapped her holster and laid it on the belt with her purse before entering the metal-detector. A PC did a double take at the pistol.

Benton stared at it with his mouth open. "Firearms are banned in the UK. Unlike you Yanks, we don't fancy mass-shootings here."

Pia and Jacob pulled their special permit cards and handed them to the officer working the metal detector. Benton snatched the cards from his man.

"MI5 lets your lot carry weapons?" Benton stared at them in disbelief before handing the cards back. "Bloody hell, that tosser was right about you and your privileges."

"Does that mean you can't spare an ice pack?" Pia asked. She stepped through the metal detector and scooped up her things.

Benton shook his head in disbelief and gestured for them to follow him. "What is it you're after?"

"I came to offer my assistance in the search for Chloe's killer."

He marched them to an infirmary, where he pulled an ice pack out of a fridge and unceremoniously lobbed it to Pia. He offered one to Jacob, who shook his head. He shoved it back and slammed the door.

"Someone killed one of our own." Benton crossed his arms and leaned his back against the fridge. "We'll handle this, thank you."

"Chloe was one of our own," Pia said. "One of a few women on Earth to play World Cup football."

"You bring too much of a spotlight with you, Ms. Sabel. You're a lightning rod of controversy. You couldn't manage the door without a brawl."

She considered pointing out they were protesting before she arrived, but he knew that.

"You don't have anything, do you." She delivered her question as a statement.

"If you have anything new to offer, I'm all ears."

"Had I not sent you the message, you wouldn't have that much."

"We have plenty. My team is sorting CCTV footage as we speak."

Pia wanted to see that video. Somewhere on it would be Chloe's killer. She said, "My team has some early analysis."

"As do we."

Pia didn't believe him. Nor did she understand his reticence to accept her help. She said, "I know a couple notorious Russians who might shed light on Anton Petrova."

"Will the Russians talk to you? Everyone knows you killed Viktor Popov in cold blood and got away with it." Benton thumbed at the plaza outside. "That muppet was right about your kind. You can cover up anything you want."

She considered arguing the point, but it was one of those cases where the rumors were true—she had actually covered up the killing of the murderous Russian. "Fine, I'll track down Petrova myself. Maybe the press will take an interest."

In the hallway outside, an officer called out for DI Benton. He opened the door and shouted, "I'm in here."

"I'll find Chloe's killer, I promise you that," Benton said.

Someone trotted toward them, their footsteps clicking in the hall.

Benton continued, "I've got more important things to worry about than the list of twelve, for the record. On the off-chance it should prove useful, tell me everything you know."

"It's a two-way street, Detective Inspector Benton." She adjusted the ice pack on her face. "Where are you on the investigation?"

An out-of-breath PC stepped to the door. "Video's been chopped to the relevant bits and queued in Room 115. Ready when you are, sir."

"Right, I'll be along in a minute." Benton sent the man off and held the door open. "We'll have to take this up another time. Where are you staying?"

"A place called Padley House."

"Dame Millie?" He stepped back, his face betraying his surprise. "You're her guest? Is she waiting for you now?"

Pia nodded.

"Damn," Benton said and rubbed the back of his neck. "I suppose she used to be one of your World Cup footballers back in the day. Should've known. Alright then. If we have a bit of an exchange, you'll leave us to our jobs?"

Pia shrugged.

"Here it is," Benton said. "We don't know more than Chloe stated on the voicemail about the twelve. The names are common enough around the world. Even 'Sabel' brings up fifty families in five countries once we skimmed off your ten thousand Google entries."

"What about Eden-Sonnet? We found—"

"You're not to go near Lord Eden-Sonnet, do you hear me?" Benton's face reddened. "We can't mither him about any of this until we know what we're dealing with. Right?"

"And the Morpheus Institute?"

"Another well-connected brick wall. We need more information before we have a chat with them."

Pia saw the truth in the Manifest Morals leader's complaint. After mentioning two important families and an institution, the air in the room had changed. She said, "Dame Millie's arranging a tour for me."

Benton stroked his chin. "Now that might be interesting. You can get something on Petrova as well?"

"Two-way street," Pia said. She pushed forward. "Let's check out the video."

Benton frowned and blocked the doorway. His face scrunched as if he were going to say *no*. He hesitated, then unfolded his arms. "Alright, this once—but this is police business. You can attend as an observer. I'll not have you interfering with the discussions."

He led them down the hall.

Jacob's phone buzzed. He checked it and held the caller-ID where Pia could see it. It read: Daniel Shikowitz. The long-serving FBI Director had been like a second father to her growing up. She couldn't imagine why he was calling Jacob.

Jacob answered the call and stayed outside when Benton led Pia into a dark room.

CHAPTER 15

SEVERAL MEN AND WOMEN HUDDLED around a large computer monitor at one end of a room full of desks.

Benton nodded to a young constable in a suit and tie and said, "PC McDonald, go ahead."

"This has been edited to show all street angles with Chloe England," the officer said. "There are no cameras on the street where she was murdered. We'll be looking for anyone suspicious. They gave us sixty seconds lead up and as much after. We know she left the Royal Infirmary at nineteen twenty-one. Her path was mostly on Oxford Road. She was alone until she came to the shopping district. Foot traffic is medium to light from there. We concentrate here, the four blocks before she pops down St. George's, the pedestrian lane where she was murdered. We'll go through this compilation once at real time, then come back to examine frames as we see fit. Note your time stamps for points of interest. Right then."

With palpable anticipation, everyone leaned forward as he pressed play.

A stout woman squeezed in front of Pia. Since she could see over the woman's shoulders, she let it go and adjusted the icepack on her eye.

On screen, a uniformed figure appeared striding at a determined pace. The back of a man with dreadlocks flowed down the sidewalk on a skateboard and passed her by. As she came under the camera's lens, a couple appeared behind her. The man wore a suit under a long raincoat. He carried shopping bags with a logo Pia didn't recognize. A VW Golf drove by on the wrong side of the road, alarming Pia until she remembered she was in England. Chloe disappeared from the frame. A man in a sport coat and sunglasses stepped out of a store and got in a red Vauxhall Corsa that pulled to the curb. Sunlight glinted in the windshield. A sharp glint. A panel van slowed, the driver taking a long look at Chloe. He shook his hand, gesturing that he considered her *hot*.

The video switched to the next camera. A skinny homeless person, the gender difficult to determine due to the baggy clothes, trotted up to Chloe and spoke. Chloe smiled and said something that disappointed the vagrant. A rough-looking man in a pea coat angled between the two.

"I don't like the Scouser," someone said.

Pia thought for a moment before recalling *Scouser* was a term for people from Liverpool.

"Quiet yet," Benton said. "Note the time stamp and we'll come back to it later."

The beggar was a woman with scraggly hair, Pia decided. She held her hands out to Chloe as if to say, *C'mon, a pound for a pint.* Pia had heard that phrase from street people once or twice. Chloe waved dismissively over her shoulder and continued on. A white A-Class Mercedes pulled up next to her. A woman got out and hurried in the opposite direction. A group of college kids ran by Chloe, chasing each other and laughing. A blue Ford Focus pulled to the curb ahead of her as she kept walking. A man with a sparkly earring hopped out, dressed in an expensive wool overcoat with a fashionable scarf around his neck, and went into a store. A woman in Lululemon jogged by in the opposite direction.

Jacob opened the door, the light from the hall dragging everyone's attention away from the screen for a moment. He tossed a nod at Pia that led to the hallway and held up his phone.

Slightly embarrassed, she slipped out to the hall.

"Director Shikowitz wants to speak to you," Jacob said.

She shifted the icepack on her cheek to her left hand and took the offered phone. "Hello, Daniel. What's up?"

"Sorry to bother you, Pia. I understand you're going to a funeral, so I called Jacob. We could use his help on this kidnapping situation you referred to us. He said you have him on a short leash."

Pia looked at Jacob. His blank, emotionless face stared back at her. "I wouldn't put it like that, exactly. What do you need?"

"My people tell me this friend of yours, Rafael Tum, is being held for ransom in Brest, Belarus. Not our jurisdiction and not a friendly country. We've made overtures to the locals, but they've shown no interest in the case. We can't mount an operation in Belarus. And the victim isn't even a US citizen. I'm afraid your friend Professor Tum is beyond our reach."

Pia looked deep into Jacob's eyes. Had he engineered the call so he could take this assignment? Belarus made it sound even more like a suicide mission. He stared back. Blank as stone.

"Tum is not my friend," Pia said. "I ran into him last month at the G20 Summit. You can't help him, and I can't help him—and he's in a foreign country. It looks like the kidnappers chose the wrong victim to ransom."

"Well, that's where it gets interesting," Shikowitz said. "When my people made a call to the embassy in Minsk and realized we had nothing, we pulled the plug. That's when the Secretary of State called me and insisted we get Jacob involved. He told me to tell you, and I quote, 'The Keepers need Tum back.' Does that mean something to you?"

Pia muted the phone and looked at Jacob. "The Secretary of State is a member of the Keepers?"

Jacob shrugged. "At the moment, you and I are the only two people on Earth not involved in a secret society."

"You joined a fraternity before you traded college for the Army. That was a secret society."

Jacob rolled his eyes in admission. "OK. You're the only person on Earth not in a secret society."

"They're holding Tum in Belarus."

"He gave me the deets." Jacob returned to his nearly catatonic state.

Pia looked him over. She knew it was a bad idea. She knew she would regret it. She took the phone off mute but kept her eyes on Jacob. "He's ready. He can take Sabel One to London, pick up Miguel and Dhanpal there, and be ready to cross the border before dawn."

A smile slid across Jacob's face. He wrapped his arms around her and squeezed her hard. Then he let go, took his phone, and bolted for the exit.

Pia exhaled her misgivings and marched back to Benton's meeting.

Several constables had stood, blocking virtually all of Pia's view. It might've been incidental, but it felt purposeful. Especially when Benton gave her a smug nod. Everyone thought she was a figurehead. She moved to one side and got a bad angle.

She texted Bianca, "Does our MI5 contract give us access to GMP's video server? I'd like to look at what's playing in room 115."

Bianca shot her a link twenty seconds later. Pia leaned back against a desk and watched the same video as the police from the comfort of her phone. She scrolled ahead to match the time stamp on the big screen.

Chloe had her phone to her ear. She approached the turnoff for the pedestrian lane at the top of the video frame. Were it not for her uniform, and the checkered band on her hat, she would be difficult to identify. A group, five men and three women, spilled out of a pub and walked toward Chloe chatting amongst themselves and swarming around her. She disappeared for a moment. A gray Toyota pulled to the curb. One of the pub people said something to the occupant and got a laugh from his mates. A red Corsa stopped next to the Toyota. The group obscured Chloe again. A man in a denim jacket got out of the Corsa and walked out of camera range. The video stopped there.

"First impressions," Benton asked.

Pia looked up and said, "Yes, the red Vauxhall—"

"You're an observer, Ms. Sabel. Thank you."

"I'd like to go back to the Scouser," a voice said and gave the time stamp.

Pia considered pointing out the Scouser might look rough, but he'd walked off camera in the opposite direction from Chloe. Benton was staring at her as if telling her not to say a word.

Dame Millie texted that they were outside waiting to pick her up.

Pia nodded at Benton and shouldered her purse. She said, "Thank you, Mr. Benton. I've learned a good deal. I must be off."

"Cheers." He nodded, bemused.

Benton turned back to his crew. "Indeed, that man caught my eye as well. Back it up, let's have another look, shall we."

Pia walked out, the machinery of her mind churning. Crossing the plaza, she got in the car, and huffed. In his condescending dismissal,

Benton was overlooking one crucial detail. Benton thought he'd won that round. She hated that he had that impression. She hadn't lost. She'd seen something and he ignored her. It was he who lost. He just didn't know it yet.

As they pulled away from the curb, Dame Millie said, "What the devil happened to your eye?"

"Rough crowd."

Dame Millie faced front and began an extravagant description of the finest restaurant in Manchester and how she was able to secure a reservation against impossible odds. She'd had to become rather pushy, you see, because people at their level simply couldn't let a random maître d' turn them away.

Pia didn't hear her. She was pissed at Benton. Did she have any right to be? Could a figurehead, even a good one, see something experienced policemen missed? Or was she ticked off because Benton bruised her ego? Surely Benton would see what she had seen. Eventually.

But it would be diplomatic to offer her thoughts on the off chance his people had missed it.

She pulled out her phone and texted Benton, "Chloe's killer was not the Scouser. But they were in that video. Let me know if you need any help finding them."

He responded a few seconds later. "I appreciate the offer, but this is police business. We'll manage somehow, Miss."

CHAPTER 16

PIA FOLLOWED DAME MILLIE AND Albert into the church and down the center aisle for Chloe's funeral. Self-conscious about her swollen eye after waking, she'd applied a little makeup. From the looks she was getting as she entered the church, it hadn't been enough.

Her hostess marched them straight to the front and stopped at the second pew, scowling at the occupants. She waved a hand and said, "Albert, find an usher. They should seat us here."

Pia spotted Jeff Benton, wearing a crisp, formal uniform complete with medals and epaulets, among the other police in the pew Dame Millie wanted. He was leaning over the shoulder of a man in the front row. Pia took Benton's confidant for Chloe's father. Seeing Benton flared her anger about his last dismissive text. She tamped it down and looked around. The first pew was family. The second to the fifth were awash in uniformed officers.

Pia touched Dame Millie's shoulder. "I think we should sit with the athletes, a bit farther back."

"Nonsense," her hostess replied. Dame Millie waved to an usher at the back.

Pia had no interest in being part of whatever would happen next. She marched back to where she found a few familiar faces. A Brazilian striker she remembered patted a small space next to her. Pia squeezed in and quietly muttered thanks.

The woman stared at Pia's eye until realizing it was impolite. With a small laugh, she whispered, "Your eye. You were playing France?"

Pia gave her a smile before getting in the right frame of mind to pay her respects to Chloe England. As she always did when settling into her pew at church, she took a deep breath and closed her eyes. She tried to think of the murder victim.

It was the fact that he'd capitalized the M in Miss that torqued Pia the most. Benton had texted, "We'll manage somehow, Miss." He'd intentionally played her age, gender, and lack of experience into a single sentence. Bastard. The fact that she'd let it bother her all the way through dinner last night was equally appalling. Not that she had wanted to be in the moment for Dame Millie's rants about the lazy people who drag down British society. But she'd come here to find out who killed Chloe England and she'd be damned if she'd let Benton stop her. *Aut inveniam viam aut faciam*, I'll find a way or make one.

The Morpheus tour. Millie had that arranged. If she uncovered something there, she'd have a bargaining chip to use with Benton. Then there was Anton Petrova, whoever he was. She'd leave another message for her favorite Russian mobster, Mikhail Yeschenko. He would know.

Again, she quieted her thoughts and tried to think of Chloe. Eyes closed. Another deep breath.

Followed by another distraction. Someone excusing themselves down the pew, stepping over knees and feet, getting closer. Pia opened her bad eye.

Abby Stokes stared down at the woman next to Pia. She said, "Go on, then. Scooch, will ya?"

Pia thought Stokes still looked like a young Mary Lou Retton with her auburn hair and irresistible smile. She closed her eye quickly.

The woman scooched and Abby plopped down next to Pia. She wrapped an arm around Pia's shoulder, the other arm around Pia's waist, and nuzzled her cheek to Pia's breast. She said, "Tell me you've seen the light, Sabel. Tell me you've come to accept my hand in marriage."

Pia peeled the hand off her stomach. "Sorry, Abby. But if I ever decide to go gay, you'll be my first call."

"You mean it?" Abby raised her cherubic face to Pia. Her collar-length hair fell away from her big brown eyes. "You know I'd give Queen E. the heave-ho for you."

"I heard you were married."

Abby sat up and faced the altar. "Didn't last."

A moment of silence passed.

Abby leaned over and whispered, "She knew I was thinking of you every time."

"Stop." Pia almost laughed, which would be the wrong thing to do at a funeral.

"No, it's true," Abby said.

Another silence passed.

"What the bloody hell happened to your eye?" When Pia didn't answer, Abby continued, "I know ten women would've loved to do that back in the day."

"You first among them."

Abby snickered.

Once again, Pia took a deep breath and closed her eyes.

"Remember that time you guys beat Thailand nine-nil?" Abby's whisper tickled Pia's ear. "The press was having a go at you about running up the score. What was it you said after? Something about drinking your enemy's blood?"

Pia almost laughed. "Thirteen to nothing. Something about the skulls of my enemies. Oh, I forget. Seemed funny at the time."

"Got you trolled something awful on Twitter. That I remember. Thought you were calling them cannibals or something."

"I was thinking of my Viking ancestry. But I guess it was a bit tone-deaf."

Together they quietly laughed at the memory. *The good old days*, as Chloe had said.

The service began. A soloist sang "Amazing Grace." As the choir proceeded in, the congregation joined their voices to the familiar hymn. Abby shared the hymnal with Pia—opened to the wrong page. When Pia realized the prank, Abby giggled and flipped to the right one. By the second stanza, Pia sensed her friend's mood changing.

Abby's eyes filled with tears as she picked up Pia's hand. "I can't believe she's gone. Just like that."

Pia felt a contagious emotion cross between them. Tears filled her eyes too. They hugged.

After the clergy took their places near the pulpit, Tania appeared in the aisle. She asked the Brazilian striker for space. The Brazilian huffed, grabbed her purse, and left for a different pew.

"Thank you for the rescue," Tania said as she took her seat.

"Rescue?"

Tania leaned close to Pia's left ear and whispered, "I'm done with that man. Won't even tell his daddy about me. What am I, his colored girl on the side? No thank you. Men suck and white men suck worse. Never again. Now I got me a non-refundable bed and breakfast in the Shenandoah."

As the officiant began the liturgy, Abby tugged Pia's arm. She pointed across Pia at Tania and whispered, "You said you weren't gay. What's with—"

"Vice President of Personal Protection at Sabel Security."

"You mean, bodyguard."

"That too."

"Oh, well, that's alright then." Abby thought for a second. "Looks like you're one up on Dame Millie, eh? Bet she has a bodyguard of her own by week's end."

Pia liked that. Dame Millie might have a title, but she didn't have bodyguards. That put Pia in the lead. She reminded herself not everything needs to be a competition. As long as she had the lead.

Tania looked the boss over and said, "Got another black eye, I see. Jacob's shit for personal protection."

While the service got underway, Tania read Pia's notes on the investigation and thumbed out responses. The most interesting was one Pia had missed: Bearded-Man had made statements that corroborated Chloe's voicemail.

Pia noticed Tania absent mindedly massaging her burn scars again. She whispered, "Do you want to try another burn specialist?"

"No." Tania's answer was quick and final.

Some problems are unsolvable, Pia thought. Sometimes we plow ahead, dealing with the pain as we go.

A young female priest who'd grown up with Chloe delivered a poignant sermon. She was followed by three speakers who shared their experiences. The first was Chloe's sister, representing the family. The second a coach, representing her first career. And the last was the Chief Constable of the Greater Manchester Police.

The service ended with the upbeat hymn "Lift High the Cross." The crowd began following the recessional and Pia felt a small portion of weight lifted. Still soaking up the ambiance, she remained in her pew while the organist played a Bach funeral cantata. Tania and Abby stayed with her. The recital ended and Pia joined the flow of exiting mourners.

When they reached the outdoors, a strong midday sun lit them. Most of the church steps were crowded by TV cameras and reporters shouting questions at the Chief Constable and DI Benton.

Across the crowd, Pia saw Liam Pickford squeezing his way through the press, heading for the street. She hadn't expected him.

A microphone pushed into Pia's personal space. "You're Pia Sabel, aren't you? What happened to your eye?"

"Not everyone's a fan," she deadpanned.

"Oh," the reporter said. "Come to gloat over your archenemy then?"

Behind the mic was a woman so young, Pia wondered if she were in high school. She glanced at the crowd facing Benton and realized the novice reporter had been shoved out of the big story. She felt sympathy for her. "I came to pay my respects to England's finest defender."

The reporter brightened, grateful for Pia's attention.

"Amen to that, sister," Abby said.

The reporter recognized Abby and asked her questions about Chloe. Pia surveyed the sea of people and found Liam waiting for the light at the corner. She waved, hoping to catch his eye. He missed her. To her right, the press was losing interest in Benton. From their disappointed posture, she guessed he'd given them the politically safe line about this being a time for remembrance and respect, not for listing clues and suspects.

A few of the reporters noticed Pia and Abby with a mic in front of their noses. They trotted over hoping for a fresh sound bite. They recognized Abby right away.

Squeezed out in the rush, the young reporter switched from Abby back to Pia. She asked, "Ms. Sabel, you've grown your business beyond what your father built. What is the key to your success?"

Pia suddenly recalled the Thailand-game incident Abby had reminded her of. She said, "I drink from the skulls of my enemies."

Abby burst out laughing. The reporter laughed. Pia laughed.

Then she remembered the social media beating she'd taken for that statement. That sound bite was going to go viral—again. She winced.

The young reporter said, "Is that why you came to Chloe England's—"

A new reporter pushed the young one aside. "Is that your way of admitting Rain Meyer's charges?"

"Who?" Pia asked.

"The founder of Manifest Morals. Rain Meyer accused you this morning of being complicit in murders for the rich."

"What?" Pia waited a beat. The reporter waited her out. "I have no idea what you're talking about."

"He read a statement this morning, posted it on YouTube, Facebook, Twitter, and a few other places."

"I've been busy paying my respects to Chloe England, one of football's finest."

Pia had a bad feeling about the direction of the next question. Tania tugged at her elbow. One of Tania's indispensable skills was finding an exit through a crowd. Pia stepped back into the space she knew from experience Tania had cleared behind her. When confronted by a crowd, a tactical retreat followed by a sweep to the left was standard procedure.

The reporter's voice rose with a hint of anger and self-righteousness. "Rain Meyer said you've been covering up murders all your life, from your mother to the Morpheus Institute. And now you're offering it as a service to billionaires everywhere."

Pia froze. The shock of the accusation was overwhelmed by the mention of the Morpheus. Incredulous, she snapped, "He said what?"

"Here now," Benton waded into the gathering crowd from the right. "We won't besmirch our local institutions with wild accusations from foreigners."

Pia felt a touch of gratitude and looked at him.

He faced the reporters and added, "Whatever Mr. Meyer has on Ms. Sabel has nothing to do with the Morpheus."

CHAPTER 17

PIA MADE HER WAY TO the reception in the parish hall next door. On the way, she made another call to Mikhail Yeschenko. The Russian usually called her back right away. She hated calling him, but he could shed light on the elusive Anton Petrova. Without time to play cat and mouse with Yeschenko, she left a message.

The line to pay respects to Chloe's father wound around the room. Populated with constables, officials, former teammates, and coaches, everyone waiting traded stories about the deceased. Pia found the end of the line and joined. Tania and Abby chatted behind her with several former teammates. Overhearing their conversation, she learned Chloe's mother had been killed at the Manchester Arena bombing when a terrorist had attacked an Ariana Grande concert. Chloe's mother had been one of twenty-two victims. In light of that, Pia tried to think of what she would say to Dominick England. The man was suffering more than she imagined. She thought of the platitudes people said to her at her father's funeral. She picked one of the least obnoxious and rehearsed it in her mind.

When her turn finally arrived, she introduced herself, shook his hand, and looked into his eyes. Words failed her. She wrapped her arms around him and held him tight. He stiffened for an instant, then gave into the hug and squeezed her back. They rocked from side to side for a moment, then pulled back. His eyes filled with tears. They shared a mutual understanding: the bereaved stand in the isolation of grief and see the world passing by outside, their words nothing but muted noises. He nodded, knowing she'd once felt his anguish. Without saying a word, they shared an epic poem on sorrow. She gave him a final squeeze and moved on.

It made her feel good to have a moment with Mr. England. In her experience, events like this always became hectic, with conversations half-finished and people pulling you one way then the other.

Food of all kinds overflowed several tables. Famished, she took a plate and a bagel, slathered on some cream cheese, and added lox. As she hunted for the onion and tomato, Liam Pickford appeared by her side.

"Quite a shiner," he said. "What's the other bloke look like?"

"Liam," she said. "I didn't know you knew Chloe."

She quickly stashed her plate under a warmer.

"I had a wee crush on her when I was at Oxford," he replied in his Scottish brogue. "Came to pay my respects."

"You knew her?"

"Not personally, no. I was working on my Master of Mathematics when she lit up the Olympics back in the day. Everyone in the department thought she was the finest lass on the team." He smiled. "Lot of strange guys in math, y'know."

Pia laughed at his self-deprecating humor and imagined socially awkward grad students huddled around a few screens in a windowless basement.

"I cannae stay long," he said. "Your Major is raking my people over the coals. I feel bad leaving them. But I did want to say hello." He punctuated his words with a sly grin. "And I thought I might give destiny a wee push."

"I'm glad you did. I was hoping—"

Benton stepped between them, showing his back to Liam. "What was that all about then, that text last night?"

Over his shoulder, Liam raised a brow and turned away. Pia sighed. "I was talking to that man."

Benton glanced over his shoulder, but Liam had moved off. He turned back. "What were you on about?"

Starving, Pia looked for her bagel plate. "I thought you'd manage somehow."

"Maybe you get away withholding evidence in the States—"

"I'm not withholding anything." She gave up on the bagel and faced him. "They were right there on the video."

"Who was?"

"The men in the red Vauxhall."

Benton leaned back, appearing to replay the video in his head. Then he frowned. "The Corsa? A man walks out of a store, gets in a car, and drives away—and you think he's a killer? Ah, total rubbish. Should've known."

"That wasn't the only—"

An older man in a serious uniform with medals and epaulets rivaling Benton's touched his arm. Benton looked up and straightened as if he were about to salute. They walked away without another word.

Pia felt her fists clench as she watched him leave. The arrogance of that man.

She started looking around for the bagel when Abby bounded in front of her. Tania followed with a wide grin. An older man, relying on a cane with a silver handle in a way that made him look like a car with a flat tire, kept up as best he could. He smiled at Pia with a charming and confident twinkle in his eye.

Abby said, "I want you to meet Eric Stone. He lives in the Peak District not far from Padley House. We'd love to have you for a cuppa later."

Pia shook Eric's hand and wondered when Abby had grown so fond of men.

Before she and Eric could exchange greetings, Dame Millie added herself to their circle. She glanced at Abby and said to Pia, "I see you've met Eric's gardener."

"Horticulturist," Abby said with ice.

The two women side-eyed each other. Pia knew they'd been teammates for years but had never heard of a rift between them.

Eric opened his mouth to speak but Dame Millie beat him to it. "Oh, yes, Eric has a scaled replica of the original Crystal Palace. He's let Abby have the run of the place. Isn't that sweet? She's turning it into Biosphere 3, I think."

"It's a certified research facility," Abby snarled. "An extension site for the Royal Agricultural University, thank you." She turned to Pia.

"Eric was the professor of toxicology there when I got the grant for my project. He very kindly offered to rent his place for the duration."

Eric said, "The university made some overdue repairs to the conservatory, so it worked out quite satisfactorily for everyone."

"I'd love to see that," Tania said. "Sounds fun."

Abby nudged Tania's shoulder in a thanks-for-backing-me-up gesture.

Everyone turned their eyes to Pia. For a split second she wondered if a toxicologist might be behind the mysterious deaths of Breach and Yang. Those thoughts disappeared as quickly as they came. Nothing more than unfounded paranoia that might require a whole session with Dr. Harrison to unpack. The Morpheus was top on her list, but there was time for a social visit with Abby before the tour. She said, "I agree, it does sound fascinating. You're talking about a greenhouse, right?"

"A rather large one," Eric said. "Four acres under glass."

"Tea sounds wonderful. Thank you for the invitation."

"Well, that's settled then." Dame Millie raised her shoulders and gazed across the group at Eric as if dismissing him. "We'll see you at four."

Pia found her missing bagel. Just beyond it was the platter of tomato and onion slices. She reached out for her plate but felt someone touch her opposite arm.

Albert Tindall pulled her elbow. "Excuse me everyone, I'm stealing our guest for a moment."

He gently tugged Pia to him and guided her through the crowd to a group of young men in crisp business suits. Two of them left as she and Albert stepped up to the third.

Blue eyes set deep in a round face locked on Pia as he clasped his gloved hands behind his back and bowed. Germophobe? Namaste? She couldn't tell. He smirked with the smug arrogance common to young men who'd lucked into early success.

"You must be Pia Sabel," he said. "Albert's told me you were lovely and he's not wrong. I'm Wayne Walker, of the 'Walking with Walker' podcast. You must do my show."

There were many forms of press these days, some legitimate and others less so. To keep on the best side of journalism, she had her people vet any interviewers for intellectual capacity. She didn't mind being grilled so long as it was done honestly and with regard for truth. She smiled. "Call my public relations officer, Emily Dominguez. I'm sure she can find a time."

"Oh, you misunderstand me." He leaned back, his round belly swelling between them as he did so. "I want a meeting right away. I interview all the top people in business. Surely you've heard of me."

"Sorry, I've not."

"Albert arranges most of my interviews at the highest levels, he'll vouch for me."

Pia wondered why Albert would be involved with a podcast if he did M&A work and had a private equity fund *on the side*. Both of those endeavors were fulltime jobs. Maybe it was a cover story. He'd been extra protective of the Morpheus. Could he be involved in Chloe's murder? She slowed her thinking. Once again, there was nothing behind her questions. Unfounded ideas. She dismissed them and admonished herself. Unlikable is not evidence of guilt.

Wayne appeared to sense her hesitation. He said, "I've interviewed Warren Buffett, Meg Whitman, Bobby Jenkins, David Breach, Tim Cook, Mary Barra. We walk and talk, Walking with Walker, right? That's how it works. As a matter of fact, I just took a walk with your friend Dave Krueger at McDowell Aerospace. I had to fly out to sunny San Diego to meet him. He had some strong opinions about the future of your company."

"Is he still pissed off about losing his bet?" she asked. At the same time, she made a mental note that her father's mentor, Bobby Jenkins was on Walker's list.

Wayne leaned in with curiosity and arched a brow. "And what bet might that be?"

"He made a public bet in Vegas that my company would be sold off within weeks of my father's death. He lost a million."

"He never mentioned it."

"Shocker. What kind of questions do you ask?"

"More philosophical in nature," he said and added a sardonic smile.

"For instance, I would ask you what it's like 'to drink from the skulls of your enemies.'"

As much as she tried not to, she did a double take. Had her remark gone viral already? Pia looked back across the room for her bagel. Her stomach growled.

Wayne went on. "Or perhaps we could talk about your qualifications for the job."

"What did the Queen say when you asked her?"

To the side, Albert snickered. Wayne cut him a glare and Albert rolled his gaze away.

Something about Walker's presence set off Pia's paranoia alarms. Assumptive men always bothered her and his assumptions about her qualifications pissed her off. Or was she running into Dr. Harrison's evaluative scrutiny? Something about asymmetrical relationships.

She took a deep breath. In the space of a few minutes, she'd suspected three people without a sliver of evidence. Maybe Dr. Harrison was right that leaving emotions unresolved had a detrimental effect on her mental health. If she kept it up, she'd be involuntarily committed in the morning.

"Let's us take a walk round Padley House this afternoon," Wayne said.

Albert grinned and nodded enthusiastically.

She wondered about the dynamic between these two. She didn't like either of them, yet she felt a minor obligation to let her host save face.

"This weekend's for Chloe," she said.

CHAPTER 18

PIA WENT IN SEARCH OF her bagel before everyone heard her hunger pangs howling like a lonesome coyote. As she crossed the room, Abby held up the plate. Tania stood next to her, smiling. Abby had finished topping the lox with a slice of tomato and onion. Pia took it with gratitude. There were even a few capers rolling around on top.

"Oh, you saved me," Pia said. "Thank you."

As she took a big bite and chewed, she noticed Abby casting a bored gaze across the crowd. Next to her, Tania's smile had turned mischievous.

That's when the taste of cinnamon hit her. Heavy, dry, powdered cinnamon—and lots of it. It coated her windpipe and made her choke. Pia spat out the bite onto the plate and saw a thick layer of red powder hidden under the lox. Abby and Tania cracked up into each other's shoulders.

"Thanks, guys." Pia put the plate on the table. "Dame Millie doesn't eat breakfast, so there was nothing—"

"Sod it, Sabel," Albert gripped her arm as he rushed in. "Did you have to be so rude to my friend? Would it hurt you to do one interview while you're here?"

Pia twisted her arm free. Did he really think of her as a trophy to be paraded in front of his business contacts? She considered telling him where he could take a flying leap. Then she remembered her father's constant business proverb, *Make no enemies.* She reset herself and said, "I came to bury Chloe England."

"Well." He stiffened and sniffed. "I suppose that's right then. Even if you hardly knew the girl."

Pia squinted at him and considered telling him she'd stay in town the rest of the weekend. Surely Manchester had nice hotels. Then she recalled Dame Millie having added her to the fête's roster. There was an appearance to make for the children. She would have to tough it out a little longer.

"Let's just set some boundaries, Albert," she said. "My time is my own. If you have an opportunity you would like me to consider, discuss it with me first."

Behind him, Tania picked up a new plate and found a bagel.

"If you insist," Albert said. "Since you're here for Chloe, I'll assume you'll not deign to meet the Morpheus Institute's founder, after you badmouthed them."

"I disparaged no one." She scowled down at him. "I told you—in confidence—what Chloe said in her message. I know nothing about them." She held his gaze. He tried to look away. "Since the Morpheus was on her mind at the end, I would like to meet them. Thank you."

From the corner of her eye, she noticed Tania offering a loaded bagel on a plate.

"Very well, then." Albert raised his nose. "Just understand, this is different. Edward Rohan is a great man. He specializes in people at the highest levels. He trains you to take control of your subconscious where your vagrant fears linger and snicker like dangerous thieves."

It had been many years since she'd slept like a normal person, and she wasn't taking Dr. Harrison's advice. Maybe Albert was on to something.

He began moving through the crowd. Pia glanced at Tania and the mouth-watering bagel, shrugged, and followed Albert.

"Sounds like a cult leader," Pia said.

"Believe it or not, there are people smarter than you, Sabel." Albert stopped and spun around with angry eyes. His voice softened. "He's not a cult, he's just … well, miles ahead of you. And me. And everyone else. You'd do well to listen to him. One day, he grabbed me and said, 'You worry about *ifs*. *If* you can fix this problem, *if* you can make this deal, *if* you can save this patient. But none of the *if's* matter. All that matters is what you *do*.' He broke through to me, Sabel. He's taken ancient ideas and used science to broaden them. He's on a new level. One that's never been imagined before. We're nothing, we're … oh, we're just crabs picking at algae in the sands beneath his feet."

Her host turned around and slipped through the throng.

Albert's manner was so odd, she considered walking away. But Chloe had mentioned the Morpheus and it was her only thread to the story. Putting her head down, she charged ahead and caught up with Albert.

They came to a cluster of people focused on a couple. One half of the couple was a dark-haired woman wearing a dark gray pantsuit and a pleasant smile. The other was a short, muscular man whose thick, wavy black hair swept back to clever curls over his collar. He wore a fashionable but dark banker's suit and moved with the grace of a dancer as he left the circle and greeted Pia with open arms. Albert melted away into the crowd.

"Meeting you," he said, "Ms. Sabel, is the greatest of pleasures." He did a quick assessment of her black eye before focusing on her good eye. He held her gaze with a rare intensity. "Edward Rohan, ma'am."

"I like you already," she said with a smile.

"I mean it. You know, I've studied you." Rohan held her attention as if no one else in the room mattered. "From your tragic childhood to your fight yesterday, yours is a remarkable journey. Recently, I've heard from many sources that you've doubts about my life's work."

"You're wrong to listen to others."

"Ah. Quite so." He smiled graciously and nodded, still not breaking eye contact. "I apologize. I should ask you, is it true the dearly departed left this world with the name of my institute on her lips?"

"Not exactly," Pia said and noted the open channel between the Rohans and Tindalls. "She interviewed someone who made extraordinary claims about your institute. She did not finish her message to me, but I did not have the impression she'd formed any opinion one way or another about your work."

"Then you've formed no opinions either?"

"I have no idea what the Morpheus Institute does. All I know is that Dame Millie said I would benefit from your methods."

"Yes," he said. "You have a rather famous case of insomnia. Walk with me and I'll explain the Institute."

They began a tour of the room.

He said, "In the second century, Neoplatonist philosopher Plotinus posited that two universes exploded into existence from a single burst of light. Today, astrophysicists have determined there was a Big Bang, a single spark of light. We have learned that in that instant, the universe was filled with matter and dark matter. The former is what we see, touch, and feel. The latter comprises 85 percent of the known universe, but only 25 percent of its mass. That is to say, there exists a larger universe around us that cannot be seen, touched, or felt. For centuries, mystics all over the world have traveled this parallel universe. As do you, although you never understood what it is."

"When do I access a parallel universe?" she asked.

"Every night, when you fell asleep." He spread his hands before them as if it were obvious. "But we'll get to that. You see, every ancient religion refers to this parallel universe, the plane of dark matter. There are thousands of ancient texts about it on every continent. It appears in the stories of the Hermetics, Buddhists, Theosophists, and Hindus, to mention a few. Judeo-Christian history separates heaven and Earth. Every culture refers to a spirit world separate from our world accessed by out-of-body experiences. A place inhabited by ghosts, demons, and angels. The truly enlightened move between the two at will."

He stopped walking and stared at her. She felt as if they were alone in the room.

"When you first fall asleep," he said, "you can control the direction of your dream because your ancient and instinctive soul knows the world you've entered. But then your modern self—she who flies on airplanes and watches television—refuses to believe in the universe of dark matter. You lose control and become a passenger in a dreamscape filled with familiar people and places behaving in ways you cannot understand."

"Are you talking about astral projection?" Pia recalled her teenage fascination with the concept. Something she'd tried but didn't find useful or effective in curing her insomnia.

"That is one of many attempts to understand how to access the other world. Without training and supervision, your subconscious will destroy your feeble attempt to set foot on that plane."

Pia had read a book about astral projection and tried it. He was right, though; she'd had no training and abandoned the idea. She'd considered it nonsense.

He stopped again. He faced her, this time taking both her hands. "Pia, you are one of a small cadre of unique people who struggle with responsibilities far beyond what any one human should. You carry the weight of all those people who count on you for their livelihoods. It strains your soul. When you lay your head on the pillow, you fill with worries and cannot sleep. It causes you to lash out and say, 'I drink from the skulls of my enemies.' A cute and pithy statement that would be harmless at any time—other than your rival's funeral."

Pia's eyes involuntarily closed. She inhaled her embarrassment. There was no need to look at her phone. If this stranger knew about it, and Wayne Walker knew about it, her effigy would be roasting over the open flames of social media bonfires.

"There is no reason for such a beautiful young woman to be so burdened," Rohan said. "At your age, life should be filled with romance, magic, and wonder."

"I suppose you have a way to unburden me," Pia said. "How much?"

"The Morpheus Institute is a non-profit supported by a benefactor who sponsors the worthy. There is no cost." He gave a slight bow of humility. "Let us show you how to balance your soul in your dreams."

Her previous suspicions had been unfounded but now her paranoia was flaring. This guy's bullshit was so deep, she couldn't imagine he wasn't involved in something. But she had one big problem: What criminal conspiracy worked for free?

Edward smiled up at her, then glanced at someone waiting nearby.

"I've taken too much of your valuable time," he said. "You have an admirer vying for your attention. Dame Millie has scheduled a tour for you later this afternoon. I await our next meeting with bated breath."

He kissed her hand and left.

Liam Pickford watched the doctor walk away. Then he turned to Pia. "You're a popular lass."

"He's a salesman," Pia said. "But I'm having trouble figuring out what he's selling."

Pia wondered if she would allow herself to undergo Rohan's treatment. Maybe she needed what the Morpheus offered. No. Not maybe. She definitely needed what the Morpheus claimed to offer. She questioned the reality of his cure. Was it science-fantasy or real?

But that would come later. Right now, Rohan was right. She deserved a little romance, magic, and wonder. And Liam—either green-eyed devil or angel—had made an effort to find her and spend time with her. That counted for something, didn't it?

"I'm glad you gave destiny a push," she said.

"That fella you were chatting with earlier about last night's texts, is he your—"

"No. He's a cop. And a rude one too. Had some questions about Chloe's murder."

Liam watched her closely for an awkward moment until he appeared satisfied.

"I've come to say goodbye," he said. "I've got to be back in London shortly. Your Major won't let up on McKenna Engineering."

"Destiny is proving a bit elusive for us, isn't it?" She tried to laugh but he was melting her heart, and with it, all her reservations about him.

"Well, about that. Uhm. Perhaps you'd fancy dinner in London?" He blushed again.

"I'd like that very much." She squeezed his arm. "I'm committed through the weekend, but I'll figure something out and get in touch."

She hesitated and bit her lip as she pieced together the next sentence in her head. "Just to be clear, Liam, I've given all authority for the deal to the Major. I'll not have any effect one way or the other on the business side of things."

"Honesty looks good on you." He put a knuckle under her chin and raised it. An unexpected smile spread across his face. "I'd give up the whole business for a quiet evening with you under the fateful stars." He paused as if holding back the punchline. "By recusing yourself from the deal, you've given it away that I've a good chance to gaze up at Orion with you. Cheers."

CHAPTER 19

PIA WATCHED HIM WALK AWAY through the crowd. Why had she been so dismissive of him? He wasn't a cad, a rake, a Casanova. He was a businessman trying to do the right thing for his employees when their paths had crossed. She knew it in her heart. And he was making a great impression.

Maybe.

"Fancy a chap of his sort, do you?" Benton asked. He stood next to her, watching Liam make his way to the exit.

"His sort?"

Benton faced her. "Y'know. Minted, posh."

"I've more money than any ten people could spend in a lifetime. None of it will bring Chloe back. 'Minted' is useless. No, I don't fancy posh."

Benton looked both surprised and pleased. "What do you look for?"

"Men who keep their promises." She folded her arms. "You promised to find Chloe's killer."

"You're like the bloody brass holding that over my head." His jaw clenched. "I'm keen on what you said about the cars in the video."

"They changed cars to a blue Ford. They changed clothes and drivers. But they didn't change the diamond earring one of them was wearing."

Tania approached and waited at an arm's length. Behind her stood the Tindalls, Abby Stokes, and Eric Stone. They watched her.

Benton glanced at the group, then faced Pia again. "You're saying they staged cars and clothes along a path she could've chosen at random? Bollocks. They'd have to be clairvoyant for that."

"Basic tradecraft in the covert world," Tania chimed in. "We look for that kind of thing when we're tracking Russian agents. Or British, for that matter. A two-man team will take two cars on a mission. They travel separately, bring a grab bag full of clothes, glasses, accessories. Maybe they need to split up and follow two people. Or maybe they need to follow one without being seen on public cameras. They drive ahead of the target; one hops out, goes in a store, keeps an eye on the target, then reverses his jacket; the driver goes three blocks to where the other car's been stashed; swaps cars, positions the first car another five blocks ahead; change jackets and scarves; circle back with all new looks; swaps places with his friend; repeat. Two men in two cars ends up looking like eight different people on camera."

Tania glanced at Pia and nosed toward the exit. Time to go.

Benton frowned. "Bloody hell, you're right. There was a blue Ford. Spies really do all that?"

Pia said, "Remember when the Russians poisoned the Skirpals in Salisbury back in 2018? That's how their assassins operated. My people helped MI5 dig through hours of video to find them."

Benton leaned back, observing her with new respect. "You think they're Russian?"

"Could be anyone. They're definitely familiar with covert operations, though. One man wore his coat collar over his chin, the other had his scarf covering the side of his face. Then he used glasses with Fresnel lenses. They're professionals."

"What kind of lens?" Benton asked.

"Fresnel. Concentric grooves in the glass. If you look straight through, everything looks normal. If you look from an angle—and security cameras are usually looking down from above—the lens distorts the light. Measuring the eyes becomes impossible. They were defeating facial recognition software."

"Thank you." His sincerity showed in his expression. "You've been most helpful."

"I'll keep my promise about Anton Petrova," Pia said. "I've not connected with my Russian contacts yet."

"Keep in touch." Benton gave her a casual salute. "Cheers."

Tania motioned to the door and Pia followed her to the street.

The entourage waited next to the limo. Abby pulled her car to the back of the line.

Pia's limo driver opened the door. Albert got in first. Dame Millie started to get in after him, then looked over her shoulder at Pia. Nodding at Tania, she asked, "Is she riding with us?"

"Who else would *she* be riding with?" Tania snapped. She pushed around Pia to confront Dame Millie, then checked herself mid-step. She leaned back. Anger rippled through her posture and the pain of ten thousand exclusions flared in her eyes. "Screw this. I'm riding with Abby."

Tania spun around, tossing her big hair in Dame Millie's face, and stormed away.

Pia turned to the driver. "Take the Tindalls back to their house and retrieve my things. Pick us up at the Morpheus."

Pia followed Tania.

"Oh, don't be childish about this," Dame Millie called after Pia. "I simply assumed bodyguards rode along in a separate car."

Pia stopped and replied over her shoulder. "Jacob rode in your passenger seat—at your invitation."

Dame Millie's face twisted up as she thought of an answer. "I rather liked him. Pleasant fellow."

"He's gone. She's my best friend. You don't want to ride with her, you won't ride with me."

"Well, it certainly wasn't my intention to offend."

"And there's your problem. It's not your intention that matters, it's the results. Did you stop to think what your words feel like?" Pia resumed her march to Abby's car.

"How rude!" Albert stuck his head out. "You simply can't walk out on us, Pia. You're our guest. How would it look?"

"I don't associate with racists," Pia called out while walking backwards. "I'll find a hotel."

"You won't find anything in the Peak District this time of year," Dame Millie said. "Sold out months in advance."

Ignoring the woman, Pia hopped in Abby's backseat and closed the door. Tania sat across from her looking out her window. Eric rode in front.

Abby pulled into traffic.

"Didn't mean to cause a scene with your friend," Tania said.

"She's not who I remember." Pia tried to catch Tania's gaze, but her friend kept her face to the glass. "I would've backed you up if you'd slapped her."

"Not at a funeral."

"Millie was never an asshole until the Queen tapped her shoulders with a magic sword," Abby said. "Good thing that happened after she retired or I'd've decked her and got benched for it."

Eric twisted to face them. "I'd offer you a place to stay, but I'm afraid Sonse End is torn up for renovations at the moment. Mother left me a grand estate and only my grandfather's silver handled cane collection for maintenance."

"You'll stay at Claigeann Cottage, my place," Abby said. "That'll torque ol' Millie, eh? But, fair warning, I've only got a couch and a fur rug by the fireplace."

"Dibs on the rug," Pia said and nudged Tania.

Tania collected herself and said, "Nice move making them ride home alone in *your* limo."

CHAPTER 20

Sonse End stood near the eastern end of Peak District National Park. Secluded in the rolling hills and surrounded by trees, the home looked like a giant brick dropped from the sky—in 1650. A three-story rectangle with a balustrade façade hid a shiny new zinc roof, the peak of which could barely be seen from the ground. The prominent front door might have been used on Downton Abbey, but the rest of the place sagged and peeled. Two hundred yards across a wild, sprawling meadow stood a colossal, gleaming greenhouse.

They bypassed the dilapidated home and drove straight to a loading dock. Eric waved goodbye and walked to his house.

A large metal roll-up door allowed trucks inside. They went through the regular door next to it. Inside the loading area a Bobcat with a scoop waited for an operator. Next to it was a large workbench and tools.

Pia pointed at a box on the corner of the workbench featuring a skull and crossbones warning label. "What is that?"

"A horticulturist's chemistry lab," Abby said. She opened it and pointed. "All kinds of nasty things in there. Potassium chloride, ammonium nitrate, and so on."

"Are any of them deadly?"

"One will give you a heart attack if you inject it and the other can blow you up, so, yeah—deadly. But, don't worry, Sabel, I'm a professional. You're safe with me."

Pia smiled and looked around.

Beside them was a significant stone building. The greenhouse glass towered above the structure as if protecting it.

"That used to be the servant's outhouse," Abby said pointing to the house. "Sonse End is a Grade II Manor House, so they had to build the greenhouse around it. I use it for an office. Oi! Don't look at me like that. It's had plumbing for a century."

Pia turned her gaze to the glass high overhead.

"The original Crystal Palace was 168 feet at its highest point. This one is sixty, with the low points being forty-eight at the walls. We needed height for the trees. Each of the four acres is a different ecosystem. Perfect little world for me."

An aisle ran down each wall with a large central aisle in the middle. Several crossing aisles formed a grid, each large enough for the Bobcat to maneuver.

The interior was so hot and humid Pia felt dew forming on her nose. Abby pointed to a map of the building pinned to a steel pillar. She said, "The project I'm fleecing the university for—I mean, studying for the university—is research into what England might look like in different climate change scenarios. If the Gulf Stream continues to warm our bit of island, we might become somewhat tropical. Eric generously rents his greenhouse to us for the purpose. The four zones are planted with natural flora from different temperate zones."

They started down the aisle with Abby in the lead. Pia overtook her. Abby picked up her pace, her shorter legs working hard to keep up. Pia matched her and accelerated, nearly jogging.

"Stop!" Tania laughed. "You don't have to compete on a freaking greenhouse tour. It's not like there's a finish line, y'know."

Pia and Abby glanced at each other and smiled.

"You two didn't even know you were doing it, did you?" Tania scoffed. "Athletes."

"This section represents the Negro-Branco moist forests of northern Brazil." Abby walked on a path that disappeared into dense leaves. "These *Lecointea amazonica* are thriving but the *Clathrotropis glaucophylla* and *Peltogyne venosa* keep dying. The first time we lost some of these buggers, I thought they shipped us right dead plants. But the same thing happened with two more, um ..." She turned to them. "I'm getting a bit nerdy, right?"

"I never expected you to spout Latin," Pia said.

"That was fire," Tania said. "I didn't understand a word of it, but I'm down with the enthusiasm, girl."

Abby blushed and studied a leaf. She stole a bashful glance at Tania, then snapped her gaze back to the leaf.

"Mold," she said. "Damn English rain. Biodiversity in the natural environment takes care of this problem. We think. Might be the ants. Still studying."

She took out her phone and snapped a picture of the leaf. "Anyway." Abby trotted forward. "You've got to see this."

As she got ahead of them, Pia tugged Tania's arm. In confidence, she said, "You know she's a notorious womanizer, right?"

"Yeah, I'm sure …" Tania grinned at Pia. Slowly her mouth fell open. "Oh. Hold up. You saying that girl's hitting on me?"

Pia nodded. "Dated half the gay women in UEFA. And some that weren't."

"Holy … I thought she was fun. Hell, she is fun. Oh, you shoulda seen your face when you bit into that cinnamon. She's a riot." Tania watched as Abby stuck her hand into the dirt beneath a bush and pulled up a weed by its root. "Yeah, guess we gotta have an understanding."

"Check this out." Abby waved them over to a bright purple flower. "*Cattleya labiata*, the corsage orchid. Sometimes we get shipments of plants and there's a hitchhiker onboard. Most are useless weeds, but this—is this sweet or what?"

She plucked one of the flowers and handed it to Tania.

"Uh." Tania took it with a quick glance at Pia. "Abby, we should talk about—"

"About the Cockscomb Basin in Belize." Abby bolted ahead to the next section of the greenhouse. "I'm chuffed about this section. We've got elfin scrub and broadleaf and, and …"

Abby caught the look in Tania's eye. She turned to Pia. "You brought her up, didn't ya, Sabel? Oh, you're rubbish as a wingman."

"It was the cinnamon. Had to get even."

"Ah well, no harm done, eh?" Abby gave Tania a hip bump.

"Love the orchid," Tania said with an apologetic smile.

Abby's phone chirped. She answered it and started walking quickly around a corner to a different wing. She pocketed her phone. "Got an off-hours shipment coming in. Have a look around. You're in the Utría, Pacific Colombian section here."

Abby disappeared between plants quickly.

Pia tried calling Mikhail Yeschenko again. And got his voicemail again. She clicked off without leaving a message. She knew what he was doing. Reaching out to whoever Anton Petrova was to see what should and should not be revealed to Pia. Everything in Russia tended to stay in Russia.

They walked and talked through dense, wet foliage. Pia brought Tania up to speed on what wasn't covered in her notes, the fight outside town hall, the street videos of Chloe, and Rain Meyer's accusations.

Tania said, "You're leaving out Liam Pickford following you around the reception like a lovesick puppy."

"I was attacked by an angry mob, and that's what my VP of Security wants to talk about?"

"Angry mobs are boring. Pickford is a hottie. So, here's the question: is he after you hoping you'll pay too much for his company, or is it kismet? I mean seriously. Did he prepare for the biggest meeting of his career, meet you in the coffeeshop, and not know you on sight? C'mon, even if you weren't on Forbes' list of stinking rich, you stand out in a crowd. Literally. And the internet is crazy with pictures of you. Not all of them in a soccer kit, either. So, was he playing you like Abby was playing me?"

"The downside to being me." Pia blew out a breath. "You never know."

"Sounds like your paranoid social cognition talking."

Pia squinted at Tania. Was her doctor talking to her friend behind her back? Before she could think about it much, something bright yellow caught her eye. Just above the milky-brown clay, deep in a shadow, sat a bright yellow frog on a leaf the size of a coffee table.

"I can't believe some people," Abby said. Still in her pantsuit from the funeral, she brushed dirt off her leg. "We imported a ton of dirt from Colombia to make sure the setting was perfect. And every month, they send us another ton. We only needed the one. I keep telling them, I'm not paying for that. And they tell me it's paid for. How do they stay in business making mistakes like that, you wonder."

She looked at her hands. Covered in dirt. She dusted them against each other.

Pia pointed at the leaf behind her. "What kind of frog is that?"

"Frog?" Abby asked. She peered into the dark recesses of the plants. "I don't know about frogs. I'm a horticulturist. What'd he look like?"

"Bright yellow." Pia looked over her shoulder. "Oh, he's gone now."

"Was it gold, maybe?"

"Yes, gold. Almost glowed in the dark."

"That would be *Phyllobates terribilis*, the poison dart frog." Abby reached in and gently moved some leaves. "We never ordered any because touching their skin is deadly. But they hop a ride on the plants now and again and wind up in here. Gotta be careful with those."

She turned around quickly and tossed a golden frog on Pia.

Pia shrieked and jumped back.

"Don't step on the poor little bugger, Sabel!" Abby laughed. "Don't worry, love. They're not poisonous in captivity."

Pia took a deep breath and scowled at Abby. Tania snickered behind her. Pia asked, "Are you sure?"

"No one's sure about them. They're so poisonous no one wants to study them, but yeah, they're harmless here. Theory is there's something in their diet sets the poison, maybe bugs. We don't do with a lot of bugs. Too many invasive species, and the Royal Agricultural University doesn't fancy being the ones who brought in the beetle that ate England."

"Still kinda dangerous, though," Tania said suspiciously.

"Danger's my middle name," Abby grinned. "We've got *Hippomane mancinella*, Manchineel, in the Negro-Branco section. Much worse than any frogs. That stuff'll burn your skin just touching it. Eric, the toxicologist, says he can make a nasty balm out of that. But if you ever cross me—" Abby playfully shook a finger at Tania "—I've a couple *Dendrocnide moroides*, suicide plants, that came with the Belize shipment. They've got tiny needles full of poisonous sap. They touch you, you're a goner."

"Oooh," Tania said, "I'm scared."

They laughed.

Eric shouted for them from the loading dock. "Hurry, ladies! The Morpheus tour is next, but we must leave right away."

Abby answered him and they set off back through the other sections.

"I'm going to find one of those frogs in my sleeping bag, aren't I?" Pia asked.

"Nah. Never pull the same prank twice, I say."

CHAPTER 21

With Tania by her side, Pia followed Eric and Abby to the Morpheus Institute's grand entrance. A gentle dome sat above curving walls in a white and navy-blue work of art. On the drive over, Eric had explained that a Saudi Prince built it as a private museum before falling out with the Crown Prince and winding up incarcerated in Riyadh. The Drs. Rohan had taken over as caretakers and renters, getting an architectural masterpiece for pennies.

Pia's limo and the Tindall's Bentley sat quietly in the small parking area.

Dame Millie intercepted Pia before she reached the entrance. "If I said anything that sounded racist, I apologize. I'm certainly not prejudiced. I never meant to say anything wrong. What will people think if my guest walks out on me?"

"Deeds are portraits of the soul," Pia said without breaking stride.

Albert walked alongside his wife with an angry mien.

"I didn't mean anything by it." Dame Millie pleaded. "Really, I'm sorry."

"Why are you apologizing to *me*?"

"What can we do to make it up to you? When the tour is over, we need you back at Padley House."

"Are you listening?" Pia stopped and faced Dame Millie. "Imagine how you would feel if I said, 'No *Dames* allowed.'"

"Just a minute," Albert stepped up. "There's no need to be spiteful. She said we'd make it up to you."

"Making it up to me is not where you need to start. I'm staying with Abby." She started to walk away. "When you understand 'love your neighbor' doesn't have qualifiers, and 'race' is nothing more than a social construct, we'll schedule another get-together."

"Well that's a bit much," Albert said. "Especially coming from someone who runs around with a figurehead like Liam Pickford."

Pia felt her anger flare, a rush of blood flushing her face and a scowl creasing her brow.

Dame Millie reached out and touched her arm lightly. Her jaw worked, but no words came out for a long time. "You will attend my fête tomorrow. There are busloads of young girls coming."

"I wouldn't disappoint the kids."

"What about meeting Wayne Walker?" Albert demanded. "An interview with him would be a great opportunity for you to set the record straight."

She almost told him to take a flying leap, but she caught herself. They had been her hosts. While she didn't feel indebted to them, they might come in handy if she had more questions about the Morpheus. She could use Walker as leverage.

But who was Walker and why did Albert feel so strongly about an interview? Wayne Walker had mentioned an interview with Bobby Jenkins, founder of Jenkins Pharmaceuticals and an old family friend. Checking the time, she dialed Bobby.

He answered right away. "About to join a meeting, Pia. What's up?"

"Wayne Walker wants to interview me. He mentioned you were one of his subjects. Worthwhile?"

"Was it ever! That young man did his research. Quite impressive. He knew the date of all my milestones and every achievement. It was so good, everyone in the company listened. I've saved that one for posterity. Highly recommended."

"Have you ever heard of the Morpheus Institute?" Pia turned her back on Albert who'd leaned in as if trying to hear Bobby.

"I have. The same fellow who put me in touch with Walker wants me to take a tour. It's a bit out of the way from my usual European haunts. Haven't worked it in yet."

"Who made the recommendations?"

"Nice Brit named Albert Tinsel … or something like that. The man has good ideas. Listen, I've got to go. Call me when you get back in town, we'll do lunch."

They clicked off.

A much heartier recommendation than she expected. She turned to Albert. "Tell him day after tomorrow. I'll make a time in my schedule."

Albert looked practically orgasmic.

Pia strode quickly to catch up with the others in the lobby. A paper appointment book was the only tool used at the receptionist's stand. There were no phones or computers in sight. A security guard of dubious qualification watched them but made no effort to scrutinize them.

Drs. Edward and Sybil Rohan waited for them with open arms. The couple had changed into more casual versions of the same fashions they'd worn to the funeral. Edward led the group through the lobby with a short lecture on architecture.

Sybil Rohan took Pia's hand. "Could we talk about your case, privately? Or do you need a bodyguard at all times?"

Pia gave Tania a nod that told her to stay with the group.

"More than a bodyguard," Pia said. "She's the VP of Personal Security."

"Really?" Sybil took a second look at Tania.

"Yes, really." Pia was ready to go a round with Sybil as she had with the Tindalls, but the older woman looked genuinely chastened.

Sybil threaded her arm inside Pia's and nudged her off to the side while staying within sight of the group. She said, "You've heard my husband talk in broad strokes about the Institute and our methods here. I'd like to talk more specifically about you. Women at our level have so much to deal with, we end up focused on the hardest decisions. What's it like for someone as young as you?"

Sybil slowed their progress to an unhurried stroll. Pia found the pace limiting at first. She never went anywhere without her long, quick strides. This easy tempo felt more peaceful.

"I'm not sure what you mean," Pia said.

"Well, I read that Sabel Industries buys a company every month. And that's after rejecting fifty others. Weighing those decisions would crush me." Sybil let out a giggle. "But for someone who drinks from the skulls of her—"

"Poorly chosen words in a candid moment." Pia's thoughts turned to the Major and how she weighed most of Pia's decisions for her. Jonelle deserved a weekend off more than Pia. "That's not how I conduct business."

"Are you the kind to internalize those decisions? Do you identify with TS Eliot's verses: *And indeed there will be time / To wonder, 'Do I dare?' and, 'Do I dare?'* Or do you simply forge ahead?"

Pia observed Sybil closely. Her style was timeless, simple, and elegant. Her hair and makeup were equally uncomplicated. She appeared purposely enigmatic.

"I favor 'Invictus'," Pia said. "Out of the night that covers me / Black as the pit from pole to pole, / I thank whatever gods may be / For my unconquerable soul."

Sybil smiled up at her and squeezed their arms together. She said, "That speaks volumes about you, Pia."

They walked in silence through a maze of corridors that gave Pia a feeling of spaciousness and calm. There were no doors, no hallways, each space opened to another through interlocking arcs of fabric. As they rounded a curved wall, Pia touched one of the barriers. Fabric was stretched tight an inch from the ordinary plaster wall behind it. It gave the space the same quieting effect as snow in the woods. Indirect lighting bounced off the dome overhead. Air, neither warm nor cold but fresh, cascaded from the gap between walls and ceiling.

"You're a conqueror." Sybil stopped and held both Pia's arms. "You're at the level of Alexander, Genghis Khan, no—you're like Catherine the Great. A woman with your energy can change the world."

"We call that brown-nosing on the other side of the pond."

"Yes," Sybil said. "It sounds that way, but it can't be helped. It is who you are." She laughed. "A lesser woman would never have challenged me on that."

They continued walking. Sybil wound her arm around Pia's again and leaned close as if they'd been friends since childhood. Pia found her familiarity both charming and suspicious.

"You know what the great conquerors of history had in common?"

Sybil asked.

"A merciless, vicious personality photoshopped into boldness by historians?"

Sybil squeezed her arm. "Someone to guide them into the realm of dark matter, a place we call the Rational Light."

"And you can do that for me?"

"Amazing. So direct. No wasted breath. You truly have the heart of a conqueror. I don't doubt you would indeed drink from the skulls of your enemies."

"I might drink from yours if you don't get to the point," Pia said with a disarming shoulder bump. "What did these conquerors do in Rational Light?"

"They controlled the dreams of their enemies."

"The historians definitely glossed over that one," Pia said.

"Oh no. It's in the ancient texts. It's like the fight Saint Peter had with a non-believer in which they rose off the ground and shot lightning bolts at each other. The texts rest at the Vatican for anyone to read, but they were a bit over the top and were left out of the New Testament. Similar stories abound about Alexander and Catherine. Virtually all the great conquerors projected themselves into the dreams of their enemies."

"And this form of astral projection did what, exactly?"

"Some, like Julius Caesar, used it to plant bad ideas in the minds of his enemies. Just look at the list of his battles—virtually every one of Caesar's enemies made a fateful mistake, all of them contrary to the tactics of the defeated general's known methods. Alexander was less subtle. He killed his enemies in their dreams, sometimes long before he arrived in their country. Most of his victories were mop-up operations in a leaderless city-state."

"Killed someone in their dream?" Pia stopped and peered into Sybil's eyes.

Sybil's pupils had not dilated, a basic but not perfect way to gauge a lie. In fact, Sybil showed none of the physical characteristics Pia associated with lying. The woman fully believed killing people through dreams was not only possible, but a moral imperative.

Hadn't Rain Meyer said something about this at the Manifest Morals rally?

"That would be illegal and immoral," Pia said.

"Illegal? What charges would the Crown file?" Sybil let go of Pia and began walking away. "As for morality, tell me how moral was Adolph Hitler? If you could eliminate a dictator who slaughters his own people, would you?"

"Why haven't you?" Pia picked up her pace to catch up. "There are plenty of candidates for that in the world."

"I am not Pia Sabel. I have no gold medals. I have no World Cups. I am not fast. I am not strong. I am not a conqueror." She deepened her voice. "I could never drink from—"

"Don't say that again."

"It is your destiny, Pia." Sybil searched her eyes. "Using Rational Light, you can rule over all you survey. In today's world, you won't order a battalion to capture your husband and force him to abdicate the Russian throne leaving you the sole monarch—as did Catherine the Great. But you deserve to send Krueger to his just deserts and buy McDowell Aerospace for pennies on the dollar."

Pia inhaled sharply, giving away her shock. Her mind reeled at the knowledge Sybil had of her business. And staggered at the insinuation that Pia would kill to beat a competitor.

The fog surrounding Chloe's list was beginning to clear. Bella Davis, the lady Chloe interviewed, had not been crazy. The Morpheus did offer a murderous solution to real-world problems. But. How the hell did that work? There was no way Pia could bring herself to believe in murderous dreamscapes. She said, "Sorry, Sybil, but this sounds like a load of bullshit."

"Everyone says that." Sybil smiled. "Sleep on it. Think about it. Imagine buying McDowell Aerospace."

"Are you talking about figuratively killing someone or what?"

"That's your choice." Sybil held her gaze. "All your problems melt away, that much is guaranteed. And then you can sleep at night. Imagine, Pia, a full night's sleep. How long has it been?"

Pia had no idea when she last slept more than three hours. Her nightmares had nothing to do with Dave Krueger, though. They were about the kitchen knife she took from the table and stabbed into a man's leg when she was four. They were about Pia shaking her mother's lifeless body and screaming pain from the bottom of her soul. They were about watching the only parent she'd truly known—Alan Sabel, her model of an unconquerable soul—die while she was powerless. If she could have killed the lone perpetrator of all those nightmares in his sleep, she wouldn't have hesitated.

CHAPTER 22

Claigeann Cottage, Abby's place, sat beneath an oak at the end of a gravel lane lined with a weathered split rail fence. Ivy ran up its stone walls to the thatched roof. Warm light poured out of the two windows like golden tea as dusk sank down around it.

When she stepped from the car, Pia said, "How wonderful."

Her hostess looked as surprised as the limo driver. Quaint as Claigeann was, it had never attracted a billionaire to its door before. The driver deposited their luggage inside and left.

Entering with a grand welcome, Abby waved her hands in her small, low-ceilinged home. "It's not Padley House."

"It's not the size of the house that matters," Pia said. She started to say something else, then stopped.

"Oh, it's the size of the hostess, is it?" Abby laughed and shoved Pia's shoulder. "Is that where you were going? Millie's got two stone on me, easy."

"Uhm." Pia couldn't find a way out of it and just laughed. She hadn't felt relaxed like that in years. Abby made it easy.

She and Tania followed their hostess to the kitchen to make a dinner of salmon, salad, and peas. Abby poured wine into water glasses that looked as if they'd been stolen from a motel.

"I can't believe she was so brazen about it," Pia said. "She called me a conqueror. And she flat out told me I could 'send Krueger to his just deserts' and get away with it."

"Sybil's not wrong," Abby said as she chopped bell pepper into bite-sized pieces and tossed them on the salad. "You're a conqueror, alright."

Pia and Tania looked around for ways to help.

"Just don't turn the toaster on same time as the stove," Abby said. "Blows a fuse. Old house, you know. I've almost saved enough for a historic restoration. Let's not burn it down just before."

"Historic restoration?" Pia asked. "Sounds expensive."

"You don't get to use the word expensive, Sabel."

"But do people believe all that crap?" Tania asked. "I'm talking about the others who've hired them. They really gonna believe Sybil taught them how to kill their enemies while they dream? Or they just giving a wink to the same old killer-for-hire business?"

"Must be assassins," Abby said. "But how?"

Tania washed lettuce for the salad. She said, "They gotta mastermind behind all this. Someone dreamed it up and pulled in different people for different jobs, keeping everyone separated. A firewall of plausible deniability. The Rohans ain't going around killing business owners, and they ain't gonna pop Chloe England neither."

"Why do you say that?" Pia asked.

"The kinda guy who's brutal enough to crack skulls open with a baton is never gonna get near an executive like you or David Breach. Ain't gonna happen."

"You're saying there's high-class killers and low-class killers?" Abby asked.

"More like rich killers and poor killers," Tania said. "When the rich get killed, it's usually someone in their peer group doing a soft-kill, like drowning, overdose, suffocation, stuff like that. When the middle class or poor people kill each other, it's brutal stuff like gunshots, blunt instruments."

"Your lot goes around killing each other, do they?" Abby asked Pia.

"Xerxes was murdered by his head of personal protection," Pia said, nudging Tania. "Not to mention Emperors Galba, Pertinax, Didius—"

"I'm serious here," Tania said. "The guy with the diamond earring, Mr. Bling, he's the street muscle. He keeps everyone in line. But the mastermind flows like water through high society, hopping continents and walking into executive offices. He can't get mixed up in killing a cop or intimidating his business partners. And that's why it isn't the Rohans. They're tied to that spot. Anyone notices a string of killings tied to their customers, they have to say, 'I was here in England, not in Hong Kong.'"

Pia thought about that one while she took a knife and second cutting board. She sliced cucumber into pieces to match Abby's bell peppers.

Abby heated a pan and tossed in the salmon filets. She went back to chopping vegetables, working quicker this time.

Pia glanced at her and picked up the pace of her chopping. Abby accelerated hers.

"Hey!" Tania barked. "Chill, people. Chopping veggies is not a competition. Somebody gonna cut a finger off."

"Just a bit of fun," Abby said. She and Pia hip bumped.

"Athletes," Tania rolled her eyes. "Sheeyit."

"How do they get paid?" Pia asked, chopping at normal speed. "There's no way the Morpheus works on donations."

"You said they had a benefactor," Tania said. "Can't we track that guy down?"

"If they list him somewhere," Pia answered. "Given what they're doing, I'll bet whoever she is, she doesn't want her name on the building. That benefactor thing is a screen for someone else."

No one spoke. They kept working while they thought.

"Follow the money," Tania said. "This operation is compartmentalized. The Rohans know who the target is, but I'll betcha they don't know who pulls the trigger. Or whatever they do to cause the heart attack. The money is also compartmentalized. Whoever does the killing probably never sees the customer or the money. All very neat. But in the end, someone takes the money from the customer, launders it, then pays the assassin and the Morpheus. So, the benefactor is the back end and someone else is the front end. If we can find either of those people, he'll lead us to the other."

"Dame Millie's gotta be one of them," Abby said.

"Based on what?" Tania asked. When no one replied, she said, "Being an asshole isn't a crime."

"Well, it should be," their hostess said.

Tania's phone buzzed. She looked at the caller ID, then stepped into the next room to take the call.

Pia went for the mushrooms next.

Abby leaned against her. "You're my conqueror, Sabel."

"Same line you used on Sabrina Chapman in the Olympic Village." Pia nudged her back.

"She tell you that?"

"I heard you. I was standing right behind her."

"Eavesdropping on my private conversations? You should be ashamed."

"You're the one who should be ashamed. You need new material."

"Why? It worked on Chapman."

Pia laughed and rolled her eyes.

"Bloody hell, Sabel." Abby sighed. "Think about that. 'Same old line.' Did they use the same line on all the other customers?"

In the other room, Pia heard Tania say, "Pia's keeping her phone off. She wants to be present for a change. Why?"

"Top executives rank high on the psychopathy chart," Pia said. "Blowing smoke up their butts would be effective. Why?"

"What if the customers do believe it?" Abby asked. "What if they buy that line about Caesar and Alexander using it against their enemies? They think they really did the killing themselves. It's the perfect cover for the whole operation."

Pia thought about Tania's analysis of the conspirators' structure. Any murder-for-hire scheme required three people: the employer, the assassin, and the victim. If either the assassin or the employer gets caught, the prosecutor tries to flip one against the other. That wouldn't work in this case. There are four involved: employer, assassin, front man, and victim. No pair of them knows the other two.

She said, "You're right. If anyone testified, the Rohans would say, 'That's the wildest dream I ever heard.' You could never take it to court."

"In that case," Abby said, "it doesn't matter if they believe it or not."

"Even if the customers don't believe it, they'll convince themselves it works. It only helps their defense. They'd say, 'They helped me get some sleep. I had no idea the guy would die.'"

From the other room, she heard Tania say, "Problem solved then. He's a good guy."

Abby turned the salmon over. She tossed the mushrooms in a frying pan with butter and onions. She said, "So how do they kill and how do they get paid?"

"Those are the two big questions. And finding the answer to one won't necessarily help with the other."

"Oh, that's not good," Tania said as she walked back in the kitchen. "I'll tell her."

Tania clicked off and looked something up on her phone. While she thumbed, she said, "Emily called. Dominick England got on Twitter a couple hours ago and slammed the trolls. He posted your 'Skulls' quote and said, 'Talk like that is what Chloe loved about Pia Sabel. So pick up the nearest skull and toast with Chloe.'"

Pia and Abby shared a pleasantly surprised look.

"That was nice of him," Pia said. "What's the 'not good' part?"

"Dave Krueger wrote an op–ed for the *Journal*." Tania held up her phone for Pia.

The headline read, A blight on American business: Sabel Industries.

Pia took the phone and clicked on the article as Tania and Abby leaned in from each side. Krueger's editorial was worse than his rant. He built on the same language he'd used in their call, referring to her as an overprivileged brat who'd combined her connections in Washington with predatory pricing to drive every competitor out of business. His solution: the government should break up Sabel Industries and auction off the assets.

Abby snorted. "Guess England's not the only team that hates you, Sabel."

She went back to work plating the food. Tania grabbed tableware from the mismatched collection and set the table.

Pia stared at the article. That Krueger guy really pissed her off. Which Sybil Rohan seemed to know. She looked at the time stamp on the editorial. It was an hour old. The *Journal* editors would've gone back and forth with him to fine tune it to avoid libel charges, making it a two-day process. Had he been working on it since they spoke on the phone?

Then something else occurred to her.

"Sybil knew about this op-ed before it came out," she said, as much to herself as the others.

"Let's eat," Abby said. "Tell us about that."

All three took the rickety wooden chairs at Abby's tiny table.

Pia picked up her wine and toasted Abby, "To our hostess, who saved us from *Dame* Millie."

They clinked glasses and sipped. Then they dug into the food.

Abby asked, "Why do you think Sybil knew about the article?"

"She used the imagery of killing Dave Krueger as one of her examples."

"Ooh, she knew you'd be gutted by his post."

"You're on the list. And so is Krueger." Tania sat up quickly. "Sybil Rohan knows too much about you."

She and Pia stared at each other as they tried to figure out what that meant.

"What list?" Abby asked.

"Can't tell you," Tania said without breaking her gaze with Pia.

"I'm a lesbian, not an idiot."

"Police have it gagged," Pia said. "Short version is: Chloe had a list of victims."

"They're not all victims," Tania said. "Didn't you read my comments on your notes? You quoted Rain Meyer as saying you were on a list of 'billionaires and their victims.' Half that list are the Rohan's customers and the other half are the victims."

"Oh, right. I missed that." Pia was stunned. "That guy knows more than I thought. But there's a problem—Chloe had the list before I ever came here. They couldn't have counted on talking me into hiring them to kill Krueger."

Abby snapped her fingers and pointed at Tania, then Pia. "Krueger's the customer—you're the victim."

Pia sat back and thought about it. "Then why give me the full sales pitch?"

"Don't ask me, I'm just a horticulturist."

They sipped their wine and ate and thought. They finished the salmon and dug into the peas. Then the salad disappeared. Pia's exercise regimen burned tons of calories. She never shied away from the table. Her hostess was much the same. Tania picked at hers like a normal person.

Abby refilled their wine before anyone spoke again.

Tania said, "Abby's right. Krueger's the customer, you're the victim. We'll have to figure out their angle."

"Sybil Rohan is a right nasty bitch." Abby blew out a breath. "Whatever they're up to, they've got to be the ones who killed Chloe. Oh, you've got to do something about this, Sabel."

CHAPTER 23

Padley House was crawling with vendors and caterers and rental companies when Pia and her friends arrived the next morning. Puffy white clouds sailed across a bright blue sky, perfect weather for a game. Pia and Abby came decked out in their national team kits. Tania wore her most menacing black skinny jeans, black t-shirt, and jacket. Dame Millie ran from one supplier to another, pointing and snapping instructions at them. Unsure what was expected of them, Pia and her friends followed the flow of workers around the back. A small circus sprawled across one end of Dame Millie's immaculately groomed acres of lawn. Beyond that, a good-sized pitch had been laid out with white lines for 3 v 3 games. Small, portable bleachers lined the sides.

A good shiver of anticipation ran through Pia. The smell of freshly mowed grass, the thrill of powering past old foes and friends, the joy of scoring a goal. Better than sex. Almost.

Several former players from England, Brazil, Germany, France, and Mexico chatted beneath a popup tent. A long way for a fête, Pia thought before remembering some of them still played in the European leagues. Pia and Abby joined them while Tania gave the grounds a security check.

Germany's Lena Schuller greeted her first. "A black eye? Is that from shoving your foot in your mouth at Chloe's funeral?"

The others laughed.

Pia smiled. "Good to see you, too, Lena."

They hugged and teased until the first busload of schoolgirls arrived. Decked out in the kits of their favorite players, the kids ran to the pitch.

Several more buses arrived, and a referee started the exhibition games. Teams were drawn by lots. Pia drew two competent Dutch and faced Abby with a Norwegian and a Mexican. Digging her cleats into the soil, she felt that pregame high that powered her through good times and bad. Her muscles tingled, her mind raced through moves, her feet twitched. God it was good to be back on the pitch. Then the whistle blew. Abby took the ball from Pia's surprised teammate. The game was on!

On the next pass, Pia stole the ball and darted toward Abby.

As she got around Abby's defensive move, Abby said, "I was a client of the Rohans."

Pia stopped in her tracks. Abby's teammate stole the ball from her and fired a long shot for a goal. Abby howled with laughter.

Pia stared at Abby, "You didn't think to mention that last night?"

"Saved it for the game," Abby said with an impish grin. "One-nil, Sabel."

Abby's trick only worked only once. It ended 3-1 for Pia's team. They went to the tent as others took the pitch. A pair of brave five-year-olds brought soccer balls for autographs. Once the ice was broken, the two were followed by a small horde.

As Pia signed, she asked Abby, "What was the Morpheus like?"

"This was more than three years ago. Before they went for Arab princes, Russian oligarchs, and your lot, they did regular people for sleep disorders. And they charged cash up front. Finished up my PhD and started realizing there wasn't much use for it. That kept me up nights. When I went to them, they were holding group sessions. Whole lot of *namaste* and *anjali mudra,* far as I could tell. Nothing about Alexander or Catherine the Great."

"Why the PhD and not coaching like everyone else?" Pia asked.

Abby nodded across the sea of kids at a mother who corralled her daughter and pulled her child out of Abby's line. "When your American pals came out of the closet, I felt emboldened and did the same. Only I wasn't living on endorsements like your girls. I did a bit of coaching and kept seeing mums like that one. Think I'll molest their daughters. They don't say anything out loud. Just give me the sideways looks. Always loved gardening anyway. The plants don't care about gender orientation."

With time between games, Pia took a stroll through the rest of the event. Lines of little girls in uniforms waited for their turns at attractions. Suddenly, several girls broke ranks, ran to another line, pulled a girl out, and herded her toward Pia. The shy youngster wore the only Pia Sabel kit in the crowd. Pia knelt to her, pulled out a marker, and asked where she could sign the girl's jersey.

"Could you write that bit about skulls?" the girl asked.

Pia hesitated, looked around for a mother to get an approval first. Before she could find anyone, the other girls joined in with, "Oh, me too!"

She wondered if this would be her fate. Remembered through eternity for a tone-deaf remark—made twice. She took a knee and started signing. A line formed immediately.

While she worked, Albert and the caterer squared off behind her.

The vendor poked Albert in the chest. "Y'haven't paid the bloody bill yet, Tindall. Where's my money for all this, then?"

"I'm getting a commission next week, Henderson. You'll be paid soon enough."

"I've a good mind to pull out now."

"You would never." Albert walked away.

Pia stole a glance over her shoulder.

The caterer caught her gaze and snarled, "Pitiful. The toff's gone skint." He stormed away.

When she finished autographs, she went back to the pitch to watch a game. A large man with a soccer ball under one arm stood nearby. He looked familiar. She said, "We've met, right? Are you Wayne Walker?"

He smiled and folded his gloved hands in prayer and bowed. "Namaste, Ms. Sabel. I'm honored you remember me."

"What brings you out here?"

"There are many Walkers in this world," he smiled mischievously, "but that one is my sister."

Pia followed his nod to a player on the pitch. "Susan Walker is your sister? What a small world."

"She didn't last long as an international. A couple months called up, a couple bad games, and off she went." He patted his big belly. "Not many people guess we're related to look at us."

Pia laughed at his humor.

"Say, would you mind?" He held out the ball under his arm. "If you could write that bit about skulls …"

"You did say you'd ask me about that in the interview." She laughed and signed it as requested and handed it back.

He wiped it off with a handkerchief. "Are we on then?"

"Albert hasn't told you? I don't have a time yet, but I'll figure that out and get back to you."

"Brilliant." He smiled as if he'd won a prize.

Then he leaned in conspiratorially close. "Say, I saw you talking to Liam Pickford yesterday. If you're planning any business deals with him, I've some interesting news about him—might affect your thinking."

His offer took Pia by surprise. Business intelligence is a murky field resembling the drama of middle school whispered secrets more than actionable information. But the fact that he trafficked in rumors caused her to wonder if he had anything on the Tindalls. She pushed that aside. "We rely on facts not under-the-table speculation. Thank you for the offer."

"Well then, until the interview." He gave her a playful salute. "Cheers."

He walked off to greet his sister as her game ended.

Pia headed back for her next round of 3 v 3. Along the way, she found herself walking past Eric Stone, who was on the phone. He held up a finger, asking her to wait for him. She slowed her pace to match his and tried unsuccessfully not to listen in. She noticed the handle of his cane was a silver duck's head, polished to gleam.

"It's not until January," he said. "Listen, I've some things in the works that'll pay off shortly. You'll get your money."

He offered some exit pleasantries, clicked off, and pocketed the phone. Leaning on his cane, he smiled up at Pia.

"What kind of professor were you?" she asked.

"A grumpy one," he laughed. "Forensic toxicology. The clinical chemistry of investigations. Mostly, research into the leading causes of poisoning. Which—to answer your question before you ask it—is alcohol. Not in nefarious uses, but in stupid ones. Close behind that, opioids. Equally stupid."

"You could answer a question for me. What is Anectine?"

"Anectine, Scoline, Suxamethonium chloride, commonly known as SUX? Never heard of it." He waited while she laughed. "A short-duration anesthetic. It's used in specific situations. What's your interest?"

"I sat on a bottle in a friend's car. Is it deadly?"

"Everything's deadly in the right doses. Anectine will stop your heart if you get a large enough injection. In days gone by, there were rumors the Mossad used it to kill their enemies because it dissolved in the bloodstream. Theoretically, that rendered it untraceable. But no one's ever proved that. About the Mossad, I mean."

They walked a little in silence. Pia didn't like silence much. She asked, "That's a nice new roof you have. I just replaced mine with zinc and even for me that was a breathtaking bill."

"Indeed." He laughed. "But, had to be done. There's no point in replacing an oak banister if the roof is going to leak on it. The university's grant helped but I still had to raise funds."

"Oh, something like this?" she asked, waving at Dame Millie's fête.

"I'm too shy for this sort of thing." His limp appeared more pronounced. "My family once held a considerable collection of eighteenth-century British art. Not a popular era these days, but I've retained a bit of expertise and broker the odd sale now and then."

"That's interesting. Is Albert in business with you? I just overheard him talk about a commission coming in."

"If he's getting a commission on anything, it must be related to those god-awful Rohans. Or maybe that Walker-the-wanker."

Pia frowned at him and started to ask a question.

He realized the impropriety of his outburst and stopped, pulling her elbow. In a hushed tone, he said, "Mustn't talk like that about the Rohans. Forget I said anything. I've no idea about Albert's income."

"You don't like them, though."

"Sybil took you for a chat. What did you think?"

"A lot of psychobabble. But why would they pay him commissions? They said they run on donations."

"Oh, I'm just an old man talking too much. I've no idea, but he's always putting people together and asking for a fee or commission, what have you."

Someone called to Pia. Her next game was starting. She thanked Eric and ran to the pitch.

When her second game ended, Tania waited on the sidelines with a phone outstretched. On the display was the name Mikhail Yeschenko. Pia wiped the sweat off her face and slammed down a bottle of water before taking the phone.

She said, "Mikhail, thank you for returning my call. I wondered if we were still on speaking terms."

"Why I would be angry with you? Oh. Do you worry because you help US Treasury with sanctions against me? What is few sanctions among friends? You need help. Mikhail Yeschenko always willing to help, my friend. What do you need?"

"I'm worried about a friend of yours, Anton Petrova. I found his name on a list of assassination targets. Is he alive?"

"Very much alive. I tell him of your concern."

"Would he have any connection to a place in England called the Morpheus Institute?"

"You make joke, *da*?" Yeschenko laughed. "British still hold Anton responsible for Skirpal poisoning. Silly, am I right? He never leave Moscow. How he do such a thing? And yet British demand extradition. Now, Pia, darling, it is your turn to help me, your old friend. You sent me twenty-eight million dollars US—but you send with trace request. How I get money out of Cyprus with trace request? You cancel trace. Then I consider your debt to me repaid. This is good deal for you."

"Great talking to you again, Mikhail," she lied. Talking to a man who once threatened to throw her off a cliff while his men held her at gunpoint was not great in any sense.

"Before you go," he said, "It is only fair to tell you about my ... what is quaint American term? Collectors. Yes, my collectors have the eye on Padley House. Remove the tracer so I can get my money out of Cyprus.

Then my collectors can come home, be with children. Good for everybody. I know you. You like doing good thing. I like these little chats with you, Pia. Call any time."

He clicked off.

And Dr. Harrison wondered why she was paranoid.

Pia scanned the area as she relayed his threat to Tania. The massive lawn was surrounded by a forest of old-growth trees. An English jungle thick and dense. Yeschenko was an old-fashioned oligarch. He preferred assassination by sniper. None of this Novichok poisoning for him. Tania reassured her that the local police had taken it upon themselves to secure the area. Not only to thwart a possible terrorist attack, but the English themselves were sometimes overwhelmed by emotions surrounding international players. A team of constables had circled through the woods twice.

Dame Millie stood nearby, watching the game.

Pia approached her. "Thank you for introducing me to the Rohans."

"I thought you weren't speaking to me." She looked Pia over with disappointment. She turned back to the game, softened. "You're welcome. I'm glad you liked them. They've done tremendous things for Albert."

Pia considered Chloe's killers, the man with the diamond earring. Yeschenko's threat brought to mind her assessment of the killers as covert operators. They could've been Russian. They could've been from anywhere. But somehow, they must've been connected to the Morpheus.

"She spoke of many people they've helped," Pia said. "I forgot to ask her—do you know if they worked with a wealthy Russian named Anton Petrova?"

"Never heard that name." Dame Millie shook her head. "Who is he?"

Pia considered how most Russian mobsters traveled Europe, as attachés for the Russian Embassy. "He may have been a diplomat."

"Diplomat?" Dame Millie gave her the side-eye. "What're you getting at?"

"Just a hunch, but I think there are some foreign assassins in the Manchester area working under diplomatic immunity. You might expect killers to have trouble sleeping. Just a thought."

"You're on about something, Sabel. Out with it."

Pia faced her and crossed her arms. "A Russian businessman just threatened me. His people often travel under diplomatic immunity. It crossed my mind that since they have so many international guests, these men might hide at the Morpheus under the guise of sleep disorders."

"You've made your disdain for the Morpheus quite clear since your arrival. I'll not hear any more of it."

"Does Albert get commissions for bringing donors to them?" Pia asked.

Dame Millie raised her nose, spun on her heel, and left.

CHAPTER 24

ABBY DROPPED PIA AND TANIA at Manchester Town Hall, where Benton and his task force worked round the clock. Due to Abby having only one shower, it had taken until midafternoon to get cleaned up from Dame Millie's fête and drive to the city. Which meant Pia was once again late for a meeting with DI Benton. She pushed through a less-agitated Manifest Morals crowd unrecognized. Their riot-inciting leader being absent helped.

Inside, she placed her purse and pistol on the x-ray belt, handed her MI5 permission-to-carry card to the attendant, and stepped through the metal detector. Benton, wearing the same clothes he wore to the funeral, only more rumpled and wearier looking, waited for her on the other side with an unamused scowl.

Something violent erupted behind her. When she turned, instinctively ready to defend herself, she saw Tania on the floor, a constable jumping on her with his knees. He raised a baton to strike. Tania twisted to her right. His club hit cement.

Pia instinctively moved to help, then stopped. Tania could handle a PC.

Benton ran through the metal detector. Pia slammed her arm into his chest stopping him.

Tania trapped the officer's left foot with hers, then pushed off the opposite side, a standard self-defense move that flipped them both over. She landed on top, ready to rain blows down on him. She hesitated when she realized he was a cop.

The PC swung his club at her head. When she ducked, she lost her balance. He threw her off. They rolled away from each other, jumped to their feet, and faced off. Another swing at her head missed, leaving his shoulder exposed.

"McDonald, she's a guest," Benton yelled. "What the hell are you doing?"

Tania swept in behind McDonald, put him in a headlock and bent his head back. She said, "Drop it! Drop the club."

Instantly, five PCs flooded the small foyer and attacked Tania like a mad mob. She struggled as the men grabbed at her and tried to throw her on the floor in what became a violent wrestling match.

Pia and Benton immediately waded in. Pia grabbed an officer by the collar and dragged him back. When his eyes swung to hers, he straightened up as if standing at attention. She pushed him against the metal detector. Benton kept shouting at his PCs, only managing to get one out of the brawl.

In a writhing mass, the officers fell to the floor with Tania still holding McDonald in a headlock. One of them tried to get his arm around Tania's neck, but she kept her chin hard over McDonald's shoulder.

Benton grabbed another officer and pulled him out. Pia wrenched out a fourth. Like the first, he stopped struggling when he saw Pia's face. The last man trying to free McDonald from Tania's grasp heard Benton's shouts and rolled out. Leaving McDonald, red-faced with rage, struggling for air in Tania's grip.

Pia gave her VP the all-clear signal and Tania released the PC.

"What the bloody hell is wrong with you?" Benton howled at his PCs. "That's not how we respond—"

"I'm suing!" Tania turned her angry glare around the room. "If that's how you treat a visitor, how do you treat your citizens?"

"She had a gun," McDonald said, addressing Benton.

Tania stepped between them. "Did you throw that white lady to the ground when she handed you her pistol?"

PC McDonald shook his head.

"Did you look at her permission card?" Tania asked.

"She came in the other day." McDonald's voice shook. "I already saw her card."

"Yeah, she came in the other day—with a big-ass white boy named Jacob Stearne." Tania pointed at the camera in the corner to remind him everything was recorded. "He had a pistol and a card. Did you try to beat the shit out of him?"

McDonald shook his head.

"What's it called when you assume a white lady with a 9 mil is OK but a black lady with one is not?"

Library silence filled the room.

"Did you ask if I had a permit, McDonald?" Tania didn't wait for him to answer. "Did you ask if I went to West Point and graduated with honors? Did you ask if I was a captain in the US Army MPs? Did you ask if I ever had to walk into a British combat base manned by a thousand teenage boys armed with deadly weapons and pull out a serial rapist?"

More silence.

"I'm sorry," a different PC said. "We've had threats since Chloe's murder and we're taking precautions."

Tania turned in the direction of the voice. "And that's why it's called institutional racism—you're taking precautions with people of color when the only damn lead you have for Chloe's killer is a white dude with an earring."

An audible exhale indicated they conceded her point.

"That's why I'm suing," she said. "Make some institutional improvements around here."

"My fault," PC McDonald said. "I'm sorry. But you fought back. What was I supposed—"

"You tried to kill me—and it's my fault for defending myself?"

Benton turned to Pia and quietly asked, "You're not really going to blow this up in court, are you?"

Pia asked, "Have you met my VP of Personal Protection? She makes her own money, makes her own decisions, and hires her own lawyers— when she's the one assaulted."

"Sorry." Benton shook his head slowly. "Stupid thing for me to say. She has every right."

Tania picked her permission card off the floor and handed it to

McDonald with a glare. She marched through the metal detector and gathered her things. Benton and Pia joined her. He motioned down the hall.

"Please accept my apologies," Benton said as they walked. "They were completely—"

Tania held up a hand to stop him. "If things work here the way they do on our side of the pond, those men don't report to you. They complete tasks for you, but they're not your personnel directly. Is that right?"

"Quite."

"Then I appreciate your apology. But what did that fix for Manchester's tax paying people of color? If they pay the same taxes as white people, don't they deserve the same treatment? Not to mention the same respect. Don't assume I didn't notice those PCs jump to attention when Pia grabbed them."

"Point taken," Benton said. "I'm looking for a simpler solution than a lengthy proceeding, that's all."

"And I'm looking for a simpler solution to entering a building without getting my skull cracked open. What can you do to assure your citizens that won't happen again—and guarantee it with your life?"

She stopped and tugged Benton's arm. "Look, we're both professionals. We take pride in our work. We represent the vast majority of police officers. But we also know the pack mentality that takes over when one of us is threatened. You saw it out there. Only this time, you were one swing of the baton from an ugly international incident. And I was one swing of the baton from becoming a victim. Let's let this play out. Proceeds from my suit will go to the local community."

Benton pursed his lips and worked his jaw and thought before saying, "Right then. Let's get to work."

He led them to a cramped meeting room with laminated tables and mismatched chairs. He took a seat and motioned for Pia and Tania to join him. He said, "You promised me intel on Petrova. What do you have?"

Pia said, "I've come to believe he's a customer of the Morpheus Institute."

She proceeded to explain Sybil Rohan's remarks about Rational Light and how Pia could destroy her enemies. That the list of twelve might represent six customers and six victims. Tania explained that Sybil knew about Dave Krueger's incendiary opinion piece in the *Journal* prior to publication. And how Rain Meyer accused Pia of some yet-unexplained collusion with the Morpheus Institute.

"My tech people tried matching the names on the list of twelve in any combination of customer and victim. Most of the names are too common to narrow it down, with two exceptions. One pair that came up is Kusumawati, a businessman in Singapore who bought the assets of a company from the heirs of a recently deceased Jiali Yang of Hong Kong."

While Pia spoke, Benton took copious notes in a pocket-sized notebook using an old-fashioned fountain pen. When she finished, he re-read them.

He frowned, started to speak, then stopped. He looked at his notes again. Then he said, "Singapore's a bit out of my jurisdiction. Even so, that's not a connection."

"It gives me confidence in our analysis of the list being customers and victims."

"I concur. But that's not evidence." He nodded and scanned his notes again.

"On another topic," Benton said. "Rain Meyer has asked us to press charges for assault and battery."

Pia held out her wrists.

"We declined," he said. "We mentioned that he started the melee. Just so you're aware, he plans to sue for damages."

"Screw him." Pia shrugged. "Are you going to investigate the Morpheus?"

"Investigate what, exactly?"

"That's the problem we had. But every time something turns up, it's connected to the Morpheus. And then she tells me she can kill my enemies. We have a list of names, and I'm sure they'll be on the Morpheus' guest list. You have the power and authority to look deeper."

"Get a search warrant or a phone tap, maybe? 'Your honor, they teach you how to kill in your dreams.' The judge would think I'm taking the piss." He rubbed his face.

Pia leaned closer to him. "You didn't go home last night, did you?"

He looked up with bloodshot eyes and didn't answer.

"The other pair of names my people lined up was Eden-Sonnet and—"

"Look here," he said loudly, "I'm not going to the House of Lords with this rubbish. I'd get sacked at the door. No, it won't do. You've not given me enough to even open an investigation. This isn't the movies, you know. I can't just arrest people, shine a harsh light in their eyes, yell at them without a solicitor, and pop comes the confession. This is my life. I need this job."

Pia drummed her fingers on the table between them. What he said was true. She had nothing. Dame Millie had been right at the beginning: it sounded like the idle chatter of schoolgirls. Pia said, "Chloe was in the middle of leaving me a message about the Morpheus when she was murdered. Only her phone was taken, not her wallet, credit cards, anything else. It had to be the Rohans."

"I'm not saying you're wrong," Benton said. He put his hand on top of her drumming fingers. "I've a feeling you're right. But I need evidence. Facts. Proof. Of anything. Can you tie the operators who killed Chloe to the Rohans?"

Pia shook her head.

"You were spot on about them," Benton said. He pulled his hand off hers. "We checked the CCTV from the surrounding blocks. It was like you said. They positioned the blue Ford in a car park three blocks away. You can see them swapping clothes and number plates. Not that it got us anywhere. They parked too far from the cameras for facial recognition, paid in cash, and used dummy numbers."

Pia started drumming her fingers again.

A constable leaned in the door and pointed at his wrist, then left.

Benton put his hand on top of Pia's again. "I'm after the man who killed Chloe England. I've not the time or manpower to chase these dream-killers. If there's anything to it. There's nothing I can do. I'm sorry."

He let go of her hand, rose, and headed for the door. He walked them to the side exit and waved them off with muttered pleasantries.

Abby pulled to the curb. Tania scanned the landscape, then gave Pia the nod. They strode to the car, got in, and drove off. Within a few blocks they had Abby caught up.

"Bollocks," Abby said. "Obviously the killers work for Sybil or Edward. Whichever one of them wears the pants."

"You don't think it's Sybil?" Pia asked.

"I did last night, but I've been thinking since. It's dodgy enough, but each of them tells you only half the story. If you're wearing a wire, you've got nothing."

"Sybil said plenty."

"Not really," Tania said. "She told you what Alexander the Great did. What you could do. She never said what she could do."

They drove in silence out of the city, each thinking hard. They stayed silent until Hattersley Roundabout, where Pia came out of her deep thoughts and flinched at all the cars flying around the circle the wrong way. She was glad to be in the backseat, where no one saw her.

"I got it," Abby said. "We break in, take a look at the calendars and books."

"Can't," Tania said. "They have sensors and cameras half a mile out. Only way in is dig a tunnel."

"How do you know that?"

"It's my job."

"Oh, right," Abby said. "Well then. You know what you've got to do, Sabel."

"What do you mean?" Pia asked.

"You've got to conquer the world."

Tania smiled at Abby. "Amen to that, baby."

They bumped fists over the gearshift.

"What are you guys talking about?" Pia asked.

Tania leaned around the headrest. "Engage Morpheus. Make them show you how it works."

CHAPTER 25

THAT EVENING, PIA CAUGHT THE Major coming off the elevator at the fanciest hotel in London, the Lanesborough. The Major wore a perfectly fitted pantsuit that resembled a tuxedo without being one. A series of gold chains replaced what might've been a bow tie on a man. Before Pia could finish greetings, Abby Stokes started to wander away, amazed by the hotel's extravagant opulence. In particular, the massive crystal chandeliers caught her eye. Pia grabbed her sleeve, tugged her back, and introduced her. Tania ignored them while keeping a sharp eye on the well-dressed passersby.

"Is that look for dinner?" the Major asked while studying Pia's little black dress with a diamond necklace. Then she turned her assessing gaze to Abby and Tania. "Or an evening out?"

"Both, actually," Pia said. "But I'm here, so I thought I'd make an appearance at your reception. Why are you looking at me like that? Is the dress too casual?"

"You're showing a lot of leg considering these are our top executives in the London office," the Major said. "And you're in heels. At least the necklace fits."

"I'm having dinner elsewhere."

"Yes. I read your text," the Major said. She gave Pia a tired but patient look. "Take me through your plan again while we walk. What do you want from me?"

Strolling down the hall, Pia brought her up to date on the Morpheus Institute and Sybil Rohan's offer of murder. They walked into the Belgravia room, where sixty of her top executives were having cocktails. She stopped to finish their discussion in the doorway.

"So these two—" Pia waved at Tania and Abby "—talked me into this plan. I want you to talk me out of it."

"You flew to London. You have a dinner reservation with Liam. You don't want me to talk you out—"

A young woman politely shrieked with excitement and ran to Pia and the Major. "Ms. Sabel! You're here, in person. What a lovely surprise! I just came on board in January, but I've always wanted to meet you. Bethany Palanski, Sabel Capital."

Bethany stretched her empty champagne flute to her left as if handing it to the Major and pushed a bright smile up at Pia.

"Nice to meet you, too," Pia said and held out a hand.

Bethany blinked with her empty glass still stretched out. She took Pia's hand, shook enthusiastically, and smiled like a rabid fan. Bethany was so star-struck, she didn't know what to say next.

"Oh. Uh. Have you met the Major?" Pia asked.

"I've heard she's here." Bethany looked to her right, scanning the crowd. "But no, never met her."

Pia drew Bethany's attention back to her. "You're trying to hand her your empty."

Bethany's face fell as she slowly turned to her left. Her flute was at the end of her extended arm, two inches from the Major's chest. The Major's face was blank. Bethany yelped in shock and shame. Everyone in the room glanced their way.

"Bethany," Abby asked, "how long have you worked here, not counting tomorrow?" She slid between Pia and the Major, took Bethany's elbow, and steered her away. "You know what we're going to do, Bethany? We're going to take a tour of the room, then we're going to come back, pretend this never happened, and start over all nice and fresh."

Bethany said, "Who are you?"

"Your guardian angel." The pair disappeared into the crowd.

"In this modern, enlightened era—" Pia held up her hands in disbelief "—how does that still happen?"

"I like her," the Major said. "Abby, that is. She knows how to solve problems."

Tania watched Abby for a moment, then faced Pia. "She's competing with you. First to get a date."

"I already won," Pia said, questioning Tania's logic.

"As I was saying," the Major continued, "you came here to get my permission. You can't have it. You're an adult. Liam's an adult. Instead, I'll give you boundaries: As long as you're clear about the risks, and you keep the business negotiations separate, then it's up to him. Not me. I'll say this though: if he agrees, he's a damn fool."

Once again, the Major proved a hard and wise counselor. Pia gave her a quick hug of thanks.

She found a glass, clinked it to get everyone's attention. She made a speech, thanking them for their hard work and devotion, singled out a few of the names the Major had asked her to recognize, and promised to return for a proper dinner at a nice hotel. Which earned a laugh.

After forming a receiving line and shaking hands with all sixty, she gathered her coconspirators and headed for the exit.

CHAPTER 26

HALF AN HOUR LATER, LIAM Pickford sauntered to Pia's table-for-two at Hide Above in Mayfair. Pia looked into his green eyes and greeted him with a peck on the cheek—which he took a moment to appreciate.

Before sitting, he looked around the room and said, "Your lovely VP is here; I feel safer already. Is the other lass a bodyguard too?"

"Horticulturist. One never knows when one might need a plant identified in Latin."

After a curious glance at Pia, he turned around and took a longer look at Abby. He faced Pia again. "Aye, you're having me on. She's an athlete."

"Abby Stokes. Used to give me hell in the game."

He took another look around the space, then came back to Pia. "Everyone in this end of the place is young, athletic, and keeps a keen eye out. Tell me, are they all your people?"

Pia nodded.

"Is there a chance we'll end up in casualty, then?" he asked.

"For what I pay them, we'd better not."

"I'm thrilled you rang me up for dinner." He put his napkin in his lap and smiled. "Shame it's a wee bit wet out. I hear you can see Her Majesty's croft from here."

Pia glanced at the window where the drizzle had picked up to a soaking rain, obscuring Buckingham Palace. She said, "Blocks out the stars, too, unfortunately."

The waiter came by and Liam stopped him from making his speech. He said, "Whatever your chef thinks is best in his scullery, I'll have that."

Pia added, "Do the same for me, only make them complementary so we can share. Pair the wine as well."

The waiter nodded and left.

Shut Up and Drive by Rihanna came on. Liam whisper-sang along with it. Pia started singing along too.

She said, "I grew up with this. You like it?"

He said, "She's my favorite from when I was a teenager."

They sang while the agents stared at them. When it was over, they laughed and bumped fists.

Liam gave her a long, luxurious look. "My chances are looking good."

"Um, well, maybe," Pia said. "I came for a reason. There's this place called the Morpheus Institute. Ever heard of it?"

"Cannae say I have."

Pia told him about meeting Edward and Sybil Rohan, her tour, their methods, and their claim it was the way of the conquerors. She explained how they buttered her up by calling her a conqueror and how Sybil proposed to teach her how to kill adversaries through her dreams. She told him how they mentioned Dave Krueger.

"This Edward fella, is he the same one took you for a wee dauner at the reception?"

"Dauner?"

"Walk, sorry."

"Yes, that was him."

"And this Krueger—" Liam frowned and straightened his silver "—he's the one that wrote that nasty bit in the *Journal*?"

"Right."

"Hardly worth killing a man over. Do they think you're daft?"

The wine arrived. They paused while the sommelier started to give the family tree of the Margaux 1996 to justify the price. Pia waved him off and asked him to pour. They toasted with sparkling eyes. Then they sipped.

Liam leaned back and appraised Pia. "Those Morpheus lads were tied to Chloe England's murder, then?"

Pia nodded. "I have no proof, not even a link, but if I can get inside,

I'll bet I'd find them."

"I wouldnae take that bet." Liam leaned forward. "Ah. So you need to get inside. Aye, that's why ye came out for dinner tonight."

He watched her reaction.

She took too long to form one. He was a step ahead of her and she didn't have a plan for that.

He picked up her hand. "I want to help. You go back there and tell them you want to do me in. Don't shake your head like that, we're just having a blether now. Hear me out. You tell them my price is too high—the Major already told me that was the problem, no secrets there—and you can get it cheap if I'm out of the way."

Pia had hoped to explain her plan in more detail before asking him to help. Now all she could think about was the Major's warning—*if he agrees, he's a damn fool.* What if he suggested it? What did that make him? And why would he jump to the idea so quickly? Was Liam the mastermind, working with the Morpheus? Her head began to fill with scenarios.

What if Tania and Abby were right about Pia being a victim? Was Liam her assassin? Suddenly, she wanted to drop the whole idea. It was bad enough putting his life at risk. Was she also risking her own? Or was this the moment where paranoia took over her life, as Dr. Harrison predicted? Her plan was a crazy idea from the start. She should leave the whole thing to the police.

Except the police had nothing to go on. Chloe's killers were tied to the Morpheus. Tania could keep Liam in check if he was a threat. Right? And the Major was going forward with the deal, so her death would work against his aims.

She decided to trust him.

Maybe.

She took a deep breath and thought up her next sentence.

Before she could speak, he waved a finger at the three nearest tables, smiled, and said, "These lads and lassies of yours; this was your idea from the beginning, to get me onboard. You've even arranged security for me. Some of these people are going home with me tonight."

"True," she said with a blush she could feel.

"Now aren't you the boldest lass in the glen?" He laughed and slapped the table.

The waiter appeared with a dish for each. Hers was called Flesh and Bone, sharpened animal bones with grilled meat skewered on the end and long quills with mushrooms impaled on them. His was an iron pot called Bread and Broth.

"Appropriate," Liam said and pointed at her dish.

"Don't say anything about drinking from the—"

"I imagine you're as tired of hearing about that as I am about being asked what a Scotsman wears under his kilt."

She smiled and ate a slice of meat off the bone with dramatic gusto.

"It'll be dangerous," she said. "I doubt very much they can kill people through dreams. But they are killing people. The people who've died already had personal security, too. I still don't know how they do it— your life will be at risk."

"We Scots have an old saying: *Whit's fur ye'll no go by ye!* What's coming for you will not miss. Whatever will happen will happen."

They ate half their appetizers each and, as if on cue, they traded plates.

When he finished, Liam said, "Well, then, I fancy a negotiation is in order."

Pia looked up quickly. "What did you have in mind?"

"I'll be your bait, gladly." He took a bite of meat from a skewer. "If you get rid of my wife."

Pia sucked in a shocked breath. Too late, she realized she should've done a background check on him before the first date. She'd read her people's backgrounder before the business meeting, but it didn't delve into personals. It covered his resumé and his career. She hated background checks for dating. While they made her feel safe, she'd always learned too much. Proclivities and prior relationships, failed or not, were best discovered in real time. But a wife? And one he casually wanted to get rid of?

"Oh, not like that!" He laughed after observing her face twist up. "Get clear of. Sorry."

"Didn't know you were married."

"Neither did she, apparently."

The waiter cleared their plates and brought the second course. Langoustine, Norwegian lobster, with veal fillet for her; lamb ribs and artichoke for him.

"What does that mean?" Pia asked.

"I thought we were happily married," he said. "For the first year, we were. We were young, though. Everything's an adventure early on. Then I started working for my dad. We moved to London and suddenly she goes a wee bit Edinburgh. Oh, uh, posh. Thinks she's all that. Yeah, anyway. Suddenly she's a right case, disappearing for three, four days at a time, no excuse. We're Glaswegians, not the kind to be putting on airs. Then, my dad is bad off. She thinks his money's all hers. Pops off to Sardinia and refuses to come home. I filed for divorce a year ago, but then she can't be found. Phone's been off the whole time. Not a word out of her."

Pia sipped her wine while she thought. She was dating a married man. That was bad. But they hadn't spoken in a year. That made it OK. Slightly. She was already in deep. She needed him. And she wanted him.

They traded plates wordlessly as if they had been married fifty years.

She hadn't looked closely at ownership of McKenna Engineering since giving the Major the whole task. She remembered a few details. The venture capitalists had just over half the shares. After that, she knew Liam had a sizable chunk, but his dad had far more. Whatever Liam had would be split with his wife in a divorce. Did he want Sabel Security to locate his estranged wife so he could buy her out before settling the deal? If that was the case, it would indicate a Machiavellian side of him she found disappointing. Then she realized he couldn't be expecting that because he needed the business deal done this week. Even if Pia's people tracked his wife down, he'd never get clear of her in time.

"It's the inheritance, you see." Liam tipped his wine glass at her. "I'd give her half what I own now, and gladly too. But my dad's not got long. She doesn't deserve to take a share of that from my sister and me."

"Fair enough," Pia said. "We'll find her no matter what. But I'm going to give you one last chance to back out of the Morpheus project. It'll be dangerous. Uncharted territory. And I'll end up knowing more about your wife than you do. So, here it is. Are you sure you want in?"

"Aye." He smiled. "An adventure with you? Wouldn't miss it for the world."

She extended her hand over the table. He shook enthusiastically.

"What's the plan then?" he asked.

"I don't have a plan," she said. "Yet. But at least I have a partner.'"

They finished dinner chatting about little things, like why he moved to London. It was that or Silicon Valley because he needed programmers and that's where they live. They chatted about why she left soccer. She gave the easy answer: Dad needed her in the business. They chatted about favorite books and movies. They had compatible tastes.

When the wine was gone, Liam looked around for the waiter and signaled for the bill. The waiter whispered to him, "The lady took care of it before you arrived, sir."

He looked back at her, surprised and mildly hurt.

She waved at the five Sabel Agents who had gathered by the stairs and were clearing their exit. "You don't have to pay for my entourage."

He conceded the point.

They walked down the spiral stairs that looked like something one might find in a hobbit-hole, beautifully carved wood in sweeping curves. Outside, the agents scattered in a protective formation at a distance conducive to privacy.

Liam glanced at them, then back at Pia. "They've got their backs to us."

"Personal security takes a little getting used to." She stood still, waiting patiently. "Especially the body armor."

He said, "You're a bonnie lass, y'know that?"

"You're not bad looking yourself."

He whispered, "Do I need their permission to give ye a wee kiss?"

"You have my permission," she said.

He winked. "Aye, I had that back in Bethesda."

A blush rose up her neck. She considered asking him where he planned to give her this kiss, on the street or in his bedroom. But she couldn't quite bring herself to say it out loud. She didn't feel like a conqueror in every aspect of life.

He cupped her cheek and turned her to face him directly. She watched his lips. He watched her eyes. Then he moved slowly, brushing his lips to hers lightly before pulling back. She didn't want him to leave it at that. She feared her breathing might give too much away. She started to lean forward to kiss him. He leaned farther back.

The bastard was toying with her.

She wanted to play-slap him for that, but his arms swirled around her back and waist. His next kiss came in uninhibited and with more purpose and intent.

She longed to immerse herself in passion. Tania had been right: it had been too long. She kissed him back hard. She wanted to lose herself in him, to seek that oblivion she knew he could bring. She wanted many things and sensed he did too.

He broke it off and stepped back.

He took a deep breath and said, "Ach, if only you were a first-date kinda lass, Pia Sabel. G'night."

CHAPTER 27

WHERE THE HELL DID LIAM get the idea she wasn't a "first-date kinda lass?" How had she unintentionally sent that message? Besides, it wasn't a first date. Not technically. If you counted the coffeeshop and the business meeting. Not to mention a funeral. None of which were actual dates but added together meant something. Was he not interested in her? No. He was interested. She'd felt his interest press against her. He was being a gentleman.

Damn it.

Maybe her heels were too high. Maybe he preferred normal-sized women. Or was she not sexy enough? Tania once told her to touch the guy she wanted. His hand, his leg, his shoulder, just a gentle and familiar touch. Had she touched Liam? Oh. She'd offered him a handshake. That was cold. Pia resolved to take Tania's advice next time.

She'd have to engineer a second date. Quickly.

Tania and Abby were out front, walking down the sidewalk. Agent Cody followed behind. Pia savored Liam's kiss while she dialed the Morpheus Institute for the third time. The call finally went through to an answering service. She left a message.

Just as she ended that call, a new one came in from Albert Tindall. He said, "Sorry for the short notice. Wayne's been called to the Americas; we'll have to reschedule his interview. Can we move it back three days?"

For all their efforts to interview her, Walker bails the night before? Bad planning. But then, he was just a podcaster, not a network anchor. She thought about dropping altogether. She said, "I'll have to check my schedule. I'd hoped to be home by then."

"No worries, he can go to DC. He'll go anywhere you are."

She thumbed out a quick message to her PR manager asking about Walking with Walker. The reply came quickly, "Respectable list of interviews. He gets 5-10,000 downloads per episode but has few subscriptions."

Pia figured that was a lot of listeners. And Bobby Jenkins had recommended him. Not to mention she considered it a favor to her former hosts for putting her up the first night. A social debt now paid in full, as far as she was concerned. But she still wanted the leverage over Albert. She said, "Fine. Let's pencil it in. I'll confirm it later."

He thanked her and dropped the call.

Then the Morpheus Institute called back. The noisy traffic made her regret walking the A4 until she saw an old-fashioned English phone booth. Nothing more than a backdrop for tourists but convenient, nonetheless.

She stepped in and answered.

"This is Edward Rohan," he said. "I'm glad you called, Pia."

"I want to know more about your methods and how you might help me get some rest. Can we meet tomorrow?"

While she spoke, she saw a man with a diamond earring pass by on the sidewalk. Was it Mr. Bling, the man who killed Chloe England? There were many pedestrians, and diamond earrings were neither common nor unheard of. It was dark. She tracked the man for only four steps. Then he was gone behind others in the dark.

"Yes and no." Dr. Rohan paused a moment. "You've heard everything we discuss in public. Before we invest any more time in you, you'll need to speak to our development director in London. Can you get there tomorrow?"

Development director is nonprofit-speak for the man driving donations. How the operation made money started to click for her. "I'm in London now. Who do I meet, and how soon?"

"My wife was right; you are a conqueror. You want it all right now, not a minute later. He'll be in touch. Can you keep your morning calendar open?"

"I'll clear it when he calls. Who should I expect?"

"He'll mention the Institute. If you're satisfied with his terms, we can see you tomorrow afternoon. We're looking forward to working with you, Ms. Sabel. Good night."

As soon as he clicked off, she filled in Tania and Abby. She told them she'd get rooms at the Lanesborough.

Abby covered her face in shock. "No. I can't. I've got to be home tonight. Straight away, in fact."

Tania looked confused. "You're turning down a night in a five-bedroom suite at the fanciest hotel in London? Girl, what's wrong with you?"

Abby worried her fingers. "I thought we would be back, is all. I've got … like plans. Maybe."

"Oh, is it something to do with the greenhouse?" Pia asked.

"No. Yes. Kinda." Abby looked up the road and back with a long, labored breath. "Promised Bethany a look round the place first light, is all."

Pia and Tania shared a shocked glance.

"That girl did not look gay at all," Tania said.

"Oh? What does gay look like then, eh?" Abby pushed into Tania with clenched fists at her side and a scowl on her face.

"My bad." Tania put up her hands in surrender.

"She might not be gay," Pia said. "Not everyone who falls for Abby is. There tends to be a vortex of sexual fluidity wherever Abby goes."

"Yeah," Tania said absently, "I noticed that."

Abby smiled bashfully and toed the sidewalk.

Pia touched her shoulder. "Why don't you and Bethany take the jet back tonight. I won't need it until tomorrow."

"You mean it?" Abby lit up. "Oh, boy. You can be a damn good wingman when you're in a mood, Sabel. Um. Is it private? In the back?"

"It's a short flight, Abby."

"Just a thought." Abby pulled her phone, called Bethany, and danced into the dark ahead of them.

After a moment, Abby waved her phone in the air and called out to them, "I win!"

Pia's competitive nature flared. Her hands balled into fists.

"Don't let it get to you," Tania stepped in front of her and grabbed both Pia's arms. "She didn't beat you. She didn't win. You loaned her a jet and gave her an edge—that's all."

Pia accepted Tania's explanation with a nod. "Yeah, you're right. I let her win."

"Working with freaking athletes is gonna drive me to drinking." Tania blew out a breath. "Now tell me what the Morpheus said."

"Rohan wants me to meet with their development manager. If they want me to make a donation, that would be easy to trace. We could have the evidence Benton needs by this time tomorrow. So. It can't be that easy."

CHAPTER 28

PIA GOT BACK FROM HER run before dawn and checked in with George's night crew in Bethesda. She reminded them to let anyone using the word "Morpheus" get through to her directly. They patiently replied they'd been made aware—several times over. She showered and put on fresh leggings and athletic top. She picked up a copy of *Death and Deception* and sat in the bay window. After losing her concentration, she went to the suite's oval-shaped foyer.

Sabel Agent Cody Jefferson leaned his chair against the wall, reading. When she entered his peripheral vision, he dropped the chair to the floor and stood at attention. He'd been with Sabel Security over a year and still reacted like he was back in the 101st Airborne. He was short and built like a bantamweight fighter. He kept a picture on his office desk of the two of them that looked like the famous picture of Maria Sharapova standing next to Floyd Mayweather.

"What are you reading?" she asked.

"Um." He glanced at his book's cover. "*The Geneva Decision.* Pretty good. The heroine reminds me of you."

"I'll trade you when you're done." She held up her book. "Tania up yet?"

"Ma'am?" He glanced at his watch.

"Sorry, bored and waiting for a call." She tracked back down the hall and found her page.

Not long after, the call came in.

"Heard you're an early riser," the voice said. "Most who seek help from the Morpheus Institute are. We'll meet at half six."

He gave an address off the beaten path in Camden Town, near

Roundhouse, a famous music venue. He said nothing else and clicked off.

Tania came in from her room still in PJs, scratching her wild hair. "Is the morning butler in yet? Starving. I couldn't eat that stuff last night. Too fancy."

"Get dressed," Pia said. "We're meeting the money man in half an hour."

"That's moving fast. I don't like it."

"What do we have for self-contained recordings?"

"You wearing that?" Tania's face contorted while she thought. "I got a button camera, would clip on a zipper. What is that brand, Alala? They don't do much in the way of zippers. What else you got?"

Tania followed her to the bedroom where she dug through the suitcase. Tania reached around her and pulled something out and held it up. "Dude, a lace sports bra? Since when do they make … oh, hold up. You was planning on going home with Mr. Liam? About time you did something proactive. What happened?"

"He didn't invite me." Pia shrugged.

"Ain't that a shame. You all ready and waiting for—"

"How about this one?" Pia held up a zippered jacket from Unbridled Apparel.

"That'll work." Tania took it back to her room and returned a minute later. Attached to the zipper pull was a camera the size of a small button. "Just don't unzip halfway. Guys always check out your boobs."

"Men don't stare at mine." Like many athletes, her A cups didn't hold a lot of attention.

"Men always check anyway. He'll see it. Keep it zipped up. They don't care about necks."

They holstered their pistols and checked their looks and headed for the door. Cody fell in at the back.

CHAPTER 29

A LIMO TOOK THEM TO Camden Town. As a security measure, they walked the last three blocks. Nothing looked out of place. Nothing particularly prosperous either. A town in the process of gentrification with shiny, trendy shops next door to vacant storefronts bearing a realtor's number. A stark contrast to the opulence of the Morpheus Institute.

The meeting address led to a nondescript door next to a shiny new art gallery. They found a narrow stairway that led to a renovated second floor. The only door had an impressive, brushed aluminum plaque that read, "Skilling and Veld Investments, Ltd." Cody checked all the entrances and exits, found them secure, and took a position at the base of the stairs.

Tania led the way into the one-room office.

"Who the bloody hell are you?" a man inside asked.

"Security," Tania said. "Step aside or Ms. Sabel goes home."

Pia stood just outside the door and listened. In his line of work, security people were routine. She guessed his surprise came from meeting a tough-as-nails woman like Tania instead of a big, dumb guy. Pia rounded the jamb and watched the man, freshly shaved and hair glistening from a recent shower. He stepped aside to give Tania room to work.

He wore a bespoke suit worthy of a broker in the financial district. Skinny, the man moved in awkward twitches like a Claymation figure. He saw Pia and gave her an annoyed nod.

He stayed behind a large oak desk that reminded her of the Resolute Desk in the Oval Office. The walls were matching honey-hewed oak panels, replete with chair rail and moldings. Diplomas lined the wall behind him. A bookcase crammed with what looked like law books flanked the desk. A few silver-framed pictures of famous people with her host punctuated the shelves. At least one of the famous people was a former Prime Minister. In all, an impressive place.

Tania tested the windows, each a heavy piece of glass embedded with copper wire. She patted the man down. He held out his hands patiently. He'd been through this before. Tania swept the room for electronic bugs and checked her meter readings. Then she looked the man over closely.

"OK." Tania nodded the all-clear at Pia and took up a position by the door. She planted her feet wide and clasped her hands in front of her.

"This is a private conversation," the man said.

Pia gave her the go-ahead and Tania circled outside. As she closed the door, Tania tapped her finger on the edge, drawing Pia's attention. Copper threads protruded from the door's core and tied off at a feeder wire running the length.

"I'll need your phone, Ms. Sabel," the man said and held out his hand.

"Why?" she asked. "This office is a Faraday cage."

"Keen eye." He bounced his hand waiting for the phone. "Nonetheless."

"Who are you?"

"Pardon my manners," he said. "Geoffrey Skilling at your service, ma'am." He pronounced it J-OFF-rey.

"Any relation to the Enron guy?" she asked. Not his real name, she guessed, but her people could run the video through facial recognition.

He stared hard, indicating he'd heard the joke before. She handed over her phone. He placed it in a metal box and tilted it for her to have a look. She did. Inside were two phones, his and hers. The box was an additional layer of Faraday shielding. He closed it and set it on the floor.

Geoffrey held up an electronics-sweeping device of his own. Pia recognized it as off-the-shelf spy hardware. Easily five years behind her technology. It searched for radio frequencies within the room. Most recording and eavesdropping devices can't record locally due to battery and storage limitations, so they use a wireless signal to reach a device, usually a phone, outside the room that then relays the information to others. A standard setup for FBI and MI5 undercover operations. Her button camera was safe, being self-contained. Once he was satisfied, he motioned for her to sit.

They both took their seats.

Skilling said, "It is my understanding you seek a form of insurance for certain business deals."

Pia said, "I thought we were going to discuss a donation to the Morpheus Institute."

"Why would we do that?" he asked. "If you have a sleep disorder and they help you, that's certainly worthy of a donation. That would be between you and them. No. We're here to talk about something else entirely. I offer what are called 'complex instruments' for those involved in corporate events like mergers or takeovers, business opportunities of any kind."

"I don't understand what you mean. I was given to understand they could get rid of my enemies—"

"Mergers and takeovers—hostile or friendly—are perilous things. Anything could throw a spanner in the works. You need to protect yourself from disaster, and for that, you have insurance. But how do you protect against a windfall?"

"Why would I?"

"Let's talk about a hypothetical situation. Just hypothetical now. If anything I say comes to pass, it's coincidence. You alright with that?"

"Go on."

He produced a charming smile and turned his gaze to the ceiling. "Suppose you wanted to buy an aerospace concern. One that's publicly held, where the CEO doesn't like you, but the Chairman is more amenable. Suppose you start buying up shares, hostile takeover-like, and the CEO starts whinging and writing nasty bits about you in the papers. Suppose your bid is already high, but he wants it higher. At some point, you'd cut your losses and move on. That CEO is likely to write nastier bits about you. Your reputation sinks."

He turned back to her and waited for a response.

Pia hated theatrics. She stared at him and rolled her hand.

"But what if—just a simple hypothetical here, nothing more—

something happened to the CEO and the Chairman dropped the challenges and accepted your lower bid? That would be a windfall success. You don't have insurance for that. Everyone who read his article would think you're a bit dodgy. The authorities would go over every email and phone call, looking for anything off."

He held her gaze, expecting her imagination to take over from there.

She said, "But if I didn't do anything wrong, I wouldn't mind."

"How long would that take? Investigations? Rumors? Employees on both sides fearing they'll be made redundant. Situations like that, your best talent would leave both places. Would the company be worth what you paid for it? Would the time?"

Pia considered the implication. She didn't see how his offer tied into the Morpheus. Moreover, she didn't have anything incriminating. "I'm no good at hypotheticals. I'm an athlete with a big headache. Explain it to me."

"Alright." He appeared uneasy. Uncertain if she were dim or playing him somehow. He tugged his jacket when he made up his mind.

He leaned over the desk in a conspiratorial posture. "Let's say you wanted to buy McDowell Aerospace, right? And everyone knows Dave Krueger is not a fan. The chairman is a bit more pragmatic. If you made a bid, what would Krueger do?"

"Tell me to fuck off."

"You don't mess about, do you?" Skilling chuckled. He leaned back. "That's right, he'd try to toss you over by insisting his company's worth twice that. But what if something happens to him? Gets hit by a car, let's say. Then the chairman rings you up, takes your offer, and everyone's gobsmacked. Everyone, that is, except the regulators. Am I right about that?"

"Oh," she said and covered her mouth with her fingertips. "I see what you mean."

"They come in, take all your phones and computers, tie you up in an investigation. What's the *Times* or the *Journal* going to say, eh? They've gotta sell clicks on the website, don't they? They'll write up some juicy stuff about a young girl like you taking short cuts. No one'll believe a word you say for a year. If not two."

"What should I do about that? I can't prove I'm innocent until the dust settles. I think."

"Exactly." He focused on her more intently. "You need insurance against sudden success. Something you can point to and say, 'See? I bet on this deal to go through the long way round, not this. I just lost money.'"

Pia processed his words twice and still didn't get it. Why would anyone bet they would be more successful than planned? You insure against accidents, disasters, bad things.

"Y'see, what we offer is a derivative called a merger-default swap." He looked pleased with himself. "You've heard of credit-default swaps? That's where Joe borrows money from Mary, and you bet me he's going to pay her back, but I think Joe's no good for it and I bet he's going to scarper."

"Credit-default swaps are what brought down the global economy in 2008."

"Indeed. Well done." Skilling pointed at her. "Funny thing is, they're still in use today. This is the same thing, only aimed at a niche. You put up £5 million in cash. If the deal goes down as planned, no problems good or bad, then I pay you £20 million."

Pia thought for a moment. "And if something goes wrong, either way, good or bad, I lose the £5 million?"

"Exactly."

"So, if I want to go after McDowell Aerospace, I give you £5 million. Then Dave Krueger gets hit by a car. I lose the £5 million?"

"Hypothetically speaking. I've no idea about the man's jaywalking habits or his health or anything else. I've never met him and doubt I ever will. But if he stays healthy, and the deal goes through, I pay you £20 million."

She sat back. Not what she expected. Not at all. She was sure there was no such thing as a merger-default swap, but financial markets invented new ways to gamble other people's money every day. There was nothing to stop anyone from creating such a thing. Regulators were constantly playing catch-up with the financial industry.

It presented a clever ruse. Nothing about it was illegal. It wasn't tied to the Rohans. Skilling would keep the money, distributing a share to the Rohans through a shell company that would donate to the Institute. Another share would go to the killers, since she doubted he or the Rohans were the types to get their hands dirty. Her friends at MI5 would trace the money if she could explain any of this without sounding like a lunatic.

"I want to be clear," she said. "There can't be any connection between me and what happens to anyone else."

"You don't want an earthquake to destroy your plant in Winnipeg, either. But you have insurance for that. No one is going to hurt Mr. Krueger—as far as I know. This derivative insures you against anyone suspecting you of hurting him."

He gave her nothing she could take back to Benton to prove the conspiracy. She said, "So it's only worth making that investment if the windfall would be worth more than £5 million."

"Exactly. At today's price, McDowell Aerospace—our hypothetical example—has a market cap of £2.7 billion. Something unexpected happens to the CEO, and it could drop 5 percent overnight. That leaves you with a savings of £135 million on the purchase price. Tidy sum, that. What do you say, worth your five?"

Everything he said kept pointing to McDowell Aerospace. Using them to draw out the Morpheus would only endanger Dave Krueger. Even if he was an asshole, he didn't deserve the death penalty.

"I should say so." Pia pursed her lips while she thought. "Are the merger-default swaps always £5 million?"

"Oh, no." Skilling's eyes lit up. He saw bigger fish than McDowell. "It depends on the game. A bigger company, a bigger payout, and naturally a bigger merger-default swap."

"And if it's smaller?"

"Sure," he gave her a curious look and tilted his head. "McDowell is a sizable company, though."

"McDowell Aerospace means nothing to me," she said. "Krueger's piece was just sour grapes. He wanted to buy my satellite division, but only an idiot would do business with him. Everyone knows he never pays his bills."

Skilling must have seen a ghost. He rolled his chair back, staring at her, and slowly rose. "But … but everyone knows you hate Dave Krueger."

"We took all his customers from him because he treats them badly. Buying McDowell would only bring down the anti-monopoly crowd. They're worth more to me stumbling along on their own."

"He certainly hates you. Doesn't that bother you?"

"Never met the man," Pia said. "Spoke to him once on the phone. Not a nice guy. But I don't care what happens to him."

His mouth fell open. "Well, then. What kind of help were you seeking from the Institute?"

"Oh, this is about the Institute?"

"No." He paled further and turned away. He stared out the window. "Just to be clear, I don't have anything to do with them. I've never met them. I've never been there. I've never spoken to them. It's just that … uh, their clients are often involved in high-stakes business deals that keep them awake. My … offering, if you will, is a parallel thing. Are you involved in any deals that might warrant a merger-default swap?"

It wasn't what she wanted. It wasn't incriminating. But she had to take it or wind up with nothing.

"Well. There is one deal. Liam Pickford of McKenna Engineering is asking four times what his company's worth. Ever heard of him?"

"Never," Skilling took his seat. His smile crept back slowly. He pulled some papers out of the desk drawer. "Tell me all about McKenna."

CHAPTER 30

AFTER SHE TOOK COPIES OF the merger-default swap contracts for legal review, Pia made plans to finalize the deal. She waited for the limo at the bottom of the stairs. Tania pointed at the ceiling where a clean and shiny camera watched them. Outside, Cody watched for their limo. It had circled the block and gotten stuck in traffic.

Pia thumbed out a text to the head of Sabel Capital to review the contracts and set up a wire transfer with a trace.

He texted back, "I know just the person for your project: Bethany Palanski. She's new, but bright and eager."

Pia texted back, "I remember her. She's perfect. Have her meet me at the airport this evening. She'll get the assignment on the jet to Manchester. They'll have her home by bedtime."

She pocketed her phone and watched the street through the smudged glass.

"Back home," Tania said, "Black people make up 16 percent of the population."

Pia glanced at her.

"Here," Tania continued, "we're only 3.5 percent."

Pia waited a moment to see if Tania would explain herself. She didn't. Pia prompted her. "And?"

"Your desire to be colorblind is appreciated." Tania pointed to the white pedestrians walking past Cody on the street. "But your security detail should blend in, not stand out."

"I like Cody. He almost died saving my life in Mumbai. Just like you did in Cameroon and Geneva."

"Yeah, and Jacob did the same despite being glacier-white. Plenty of us are willing to die for you, girl. That's not the problem. When your detail stands out, you put your people at risk. When Jacob was here, you had a little balance. You pulled me in to replace him and that makes things different. Ima add Tanner Wyatt to the team. He's as white as Pepperidge Farm cookies. When he stands on a London street waiting for the limo, nobody notices him."

Pia faced the traffic again. Pedestrians kept a wary eye on Cody as if he were about to jump them. "Is someone specific noticing Cody?"

"That Corsa," Tania said. "Third go round. Didn't you say Chloe's killers drove a Corsa?"

"Get a picture—"

"Cody's been briefed. He's taken a few. Only one guy in it and he doesn't have a diamond earring like Mr. Bling. There's more than one car like that in England. Could be someone with an eye on us, could be a lost Londoner, could be a racist thinking about calling the cops. Oh, hey. Here's the limo."

When it pulled up, Cody scanned the area, readied the door, then waved them out. Pia came first and slid in. Tania followed. Cody rode up front. A blue Ford drove by. A significant diamond earring flashed in the morning sun. In another second it was gone. Then the limo pulled out.

As they drove back to the Belgravia district, Bianca called. Pia put her on speaker.

Bianca said, "The team's been searching for pairs off the list of twelve and found one. A man named Martin Vermeer died in Vancouver yesterday. Charles Eden-Sonnet bought the man's company from his wife by the end of the day."

Her words fell on Pia like an imploding building. Until now, she had considered her inquiries as a way to finish Chloe's last case with the hope of uncovering her killers. Involving Liam seemed like a fun way to discover more about him. The whole idea of killers for hire hiding behind a sleep center sounded so abstract it felt like a game. Worse, this was an operational murder conspiracy. People were dying while she tried to figure it out. Suddenly, everything had turned as real as the first flash of steel in a knife fight.

"He couldn't buy the company the same day the owner died," Pia said. "There's probate first, then the estate has to settle."

"Vermeer Commerce Bank was wholly owned by the wife."

"That's odd," Pia observed. "Was it hers to begin with?"

"We haven't figured that out yet. Canadian corporations are murkier than American or British."

"What business is Eden-Sonnet in?"

"Vulture capital. This is the third postmortem deal he's done in three years. The first went through an estate settlement that took a year. The other one and this were a same-day deal. He learned from his mistake."

"How long has the Morpheus Institute been operating?"

"Five years."

As if more bricks were falling from that collapsing building, Pia considered the ramifications. Abby said they were a legitimate sleep center just over three years ago. Eden-Sonnet began acquiring companies from heirs three years ago. The Morpheus had been at this longer than she realized. Which meant they had operated undetected for quite a while. Their connections protected them. And they had ruthless operatives, the kind who weren't afraid to kill cops.

"Can you hack into the Morpheus Institute's scheduling system? I'd like to see who's on their calendar."

"Without a warrant?" Bianca replied. "I can see if any of our contracted agencies can give us cover, but we can't play games in the UK. We're in tight with MI5, but their version of the FBI is called National Crime Agency, NCA. The two groups are rivals, and the NCA hates us."

"OK," Pia said and silently cursed her brilliant executive for being a rule-follower. Of course, without people like Bianca, Pia could easily become the corrupt, problematic billionaire Rain Meyer believed her to be.

She complimented Bianca on the great work and clicked off.

"Why did Vermeer's wife own the business?" Tania asked.

"Usually, it means he was getting sued and transferred the ownership to avoid losing it. Or it may have been hers all along and he ran it." Pia thought for a moment. "Do we have enough evidence for Benton?"

Tania shook her head and absently massaged the scars that never healed. "To get the NCA and Benton involved, we need something stronger than guesses."

"I never asked you about the incident. Should we work with Benton at all?"

"He texted me," Tania said. "Wanted to know if a diversity training would help."

Pia waited a beat, hoping for an explanation. "Would it?"

"Are you kidding me? He's trying to protect his institution from a lawsuit instead of fixing the rank and file."

"I almost understand what you're telling me. Almost."

"They done diversity training last year. How'd that work? Cause that pack of cops overreacted and were ready to kill me." Tania breathed and thought. "Honestly, I think Benton gets it. He don't get the urgency, but he understands the problem. Maybe his bosses get it, too. There appears to be an effort underway—minimal as it is. But there's been no follow up, no reporting on good and bad, no one holding the PCs accountable on a day-to-day basis. And that's how you end up getting protestors out front of your building holding signs that say *Remember Tania Cooper*."

"Should we work with him or go it alone?"

"Sure, we can work with him." Tania smiled. "You mean in case Liam doesn't work out? Oh, don't give me that face, sister. I saw the inspector holding your hand. Don't pretend he didn't."

"My drumming fingers annoyed him."

"Oh. OK. Musta forgot how to use his words then. We'll go with that." Tania nodded slowly. "He also asked how come you're nice when most rich people are assholes."

"That's because he's a socialist."

"OK, then, talk about finding Chloe's killer," Tania said. "Notice he told you to stay away from that British upscaler?"

"He warned me off, yes."

"So you're gonna call *Lord* Charlie, right?" Tania asked. "Offer to take Vermeer off his hands?"

DI Benton had been adamant about not implicating Lord Charles Eden-Sonnet. Dame Millie Tindall had been equally steadfast about the propriety of the Morpheus Institute. While Pia had a weak grasp on English class system, it was clear these people feared the Morpheus and its customers. Pia didn't.

CHAPTER 31

PIA TEXTED GEORGE'S TEAM TO track down Eden-Sonnet and Rain Meyer. It took them three minutes. First, she called Lord Charles Eden-Sonnet.

He answered with an aristocratic and bemused voice. "What a lucky man am I to get a call from the illustrious Pia Sabel."

"Flattery is always nice—if not suspect. I'd like to discuss some business opportunities. Are you free today?"

"Charming presumption, but I haven't any opportunities to offer, nor am I interested in any new ones. Thank you for thinking of me."

Pia felt him slipping away. She thought fast. "Vermeer took all your capital then?"

He hesitated. "I've no interest in discussing any opportunity."

She only had a split-second left before her only lead evaporated. What would appeal to an old school patrician? Status.

"Even if it includes an invitation to White's?"

An invitation to the ancient and exclusive club was desperate, but the only thing she could think of under pressure.

Another hesitation. "I'm not a member of White's and you couldn't be. Only royals and men are allowed. Certainly not Americans."

"They made one exception on all three counts," Pia said. "The issue was forced by an outstanding loan for an extravagant renovation. But my membership is only good until they pay it back. They want me out so badly they might make you a member if you would refinance the loan for them."

"Interesting proposition," he said tentatively. "How much do they owe you?"

She told him. He gasped.

"Be there at seven for cocktails," she said while he continued trying to find air. "Their gimlets are remarkable."

"Intriguing offer. One mustn't turn down a gimlet at White's even if one prefers a Vesper martini. Seven it is, then. However, I must repeat that I've no opportunities to discuss."

She clicked off and gave the limo driver the address to Rain Meyer's flat in Wembley. They found him getting out of a car in front of a modest duplex on a tree-lined lane. A silver brace covered his nose, held in place with white medical tape. A bag of groceries hung from one hand. He stared at the limo first with curiosity, then fear.

"Is that your real name," Pia asked when she popped out.

"You can't talk to me," he snapped. "You have to talk to my lawyer … I mean, solicitor, or whatever they call them here."

"About your little nosebleed? My legal team handles that. I'm here to ask if you want to change the world or just whine about it."

"Don't think you can corrupt me with whatever you're offering." He huffed a couple times. In a higher pitch, he asked, "Are you offering something?"

"Possibly the head of Charles Eden-Sonnet. But only if you have substance behind your cynical, fact-deprived soapbox speech."

"I might. Why?"

"Because I believe he had a man named Martin Vermeer killed so he could buy Vermeer Commerce Bank of Vancouver."

"W-wh-what?" Rain choked and swallowed and finally said, "Why are you telling me this?"

"Do you have dirt on him or not?"

"Yeah. How did you find me?"

"Grow some balls and talk to me, Rain. Do you have something concrete? Was your speech just your way of jerking off in public or do you stand behind your bullshit? I'm going to need some ammunition when I confront the guy later today."

"You're going to meet him? He doesn't meet with anyone. He's a hermit."

"Answer the question."

"Yeah. Um, a former employee of his told me some stuff. Actually, she posted it on Reddit. She sounded crazy but everything I checked turned out to be true. But … how did you find where I'm staying?"

Pia leaned in, an impatient look on her face. She rolled her hand.

"She said she was a contractor involved in some dealings, said there's a place that arranges murders for the rich." He looked skyward. "Like I said, it sounds kinda crazy."

"This contractor have a name?" Pia asked. "Will they talk to me?"

"Bella Davis, but, um …"

"She died last week." Pia blew out a breath of frustration.

"Wait," Rain said. "How did you know?"

In brief, Pia explained about Chloe England's fateful visit with Bella Davis and how it led Pia to Manchester. He explained how he'd come directly from Boston to record Bella Davis's statement on behalf of Manifest Morals only to find she'd died. He was staying with friends while trying to raise funds on social media to get a flight back home.

"You still haven't answered me," he whined. "How did you find me?"

"Remember how you said Sabel Technologies spies on every word you say? Well, you're wrong. You're not that interesting. We don't care about what you say. However, my people are really good at finding you when you think you're offline." She pointed to his pocket. "You play *Galactic Multiplayer Dodgeball* on your phone. It's produced by Sabel Gaming."

Rain Meyer rolled his eyes so hard his face tilted skyward.

Pia observed him while considering if he could do the job she had in mind. He looked like a guy who could break in a strong breeze but had a mission burning inside him. People with fire could rise up when called. She decided to take a chance. She said, "I have an undercover job that could put you and Manifest Morals on the map. Can you handle trench warfare?"

"Uh." Rain Meyer swallowed. "What do you mean?"

"They killed a cop, Rain. Are you prepared to work inside their organization, get a peek at the books, record conversations, steal information?"

"That's what we do."

"That's what you fantasize about doing. I'm not talking about spinning up baseless memes and hoping they go viral. I'm offering you a chance to actually do something. But I'm not going to kid you: there are risks. Big risks."

Rain straightened up. "Why should I trust you?"

"Because that crap you spouted about me back in Manchester was nothing more than conspiracy theories you picked up online. I'm offering you a chance to put your threadbare organization on the map. Just don't think this kind of work is easy."

"Yeah, OK. If you're for real, I'll do it. What's involved?"

"First, you gotta man up." She laid a finger on her own nose. "See this? Broken five times. Four in soccer and once in the ring. Plastic surgery makes it look like new." She ripped the bandage off his. "If you needed this, you'd have two black eyes behind it. If there's a lump later, I'll have the guys who fixed mine do the same for you. Someone will call you about logistics, expenses, and tech gear. Be at the airport this evening. You'll get the mission details on the flight. Now shave off that stupid beard, get a couple suits, and look like an accountant from headquarters."

CHAPTER 32

PIA SAT IN A WINGBACK near a large window in a corner of the spacious Coffee Room upstairs at White's. Portraits of members hung on every wood paneled wall. Some dated to the club's founding in 1693. From the look of the patrons, a few might've been original members. As much as she hated dressing up, she saw no need to inflame the club membership more than necessary. So she'd put on a double-breasted navy blazer with nothing under it and a gray skirt from Balmain. Matching shoes, purse, and heavy strands of pearls rounded out the statement. It was the kind of thing a local princess might wear to a business meeting—only flashier. Her hair had been professionally styled and pinned back with pearl barrettes that matched her earrings and necklace.

Ignoring the cold stares from the members seated nearby, she worked on her phone, trimming an audio recording to just the right portion. She saved it and waited for her guest to arrive.

A short while later, a plump, older man with bouncing jowls waddled through the room. The manager pointed to Pia with a sneer and let Lord Eden-Sonnet introduce himself. He held a cupped hand out for her fingertips. She obliged.

"Charmed, Ms. Sabel." He kissed the back of her hand.

"You might reserve judgment on that, Chuck."

He dropped her hand and settled into the wingback angled toward her. "The proper etiquette insists you address me as Lord Eden-Sonnet."

"Insist all you want," she said. "Not many Eden-Sonnets around, are there?"

"I was an only child, the last of my line." His voice drifted back with mild regret.

Adjusting his weight in the chair, he took on the countenance of a man wanting to control the subject. "Quite a shiner you've got there. Must've been quite a catfight. How did the other lady fare?"

"I broke his pride in three places."

"Have you been interviewed by Wayne Walker?" he asked. "All the rage in the world of podcasts, I hear."

"On the schedule."

"Well, isn't that grand," he said. He glanced around to check out the other patrons and realized she'd seated him to focus on her.

A waiter arrived with two gimlets. Eden-Sonnet looked surprised and disappointed. Ordering for him was rude of her, especially since he'd mentioned he preferred a Vesper martini.

"To what do I owe my hour in your august company?" Lord Eden-Sonnet asked.

"You're going to sell me Vermeer Commerce Bank."

He smiled and sipped his drink. "You were right when we spoke earlier. When men flatter, it is indeed suspect. Likewise, women are suspect when they make demands. So rarely do they demand what they really want. I find there is often duplicity in the words of a beautiful woman. And so I marvel at what you might truly want, Ms. Sabel."

"Western Canada is ascendant. With the influx of Chinese wealth, the potential for Sabel Capital is far greater than whatever you could accomplish with Vermeer. You can name your price."

"A reasonable man might speculate about your true motives. A woman at your level would send a division president for such a small venture." He sipped his gimlet, smacked his lips, and glanced around at the portraits of long-dead white men. "Why would you personally handle something so small, I wonder."

She watched him craning to see a portrait to his right. "After expanding the Security division, we began looking to expand Sabel Capital. It's keeping me up nights. I barely get any sleep."

"What I like about doing business with men is they tell you what they want straight out." He looked at a painting farther to the right.

"That's why I'm seeking help from the Morpheus Institute. You've heard of them."

Eden-Sonnet's head snapped around to her.

A smile widened across Pia's face.

"Indeed," he said. "They did a good turn for me."

"They've led me to believe I can get whatever I want using their system."

His eyes locked on hers, he paled a shade lighter than his original pallor. "What is it you want?"

She sipped her Gimlet without breaking their gaze. "More to the point is what I don't want. I don't want to resort to the Morpheus and their radical methods."

"You poor thing," he said. "You Americans are absolutely delusional with your fixation on celebrities. Long ago your nation sank into the quicksand of mob rule—as predicted. Nothing but a bunch of overfed, vulgar, annoying mutts. It would appear you're confusing movie innuendo with reality. For your implied threat to have any weight, you must be specific. Speak into the mic, dear."

He leaned forward, his thumb under his jacket lapel as if he had a hidden microphone. He didn't. She'd already checked.

She leaned forward and said in a clear voice, "They claim I can sleep better knowing I've gotten inside the head of my enemies."

"Yes, yes, the bank. It's not up for sale, you see." He leaned back and sipped his gimlet. "And their methods are not as effective as they might lead you to believe."

Pia considered her next move carefully. DI Benton had specifically told her not to share Chloe's last message. But she saw no other way to get inside Eden-Sonnet's operation. Forgiveness was better than permission in this situation.

"And yet you've used the Morpheus quite effectively," she said. "They cleared your path so you could buy Vermeer. Sell the company to me and the evidence I have of your complicity never falls into the wrong hands."

Eden-Sonnet set his drink on the table between them. He swallowed and breathed and adjusted his suit. "I suppose you have some form of blackmail to back up your rather preposterous claim?"

"Did you hear about the constable who was beaten to death in the streets of Manchester last week?"

"Can't say that I have."

Pia nodded. "Chloe England was a friend of mine. She discovered the Morpheus had me on a list for extermination. They accepted my counterproposal and moved me from the to-be-killed column to the other one. The one you're in. How do I know about all this? Chloe collected a good deal of dirt and shared it with me. Allow me to play an enlightening portion of a report she made to me."

Pia held her phone between them. Eden-Sonnet's gaze dropped to the phone as if it were a rattlesnake in her hand. She pressed play on the audio clip she'd edited earlier.

Chloe's voice came out loud enough to startle the man. Chloe said, "Anyway, here's the list. Oh, hang on." Chloe fumbled the phone. "Gotta put you on speaker so's I can read my notes while I'm talking. Here it is, then: Yang and Breach, Anton Petrova, Sabel, Kusumawati, Wilson, Vermeer, Nhung, Duval, Eden-Sonnet, Krueger, and Santos."

The recording stopped and Eden-Sonnet's eyes rose slowly to Pia. "No doubt you have something more substantial than a list of names."

"She was murdered." Pia snapped the phone back and dropped it in her purse. She took pleasure in watching him flinch. "A Greater Manchester Police constable lost her life for telling me about the Morpheus Institute. Yes, I have a good deal more. And, in no time, the GMP's lead inspector might find it in his inbox."

"Could be anyone she's referring to in that."

"How many Eden-Sonnets are there?" she asked. "You told me you're the last of your line."

He swallowed hard.

"We can avoid a good deal of nastiness," she said. "If I get what I want, there won't be any need to involve the GMP, or NCA, or even tell the Morpheus that you're their weakest link."

"You're getting in over your head, dear girl."

"Guess how many times I've been told that." She paused a beat. "It's not a tough decision. I get Vermeer or everyone finds out you're involved. Come to think of it, I could just drop it on Twitter. Then everyone in the House of Lords could imagine whatever they want."

"Perhaps we can come to some understanding or another," he said. His lips trembled. "For now, at least. You might think you're winning, but you'll soon learn there's more to this iceberg than you can see."

Pia leaned toward him, her elbows on her knees. "This isn't a negotiation, Chuck."

"You'll address me as Lord Eden-Sonnet."

"The fuck I will."

He took a deep breath and sank back in his chair. If it had been an ejector seat, he would've taken his chances blowing through the ceiling to get away from her. He muttered, "You really do drink from the skulls of—"

"All I want from you is a fair price on the Vermeer Commerce Bank," she said. Pia shouldered her purse and rose. "My forensic accounting people will be in your London office first thing tomorrow. Make sure it's a pleasure doing business with you, Chuck."

CHAPTER 33

"WHY WOULDN'T HE TELL YOU he was going out of town for a couple days?" Tania asked as the limo crossed the apron toward Sabel One at the London City Airport. A barely audible rain pinged off the roof.

Pia hesitated, then said, "I don't want to talk about it."

"Well you sure do want to sit there and sulk about it, sister. And I gotta be with you."

"Liam's an adult. He doesn't owe me an itinerary. It's not like we're dating."

"The way you dressed for dinner, sure looked like you were dating somebody."

"I should've called earlier, that's all. Now drop it."

"We had to scramble for boots on the ground at his destinations." Tania blew out an irritated breath. "At least he took his body armor with him. Getting principals to wear it is usually a bitch. Of course, we don't know he's wearing—"

"Drop it."

They got out and strode toward the jet in the dark. Tanner Wyatt's steely gaze scanned the apron around them. He held out an umbrella. A smaller silhouette stood next to him, waiting nervously.

As they approached, Pia recognized Bethany Palanski. The woman from Capital worried her hands and stepped forward.

"Ms. Sabel, I just, just..." she stammered and stopped. Her eyes flitted from Tania to Tanner before coming back to Pia.

"Could you give us a moment?" Pia said to her bodyguards.

"Everyone's here," Tanner reported. "Rain Meyer is onboard, the specialists from Security are with him, your execs from Tech are online.

And Cody's catching some shuteye in the suite."

Pia thanked him. He took the airstair two steps at a time. Tania followed him with a curious glance over her shoulder.

"I want to apologize …" Bethany sounded like she was on the verge of tears. "I never meant for anything to … you know."

"No, I don't know. What are you apologizing for?"

"I've never done anything like that before. I'm not… I didn't mean to come between … Oh, please don't fire me. I need this job."

Pia's head snapped back trying to figure out what the woman was talking about. Then it came to her. It was almost funny, except that Bethany was trembling in terror.

Pia patted the woman's shoulder and said, "I am not now, nor have I ever been, in a romantic relationship with Abby Stokes. I've no interest in what you did last night, tomorrow, or any of your free time. You've not been asked here to answer for anything involving Abby. This evening is about something else entirely. You've been recommended for a special assignment."

"I'm not romantic with Abby either." Bethany looked up with pleading eyes, uncertain if she believed herself. "Wait. A special … what?"

Pia had a moment's doubt about picking Bethany. She didn't seem to be made of the steel required for undercover work. Still, her boss had recommended her for the job without hesitation. That said a lot.

"We have a full briefing for you onboard." Pia gestured to the airstair. "It's a special assignment that could be dangerous."

Bethany's face lit up with excitement. She grabbed the handrail and started up, then stopped. "I'm not gay, just so you know."

"It makes no difference to the mission, the company, or me." Pia followed her up the steps. "For what it's worth, I've always known Abby Stokes to be charming and irresistible."

Bethany stopped at the doorway and turned her face skyward, letting the cool rain spatter her face. In a dreamy voice, she said, "That she is."

On the flight to Manchester, a team of specialists from around Sabel Industries filled in Bethany and Rain on the many shell companies of Eden-Sonnet. Pia spelled out what she wanted, how Bethany would go over the Vermeer books while Rain pretended to be a slacker engaging the other workers in casual conversation. Both would wear a series of body cameras on site. While there was little likelihood of physical danger on the job, two Sabel agents would be nearby should they push their panic buttons.

Both had eagerly accepted their missions by the time they landed.

The jet taxied to the private facility in Manchester and the pilots opened the airstair.

Tania led the exit with Pia second, Tanner third. The others stayed on board, Bethany and Rain heading back to London.

Abby waited at the bottom step, her gaze focused past Pia and Tania's shoulders at the open doorway as they descended. She looked disappointed when no one followed Tanner. Tanner stopped and examined her as if she were a potential bomb to be defused.

Pia stopped and waved Tania and Tanner on to the car. Abby didn't even glance her way.

"Bethany's going back to London," Pia said. "She has a big job in the morning."

"Oh." Abby's face fell.

"Are those flowers?"

Abby snapped the small bouquet behind her back. "Might be."

"If you don't have a squirt bottle hidden in there, you can run up and give them to her."

Abby's face lit up like a child opening a birthday present. She started to track around Pia.

Pia stopped her. "She's special? Not one of your flings?"

"Yeah. This is the one, Sabel. I feel it." Abby's gaze found Bethany in the window. "Am I showing it too much?"

"Maybe you could do me a favor." Pia waited until Abby looked up at her. "Keep an eye on her on the trip back. The pilots will bring you back anytime, later tonight or in the morning. Whatever works for you."

Abby's smile glowed in the dark.

"If you need a place to stay in London," Pia continued, "I've kept my suite at the Lanesborough. It's all yours."

Abby fast-clapped with glee, then frowned. "Why're you being so bloody nice to me all of a sudden?"

"My plans fell through," Pia said quietly. "Like to see someone happy tonight."

"Nah, that's not it." Abby wagged a finger. "Admit it. You're pining for me, aren't cha." Abby laughed with joy and wrapped her arms around Pia, squeezed hard, tipped up on her toes and planted a wet, sloppy kiss on her cheek. "Well, you had your chance, Sabel. You blew it."

Abby bolted up the stairs, taking them two at a time.

"I'm stealing your bed," Pia called out. "I didn't want to sleep by the fireplace again, that's all."

CHAPTER 34

THE MORPHEUS INSTITUTE GLOWED LIKE a sun rising through the mist. Strong lights blazed up the walls, creating a foam of light around the grounds. Domes of video cameras hung from every corner. No dark recesses. No blind spots.

Dr. Sybil Rohan greeted them at the entrance, dressed in a white pantsuit that flowed with her movements. A security guard with a potbelly stood next to her. "Welcome, Pia. Your presence is forever enchanting. You stand unbowed regardless of the bludgeonings you suffer on social media. I am in awe."

"OK." Pia eyed her suspiciously.

"We welcome any scrutiny you may bring." Sybil examined Tanner and Tania. "It is not at all unusual. Everyone at your level has concerns. We've been vetted by all our clients."

"I keep hearing that phrase, 'at your level.' Is that British code for class or something?"

"Oh, no." Sybil looked concerned. "I thought that was an athletic term. Aren't there different levels of competition before you reach the international stage?"

Pia considered her hostess for a moment. Yes and no. There were levels but no one she knew used the phrase the way she'd heard it since she landed in Manchester. The people who used that phrase were connected. She said, "If you could walk me through the process, I'd appreciate it."

"Naturally." Sybil turned to Tanner. "I understand it is standard security procedure for one of you to proceed Ms. Sabel and the other to follow behind. Unfortunately, such behavior upsets our special guests.

I'll ask you to stay here in reception."

Tanner stared at her wordlessly.

Pia said, "Tania is in charge of my personal security. She will accompany us on the tour."

"As you wish," Sybil said.

Wordlessly, she instructed her security man to watch Tanner. Her man looked relieved that he had no more to do than stand still. Though he looked spooked by Tanner.

Dr. Rohan bowed and gestured to a wide passageway leading to an open area.

"No computers?" Pia waved her hand around the reception desk. "You don't appear automated."

"Computers." Sybil laughed. "They're only good for the people who hack them. We're pencil-and-paper here."

"How do you keep track of who's coming and going?"

"Each of our clients are special to us. Every appointment is unforgettable." She smiled and gestured to the passage again. "Come, let's get you comfortable with attaining Rational Light."

Sybil led Pia and Tania to a terrace overlooking a lily pond. Round lounging chairs overflowed with pillows. Heaters warmed the air around each one. A large overhang kept the English rain off the seating area.

Sybil said, "This is where your orientation session will take place."

Tania checked the corners and under the seat cushions.

Picking up a small stack of reports, Sybil handed them to Pia. "These are the research papers on dark matter, Rational Light, and sleep disturbances. Some are independent studies and some are ours."

Pia fanned through the pages. With every appearance of serious academic work, they conveyed the aura of deep science. The only one directly addressing Rational Light listed the Rohans as authors. She tucked them into her purse.

"A friend of mine came here a while back. Abby Stokes," Pia said. "She didn't mention a lily pond."

"I don't recall a client by that name." Sybil smiled weakly. "From here, you'll go to the preparation room."

Sybil led them around a curved wall to another space.

"Looks like a spa," Pia said.

"Indeed. A little relaxation induces a restful dream state to help you achieve Rational Light."

"Who does the massage?" Tania asked.

"Edward provides a holistic body, mind, and spirit alignment using essential oils, aromatherapy, and—"

"Eden-Sonnet went through all that?" Pia asked skeptically.

"I beg your pardon?" Obviously startled, Sybil turned away to examine something. "I don't follow."

"Chuck came for cocktails," Pia replied. "We discussed the Morpheus briefly. He told me, 'their methods are not as effective as they might lead you to believe.'"

Sybil's mouth drew tight; her face hardened to stone. "We never confirm or deny clients. In any event, we would never refer to Lord Eden-Sonnet as *Chuck*." She paused and softened and resumed her pleasant expression. "I'm sure you wouldn't want us discussing your situation."

Pointing to the only door Pia had seen in the place, Sybil ushered them through. She said, "We find the conqueror-mindset operates best in spiritual enlargement chambers."

They stood in a sand-colored control room where two workstations faced a glass window overlooking another room. Before them were monitors tracking heart rate, blood pressure, oxygen levels, temperature both ambient and body, and several other indicators. A microphone stalk could reach across the desk to either seat. The second workstation showed a set of displays labeled EEG, MEG, and fMRI, which Pia guessed were for monitoring brain activity.

"You do use computers," Pia said.

"Medical equipment only. They're not connected to the internet, so the data from your sessions remains secure."

"You keep copies here?"

"We give them to you. They are yours to keep or dispose of, as you see fit."

Pia didn't believe that for a minute but nodded anyway.

Tania squeezed by her moving to the far end, carefully examining each workstation without touching anything.

Pia turned to Sybil, pointed at the room beyond the window, and said, "That's the sensory deprivation chamber?"

"Spiritual enlargement chamber," Sybil replied.

She touched a switch, lighting the next room in crisp LED-induced daylight. A white fiberglass oval, shaped like a river rock the size of a small car, sparkled under bright lights. The Morpheus logo stretched across the side.

Sybil crossed to the entrance and waited for Pia. Tania lingered in the control room.

Sybil pressed a button. The top half of the river rock rose four feet on a hydraulic hinge. Inside the chamber, a royal-blue solution filled a space Pia estimated to be four feet by eight. Glass pebbles covered the underside of the lid.

Tania joined them and stood at ease by the door.

Pointing at the pebbles, Sybil said, "There are 2,880 LEDs in red, near-infrared, and deep violet to reduce oxidative stress through photobiomodulation."

Tania scoffed. Pia shot her a stern look.

Sybil wrapped her fingers around the edge of the tank. "Not only is the enlargement chamber sound-dampened, but the room is as well." She swished the water. "The magnesium sulfate solution is changed for every guest. Pure, warm oxygen circulates while you meditate. As you can see, Edward and I carefully monitor your vital signs from the control room.

"It takes roughly forty minutes to achieve the first stage of Rational Light. Another twenty to forty is required to move about the plane you wish to inhabit. When you encounter the source of your spiritual stress, you can conquer it rather quickly from there."

Tania stepped closer and examined the tank, the lid, and the lights. She felt the LEDs and dipped her fingers in the solution.

Pia looked beyond the floatation pod. Fabric-covered soundproofing on every surface but the floor. Behind each burning light bulb were three others in different hues. She recognized the hinted scent of a primeval pine forest, thick with moss in the humid air.

"For the true conqueror," Sybil continued in a silky voice, "this is where destiny is fulfilled. A woman like you can move up a level to dominate all she surveys, Pia. You dominated sports. You dominate your company. It's time to take charge of those poor lost souls at McKenna so you can inspire them to achieve the greatness they can only achieve under your brilliant guidance. This is your time to ask, 'Do I dare?' And you will dare. I know you will, Pia. When you rise from the Rational Light, you will truly thank whatever gods may be for your unconquerable soul."

Pia watched Sybil's eyes. They were the steadfast windows into the soul of a true believer.

"Where did you get McKenna?" Pia asked. She waited for Dr. Rohan to blink but the woman didn't show the slightest concern. "Last time we met, you told me I could get rid of Krueger."

"Rational Light is an informative process. One can travel through dark matter to discover what truly troubles another. Your concerns are visible to those who know how to divine them."

A remarkable answer. They had every excuse worked out.

Sybil raised her hands in the air and turned a circle, indicating the whole room. She said, "The world will be yours."

She looked up to Pia with the somber mien of a lovesick admirer waiting for affirmation.

"Is all this necessary?" Pia asked. "It seems kinda gimmicky."

Sybil stepped back, disappointed. "Until you've experienced Rational Light, none of it makes sense. But once you've undergone the transformation, I assure you, it will."

"Do I need to go through all this every time?" Pia twirled a finger at the room. "After McKenna, can I just call in the next one?"

Sybil darkened. "Rational Light is a serious process."

"You've made that clear," Pia said. "And while Geoffrey Skilling might fly to Moscow to pick up a few million pounds, I just can't see Anton Petrova risking a flight to England every time he wants to conquer another source of his spiritual stress."

"You sound as cynical as a journalist." Sybil's frown crushed her dark eyes to tiny dots. "As you well know, the road to greatness is littered with roadkill. Either you're the driver or you're the rodent scurrying across the cold, unyielding pavement. This is a decision only you can make. Our methods are historically proven. You, of all people, should see the unique opportunity before you. We are not people to be trifled with or belittled, Pia. We offer you the world, not to be slapped away with childish petulance, but to be honored and cherished with extreme gratitude. Perhaps you're not the conqueror we envisioned. Perhaps Rational Light is not the right solution for your problems."

They stared at each other for a tense minute.

Pia bristled at Sybil's challenge. Submitting to Dr. Rohan made her skin crawl. It felt like losing. She longed to put this pretender in her place. She wanted to throttle the woman until she answered the question, *Who killed Chloe England?*

But that would have to wait.

She said, "I'll keep the appointment."

CHAPTER 35

CLAIGEANN COTTAGE WELCOMED PIA AND Tania when the limo dropped them off. Even in the dark, the swayback roofline and rustling ivy invited them in like an old friend. Tanner left with the driver for a room in the nearby town. They lit a fire and opened a bottle of wine.

"What do you think of the Morpheus security team?" Pia asked.

"Don't expect any of them to back you up in a street fight. But they got tons of video. They'll call it in and let the local cops handle it."

"And the facility?"

Tania said, "That control room has gas valves."

"What do you mean?" Pia asked.

"It's supposed to feed in oxygen, but they have secondary hookups for something else. The valves and controls are under the control room counter. The readouts show on the screens."

"You mean like an anesthetic to put me under, so I don't know what's going on?"

"I don't know. Maybe it's a psycho-suggestive mixture. That microphone on the desk had to be hooked to the speakers in the chamber. In case you didn't see them, there were tiny speakers like the ones in your phone between all the LEDs in the top. Combined with the lights, maybe they talk you into believing in Rational Light."

"What's a psycho-suggestive mixture?" Pia asked. "Like hypnosis?"

"Yeah, only ingrained deep in your brain. When I was in the MPs, terrorists were doing it to suicide bombers with magic mushrooms. Now, most security people ain't gonna know what to look for. Some guy like Eden-Sonnet could have his bodyguard standing right in the control room without a clue about what the Rohans are up to. They suggest things to the customers in that new-age-doublespeak about rational light, dark matter, this and that, and they're the only ones who know what's going down."

Pia sipped her wine while watching the fire lap at the edges of the logs. "These people like Petrova and Eden-Sonnet might actually believe they killed their adversaries?"

They sat in silence for a few minutes, sipping wine, watching the fire, and thinking the same things separately.

"It's the perfect setup," Tania said finally. "When you were a kid, and you got really pissed off at somebody, you wanted to believe in voodoo so you could use it against your enemies. Ruin her life without ever touching her. Like witchcraft or some shit. And here they are, offering you that mystical experience with fancy oils and pine-scented air and lily ponds and high-tech machinery and drugs. Then your enemy dies. And they get you to thinking you did it. Egomaniac like Petrova thinks he's found a real science-based voodoo, the key to taking over the world."

"I paid £5 million this time. The next time they'll charge ten. It was Chuck's third. I wonder how much he paid them to take out Martin Vermeer."

"But how are they pulling it off?" Tania drained her glass. "No matter what they make you think, someone still has to pull the trigger."

"The two guys," Pia said absently. "A red Corsa and a blue Focus. Probably the same guys who used Novichok on the Skirpals."

"Except Mr. Bling was in Camden Town yesterday, watching over Skilling. Not in Vancouver killing Vermeer. Not to mention that even a lousy bodyguard would never let that guy near their principal. Nah, it's gotta be someone who would waltz by security. A lawyer, doctor, stockbroker, a police detective—or someone selling his business."

Pia's blood ran cold. "No way. He's… too nice."

"So was Ted Bundy. Handsome too. But you gotta consider all possibilities." Tania finished her wine. "What did Vermeer die of?"

"Good question," Pia said. "Yang and Breach both had heart problems that weren't diagnosed previously because … hmm. I don't remember. Was there a neurologic problem?"

"Well, you figure it out, girl. Unlike you, I gotta sleep." Tania stripped to her undies and pulled blankets over the couch.

Pia did what she always did at night: went to bed, pulled out her copy of *Death and Deception*, turned to the current page, and started reading. It usually put her to sleep right away, but she kept reading until she finished it at 2 AM. She turned out the light and cuddled Abby's blankets under her chin.

Her thoughts kept turning over in her mind. Where did Liam say he was going? Canada? It was the closest Commonwealth nation to Silicon Valley, giving him access to the best programmers without paying California salaries. A smart move. Then she wondered when he was coming back. Another day or two, maybe.

At least Abby had someone for the evening. Only because Pia let her win.

She pulled the blankets tighter and felt a little drowsiness overcome her.

CHAPTER 36

BEEP. BEEP. THE SHARP, DISTINCTIVE perimeter alarm buzzed her phone. Pia tossed the sheets, grabbed her pistol, and popped up. Crouching, she crabbed to the hallway and into the kitchen. She whispered, "Tania, I'm coming in."

"Stay low," Tania replied. She held an automatic rifle, her H&K MP7. "Shows four … no five, coming in from three sides."

Pia fumbled her earbud. It skittered across the hardwood floor into the living room ahead of her. Tania picked it up and handed it to her. Pia checked her phone's map and saw a sixth dot appear.

"Where's Cody?" Pia asked.

"Not responding. Might've gone down before the alarm. He should be out by the mailbox and on this channel."

Something smashed through the window on their right. A cannister rolled to them across the broken glass. They both took deep breaths and held them, as tear gas spewed out. They would lose their vision and be sitting ducks if they didn't move fast. Which meant diving out of the house into an ambush.

Six assassins—three times the number they'd expected and planned for. Suddenly, Pia felt her chest tighten with fear. Not for herself as much as Liam. What had she gotten him into?

Tania pointed over her shoulder, indicating the kitchen and dining nook. Pia crouch-walked her way through while Tania covered the living room. With only one door in the cottage, she went looking for the best exit-window. The one over the sink might fit Tania but Pia would never make it. She slid up the dining room window and peeked outside. No one shot at her.

Tania tapped her back, letting her know she had the inside covered. "Couldn't grab the armor. Here."

Pia reached behind her. Tania slapped a Sabel Visor into her hand. At least they could see in the dark.

Bullets raked the front door, an entire magazine expended to loosen the iron latch and lock. A boot crashed into it three times. Without a chance to scan the backyard, Pia rolled out through the window and landed inelegantly on thick shrubbery. Bullets blew through the window behind her. With her 9 mil in one hand and the Visor in the other, she rolled off the bush and into dense undergrowth. She crawled as fast as she could go into the forest surrounding the cottage.

In the comm link, Tania said, "Coming out the kitchen since you went and raised the alarm on this side. See anyone?"

Pia slipped on her night vision and angled toward the backside of the cottage. The back was clear. She said, "Clear for—"

Something large and hard slammed into her belly button. She bent in half and fell backwards. Pain shot through her core. Her lungs stopped working. She felt like a turtle on her back. A man in full night gear and body armor raised his baton overhead for a death blow. Pia fired twice, center mass.

The man spun to her left, his baton crashing into a sapling next to her. Stunned but not felled, the man struggled to keep upright while Pia jumped to her feet. He turned as she tried to kick him in the groin. Her shin glanced off his knee. Still gripping his baton, he backhanded it toward her head.

She heard Tania hammer out the glass in the kitchen window, the frame not giving enough of an opening to let her out.

Pia ducked and tackled him like a linebacker. They went over together. She shoved her 9 mil under his chin and squeezed the trigger.

Before the sear released the hammer, a massive hand grabbed her ponytail and yanked her upright. Her shot went high, missing her target. She lashed out with an elbow behind her that connected a weak blow to the new man's ribs before his other arm circled her waist. She hooked her right leg around the back of his knee to stop him from lifting her higher, twisted to her right, and slammed her left fist behind her directly into his balls. He groaned but maintained his grip. She threw her body to the left, toppling them both.

To his credit, he never let go. She slammed her heel into his groin again, connecting only with his thigh. The man wasn't dumb enough to leave himself exposed twice.

The distinctive snap of Tania's sound-suppressed MP7 echoed through the trees not far away. It sounded like Tania was in her own firefight and wouldn't be coming to the rescue anytime soon.

Pia's lungs screamed for air, reminding her she still had the wind knocked out of her from the first blow. Her head jerked back again, exposing her throat. A move usually followed by a slashing knife, but this time she considered the first man's baton. She crunched hard in a sit-up that dragged the new man with her.

The baton whipped through the air, glancing off the helmet of the man holding her. This time, his grip relaxed enough for her to spin off him. Landing on all fours as a second baton blow crashed into her thigh, she leapt forward in a dead run. Pounding boots followed close behind her.

Not far away, she heard Tania yell in pain.

Pia reached out for a tree trunk, using it to swing her direction around 180 degrees. Her first pursuer tried to adjust and slipped in the muddy leaves, falling with a grunt. The second plowed straight into her. He was shorter than Pia but forty pounds heavier. Her momentum took them to the ground with her on top. He wasted no time and landed two blows to her chin before she could react. He rolled them over in a swift move, locked his fingers together in a double fist and dropped his body weight into a blow aimed at her face. Again she sat up, driving her face to his chest, negating what could've been a death blow. Unfortunately, the move left her firmly in his grip.

He pushed up on powerful legs and held her head in a vice grip between his forearms, her body weight hanging from her jawbone. They were face-to-face for a moment before he headbutted her. Her forehead hardened on a hundred thousand headers in soccer, the net effect was bad for both. Releasing her, he staggered backwards holding his forehead while she did the same in the opposite direction.

Black flashes filled Pia's peripheral vision, the dark lights of impending concussion. She gasped for air as pain shot through her body from her stomach to her head.

Nearly blind but knowing the next blow would be life or death, depending on who landed it, she lashed out with a combination punch. Her left hand skimmed his ear. The glancing blow took off a thick layer of camouflage face paint, revealing a diamond earring.

Suddenly, her arms were yanked back in a powerful grip. A third man held her.

Mr. Bling and his diamond earring staggered away into the woods.

Using standard technique, Pia stepped her right foot back, intending to twist to the right and pull her assailant off-balance. Instead, her first assaulter stepped up and slammed fist after fist into her breadbasket as if he were working out on a heavy bag. For the second time in the space of a few seconds, she couldn't breathe.

Sirens echoed from a nearby hilltop.

Without warning, the man stopped hitting her and fell into her. His limp body collapsed at her feet. The man holding her, too short to see over her shoulders, twisted her body to peer around her side. Placing her right foot back, shoving off it, and twisting to the right, she clamped her arm around his to throw him backwards. Before she could complete her move, the man wrenched free. For a moment, they assessed each other looking for an advantage.

"Plods a'coming," a man's voice rang out. "Clear out. Clear out NOW!"

Her adversary turned and ran into the woods. She tried to trip him but missed.

Pia aimed her pistol without a clear shot. She gave chase but lost him in the trees.

She turned back to the cottage where a flame at the front rose over the roof line. Silhouetted against the weak light was Cody's diminutive frame. He was hard at work with flex cuffs, securing the wrists of the man on the ground.

"Tania, where are you?" she asked in the comm link.

Tania pushed through bramble, her cheek bloody and her shirt torn.

"Hey sister, we survived again! Just, just ... gimme a minute."

She fell to the ground.

Cody turned his attention to her. Pia realized his night hadn't gone well either. Red welts around his neck indicated he'd survived a serious choke hold. His body armor's covering fabric had ripped in three places where bullets had bounced off. One lens of his Sabel Visor was shattered. He tended to Tania.

Pia realized the cottage was on fire and ran to the front. Scrambling for a hose, she sent a full stream to ten feet of flaming thatched roof.

By the time the fire department and police arrived, the flames were out. In the blue glow of first light, Pia turned over the hose to the professionals.

A woman who identified herself as Derbyshire Chief Constable Sumithra Swann said, "These people didn't like you very much."

Pia began a lengthy explanation. They walked around the property to where Tania and Cody held their prisoner.

The chief identified Pia's captive right away: a retired airborne veteran who'd turned muscle-for-hire. He'd been hauled in several times and never cracked, never bargained his coconspirators for a lesser sentence. Sumithra gave her little hope they'd learn anything from him.

Cody explained the team had parachuted in, taking him by surprise outside their secure perimeter. Indicating it was a well-planned attack.

"Why'd they run off?" the inspector asked.

"When they lost control of Cody," Pia said, "they knew the odds were six of them against three of us—they were bound to lose."

They let the paramedics clean up their wounds and give them ice. They perched in the ambulance's opening and sat quietly. The sun warmed a distant horizon painting the eastern sky orange. The birds began chirping.

"Think I pushed Sybil too hard last night?" Pia asked no one in particular. "Did pissing her off spark this?"

"Some serious planning went into this attack," Cody said. "They landed on me. Never heard them coming. Expert jumpers, definitely airborne skills. To arrange a drop at three in the morning, get the gear and the men together, assess the approach, gotta all be former military guys. They knew how many windows, estimated where I'd keep watch. Not something they planned in a few hours. Had to take them a day. They must've had eyes on us when we landed in Manchester."

Tania held out a clenched fist in front of Pia and opened it slowly. In her palm was a single crushed orchid petal. There was no mistaking it due to its unique shade of purple: a corsage orchid. Tania said, "Stuck to the Velcro on one guy's body armor. Like he brushed by it."

Pia stared at it for a long time. Then shifted her gaze across the rolling hill sloping away from the van. The sun rose over the far hilltop. While the rays warmed their faces, Pia could think of a hundred ways that petal could've ended up on an assassin's body armor. None of them good.

"You've taken the first step into a dark and suspect world," Tania said. "It's time to face an ugly fact: Abby's involved."

CHAPTER 37

THE DAY SPREAD OVER THE land. Pia and Tania turned down a trip to the hospital. The paramedics left with Cody in the back, a broken collarbone suspected and possibly worse. They insisted on x-rays.

Pia and Tania sat on the grass near the main road, still smudged with blood and dirt, their hair smoked and caked with ashes, their clothes torn and muddy. Some of the extra PCs packed up and left. The sun rose higher and filled the morning with warm daylight. The police came back with questions and more questions. Having been through a few investigations, Pia and Tania waited and answered patiently.

An Uber pulled up to where the cottage driveway met the main road. Abby Stokes got out and stood in numbed silence, surveying the scene. Claigeann Cottage's bullet-riddled front door hung from one hinge. A fifteen-foot circle of blackened char marred her perfect thatch. Shards of glass lay beneath every window. Crime scene investigators swarmed the exterior.

Pia walked up to her.

Abby kept her eyes on her home while she said, "What the fuck, Sabel?"

"Got a bit stuffy, so we opened a window … or two." Pia waited, hoping Abby would laugh and knowing she wouldn't.

Abby teared up. After a few deep breaths, she appeared to bring herself under control. She sniffled a few times, then blew her nose like an athlete. Closing one nostril with a finger, she blew the other on the ground, then switched sides. She wiped on her sleeve.

She looked up at Pia and said, "Suppose you and your lot are OK then?" She pointed at Pia's face. "Except for that cheek."

Pia pulled up her top, revealing bruises across her midriff.

"Bloody hell, Sabel." Abby looked sick. "Like playing France then, eh?"

"We need to talk."

Abby stared at her for a long, silent moment, then backed up a step and pointed back at her house. "Oh, now hang on. You don't think I had anything to with that, do you?"

"Yes," Tania said.

At the same time Pia said, "No."

Pia shot a silencing look at Tania, which Tania returned with equal ferocity. Facing Abby, but speaking loud enough to include Tania, Pia said, "You would've been caught up in the melee if you'd been home. We're professionals and we barely got out alive. You're lucky as hell I gave you a free ride to London."

Abby stood still.

"One of the guys had this," Tania thrust the crumpled orchid petal at Abby.

Their hostess stared at it, then looked back and forth at Tania and Pia. "They were in my bloody greenhouse!"

Pia said, "Tell me you have security cameras."

"For a bunch of bushes and trees?" Abby held up her hands.

A limo pulled up. Tanner Wyatt stepped out, his silent, steely gaze surveying the land.

Pia said, "Let's check it out, shall we?"

"How do you do that, Sabel?" Abby said. "A limo shows up in rural England with Rambo standing guard like you summoned it telepathically."

Pia said, "Perks."

Abby nodded. "Must be nice. What about Claigeann Cottage? It's historic architecture. Was."

"Unlimited remodeling budget, on me. We'll get the best craftspeople."

"Yeah. That is nice." Abby's bitterness flowed through her words. "Wave your magic money finger around and problem solved. There never should've been a problem in the first place."

"It'll never be the same," Pia said and put a sympathetic hand on Abby's shoulder. "Money will never fix that part. I'm sorry." She waited until Abby appeared to accept her apology before adding, "Maybe they can get the toaster and stove to work at the same time."

Tanner held the door open. Tania got in.

Abby followed but stopped before putting a foot in. She looked at Tanner and said, "Do you ever speak? Like ask your boss how she's doing? Say hi?"

He faced her, then leveled his gaze back to the horizon.

They rode in silence to Sonse End, Eric Stone's estate. Abby called ahead. He met them and waved them through to the delivery drive. It led directly to the backside of the scaled Crystal Palace greenhouse. When they passed through, he followed them down, limping on his cane a little more than usual.

The limo stopped in the drive before the parking and delivery area to drop them off. Half an acre was filled in with gravel for delivery trucks to turn around. Opposite the glass structure sat a pile of rotting leaves the size of a shipping container: the compost heap. Next to that, the bobcat with a front-loading scoop attached. On the far edge of the gravel was an even larger pile of milky-brown clay. A series of tarps protected the top of the mound from the rain in a haphazard fashion. A couple tarps had been folded back.

Eric Stone met them at the door. He looked over Pia and Tania. "Appears you're not fairing so well in our little corner of the country, young lady. Are you alright?"

"Is this door unlocked?" Pia asked and answered her own question with a simple twist of the knob.

"What d'you think, someone's going to break in and steal a few *Brosimum utiles*?" Abby snorted.

She pushed around Pia and entered a tool and staging area. They checked the office. It hosted a battered desk with an old laptop and stacks of dogeared paperwork. On the other side, the beaten workbench where plants were lovingly examined and catalogued. Underneath was a mesh bag full of soccer balls, several Pug goals, and three pairs of women's soccer cleats. One brand new in the box. Abby was still getting free boots from her endorsements.

The inside was significantly warmer and sunnier than their last visit. And a good deal more humid. Condensation rolled down the windows and pooled on the floor. Metal support posts had a similar problem.

"A rain forest requires rain," Abby said and pointed to misters fixed to the rafters above them. "Need to simulate an inch of rain a day. The misters work all night. Gotta wear a raincoat to work late."

"How many people work here?" Pia asked.

"Just me." Abby led the group toward the Utría section where they'd found the orchid. "There's a new crop of students come every two weeks to work a week. Supposed to study, but they're usually out getting pissed all night and hanging in the morning. We're done with that now 'til the summer semester, though."

"Was there anyone here last night?" Pia asked Eric.

"Not that I saw," he replied. Not as quick as the young women, he trailed behind. "People get by me now and again, but I see the headlights coming down the lane usually. It's a quiet life we lead out here."

"This petal is one of your orchids, right?" Tania asked. She held out her evidence again.

Abby looked it over more closely. "Can't tell for certain, but not a store-bought one, yeah."

"How'd it get hooked on that guy's Velcro?"

Abby shrugged while her face melted down to one step short of crying. She didn't say a word while she led them around a corner and down a narrow gap between overgrown leaves.

Tania looked at Pia as they walked. Pia understood her methods; harsh interrogations that trapped liars were her specialty. While she usually deferred to Tania's expertise, Pia didn't want to see Abby as complicit. Was she overlooking something?

Pia fell back and whispered, "If she was involved, how do you get past the problem that she should've been home last night?"

"People willing to kill constables would sacrifice one of their own—" Tania snapped her fingers "—like that."

Ahead of them Abby stopped in her tracks. "Sod it. Someone was here last night."

She pointed to broad leaves trampled and stems snapped in the section where they'd talked on their first visit. Abby looked more upset about her violated plants than her cottage. Pulling a pair of cutters from her pocket, she snipped away at a few stems, cutting away the damage. Tania watched her closely. In front of them, the remains of an orchid clung to the side of a larger plant.

Pia peered into the surrounding bushes. The soil was the same milky-brown clay as the pile outside. Abby had said something about her supplier shipping more soil than she'd ordered for the section. A trail of large ants crawled through stems and around saplings. She pushed back leaves with her forearm and met a swarm of gnats.

"Hey now," Abby called out, "don't go in there. You got a question, ask me."

"Sorry, I thought you didn't like bugs. There's some healthy ants over here."

"Gotta have bugs. It's the beetles we worry about. Harlequin Ladybird beetles have nearly wiped out our indigenous version in little more than a decade. I find them, I squash them."

Pia asked Tania a question with her eyes. Tania answered, "Couple boot prints in there. He went in deep."

Abby turned around and checked the dirt. Pia saw them too.

"Nothing special in there," Abby said. "He crunched a lot of leaves like he was looking for something, then scarpered. Nothing in there but plants."

They stared at each other for a blank moment.

"What about that killer plant you told us about?" Tania asked.

"The what? Oh, you mean *Dendrocnide moroides*, suicide plant? Over in Belize." Abby headed down the aisle. "Most dangerous thing in here, really."

They went to the Belize section. Abby checked the ground and leaves.

Tania came up behind her and went around her, looking for boot prints.

Abby said, "Oi! Don't touch that. I wasn't kidding about them being deadly. Tiny needles that float on the air, each one's a syringe full of deadly toxin. Gotta wear protective gear around the bloody thing. You can inhale the needles without realizing it. But there's no sign of anyone being around here."

They looked around more without finding anything.

Pia whispered to Tania, "There's nothing here connecting her."

"Oh, there's something here," Tania said. "We just ain't seen it yet."

"What about Eric? He's a forensic toxicologist."

"Could be both of them," Tania thought for a moment. "They're both restoring historic homes and you said that was pricey. How bad is it, out of reach for teachers? Where are they getting the money?"

"I can't imagine either could afford it without additional sources of funding."

"We gotta look into that. But you're right, we're done here."

"Then what's next," Pia asked, "back to the Morpheus?"

"And ask what? No. We go for the weakest link, the Tindalls. Maybe we can shake a clue out of that tree."

"Well, I've got work to do," Abby said. She led them back the way they'd come in. "What about my house?"

"My damage control people landed in Manchester twenty minutes ago. They're on it."

"'Damage control people?' Happens that much, does it?"

Pia felt that one kick her in the gut harder than the man who'd pounded on her. It did happen a lot. Everyone she'd loved was dead. Her mother and father. Her adopted father, Alan Sabel. Too many employees. At this point, Jacob and Tania were all she had left. And Liam. Who she'd just put in greater danger than she'd intended. Six paratroopers dropped in on them. Not to mention she still had no idea how the operation killed their victims.

When they trooped back, they found Eric checking something on the workbench. Abby stopped as she walked by him. She leaned past him, picked up a trowel and scooped a couple dead beetles off the bench. She carried them outside.

Tania stopped and examined what Abby had called the "horticulturist's chemistry lab." She pointed the contents to Pia who glanced over her shoulder. Tania said, "Looks untouched since the first time we saw it."

Pia nodded her agreement.

They followed Abby and watched as she flung the trowel's contents to the top of the compost heap.

"Oh, that reminds me," Eric said. "There was a visitor. Not last night, though. Your bug man was here yesterday noon."

Abby's attention turned to the mound of clay where two tarps had been pulled back. She walked in that direction. Several shovel marks were dug into the mound as if someone were sampling dirt. She got up close to one of the spaded places and tilted her head. Pia and Tania followed her and checked the turned-over soil. Tania snapped a couple pictures.

"Sorry," Abby said to Eric. "My what?"

"Your bug man," Eric replied. "The man who comes Sundays. Helps you with the beetle problem."

"I don't have a bug man."

"You do, certainly. You know the man I mean. He's been coming since the beginning."

Abby tilted her head, curious, then crossed back to Eric. Pia followed her. "There's no bug man on my payroll. I don't know what you're talking about."

Pia asked, "Does he come on her days off?"

"Sundays most often." He faced Abby. "But yesterday, just after you drove to town on those errands. Come to think of it, I've never seen you talk to the man." He turned to Pia. "Is that what you're getting at? He's not supposed to be here?"

"Does he wear a diamond earring?" Pia asked.

Eric looked curious. "Now that you mention it, I believe he does."

CHAPTER 38

ABBY AND ERIC WAVED GOODBYE as the limo backed out of the narrow lane. Tania tapped the arm rest with an impatient finger.

"Go ahead," Pia said. "Tell me I'm ignoring the evidence."

"I know what you're thinking," Tania said. "She's fun, she's nice, she's cute, she couldn't be wrapped up with international assassins. But she could be deep. Maybe she's been coerced, we don't know. For what it's worth, I agree, she looked true." Tania sighed. "Every lie I ever believed was delivered with the sincerity of Mother Teresa."

Pia considered a few lies she'd believed. All of them had sounded genuine. A theory about what was going on sat on the edge of her consciousness. Like looking at a distant bluff through thick fog, the more she tried to examine it, the more indistinct it became.

"What about Eric?" Pia asked.

"You're looking for a way to clear your friend by blaming an old man with a limp?"

Pia shrugged. "As the de facto gatekeeper, he has better access to that place than anyone. The bug–man story could be a cover. And he has a new zinc roof that could easily cost £2-3 million."

With bulging eyes, Tania said, "Shut up. That's a motive. What about Abby's restoration? Remember, she was going to remodel too."

Pia shrugged. "Yeah. A thatched roof would be a lot, too."

"Eric's just as sincere as anyone. I'll consider them both. They worked together at the college, right?"

Tania pointed at Pia's phone and said, "Speaking of sincerity, are you going to find out about Liam?"

"I'm not sure I want to know anything about anyone anymore." Pia dialed anyway.

Pia put Bianca on the Bluetooth speaker. Bianca said, "We haven't found Liam's wife yet. We found a few passport entries, small debit card charges, and a new phone for her in the Balkans six months ago. She was traveling with a wealthy Iranian who paid for most everything. Then she went off the grid. We'll find her by the time Liam gets back from the States."

"States? I thought he went to Canada."

"British Columbia yesterday, California today. Babe, if you're going to date a guy, you might want to keep up on where he's going." Bianca laughed.

Tania added, "Especially since you don't know where his wife's at. Dating a married man—girl, you should be ashamed."

Pia would've laughed with them except it would tear the abrasion on her cheek. When they settled down, she asked, "What about Breach and the rest?"

"David Breach died of a rare heart condition. I've asked your doctor to review the findings because it goes into something arcane about the brain function that sends signals regulating heartbeats. That's not how Novichok or other variants work. NYC's coroner has a process if you want them to re-examine the case."

"Not exactly helpful," Pia said.

Bianca continued. "Hong Kong won't release details of Yang's death other than cardiac arrest. But, like Chloe said in her message, something caused that. They've not been helpful since Beijing took over.

"Vancouver's a different story. Vermeer died of the same rare heart condition as Breach. As soon as my team told them we were concerned about cause of death, they re-opened Vermeer's case. They'd already done the standard tests, cyanide, arsenic, opiates, methamphetamine, and a bunch of other stuff I can't pronounce. Nothing came up. If someone administered a drug, it was rare and not used in known clandestine operations. But, if you can tell them what to look for, they'll look for it."

"Canadians, the antidote to New Yorkers," Pia said. "Much more helpful but no more useful."

"Hey." Brooklyn-born Tania scowled. "Don't be bad-mouthing New

Yorkers. Wait a second. In your notes, you mentioned Anectine in the back of the Tindall's car. Bianca, ask the Vancouver ME to test for Anectine."

"Will do," Bianca said. "The Skilling video hasn't turned up much. The furniture is used and untraceable, the diplomas look fake, the photos are photoshopped. It's odd, but it happens."

"Didn't facial recognition find him?" Pia asked.

"Those things aren't the magic we hope for," Tania said. "Depends on a lot of factors. Lots of people don't show up."

"Last item on your list," Bianca said. "Your team at Vermeer Commerce Bank hasn't wasted any time. They're inside the network already. Bethany got us a backdoor and we're scouring the apps. Meyer thinks he can get into Eden-Sonnet's email."

"He's a hacker?" Pia asked.

"Amateur, but he has a few tricks."

"Tell him to stand down. These people are a lot more dangerous than we thought. I don't want one whiff of our real intent getting back to Eden-Sonnet. Do everything from your end and make the hacks look unrelated."

Bianca promised updates as they rolled in.

They disconnected as the limo pulled onto the turning circle at Padley House.

Pia and Tania walked up and knocked on the home's massive door. After a minute's wait, Dame Millie opened the wall of oak. Holding it partially open, she frowned at them.

"What do you want?" Her gaze ran up and down them and her expression changed from angry to disgusted. "What on earth happened to you?"

"We need to talk to you and Albert," Tania pushed the door open.

"He's not—"

"Who is it, dear?" Albert's voice came from a room beyond the foyer.

"You gonna be answering some questions." Tania tracked around Dame Millie. "I'll bet you gotta fucking *drawing room* where we can talk. Show me."

Albert leaned in at the end of the foyer. When he recognized them, he flushed with anger. He pointed to a nearby room. "So, it's you. Go through. That will do."

The four of them filed into a room scattered with eighteenth century furniture. The fabrics were silks of mismatched patterns, frayed in places.

Albert said to Pia, "Were you able to reschedule your walk with Walker?"

"I show up on your doorstep looking like this, and that's your first question?"

Dame Millie gave them another critical examination before reluctantly saying, "Have a seat."

The Tindalls sat in a pair of matching chairs separated by a small, empty display case that doubled as a coffee table.

Tania leaned back against a mahogany sideboard. Pia rested an elbow on the fireplace mantle.

Tania said, "Someone tried to kill us last night. Grenades, automatic rifles, surprise attack at three in the morning. We're not happy. I'm gonna ask questions and you gonna answer—straight up."

Both the Tindalls looked to Pia. She met their gaze with a cold expression set in stone.

Tania said, "What's your connection to the Morpheus Institute?"

"We don't owe you people anything," Dame Millie said. "You can't barge in here—"

"I just did." Tania pushed off and closed in on Millie. "And you're gonna answer cause you sure as hell don't want the cops coming in asking the same questions. Am I right?"

"I've already told you, I sought their services a few years ago," Albert said. "They were quite nice and very effective."

Tania turned to him. "Charles Eden-Sonnet didn't think so, despite being a three-time loser at the Morpheus."

"Charles told you that?" Dame Millie asked.

Tania kept her gaze on Albert. "He's selling Vermeer Commerce Bank, his latest acquisition, to Sabel Capital as we speak."

"Why would he do such a thing?" Dame Millie asked.

"Huh." Tania turned to her. "Now that's a strange question coming from you. Implies you find that inconceivable. Which means you know him—and you know all about his business."

Pia loved watching Tania in action. They'd walked in with nothing to go on but a dislike for the pair. In the first few seconds, she'd found a crack in their façade.

"Well, I, I don't really …" Dame Millie's voice trailed off.

"Look here," Albert said. "I arrange mergers and acquisitions. I keep abreast of all the deals going on at our level."

Tania kept her gaze hard on Dame Millie. "You haven't been involved in a merger since Nike acquired that little shoemaker in Bristol six years ago. And your private equity firm owns a landscape outfit and a billiard repair shop. Your income from that wouldn't cover my car insurance. Don't think I don't do my research, Albert."

"Nonetheless, I resent your—"

"Don't resent until you've answered her questions," Pia said. "I lost my patience at three this morning when someone unloaded a full magazine into Abby's front door."

Albert's head snapped back in shock. "Claigeann Cottage?"

Quietly, Dame Millie snickered.

"What's your deal with the Morpheus?" Tania turned back to Albert.

"We're not like you," Albert appealed to Pia. "We don't have a big company spewing endless millions out every window. We've had a string of hard luck is all. We've got obligations in the community. They expect a good deal from people at our level."

"What the hell is your level?" Tania asked.

"Well, you know, community leaders, titled people." Albert straightened his collar.

Tania squinted at him and pinched her chin while she processed his words. After an awkward silence, she turned to Dame Millie. "How'd you get to be a dame? What's that all about?"

Dame Millie raised her chin. "I helped the Crown raise funds for youth sports."

"That's nice of you," Tania said. "Charity?"

"Right."

"Eden-Sonnet in this charity?"

"No, just members of the Royal Family."

Tania bent over, putting her hands on her knees, face to face. "When we expose this operation, how're them *Royals* gonna feel about you covering for the Morpheus?"

Dame Millie turned away.

"Why did you have a bottle of Anectine rolling around the backseat of your car?" Tania asked.

"We went to dinner with Dr. Karen Kearns the night before," Dame Millie snapped. "Maybe she dropped it."

Tania turned to Pia. Telepathically, she handed off the interrogation. Tania needed time to think. Like Pia, she had a theory forming in a distant fog. They had threads. You can't hang criminals with threads.

Pia crossed her arms and caught Albert's wandering gaze. She asked, "Do you get commissions from the Morpheus?"

Albert looked away without answering.

"We certainly have nothing to do with whoever attacked you," Dame Millie said.

"You're scared of them," Pia said.

"Phht." Albert tried to scoff with his lips trembling. His gaze bounced around the room. "Not scared of anyone."

"Cornered then. You're short of cash and afraid someone's coming down on you. Do you owe someone money? Is it something I could fix?"

Dame Millie turned her face away while Albert turned the opposite direction.

Pia and Tania shared a look. Someone posed a threat to the Tindalls. Whoever he was, he was scarier than anything they could threaten. Realistically, there wasn't much more they could learn here.

"These people killed Chloe," Pia said. "When you come to your senses, call me. I'll put in a good word for you with the NCA. They tend to go easier on the first one to talk."

Dame Millie perked up. "What did Lord Eden-Sonnet tell you?"

Pia gave her a cold stare while Tania headed for the door. When Dame Millie lowered her gaze, Pia followed Tania out.

Tania stopped and stepped back to the drawing room.

She said, "Albert. *Utrinque Paratus?*"

He lit up a smile. "Ah, yes, actually. Lieutenant, 1st Battalion, four years and out."

CHAPTER 39

AN HOUR LATER, TANIA YANKED open the front door to Manchester Town Hall and marched in. Pia followed, with Tanner six feet behind her. DI Benton waited on the other side of the metal detector. When Pia's eyes adjusted to the darker lobby, she saw Tania and PC McDonald in discussion to her left.

She heard McDonald say, "I had no idea what white privilege meant. I'm sorry."

Pia handed her purse and Glock to a constable and watched Tania give McDonald a long hug.

Tania caught up and whispered, "PC McDonald did some homework. Seems Benton leant him a copy of *Between the World and Me* by Ta-Nahisi Coates. First he ever heard of 'the talk' black parents have to give their kids. It moved him. He says. We'll have to see if it lasts."

"That's a start," Pia said. "Benton had that book to lend him?"

"Like I said, I think Benton gets it. Our allies still gotta work a little harder on their end."

Pia went through and collected her things while Benton watched with his arms crossed.

When she approached him, he said, "England's no good for your complexion."

"Funny."

"D'you need another ice pack?"

"Nah. Thanks though."

When Tanner joined them, Benton led them down the hall to a meeting room. Inside was a U-shaped conference table configuration with a collection of aging office chairs. One place in the center had a

BENTON name plate. At the other seats were stacks of photos and printouts from videos. He rolled a chair to the inside of the U and gestured for Pia and Tania to sit opposite him. Tanner stood at ease outside the door.

"Terribly sorry about the attack," Benton said. "Now, I've got your email. Could you walk me through all this?"

Pia explained the meeting with Skilling and the merger-default swap being the financing arm of the operation. She explained about Martin Vermeer dying in Vancouver of the same thing as Breach in New York. She explained how she'd blackmailed Eden-Sonnet with non-existent audio recordings. She explained Sybil Rohan's angry reactions to her provocative statements. She explained the attack on Abby's cottage and the unexplained visitor in the greenhouse. She explained her visit to the Tindalls and their non-responsive answers.

Benton jotted notes in with his fountain pen.

"I only got one thing out of Albert," Tania said. "He was a Para."

Benton nodded and looked at his notes, then said, "And that means what, exactly?"

"We were attacked by former Paras." Tania bounced her gaze to Pia and back. "Probably from the British Army's elite Parachute Regiment. I tripped up Albert Tindall by throwing the Paras' motto at him, *Utrinque Paratus*. Ready for anything. He answered with his rank and battalion. A former Para lieutenant could keep in touch with veterans and scare up a few bent Paras."

"Possible." Benton made a note, then looked up at her and waited for more.

"No, I can't prove it. But the connection's there. It's something you should watch."

"Wayne Walker claimed to have intelligence on Liam," Pia said. "He might have something on the Tindalls."

"Anything would be better than what you've got," Benton said. "Which is nothing."

Tania said, "Maybe that Walker guy would be useful."

"And your friend, Abby?" Benton asked Pia. "Someone broke into her greenhouse and stole an orchid?"

Pia wondered if he made it sound ridiculous or if she'd presented it that way. "Someone got in and took something. We don't know what. Abby has a couple poisonous plants and toxic fertilizers in there. We don't know what he was after, but the orchid stuck to his Velcro."

"I see." Benton took his time reviewing his notes.

She had to agree with what he implied: the orchid sounded lame.

Pia drummed her fingers on the table. Benton looked at her, his hand moved towards her. She pulled her hand back and put it in her lap.

"This is all very good information," he said at last. "None of it, I repeat, none of it is in my jurisdiction. London, Peak District, Vancouver, Hong Kong, New York—a bit outside Greater Manchester. You see, I'm interested in who killed Chloe England. The rest of this, well, it's huge. It's international, it's intriguing, and it's full of big splashy names. But Dominick England is a friend of mine. I've had lunch with him twice since the funeral. All I can tell him is—and this is thanks to you—we're looking for a red Corsa, a blue Focus, and two unknown men. One of whom was seen wearing a diamond earring."

"Two Paras," Tania said with a finger wag.

"Indeed, thank you. The connection's not yet been confirmed, but you've raised a good point of possibility." Benton held their gazes. "It pains me to tell Dominick we're nowhere. I can't tell him that again and then go off to London chasing a merger-default ... whatever you said. If those really exist."

"You're defeating yourself, Benton." Pia crossed her arms and leaned back. "You've dug in here for the long haul. You've accepted that it'll take forever. You even brought your name plate in here. You're letting Mr. Bling with the diamond earring win because the case is bigger than your hometown. If you want to beat this guy, you need a positive mental attitude. Winning is all in the mind."

Benton looked like she was pulling his molar without an anesthetic. He said, "I'll have to refer this to the NCA. They're the ones with the resources to go after something like this. Wait here."

Pia winced. Benton walked out and down the hall.

She could make nice with the NCA. She was sure they would act like professionals and not ask questions about MI5. The inter-agency resentment couldn't be as bad as her people in the field reported it.

Pia and Tania got busy on emails. Benton's absence grew into a noticeable length of time.

Pia learned that Cody had two cracked vertebrae to go with his collarbone and was now in a steel brace while a specialist was summoned for consultation. Pia considered firing Cody for his own good. Every time he'd been on an assignment to protect her, he ended up with shattered bones and months of rehab.

Somehow, Jacob Stearne had landed in deep trouble in Belarus and wound up in the hospital. She never should've let him go on that trip. She was so angry with herself she couldn't even read the report on his health.

She sent a message to the Vancouver medical examiner to test for the poison of the suicide plant. He replied immediately, promising results in a few days. Which was nice of him, Pia thought. Even if she wanted to catch the killer in hours. He also noted her request for an Anectine test had come in too late for conclusive results. They would have needed to test within the first twenty-four hours. She thanked him.

Loud voices erupted into shouting several offices down the hall. The shouts approached. Benton was saying, "…the bloody hell am I supposed to work with her? Have you tried it? Impossible."

A calmer voice said something they couldn't hear. Then Benton yelled, "Professional my arse! You're looking for a bloody scapegoat when this shite falls apart."

Pia and Tania stood and grabbed their purses, expecting to be shown the exit.

The meeting room door opened. An older man wearing the uniform of a high-ranking officer entered with a red-faced Benton behind him.

Mottled scar tissue covered the side of the older man's head. Running from his left eye, down his neck, and into his collar, they were the distinct type resulting from extensive burns. His ear was a patchwork of skin grafts. The injuries looked much like Tania's legs. His mouth fell open and his palms rose.

Before Pia realized what was going on, Tania rushed past her to embrace the man. Like long-lost friends, they held each other tight and rocked back and forth.

"Tania Cooper," the officer said, "I can't believe it. They spelled your name wrong on the incident report or I'd've looked you up right away. But it's you."

"Good to see you too, Crawford," Tania said as she pulled back.

Holding each other's hands, they stared at each other.

Pia and Benton exchanged looks and shrugs. Neither understood their connection.

Finally, the older man turned to Pia and said in a soothing voice, "Chief Superintendent Crawford, ma'am. I just wanted to say thank you for all your hard work, and—good lord, are you alright? Have you been to casualty?"

"I'm fine, thank you." She shook his extended hand before glancing at Tania.

"Sorry, Captain Cooper and I go way back." He smiled at Tania. "Almost died together when an IED blew up our truck and set us all on fire. I do hope the Americans gave Jacob Stearne a medal for that. Damn fine soldier, he was. He pulled us both to safety."

"You were riding together?" Benton asked.

Pia was equally interested in how a Brit ended up in the same vehicle as an Army MP.

"I hitched a ride back to her base intending to sing her praises to her commanding officer. Damn fine job she did for us. You see, we had a serial rapist in our ranks and the RMPs had a devil of a time finding him. Someone suggested we bring in outside help. The Americans leant us Captain Cooper. She ferreted out the bastard right off—our very own RMP in charge of the case! Brilliant work. Absolutely brilliant."

He gave Tania another admiring smile.

"You go right ahead with that suit," Crawford said. "Might do us some good. When your current investigation is over, I'd like to get your thoughts on community outreach. There are a few constables who aren't responding to standard programs. I need to implement something more effective than what I've got now."

"I have some thoughts on that," Tania said.

"Very good, then." He turned to Pia. "Very nice meeting you." He turned to Benton. "You'll do well to keep your ears open, Benton. Carry on."

He and Tania walked to the door together, chatting.

Benton and Pia just stared at them.

Pia broke the silence. "I knew Jacob pulled her out of a burning wreck, but I never knew the rest of that. She's not one to brag."

Tania and Crawford hugged goodbye.

"Impressing Crawford is a rare thing," Benton said as Tania rejoined them.

"What were you yelling about in the hall?" Pia asked.

Benton's anger flared back. He scowled at Pia and slapped a small stack of papers on the desk. He crossed to the lone window in the room. He let out a long sigh. "You've gotten me yanked off Chloe's murder. Crawford assigned me as liaison to the NCA. I'm to work with you to develop the case."

"Impossible as I may be to work with?" Pia asked.

He faced her. "Oh. Uh. That's not what …"

After he gave up trying to find an excuse, she asked, "Prefer to work with men?"

"No. Not that at all. It's … well." He tossed his hands in the air and turned away. "Sod it. I'll put it out there. The English system's bad enough with Lords and Dames breathing down my bloody neck. Then you come along. You've lived up to your reputation as a spoiled rich kid. A very smart, but very privileged, uhm …"

"Rhymes with rich?" Pia offered.

"No. Sorry. I'm on edge and blaming you. That's not right." He flopped into his chair. "The NCA doesn't want the case—not yet. England is a bit different from your little egalitarian village. When you go sniffing around someone in the House of Lords, you can make your career—or lose it. And when you go after an institution like the Morpheus that caters to the upper class, and a Dame, and god-knows-who-else you're going to dredge up, well, it gets a bit sticky. They want me to 'develop leads and evidence' and build a bloody case. If I come up with something solid, they'll take over. If I piss people off, I'll be pounding Chloe's old beat."

"Oh, we got some solid shit," Tania said. "If you don't mind rolling up your sleeves and working hard. We'll find you Chloe's killers—and make your career."

Benton took a long, appreciative look at Tania, then faced Pia. He said, "I am sorry for my outburst. I didn't mean all that rubbish."

"I played international soccer. I've been called worse in fifty languages." Pia smiled and took a seat. "I offer you one huge advantage: I can piss off the House of Lords and I won't lose my career. That's where being a spoiled rich bitch comes in handy."

Benton looked surprised at first, then smiled. "Might be something to that."

Pia appreciated his mood change. The room felt warmer. Maybe they could get somewhere.

He opened his notepad and checked over his notes. "Right, then, a psychological profile. We're looking for a mastermind who is probably thumbing his nose at us just now. He's been getting away with it for years and that always leads to arrogance in criminals. Enough to kill a constable. Or order her killed by Mr. Bling, anyway. They like to think they're smarter than the rest of us. He's probably leaving clues in plain sight and laughing that we haven't figured it out yet. At the same time, he's raking in money and distributing it through his financial man. So where are we? We don't know who the financial man is; we don't know who the mastermind is; we don't know who Mr. Bling is. And you think the Morpheus is involved but you haven't any evidence."

Tania said, "Yep."

CHAPTER 40

Well after dark, Pia and Tania flew to London on Sabel One with both Benton and Abby in tow. Under the guise of taking her to see Bethany, Pia allowed Benton and Tania to mercilessly interrogate Abby. Pia tried to focus on catching up with office work but kept one ear to the interview. Abby was the opposite of a hardened criminal. She broke down in tears at one point. It was all Pia could do to keep herself from running to Abby's defense. Instead, Pia remained in her seat, facing forward, letting the professionals do their job. Eventually, Benton went quiet, apparently satisfied. Tania broke things off on a skeptical note when they taxied into the London City Jet Center.

Twenty minutes later, their limo pulled up to the Lanesborough Hotel. The driver was scheduled to take Benton to a different hotel and then take Abby to Bethany's. But when Pia got out, Abby hopped out with her. "A word, Sabel?"

Abby gave Tania a shove-off look. Tania went ahead. Tanner turned his back and faced the street. Abby hesitated before deciding she had all the privacy she would get.

"After a flogging from your lot," Abby said, "I'm not in a proper mood for seeing Bethany. Mind if I take the couch in your suite?"

"We have a couple extra rooms." Pia nodded toward the elevators. "Come on up. We can talk about old times."

"I need you to know," Abby said as she followed Pia to the elevator Tania held for them, "I'm not like you. I'm not important. I'm just an aging footballer going batty with shrubs instead of cats. No one's going to involve me in any plot against you."

Tania checked her phone. Tanner faced the doors.

Pia considered her friend. Trust was a difficult commodity to weigh. While she could never imagine Abby turning against her, Julius Caesar never suspected his best friend Marcus Brutus of betrayal either. Throughout history, countless people have sold out friends and relatives for thirty pieces of silver. Pia didn't respond.

They marched in silence through the suite's foyer. Tania went to her room to shower and Tanner manned the foyer. The butler appeared and examined Pia with grave concern.

"Flesh wounds," Pia told him. "Abby, follow me."

Pia led her to the master suite while Abby stared at the gilded ceiling sconces and crystal chandeliers as if she'd never seen them before. Pia stopped in the hall and waited for her. "You didn't stay here last night?"

"Nah. Afraid I'd break something that would cost me my retirement fund." Abby snapped her gaze from a fine china vase to Pia. In an anguished voice, she said, "Oi! C'mon now. Bethany and I stayed at her place. I was in London all night, I swear."

They passed the dining room, where a servant polished the formal place settings. They trekked through the bedroom and into the master bath, where Pia turned the shower on. "Something's on your mind. Spill it while I get cleaned up."

Pia peeled off her layers. Abby leaned against the counter, averting her gaze.

Pia stepped into the shower. "Talk to me, Stokes."

"Your VP's accusing me of having something to do with the bloody attack. It's not enough they shredded my little cottage. The only thing would make Tania happy is if I'd been there last night and got myself killed." Abby's gaze fell to the toilet. She looked over the remote control, pressed a button, and watched as a small device extended into the bowl where it shot warm water upward. "Holy shite … Sabel, you've got a remote control, retractable bidet? You can't wipe your bum like a normal person?"

Pia soaped up and rinsed her hair. "What's that?"

Abby backed out of the toilet room. "I said, I'd never survive a gun battle. I'm the kind who turns into collateral damage right off. How could they think I'd be part of anything like that? You know me. How could you let them treat me like a criminal?"

Pia shut off the water and grabbed a towel. "Interrogation is not my area of expertise."

"Just leave it to the attack dogs then, eh?" Abby glared while Pia toweled off. "Nice."

Pia wrapped in the towel and checked herself in the mirror. One four-day-old black eye, one skinned cheek, a welt over an eyebrow, and a cut under her ear she hadn't noticed before. When did that happen? She put antibiotic ointment on the abrasions and cuts. She trimmed a rectangle of gauze for her cheek. Abby took the tape from her and pressed the bandage into place.

Abby asked, "How do you sleep when veteran Paras are dropping out of the sky trying to kill you at three in the morning?"

"Not well."

"What drives you, Sabel?"

"What do you mean?"

"For me, sixth grade made all the difference. I figured out I was gay and so did everyone else. They started saying things, making jokes, and leaving me out. I wanted respect. So, I turned to the pitch. While the other girls were learning makeup, I was learning back-heels and rainbows. After a while, I got good at it. It drove me. I needed to play. I thrived on the love of my peers. That came to an end. Now, I need to find Britain's eco-future. I don't need someone I thought was a friend bringing down World War III on my house. Talk to me, Sabel. What do you need?"

Pia pulled out a little black dress, simple and sexy, and slipped it on. "I need to find Chloe's killers."

"Don't be an emotional holdout," Abby snarled. "Back in the day, they said you fought every game like you were going to die. I remember most people for a play they made. But I remember every minute of every game when you were on the pitch, Sabel. It was just like they said. You weren't just fierce, you were desperate. Angry, scared, furious, horrified at the thought of losing. That made life hard for the rest of us, you know. Playing against you was like playing on the edge of a cliff. One wrong move and you're a goner. You were terrifying. What was that about?"

Pia brushed her hair gingerly, avoiding the bruises lurking unseen on her scalp, and looked at Abby in the mirror. "What's your point?"

"I'm seeing that same scared young girl desperate for the win." Abby grabbed the brush and forced eye contact. "Only this time the game's deadly. Why do you do this stuff? Why do you push so hard someone sent six armed men to take you out in the middle of the night? Why not be a normal woman and let Benton and the GMP figure out who killed Chloe England? None of this is your business. What's eating at you so bad that I not only end up in danger—but under suspicion for the danger you brought down on me?"

Pia thought about it and shrugged. She pulled the brush back and finished her ponytail.

"Tell me something." Abby kept a hard gaze. "Is it true you killed a man when you were a kid?"

Pia froze, her gaze bouncing off the mirror at Abby.

"I couldn't kill a man," Abby said. "No matter what. I don't have that kind of rage burning inside me. I don't have the nerve to hang with a bunch of killers either. And yet, here you are running around with military-trained assassins, and you go at it the same way you played football—desperate for the win. What happened to you?"

Pia reached for her makeup bag and found an eyeliner. "Where'd you hear about my childhood?"

"Rumors go around practice squads, reporters, players, coaches— what does it matter? Is it true?"

"Why do you want to know?"

"You mean besides trying to figure out why I could've died if I'd been home and now have to answer for why I didn't? Yeah. Well. Hard as it may be to believe, I care about you."

Pia finished one eye, then moved her hand to the other and stopped. "First time I killed a man, I was four. It's an indelible memory. The only one I have of my mother. It was a sunny, yellow day that smelled like cilantro. Two men broke in. One shot my dad in the study. The other strangled my mother in the kitchen, where she'd been showing me how to dice vegetables. I grabbed the knife and stabbed and stabbed and stabbed, trying to make him stop. Then I hit something. Blood poured out of his leg like a fountain. He bellowed in agony and dropped my mother. Her head hit the floor with a sickening thud. Blood was pumping all over. I'd hit his femoral artery. Everything was slick and greasy. I slipped and slid in the gore trying to crawl to Mommy. I screamed and cried and shook her, but she wouldn't wake up."

Abby winced.

Pia finished her eyeliner and put it away.

"Dear God," Abby said quietly.

Picking up one of the lipsticks, Pia looked at it, then at Abby. She said, "Alan Sabel was a graduate student who lived next door. He was the first one there. He adopted me and raised me. The people who killed my parents were looking for the plans to a metacapacitor that would've revolutionized electric battery storage, ending the oil business overnight. They didn't find it. They assumed Alan Sabel stole it. They kept coming after us. When it wasn't them, it was someone else. There's no end to the people who believe I have something that belongs to them.

"I started carrying a weapon when I was six. Dad hired bodyguards and built Sabel Security. Soccer was my safe place. On the pitch, I was surrounded by parents who were naturally suspicious of anyone hanging around girls' games. All my teammates and their parents counted on me to win the game, which meant they would protect me from anyone. Being the best wasn't just for the glory, it was for the safety. You're right, Abby. I was desperate to win."

She applied the lipstick. A sexy red.

Abby watched, uncertain what to say.

Pia continued, "Twenty-three years later, the man who'd ordered my parents' assassination killed Alan Sabel. Viktor Popov. After a lifetime of living in terror, I tracked Popov down and shot him nine times. I felt better. But not much. These days, when I see a victim like Chloe, young and innocent, full of potential—just like my mother—I can't let it go."

Deep in thought, Abby watched her. After careful consideration, she said, "That's why you're so brave?"

"Brave?"

"You took on six killers—and won."

"That wasn't brave." Pia put the lipstick away. "You've heard of acute stress response? More commonly known as fight-or-flight response?"

"Sure, when under threat, your brain makes a decision to stand or run."

"That's the first decision. There's another decision you're forced to make after that. What happens when you flee—and the threat catches up to you? Or, what happens when you fight, and you start to lose?"

"You freak out," Abby said while staring at Pia.

Pia said nothing. She let the silence stretch until Abby figured it out.

"You get angry, scared, furious, horrified at the thought of losing," Abby said. "Then you fight—desperate."

Pia reached for a box of jewelry and pulled out a thick rope of diamonds. She fiddled with the clasp, then looked at Abby. Her friend took the heavy necklace and Pia turned around.

"You don't sleep because you're scared to death all the time," Abby said. She fumbled the clasp and dropped the diamonds. "God, that's got to be an awful way to live, Sabel."

Pia caught the necklace and held her ponytail out of the way. They tried the necklace again.

Abby said, "I didn't have anything to do with the attack. I need you to believe me."

"Trusting people leads to an early grave."

"Your world sucks. It's dangerous to be around you."

It was Pia's turn to wince at the hard truth.

Watching her face in the mirror, Abby let the necklace slip again but caught it. "Bloody hell. I'm rubbish with this girly stuff."

"You're a world-class champion. Where's your positive mental attitude?"

"You're right. I can do this." Abby concentrated and tried once more. This time the clasp clicked into place.

Pia faced her, and was about to say thank-you, when Abby looked her up and down and said, "Hang on a minute. Do you have a date?"

CHAPTER 41

PIA GAVE HER A SMILE and picked up the matching earrings. "Would you mind having dinner with Tania? Liam lands in half an hour and, uhm …"

"Dinner with Tania?" Abby's brows rose. "I'd rather eat with alligators. Maybe I'll go over to Bethany's place after all."

Abby headed down the hall, then stopped. Over her shoulder, she said, "I feel bad your childhood wasn't what we all thought, unicorns and yachts. When you get done suspecting me, I'll not hold it against you."

She didn't wait for an answer. She strode out quickly.

Pia checked her look in the mirror. It had been just over two days since she'd last seen him, and he'd spent half that time on airliners. He'd probably prefer a short dinner before going home. Then again, he'd flown on lie-flat flights, so he might have had plenty of rest. Either way, she should look her best. Should she put on some heels and look him in the eye? Or would that be too aggressive? Should she leave his natural height differential alone? She put on pumps and took them off. She put on flats and took them off. She put on stilettos and took them off. She dropped on the settee at the end of the bed and stared at the scattered footwear.

It wasn't the shoes that bothered her.

Abby was right. They suspected Abby only because she didn't die. Pia's world was a paranoid dangerland. Her stomach twisted in that all-too-familiar grip of anxiety. Paranoia as a lifestyle.

Pia's phone buzzed. Albert Tindall.

"Look here," Albert said. "You left things on a rather nasty note. My dear wife is distraught at how you must think of us. I'd like to make a fair exchange, put things right between us."

"Exchange?"

"Indeed. You're looking for information about life in the English countryside and, well—as you've obviously figured out, I'm hard up for capital. A matter for which I expect your full discretion. At any rate, I have a proposal to make."

Pia felt a frown creasing her forehead. She looked out the window as the lights came on at Buckingham Palace. "I'm listening."

"As I told you, I pick up the odd commission from making introductions between important people. It's no secret that you are one very, very important person. There are many people who would like to meet you, and I would really, really appreciate it if you would reschedule your interview with Wayne Walker."

Pia waited for a moment to see if he'd expand. When he didn't, she asked, "In exchange for what?"

"Well, for example, anything you want to know that we might shed light on. You could ask questions and I could fill in any blanks—"

"I'm looking for the people who killed Chloe England. Answer that and I'll fit him in."

"Ah. Yes. Uhm, that is something I don't know anything—"

"You know more than you've offered. If you're not willing to talk about that, you'll have to answer to the NCA."

"Now hold on." Albert stammered, looking for words. "You … you needn't go to them. There's nothing we can't work out amongst ourselves. Be reasonable—"

"They are already involved. DI Benton is meeting with them in the morning. If you have something you'd like to keep between us then spit it out right now."

Albert took a moment to either think it over or get permission, she couldn't tell which. Eventually he said, "Would it hurt you to reschedule Walker? Won't take but half an hour, I'd wager."

"I'll consider it," Pia said with a quick, clipped voice. "Start shedding light."

"I'd also like you to pay a visit to Lord Eden-Sonnet. He says your people have been shoving their way around his offices all day, being quite rude and unpleasant. He's tried to reach out to you, but he can't get past your secretary, George something or other. At any rate, he'd like to have cocktails and bring this chapter to a close."

"I'll consider that too. Where is that light you were going to shed?"

"You know how these things go, Pia," he said with a sneer. "First things first."

If there was one thing that flushed out Pia's anger it was coercion. "Call me Ms. Sabel, Albert. Good luck with the NCA."

As she went to click off, she heard him protesting. No doubt he wanted to renegotiate. It would wait until morning. But she could meet him halfway. She texted him with a time for Wayne Walker. The Eden-Sonnet meeting she could leverage for her next move.

She stepped into her flats and contemplated what had motivated Albert to make that call. Sinking onto the settee again, she looked at the mirror. Abby's words came back to her, *Your world sucks. It's dangerous to be around you.*

Did Liam deserve to be in that kind of danger? Did he understand whoever was behind all this was willing to send armed assassins to shoot up an entire cottage?

She texted Tania.

The two met in the sitting room surrounded by marble columns and silk floral upholstery. Tania stared at Pia's bandage until it made Pia self-conscious. Then she looked at the black eye instead. Tania said, "Benton was right about Bella Davis's co-workers. They didn't pay attention to her cuz she was one of those conspiracy whackjobs. She'd been spouting off wild ideas for years. No one liked her enough to talk to her."

"Too bad," Pia said. "That's not my biggest concern. After last night, I'm worried about Liam's protection."

"We assigned him three with standard rotation, 24x7. His unscheduled trip across the pond took us by surprise. We let him take a commercial flight and had people from the Vancouver office meet him. They were a little late getting there and he didn't wait for them. Same thing happened on his San Diego leg. Three people met him half an hour ago at Heathrow, on time this time. And he was wearing his Sabel Armor like a good boy. They should be here shortly."

"Is that enough?"

"How deep are Mr. Bling's resources?" Tania pursed her lips while she thought. "I'm thinking he was stretched thin at Claigeann Cottage."

Pia thought out loud. "Because the local cops knew the guy we cuffed? Which means Mr. Bling is using sub-contractors. I see what you mean. Still, I don't like it."

"He's in the city. With all the cameras they got on every corner, Bling won't be so ballsy."

"You sure about that?"

"Of course not. Who could be? But you can't let your paranoid social cognition outrun what's effective."

Pia wondered when Tania had teamed up with Dr. Harrison against her. She let it go and thought back to the death of her adopted father. There had been too many armed men on both sides during the negotiation for her ransom. So many, that one of the kidnappers panicked and touched off a firefight in tight confines. The result was one dead and three seriously injured. Overdoing it was as bad as underdoing it.

"Too many guards makes it hard to move around," Tania said. "The principals be dodging their detail before you know it. Then you have zero bodyguards." Tania thought hard. "Best I can do is put on a shadow."

"I want to make sure he's safe," Pia said. Having someone follow a principal at a distance without him being aware often produced unintended consequences. People thought they were being spied on when they figured it out. It sometimes led to confrontation and resentment. "Will that guarantee his safety?"

The butler appeared in the doorway and waited for them to finish.

"You want guarantees, huh?" Tania asked with sass. "Cancel. We thought we had it under control when we turned in for the night at Claigeann Cottage."

The butler repressed a snort of laughter.

Tania turned to him. "How come people snicker when I say Claigeann Cottage?"

"Begging your pardon, ma'am." He stiffened. "I meant no disrespect. I thought you were trying to be funny. It's just a reference to Ms. Sabel's errant phrase."

"And just which phrase izzat?" Tania canted her head.

"That she drinks from the skulls of her enemies, ma'am."

Pia and Tania exchanged a glance before turning their questioning gaze back to the butler.

"Uh. She defeated her enemies at Claigeann Cottage. It's quite appropriate if you don't mind my saying so." He checked their reactions. "You see, *claigeann* is Gaelic for skull, ma'am."

"I'll never hear the end of that."

"We Brits see it as a good thing. Endearing. By the way, a Master Pickford is here to see you."

CHAPTER 42

"SHOW HIM IN, PLEASE," PIA said.

Tania took the side door, saying as she exited, "Good luck, girlfriend. I'll figure something out by morning."

Pia wrestled with the idea of sending Liam home. *It's dangerous to be around you.*

Her gut twisted into a full pretzel as he appeared in the hall following the butler. She worried her fingers. She should call the whole thing off— even dinner. Just end it all cold right now. Then the butler stepped aside.

Liam's gaze connected with hers like an electric current. He smiled with a combination of mischief and admiration. Her mind flooded with memories of their one and only kiss. That fleeting intimacy had filled her with an unexpected—and unresolved—surge of desire. Her heart rate rose. She found herself rushing to him.

They drew each other into a warm hug. She inhaled his scent and cherished his warm embrace. Even though his strong arms and broad, muscular chest gave her comfort, her stomach still did flips. Her veins ran with ice water. Her breathing came quick and shallow. The right thing to do was to send him home.

She didn't want to do the right thing.

He pulled back and looked her over, as if seeing the significant bandage on her cheek for the first time. "I heard about that. You're alright, then?"

"It looks worse than it is." She looked away. "I don't want to talk about it."

He hugged her again. This time, she tipped up and gave him a big kiss on the mouth. When it reached its zenith, she broke off and gestured wordlessly to the couch. The butler brought them gimlets. She asked him about his trip. He answered in halting sentences, his gaze returning to her bandage as if it hurt him.

The attack overshadowed the conversation, so she gave in. She told him everything, step by step. Her analysis surmised that the attack came from Chloe's killers and that she believed their resources were limited. Then she came to the hard part.

"These people are more dangerous than I thought," she said. "We have to—"

"Won't hear of it, lassie," Liam said. "You cannae leave me out of this fight. Besides, I can handle myself, y'know. I played rugby."

She almost laughed at his bravado but caught herself. He was dead serious. Everyone knew rugby was one of the roughest sports, up there with hockey and boxing, but guns and grenades are a whole different animal. She and Tania were lucky to have engaged their attackers in close quarters.

The butler announced dinner. They moved to the next room and took their places at the table. Pia found her lipstick lying next to her salad fork. She didn't recall taking it from the dressing room, much less leaving it at the table. The waiter displayed the bottle of wine for her approval. She nodded at the Chambertin Domaine Leroy, 1989. He uncorked it and poured a sample. She sniffed it, checked the legs, and sipped. With her nod, the man poured two glasses and disappeared.

"To the loveliest lass in London," Liam said and pinged his glass on hers. "I'd say loveliest in the world, but I couldnae pass up the alliteration."

Pia smiled and felt her stomach twist another notch. Rugby or not, putting him in the middle of this was a mistake.

The waiter slipped in silently and removed the charging plates. Beneath her charger was a message written in lipstick. It read, *Forget Liam, it's me you want, love. Toss him and give us a ring, Abby.* A large heart finished the note. The salad plate landed before Liam saw anything. It relieved her to know Abby hadn't lost her sense of humor.

"You've never told me your story," Liam said. "There're wild rumors about you all over the internet. I peeked at a few, the good ones, mind you, not the conspiracies. I'd rather hear it from you, though. If you're up for a blether, I'm all ears."

He asked with perfect innocence. Perhaps it was a winning line in his pursuit of women; perhaps he'd read some of the worst conspiracy theories and refused to believe them but still needed a little reassurance. In the end, it was his endearing smile and endless charm combined with her twisted gut that tipped her decision. Because of the danger she'd dragged him into, and in the interest of transparency—despite the fact it would kill any romantic mood—she decided to tell him.

For the second time that evening, she dredged up the story of the first man she'd killed. And the others thereafter.

He listened intently, never interrupting and never letting her stop. They ate and talked. The main course came, and she kept talking. Her monologue reminded her of therapy sessions. She began to feel a weight lifted in one regard, but in another, a heavier issue pressed down on her: what to do with Liam. When the dishes were cleared, and the crumbs scraped from the table, she wrapped it up. In the end, he knew more about her than Abby.

He held her gaze for a long time.

As she expected, her biography dropped a cold, wet blanket on the romantic twinkle in his eye.

"You had a wee bit of a struggle, that's for sure," he said. "Not all mansions and fancy cars. And yet here you are, pure dead brilliant at everything you do. I knew you were a remarkable woman when I first laid eyes on you."

"Yeah, well, thanks. But that story is why I'm going to cancel the project. Abby's right—I'm a danger to everyone around me."

He leaned back, observing her keenly, as the waiter poured the last of the wine. When the man removed himself, Liam leaned in and held his hands out, palms up. She took the hint and put her hands in his.

"Knowing more about you makes me want to be with you all the time, danger or no."

"I appreciate that, but I'm not changing—"

"This has been a lovely dinner. Let's not faff about arguing decisions that I'll talk you out of later."

She thought he looked scrumptious in the candlelight. Sincere and caring. The kind of man she wanted to care for. The kind of man she wanted to have care about her. Those feelings of longing and desire that stirred inside her brought back memories of the many betrayals she'd suffered in the past. Her life lay in ruins among an excess of material splendor: the first blush of passion brought with it requisite waves of suspicion.

"This would be a good time for me to take my leave," he said. "Before you close that door for good."

"No," she said all too quickly. She recalibrated her pace to slow herself down. "That door's not closed."

She rose and nosed toward the sitting room, giving him a tug with her hand.

"Seemed a bit closed when you said I was off your project."

"Maybe thinking of a door is too binary. My decision's more like a portal."

They moved like dancers gliding into the next room.

"Oh aye?" he said. "Are we talking organic or architectural portal?"

"Let's say … human."

"How deep is your decision buried in that portal? I'd like to find it and flip it over."

"Buried deep in my childhood."

"It's admirable that you've risen above such tragedy." He swept her into his arms again. "How do you cope?"

"I seek out the pleasures of each day as if it were my last." She brushed her lips against his. "I never know if I'll have another chance to get what I want."

His eyes sparkled. "And what do you want?"

She placed her palm on his chest and pushed him backward, where he dropped onto the sofa. She placed a knee on either side of his hips and ran her fingers through his caramel hair. "I want you to see me as a this-date kind of lass."

CHAPTER 43

PIA AWOKE SPOONED UNDER LIAM'S protective arm. A sense of safety washed over her as if she had suddenly achieved immortality. She took a deep breath and cherished his scent as well as the lingering memory of great sex. As it turned out, Liam had a degree in the all-important study of oral stimulation. A pleasant and rewarding surprise. He'd started out slowly and gently, then progressed at a perfectly provocative rate, building to a crescendo like Beethoven's Ninth.

She rolled out from under his arm. He snored lightly. She watched him in the dim light. Tania had been right. She needed this.

Many years ago, a college professor had stopped her Psych 101 class, angered by a student's off-topic question about relationships. "We don't need to be loved," he'd said. "Humans have a burning desire to love others. To care about them, nurture them, keep them safe, and make that relationship last. Partners, friends, children, parents, all relationships based on love. All too often, we strive to make others love us—a pursuit destined to fail."

Like most people, Pia adored being adored. She longed to be the center of attention. And yet, she had learned the professor's lesson the hard way. The more one longed to be loved, the more elusive that love became. Liam was someone worth loving first. Maybe her love would be repaid in kind. Maybe not. But she had to try. After all, he'd blushed at their first and second meetings. Destiny.

Pulling on her leggings, she read the clock: 3 AM. While the sex had been great, it hadn't changed her sleep habits. She pulled on a top, found her running shoes, and made her way outside.

At this hour, she didn't bother her guards. Few bad guys were ambitious enough to wait until zero-dark-thirty to ambush her while running a random route. Only Jacob could keep her pace anyway. Tanner was too slow, Tania was more of a sprinter, and Cody was still in the hospital. She mapped out her run: behind Buckingham Palace, around St. James Park, back toward the Lanesborough, then two laps around Hyde Park. Her map showed the course to be ten miles give or take.

Second best way to start the day, she figured.

She noticed a message from the Major asking her to call if the time difference allowed. It was still 11 PM back in DC. She dialed and the Major picked up right away.

"Our people had a breakthrough on McKenna Engineering," the Major said. "Our team figured out what Liam's dad had planned for the software. Our AI system can guide the McKenna team to finish in a quarter of the time previously thought. That makes buying the company a steal. With your approval, we'll move forward with the acquisition process tomorrow."

Pia picked up her pace at the news and made the corner by the Royal Mews, where the kings' horses were kept back in the day. She tried to hide her excitement when she said, "That's great news. Thank you for coming up with the idea and working so hard to make it happen."

"The glory belongs to the Satellite Division. Their engineers stayed up late running hundreds of scenarios until they found a path that made sense."

"I'll throw a party for them when I get back."

"Don't forget, you must remind Liam there will be no public disclosures about this until the press release, and it's not a done deal until we've finished due diligence."

They clicked off. Pia found herself running too fast for the distance. Pacing herself, she ran by the palace and down Birdcage Walk. The streets were dark and empty and the park quiet. Her thoughts turned to Liam, resting peacefully in her bed. How would she tell him? Wake him up and blurt it out? Get a keepsake and serve it with his breakfast? Would there be any flower shops open before breakfast? Not likely. Besides, you don't give men flowers. What does one give men? Other than sex. Alcohol. Yes, that was the right idea, but what kind? Scotch would be too obvious. She would have to think of something clever. With the companies merged, they might be together for a long time.

A long-term relationship would be nice.

Her thoughts turned to Bethany and Rain. It made her feel good to hear they were causing trouble for Lord Eden-Sonnet. She should take him up on the invitation to cocktails. It was his turn to host, after all. While she tucked that thought away, a text came in from Bianca, asking if Pia were up.

Pia called her. "I'm out for my morning stroll. What's up?"

"Nothing good," Bianca said. "Krueger's dead, the Brits won't give us a wiretap, and we found Liam's wife. Which do you want first?"

The wife. Pia felt like she'd run into a palace wall. She caught her breath and looked around. "What happened? Tell me about Liam's wife."

"She was murdered about six months ago on the Croatian island of Hvar. She was battered so badly, we had to send DNA to have her remains identified."

Pia stared at a lone cab driving by and suddenly felt as if all the air had been sucked out of England. She knew what it meant. Savage killings were acts of rage, usually perpetrated by a lover. "Did they have an exact date of death?"

"They do," Bianca sighed. "We don't have calendar entries for Liam that week. You'll have to ask him. But it's better to leave it to the authorities."

"That would be best," she said knowing full well she couldn't do that. Pia resumed her run with significantly less desire.

"You still there?"

"Yes," Pia said.

"Krueger died of a sudden heart attack in San Diego yesterday morning. The official report mentions an EpiPen puncture mark. We requested they double check as it could be an injection site for Anectine or some other difficult-to-trace poison. The coroner wouldn't talk to my people, so we asked Director Shikowitz to get involved."

"San Diego?"

"Right, at the headquarters of McDowell Aerospace."

Pia stopped again. She looked around. Kensington Palace on her right, the Round Pond on her left. Everything else dark. Images of Liam crept through the shadows of her mind. Why had he been in San Diego? Was her imagination playing tricks on her, or had he also been in Vancouver when Vermeer died?

"Pia? Is there something wrong?"

"What was the other thing?"

"We asked NCA and MI5 to let us tap the Rohans and the Tindalls. Neither of them would allow it. I could ask the FBI to back our request. It's thin and could tarnish our reputation. I advise against it."

"What if something pans out on Krueger?"

"You mean proof of murder? That would give us a thread. I'm not sure who it would lead us to."

Pia understood what Bianca wasn't saying. More than likely, it would lead to Liam and not the Rohans or the Tindalls. She thanked Bianca and clicked off.

Fired up by anger, she took off running. So much for the merger celebrations. What had he done? If anything. How could she have slept with him? Her lust got ahead of her common sense. She should've known something was wrong when he pretended not to know who she was in the coffee shop. *You're a strapping lass, aren't ya?* It was a pickup line. Even Tania had seen through his crap—and she hadn't even been there.

Yet he'd blushed when she entered the meeting.

When she'd asked about using him to set up the Morpheus, the Major had warned her, *if he agrees, he's a damn fool.* And what did he do? He jumped at the chance. He was no fool. Did that mean he was the mastermind of the whole operation? Skilling was the money, the Rohans were the front, and someone else pulled Mr. Bling's leash.

And now that it had become a shooting war, Liam still wanted in. Because he'd once played rugby. Would a guilty man do that? Was Liam guilty of anything? His wife had been murdered. He might not have been in Croatia at the time. Vermeer and Krueger had not been ruled murders. Even if they were, being in the same city wasn't proof of involvement. It could be coincidence.

In every bad mystery she'd ever watched, the detective always said,

"I don't believe in coincidences." Yet they happen all the time. John Adams and Thomas Jefferson, political opponents, died on the same day, the Fourth of July—by coincidence. Robert Lincoln was on the scene of three Presidential assassinations—his father's, Garfield's, and McKinley's—by coincidence. Stephen Hawking was born on the same date as Galileo. Coincidences happen.

So did premeditated murder.

Krueger had been right about her. She was a figurehead who didn't belong in her position. She was no avenging angel, and certainly no Bruce Wayne. She, like Abby, was an aging footballer with no detective skills, no special insights, no instincts, and no ideas on how to figure out if Liam were as evil as circumstances made him appear. She could be sleeping with a murderer. Lacking any special skills, the best thing she could do would be to ask him.

Looking around, she found herself on her second lap of Hyde Park at the Kensington Garden end. She cut across the grass in a beeline for the hotel. Her anger rose with each stride.

The elevator took forever, and the music was excruciating. She stormed through the suite and into the bedroom.

He lay on his side, his arm circling an empty space. He looked so peaceful and innocent that she found herself melting into the carpet.

CHAPTER 44

PIA PUSHED OPEN THE DOOR to Tania's room and switched on the light. Taking a seat on the bed's edge, she waited until Tania rolled over with one eye open.

Pia said, "I need your advice."

"Yeah, huh?" Tania pushed up on an elbow. "Remember when we talked about boundaries?"

"Yes, but this—"

"Remember when we talked about how slavery is over and just because you're rich don't mean you can come barging in my room whenever you feel like it?"

"Yes, but this—"

"I coulda had a man in here."

Pia looked around. "You don't."

"That don't matter. I don't answer to you 24/7."

"Sorry," Pia said. She stood and crossed the room.

"Besides, you stink."

"I went for a run and got some terrible news. I needed to talk to someone. I'll come back later."

"What news?"

"No, you're right. I shouldn't have woken you up. I should've called Jonelle."

"She ain't your slave either and it's after midnight stateside. What news did you get?"

"Really, it can wait." Pia pulled the door open.

"I'm done with your passive-aggressive bullshit, sister. What fucking news did you get?"

Pia blurted, "Liam's wife was beaten to death in Croatia six months ago."

"OK," Tania said and rubbed her face. "That's some shit. You might've started with that."

She pulled back the covers and sat up, her feet dangling over the edge of the high bed. Pia came back halfway across the room. Tania sniffed the air and held up a hand to stop her.

"Go take a shower and come back," Tania said. "I'll find some coffee."

Pia left and slipped past her sleeping lover with a suspicious eye. She showered quickly. Twenty years in soccer taught her how to soap up and rinse every square inch of hair and skin in seconds. She put on a fresh athletic outfit and snuck past Liam with a second wary glance. She met Tania in the sitting room.

"No guest-accessible kitchen in this suite." Tania tossed her hands up in frustration. "Gotta have a manservant do everything. I'm surprised you gotta wipe your own butt in this place." Tania frowned. "Come to think of it—you don't even gotta do that."

The night butler appeared with a silver service. He poured two cups of coffee and retreated.

Pia explained all the coincidences to Tania. Vermeer in Vancouver, Krueger in San Diego, his missing wife.

"OK, I'll talk to him," Tania frowned into her coffee cup. "Brits should stick to tea."

Pia needed answers. But when she thought about Tania's interrogation of Abby and how it soured that relationship, she shuddered. She couldn't risk ruining what she had with Liam. She felt herself tightening up with tension the more she thought about Liam's secrets.

"You're doing that thing again," Tania said. "You're seeing Liam as an asymmetrical relationship, like he holds all the cards just cause your rosebud twitches when you see him—and that sparks your paranoid social cognitive dysfunction. You're working yourself into a frenzy over—"

"No. This time it's *Stearne's Law*."

In unison they recited Jacob Stearne's maxim: "Paranoia is the result of acute situational awareness. Everyone really is trying to kill you."

They both laughed nervously.

Pia said, "So. Why do you sound just like Dr. Harrison?"

"Sat outside enough sessions. I can recite that in my sleep. But that don't mean it ain't true."

Pia grew serious again. "I've got to be the one who interrogates him."

Tania didn't hide her surprise, nor her disappointment. "I get it. You want to go easy on him. Break it to him gently. You know personal relationships are not allowed in any professional setting. And that means you know better. But I know you. You're going to do it anyway. And I know I'm not going to talk you out of it. So, I'm just gonna tell you right now, bad idea."

"Walk me through it."

Tania rolled her eyes before pouring as much of her career experience as possible into her boss. After one last protest, she went back to bed.

While Pia waited for Liam to wake, she rehearsed everything Tania had taught her several times over. She had her technique down by sunrise. But Liam still wasn't awake.

She took the coffee service to the kitchen, where she surprised the night butler. Without saying anything, she poured the pitcher's contents into the sink. Then she showed him how to make coffee her way: twice as many beans, ground finer than sand, and double the paper filters. She explained that to the British, tea is a secular communion, but to Americans coffee has a different purpose. It's an aggressive, in-your-face wakeup call. The man smiled as if she had explained how to cook children. Then he looked past her shoulder.

Liam stood in the doorway, dressed and disheveled.

CHAPTER 45

HER HEART REVVED UP LIKE a race car. Her mind went blank. Instead of asking the opening questions Tania had lined up for her, she heard a soft voice asking him, "Coffee?"

"Aye, I never pass up anything a bonnie lass offers me in the morning." He grinned. He looked ruggedly handsome. His green eyes sparkled. He moved in for a good-morning kiss.

She found herself smiling and handing him a cup to keep him at arm's length.

How could he have done any of the things she imagined?

Quite easily, she reminded herself. Or not at all.

The cup shook as she handed it off. His gaze fell to her hand. She withdrew it quickly and turned away.

"You know why Americans like coffee?" she asked, her voice betraying her nervousness.

He looked at her curiously. "Cannae say I do."

"When King George levied the Stamp Act in 1765, rather than pay the tax without representation, the American colonists boycotted tea and started drinking coffee instead."

"You don't say." He took a sip and spluttered. "Whoa. What the bloody hell is this—liquid asphalt?"

Pia couldn't breathe. Everything Tania taught her swirled in her head. She couldn't remember which question to ask first. Something about trapping the witness. Cutting off all the escape routes before asking the main question. She felt like she was trying to catch fog.

"Are ya alright?" Liam asked. "You look like you're having a wee bit of remorse. Should I have left straight away last night?"

"Nothing like that," she said quickly. She needed air. She needed sky. She needed grass. "Let's go for a walk."

She didn't look back. She reached the elevator, pressed the button, and waited. Tanner held two Sabel armor shirts when he caught up. Made of liquid metal with the thickness of a sweatshirt, they were the least obtrusive armor on the market. Pia ripped off her top, slipped the armor over her athletic bra, and slammed her top back on in a fast and fluid movement. Something she'd done hundreds of times. Liam watched her, somewhat amazed. Then he took off his shirt, slipped into the armor and rebuttoned his shirt.

He said, "Thing's not so bad when you get used to it."

He smiled at Pia, then at Tanner, and the other agent assigned to him. No one returned the smile.

Liam stepped next to Pia, watching her eyes. He said nothing as they rode the lift to ground level and stepped out to the street.

Tanner and the other Sabel agent backed off enough to give them privacy.

She led him past the artillery memorial and through the Wellington Arch. The air was brisk, and the sun was low. Traffic on the A4 rumbled through the tunnel beneath them like a distant war. She didn't know where to start. The coincidences churned together, boiling and burning like acid. A wolverine tried to claw its way out from inside her.

While she tried to formulate the right words, she heard her name called. Looking up, she saw a heavy, familiar man jogging toward her in a sweatsuit. He slowed as he approached them.

"Pia Sabel! It is you," the heavy-set man said. He grinned and pressed his gloved hands together in the namaste gesture as he approached. "Wayne Walker, the Walking with Walker podcast. Albert told me we're rescheduled for tomorrow. That time works fine for me. Shall I meet you in the lobby?"

The man had the most annoying habit of showing up at the wrong time. She was in no mood to talk—but one must never offend the press. She waved off Tanner and said, "I didn't expect to run into you so far from Manchester."

"Oh, I live just there." He pointed vaguely down Piccadilly at a block of expensive flats. "I promise a right good time. How wonderful to run into the famous Liam Pickford as well."

"Indeed," Liam said and stuck out a hand that Wayne ignored with another namaste bow. "We're on for an interview tomorrow as well. Eleven, I believe."

Pia looked to Liam and wished she had listened to Wayne's dirt on him. It was too late to ask now.

"Is that alright?" Liam asked Pia with an uncertain look on his face.

"Did Albert set you up too?" she asked.

"We were on the same flight from America last night," Liam said.

"I took the liberty of setting it up directly," Wayne said. "Anyone in your orbit is fascinating to my listeners. See you both tomorrow."

Walker resumed his jog, though he couldn't be a regular at it given his shape.

Pia pressed on at a serious stride. Liam lagged a bit behind, then trotted to catch up.

"What's this all about?" Liam tugged at her elbow. "Are you dumping me already? I didnae think you the kind."

She turned around, her eyes flashing. "We located your wife."

Wrong move. Tania had told her to ask him if he'd been to Croatia first. And a bunch of other questions that would force a verifiable answer.

"Oh aye?" Liam pulled back. "And? Where is she then?"

It was too late to regroup. Pia leaned into her anger. "Beaten to death six months ago on the island of Hvar, Croatia. Ever been there?"

"Dead? No. That cannae be. I'd've been told. Are you sure? Who identified her? Why didn't they contact me?"

"We had to provide a DNA sample to ID her." Pia's phone rang with the ID announcing Jeff Benton. She ignored it.

"DNA?" He cocked his head to one side. "Why DNA?"

"Her face was crushed. Nothing left to identify."

"Oh my god." Liam reeled backward, looking sick. "Do they know who did it?"

Pia observed him closely, hoping to read his level of sincerity. She wanted to trust him—and because of that, she knew better than to trust herself. It was time to call in Tania.

Benton called her again. She ignored it again.

"Hold on." He scowled and pointed a finger at her. "You asked if I'd ever been there. You think I did it?"

"Just answer the question."

"I've never heard of the place." His face flushed with anger. "And no, I've never been to Croatia at all."

"Croatia's police will be checking passport records."

"Fine by me. Here, see for yourself." He pulled his passport out of his pocket and thrust it at her.

The first page she opened to had USA stamped on it from the day before. She flipped through and saw only four stamps, including his previous trip when they'd first met. She flipped to his picture and saw it had been issued in January, four months earlier. "What happened to the older one?"

"What?" Liam squinted at her before checking the date. "Oh, right. I renewed it because the old one expired. They do that, y'know."

Pia handed it back as the bile rose in her throat. Regrets came up fast. She should've taken Tania's advice in the beginning. Now she couldn't find a way out. And she still had questions about his last trip. Tania's instructions came back to her. She may have blown the wife question, but she could work on the others.

"I wanted to be clear of her," Liam said. "I never wished her dead."

"Why did you go to Vancouver?" she asked.

"Spending all this time on the merger, I neglected the sales effort. Before Dad took sick, I'd been VP of Sales. Two of our customers were turning right scunners. I had to patch things up with them."

"Who?"

"What's this all about, Pia?"

"Do you know a man named Martin Vermeer?"

"Cannae say I do. Can you give me some context?"

"How about Dave Krueger?"

"Krueger? Is he that feckless bastard who wrote the piece in the *Journal*? What about him?" Liam pieced it together before she could answer. "Oh, aye. His company's in San Diego where I was yesterday.

Are you accusing me of conspiring with him? You're that suspicious, eh? If you must know, I was there to visit Qualcomm. We engineered their water filtration system."

"Krueger died unexpectedly yesterday."

Benton rang again. Third time. Pia accepted the call. Before she could say anything into the phone, Liam stomped in anger.

"Oh, now hold on a minute," he said. He pointed at her and backed up a step. "Are you thinking …"

She held up her phone. "I have to take this."

"To hell with you, lassie." He turned and stormed toward the A4. A few paces out, he turned but kept walking backward. "I thought we had something special. I thought you were different from all that shite they say about you."

"You went to Chloe England's funeral because you followed women's soccer. That means you knew it was me in the coffeeshop when we first met."

"You're full of yourself, y'know that?" He walked backwards and pointed at her. "You're not the only lass who played the game."

"Where are you going?" she asked.

"To Croatia. I grew to hate the woman, but someone's got to bury her." He pointed at his assigned Sabel agent. "Stay where you are. I'm done with your lot."

Benton was shouting into the phone. "Pia. PIA!"

"What is it?" she snapped angrily.

"Your mates Bethany and Rain were abducted a few minutes ago. A black van snatched them right in front of Eden-Sonnet's office. Your agents were tased before they could react. No plates. I've sent a police cruiser to fetch you."

"Damn it," Pia said. She calculated the distance to the financial district. "I'll run there. It'll be faster."

She made it twenty yards when she heard the distinct snap of gunfire behind her. She turned in time to see Liam fall to the ground.

CHAPTER 46

Metropolitan Police constables swarmed out of nowhere in full riot gear before Pia could cover half the distance to Liam. At gunpoint, they forced Tanner, the other agent, three assailants in black, and Pia to the ground, face down. They slapped flex cuffs on them and stripped them of weapons.

The men in black had attacked a quarter mile north of Buckingham Palace. Naturally the Met was there in large numbers. Bad planning by the perps.

Unless it was staged.

Pia marveled at the police efficiency while they dragged her to her feet and marched her to an area behind a hedge not readily visible to tourists. They pushed her to her knees. They shoved the assailants and Pia's agents next to her. Several armed men stood over them while officers sorted out the next steps.

An ambulance came for Liam. Too many people hovered over him for her to figure out his condition. They bundled him up and carted him off quickly. No need to alarm the sightseers.

One by one, Pia's confederates were taken a few yards away to a different hedgerow where they were identified, photographed, and interrogated. Pia was last on their list. The police quickly figured out the bad guys wore balaclavas, marched them to a van, and took them away. Pia's agents were taken out of sight. The constables were respectful but still took her picture and checked her special permit card. They said little to her other than directional commands. One of them took her by the elbow and led her around another clump of hedge. Her agents knelt on the grass with their backs to her.

The Sabel agent whose name she didn't know was in the middle of saying, "—always like this?"

Tanner replied, "The more you work with Ms. Sabel, the more you end up in handcuffs. You get used to it."

The constable pointed at the ground next to Tanner. Pia knelt next to him.

Tanner coughed out of embarrassment.

"Sorry to get you into this, gentlemen," she said.

They didn't reply.

Behind them, she heard DI Benton's voice. It was raised in anger with two other men. She cocked an ear in that direction and picked up some of the conversation. Benton said, "—walked into my office a few days ago and everything's gone to hell since."

"My boss got a call from the Home Secretary," another voice said. "He wants you to deal with her."

"Am I supposed to take your word for that?" Benton's voice rose a few decibels.

"And mine heard from the Foreign Secretary," a third voice said. "She's yours. Deal with it."

"Bloody hell," Benton said. His voice lowered as he headed toward her. "Sod the lot of you then."

A moment later, he rounded the corner and stood in front of her. "You know what you've done?"

"My friend was shot," she said. "How is he?"

"You've gone and shot up the Queen's Palace for Christ's sake. What hornet's nest did you shove a stick into? Three bloody Paras armed with 9 mils shooting a man in broad daylight where the Royals can watch from their bleeding windows. Who opened the gates of Hell and let you out? More to the point, how did I get stuck with you?"

Pia felt the eyes of both her agents turn to her, waiting for her reply.

"You're not stuck with me. Go back to Manchester and leave me alone. I'll figure out what happened to him on my own."

Benton bent down with a pair of wire cutters. "NCA and the Met— what people call Scotland Yard—turned you over to me. I'm giving you a choice: either you stick next to me and mind your manners or you take that fancy jet of yours and get the hell off our little island."

She sat still.

He snipped off her flex cuffs then moved to Tanner.

"You'd make my career, you said." Benton clipped the others free. "You'd deliver Chloe's killers, you said. My first meeting with the NCA brass went on hold five minutes in. Five minutes, Pia. My career is going right down the gutter."

"Those men are tied in with the Morpheus. They'll lead us to Chloe's killers."

"Right. As if three Paras fresh from serving time at Her Majesty's Pleasure are going to tell us anything."

"How is Liam?"

"Taken to casualty. He had the strangest armor on." Benton stared at Pia's chest. "What the hell is that you're wearing? Let me guess—it's body armor from the future."

"What's his condition?" she asked as her phone rang.

Benton tossed his hands up, no idea. He walked back to the other officers.

Pia took the call. Before she finished her first word, Abby Stokes was yelling at her. "Sabel! Why've I got three constables here asking me about Bethany, eh? Why'd they want to know who would kidnap her?"

"Where are you?"

"I'm at your jet—heading back to the greenhouse. I'm supposed to be at work in an hour. These people stopped me at the gate and tore into me about who'd want to kidnap Bethany. Why?"

"I understand you're upset. We're working—"

"Five days, Sabel! You're in town for five fucking days and my life is going to hell. I've been interrogated twice, my house's a right ruin, and now you've gone and gotten my girlfriend kidnapped at gunpoint. Bloody hell, Sabel."

"I'll get her back. Don't worry about—"

Pia realized Abby had clicked off. She looked at her phone. Tania was reflected in the blank screen.

"Came to say, *I told you so?*" Pia asked.

"Don't gotta say what you already know." Tania crossed her arms and stared at Tanner. "What's your excuse?"

"Principal dismissed his detail before the shooting started." Tanner maintained his statue-like stance. The other agent straightened up and mimicked Tanner.

Benton came back with a box full of weapons. "These are yours, I believe."

They hastily re-armed themselves.

Tania scowled at Tanner. "Go find out where they took your principal and get his vitals. For future reference, principals don't fire you, I fire you. You're not fired, so guard that son of a bitch like your job depends on it. Because—guess what."

Tanner took off running.

She looked at the agent with no name. "He was your principal, too. Go on now. I'll take care of the boss."

The young man took off running.

Pia sorted things out in her head. She checked the time. 9 AM in London worked out to 5 AM in DC. The Major was not an early riser and hadn't heard any of the potentially bad news about Liam nor the disastrous morning in London. She wanted to call and apologize for getting the company involved in what were sure to be bad headlines. Not a great way for the figurehead to inspire the employees. After Benton and Abby yelled at her, and Tania refused to, she didn't need another angry voice. She sent a text putting the McKenna merger on hold. Details to follow.

She took a deep breath and wondered what to do next. Her gaze wandered across the park. Tourists meandered everywhere, the sun was shining brightly, the traffic had built up, and the sky was blue. All around her people were having a nice day.

She sensed Benton staring at her.

"My career," he said. "Do you have a plan?"

CHAPTER 47

YEARS AGO, PIA HAD COME to terms with the fact that many people
hated her for no other reason than she was rich. It didn't matter that she
had no hand in creating her wealth, nor that she gave half her income to
charity. Some people resented her for having more, full stop. Oddly,
these people never complained about riding on her jet, sailing on her
yacht, or feasting at her breakfast table. Benton was one of those people.
She watched him mop up the last bit of hollandaise sauce from his eggs
Benedict and wash it down with fresh-squeezed orange juice.

Pia nursed her coffee. With all the disasters piling up, it occurred to
her that leaving the country might be the best option for all involved. A
historic cottage destroyed, an agent with a broken neck, a lover in the
hospital, a career detective on the ropes, and not an inch closer to finding
Chloe's killers. Sometimes you simply cut your losses and move on.

But for Pia, that smelled like losing.

She sure as hell wasn't going to let Mr. Bling win.

Benton leaned back, tossed his napkin on the table, and looked
surprised when the day butler appeared from thin air to remove his plate.
The butler left a cup of coffee, Pia's recipe, in front of him. His head
swiveled back and forth, unaccustomed to the perfect service.

"You get used to it," Pia said.

Tania chugged half her coffee, then said, "We gotta focus on Mr.
Bling. He's the only one directly connected to Chloe's murder. From the
video, we know his methods were professional, so we know it wasn't a
crime of—"

Benton squinted at her. "You've seen the video?"

Tania realized she'd said something out of turn and glanced at Pia.

"We have a copy," Pia said.

"How'd you get that, then?"

Pia hesitated. "MI5."

"They don't have access to my surveillance system." He took a sip of coffee and smacked his lips. "Do they? Wait, your lot works for them. Jesus, they host our servers. Let me guess, you host their servers which means you're the ones who really host ours. Christ."

"You get used to that too," Pia said. "And then you put black electrical tape over your laptop's video camera."

Benton shook his head and took a big slurp of coffee and peered into the cup. "Say, this is dead good stuff."

Tania continued, "What I was saying is, Mr. Bling's gonna be the main clue. What was he doing in Abby's greenhouse? How come she's gotta bug man showing up for a year but claims she's never heard of him? And then, why is Dame Millie and her low-rent husband holding out on us? How does the Morpheus dupe its customers? Do they really believe that Rational Light crap? Then we gotta look at Skilling. Who izzat guy? He sure as hell ain't named Skilling. Why don't the facial recognition systems identify him? Now, in my experience, that could be cosmetic surgery—or he's managed to get a bunch of passports. Getting multiple ID's into the system will trip it up. Then there's Vermeer and Krueger. We know Mr. Bling didn't kill them. He was too busy trying to kill us. Liam crossed the pond at a damn convenient time for it. Does that make him the mastermind for all of this? And that gives me another question: how do they kill people? The victims always have a heart attack cause of some unknown problem. That's interesting. More interesting is following the money. Skilling takes it in, shares it with the Morpheus through a bunch of shell companies. Who is he paying to do the murders? We gotta get all up in his shell companies to see where the money's being siphoned off."

Benton's eyes were wide, staring at Tania with respect and wonder. Then he looked at his coffee. "This stuff gives you a proper kick then, doesn't it?"

Pia and Tania shared a glance.

"The ME in Vancouver got back to me earlier," Pia said. "The suicide plant would leave a rash. Vermeer didn't have a rash. And, he says it's not as deadly as Abby made it sound. She was being dramatic."

Tania groaned in disappointment. "Well then, like I said, follow the money."

Benton gulped the rest and set down the empty cup. "We don't have probable cause to look at Skilling's books. Unless your friends at MI5 could bend some rules."

"Push your cup outside your place setting if you want it refilled," Pia said.

Benton kept his gaze fixed on her while he followed her instruction by sliding the cup six inches to his left. The butler instantly reappeared, filled his cup, and disappeared. Benton pulled the cup back to center. "You're right. A guy could get used to that."

"MI5 won't help," Pia said. "An operation like this will use Panama, Luxembourg, and Vanuatu with several shell companies going around in circles. Let's say the money moves through ten companies before landing in the Rohans' account. The fourth will keep a little for expenses to pay Mr. Bling. The seventh and eighth will skim payment for anyone else involved. But my trace won't follow it without a fistful of warrants from several countries. I'm working on that, but it'll take time."

Benton nodded his agreement. "You're sure there are others involved?"

"Mr. Bling is a professional," Tania said. "But he's no mastermind. Someone dreamed up the whole scheme. Not Skilling, because he's exposed. The guy who came up with this plan is someone you'd never guess."

Benton looked her over. "You did more in the MPs than ferret out the odd meth dealer. That was all I ever did when I was in."

Tania said, "You learn some stuff on your way to making captain."

"And I never made it past lieutenant." Benton raised his coffee mug to her as a toast.

"That's our biggest question," Pia said. "Who is the mastermind? Whoever he is, he kept all the pieces separated by a firewall."

They each sipped their coffee and considered how big and opaque that virtual wall might be.

After a long stretch of silence, Benton sighed and said, "Bollocks. We've got nothing."

CHAPTER 48

PIA'S PHONE PINGED WITH THE special sound reserved for a text from the Major. She was up and wanted Pia to call.

Her heart stopped. It was time to face up to the latest events of her disastrous vacation. How would the employees regard their figurehead if she went to another country with good intention and instead made a mess? She steeled herself for one of Jonelle Jackson's famous *directional adjustments*. She excused herself from the dining room and made the call.

When the Major answered, Pia stammered out a weak greeting. The connection had an odd sound to it, as if she were in a dark and cavernous hall of stone with the Major at the far end. The sound carried the distance without the need to raise her voice, but it echoed ever so slightly.

"What's on your mind?" the Major asked.

Pia's mind tipped over and spilled everything from Liam's wife and itinerary, to her botched interrogation, to the shooting. When she got to the end, she stopped and waited.

The Major let some time pass. Pia realized she hadn't asked a question so a response might not follow. She wasn't sure what to say next.

The Major broke the silence. "You want me to tell you to come back?"

"No. Yes. I don't know. No. I … We can't go through with the merger, that's all."

"That's not why you called."

Pia wanted to say something, but the Major's first question was the right one and she'd dodged it.

Then the Major asked, "Who do you want to be?"

Pia leaned against the sill and gazed out the window. "I don't know what you mean."

"You weren't happy when Krueger called you a figurehead. Who do you want to be?"

"You said I was a good figurehead."

"I didn't say that's what you want to be."

"I don't …" Knowing the Major would call her out on any more dodged questions, Pia thought through the next five moves and skipped ahead. "I want to be a champion. I want to champion Chloe's cause."

"What made you a champion in the game?"

"Twenty years of fourteen-hour workdays."

"No."

Pia wanted to tell her she was wrong. No one can be the best without putting in the time. It was the fixed rule in any meritocracy. *How do you get to Carnegie Hall? Practice, practice, practice.* But she knew that wasn't where the Major was going. You can't practice unraveling conspiracies. Each one is unique. A game defined by unknown players with equally enigmatic moves. Unlike soccer, there are no rules, no sidelines, no referees. Everything is freeform, spontaneous, and dangerous. Any mistake could be your last.

"You have the confidence to win," the Major said.

"I've never been confident. I was desperate."

"How many soldiers work for you?"

"Twenty thousand."

"Did any of them tell you what courage really is?"

"Yes," Pia said. "When the options are concession or death, courage is the madness that makes you choose to die trying."

"What is that madness called?" the Major asked.

"Desperation."

"Criminals thrive on bravado," the Major said. "They beat their chests and shout their insults. They make noise to drown out the truth. 'Figurehead' is what a weak man calls a strong woman. You can't come home, Pia. You're desperate to expose them. You don't need my permission. Go do it."

She clicked off.

The conspirators' bluff she'd seen earlier through a heavy fog became a little clearer. The vague outlines of a plan for taking down the Morpheus began to take shape in her mind.

She tapped her finger to her lips as she thought. Across the park, Buckingham Palace sparkled in the bright sunshine. She squinted at the distant bluff in her mind. She could see its ridges and footholds. She could visualize how to scale it. She saw vague figures standing at the top, beating their chests like ancient warrior chiefs. They thought they were getting away with it. They thought they were above the rules. They thought she couldn't scale the cliff.

She dialed Albert Tindall. When he picked up, she skipped the pleasantries. "You want to make connections. Tell Chuck Eden-Sonnet I accept his invitation to cocktails. Make it this evening. I also ran into that other guy, Wayne Walker, the podcaster, and confirmed our appointment for tomorrow. Get your ass down here to the Lanesborough and we'll work out details."

He started to thank her profusely.

She cut him off, "No need to fawn. You promised information—and you're going to deliver."

She clicked off and strode into the sitting room where Benton and Tania looked up from their coffee mugs.

"I figured it out," she said. "I've got a plan you're not going to like."

CHAPTER 49

PIA TOOK OFF HER SUNGLASSES to watch the last glimmer of a beautiful sunset fade in the west. Her ponytail whipped at her neck as the cold wind swirled through the convertible.

Tania called. Pia held her phone to her ear so Albert Tindall, her passenger, wouldn't see her hidden earbud.

Tania said, "Tanner finally got something out of the nursing staff. Liam had two broken ribs and a bullet hole in his bicep. Got his arm bandaged up. He left the hospital an hour ago against doctor's orders. He tried to ditch our boys. They let him think he did."

"Where did he go?"

"Glasgow. It seems he's breaking the news to his in-laws in person."

"Not the typical actions of a murderer," Pia observed.

"Could be a cover story. Good news is, he kept his body armor. Getting shot will sober a man up fast. I'll update you when we know more."

Pia clicked off and concentrated on the narrow road meandering through the English countryside.

"It's the road just there," Albert said. Hunkered down in the passenger seat, he pulled his jacket tight around him. "Watch out! We drive on the bloody left."

"Try not to pee your pants and keep talking," she said.

It was no big deal. She'd only swung halfway into the right-hand lane before correcting and there wasn't any traffic. No need to get excited.

He said, "McLaren's going to want their car back in one piece, I reckon."

"It's mine. I bought it."

"You can't just buy a car and have the factory deliver it to your hotel day of." He glanced at her. "Can you?"

"Ever noticed the Sabel logo on their Formula One cars?" she asked. "They love me. I've had four. Wrecked one. Trashed another. Transaxles just aren't built for street racing. Now quit ducking my question."

"I don't know anything about the man."

"I'm not big on jewelry," Pia said. "I wear it to comfort people, make them see that I value them enough to dress up. They know I can afford it, they know I have it, so they expect me to show it off. They feel honored when I trot it out for them."

"Would you please slow down?" Albert snarled. "We do have speed limits here, you know."

"I don't know much about ordinary trinkets," she said, "but I've learned my way around the impressive stuff. That man wore an extraordinary diamond in one ear. He's so proud of it, he doesn't take it off when he goes operational. That's risky. And it's a big diamond. Big enough to glint through a windshield on CCTV. It's a carat, maybe one and a half, too big to be a man's stud. Which means it's from a woman's set. Boodles doesn't make them that big without a surrounding ring of diamond chips. That tells me it's from Tiffany's. And big diamond pairs at Tiffany's are over £20,000. Where would a former Para find that kind of money? Savings? I doubt it. Which means somewhere, a once-rich lady is missing one of her earrings. And that means our guy is not wearing it to impress anyone—it's a trophy. He owns you."

The engine roared behind their heads. Albert kept his nose to his window and squeezed his arms tighter around himself. "Doesn't the heater work in this thing?"

"Your car is ten years old, your furniture is ratty, you stiffed the caterer at your fête—that tells me you're flat broke. You're a former Para, he's a former Para, he's parading around with your wife's diamond in his ear, Albert. Tell me the fucking truth. Did you give it to him? Did he steal it from you? Did it settle a debt? Does Millie know?"

"Of course she knows!" he shouted. "She's not like you, she doesn't have spares. Doesn't dial up the factory to buy a car on a moment's notice."

"What does he have on you?"

"Nothing." He raised his hands in the air, then let them fall on his thighs. "We came home one day and there he was. Sitting in the living room, gin and tonic in one hand, feet on the coffee table, and my wife's jewelry box lying there all strewn about. I knew him in the Paras, hadn't seen him since. Somehow, he knew we were a bit tight and he offered a deal. He wanted Millie's royal connections. Wanted some of them to visit the Morpheus, that was all. I'd get paid good money for bringing them in. Gave me a much-needed advance on commissions. Introductions, he said. Never told me what was to happen next. Nothing about killing anyone. I don't believe that bit, frankly."

"Rough way to recruit someone for a sales job."

"I thought so too, but one must be discreet to land the royal family. I do similar work for Wayne Walker." He twisted in his seat. "I'm quite good at it, you know. I put Walker in touch with some of the top business executives around the world. No one else could get those connections to line up. I'm a master at it."

She hadn't believed a thing he'd said since they got in the car. But his story about Mr. Bling showing up might have a kernel of truth. She asked, "And did you make the royal connections your diamond thief wanted?"

"I tried my best. Rohans didn't pass the royal vetting process. Mr. Bling, as you so inelegantly call him, wanted me to make up for it with the people I'd arranged for Wayne to interview. A few went along, others scoffed at the whole idea. Eventually, I ran out of contacts."

"And that's when I showed up."

"I thought it was a great bit of luck for all of us. I didn't know about the danger. I never expected they'd attack you. Believe me. I had nothing to do with that. Nothing at all. I'm sick about it."

"What's his name?"

Albert choked and dropped his head. "I can't tell you that."

Pia glanced at him. She waited. He wouldn't look up. She said, "I get it. He'll kill you—and you think I won't. Don't push your luck, Albert."

Was Albert the mastermind? Liars often tell a true story with roles reversed. It could have been that Albert gave him the diamond as a down payment for services. Perhaps Albert had failed to pay in a timely manner, like he failed the caterer at the fête, and the rest of the story was true. Mr. Bling had taken the diamond as collateral.

"It's just here." He pointed to a stone fence broken by a steel gate.

They were just outside of Bedford, fifty miles north of London, entering a sixty-acre estate. She pulled to the call box, pressed the button, and waited while the sheet of steel rolled to one side. No visible guards on duty but she sensed their energy close by. One on each side.

Before she could pull in, headlights filled the lane. Another car was leaving. When it pulled out of the private drive, her headlights illuminated the driver for a second. A familiar-looking face. She said, "Isn't that your friend, Walker?"

"It did look like him." Albert sounded surprised. "It would make sense; everyone wants to Walk with Walker. Very popular."

"Did you set up a meeting between Walker and Chuck?"

"Ages ago. He needn't involve me on subsequent visits."

"I thought Chuck was a hermit."

"Really, Pia," he scoffed. "You should call him Lord Eden-Sonnet. It's disrespectful."

She drove through the gate onto a farm lane with barns on one side, stables on the other, then up a curving gravel drive through a row of trees. When they came through, the house appeared. A very neat Queen Anne-style country house. An unimaginative rectangle of red brick with three windows on each side of the front door. Above that, two rows of seven windows were symmetrically aligned to the ground floor. Two chimneys rose in front and two more in back.

She took the turning circle at speed, jammed down three gears, pounded the gas, and spun up the back tires. Gravel sprayed the front door as she slid to a stop.

"Was that necessary?" Albert asked.

"I don't do doorbells."

CHAPTER 50

A BUTLER STEPPED OUT AND examined the gravel damage. With a disapproving scowl, he faced Pia and studied her black athleisure gear, running shoes, and black leather jacket. He turned, gestured for them to follow, and showed them to a drawing room crammed with worldly artifacts from the days of the British Empire. The center was open, with antique furniture facing each other around a Persian rug.

Gripping the back of the largest chair was their host, wearing a gray suit too tight for his girth. Dampness on his forehead glistened in the weak light. His sullen jowls wobbled as he rounded the chair with difficulty. He didn't extend a hand.

Eden-Sonnet said, "I wish I could say it was a pleasure to see you again, but you wore out your welcome when you set foot on British soil. Your new bandage is testimony enough to that fact."

He waddled to his seat and adjusted his slacks.

"Same to you," Pia said. She stood in front of him. "Where are my people?"

Albert crossed his arms and stood behind Eden-Sonnet. From the smug look on his face, he expected the fat man to make quick work of her.

"From what I understand," Eden-Sonnet said, "they never showed up for work this morning. Sit. I have a quick and simple offer to make and we can put this rather unfortunate Vermeer business behind us."

"The only offer I'm making is an exchange for my people in return for a reduced sentence."

"I've no idea what you're referring to, young lady. I've nothing to do with your recalcitrant employees." He gestured to a chair again. "My offer is that I sell you Vermeer only if you go back to America and never speak of me or the Morpheus Institute again."

Pia remained on her feet. "I blackmailed you. Nine hours later, armed gangsters tried to kill me."

"Such an imagination you have," Eden-Sonnet said. He folded his hands across his belly. "You presume I'm the only one in the British Isles you've angered while an endless line has formed stretching from Manchester to London. Presumptuous women never marry yet always wonder why."

"On the first day, my people were given everything they needed to complete their due diligence. But the next morning, they were abducted at the entrance to your building."

Eden-Sonnet turned to Albert, his jowls quivering with resentment. "Americans have given this feminist experiment a bit too much leash, wouldn't you say? It's melting traditional relationships and diluting their institutions."

Pia tracked into his line of sight. "That tells me you're connected to the Morpheus but have no control over the muscle. If you had any, they wouldn't have done it at your building."

"American democracy has devolved into a flailing failure." He glowered at her. "The predictable result of electing those movie stars and reality TV hosts to run the place. They make promises to the foolish masses, pledging to make them rich then do just the opposite. That's what happens when you let the uneducated rabble have a hand in distributing power and control."

"Who controls the man with the diamond earring?"

Eden-Sonnet rose and poked a finger in her chest. "You've not listened to a thing I've said. You've no respect for your betters. Exactly the kind of chaos you and your classless crowd would bring to the Morpheus if they allow it. It works, you know. Rational Light is a gift from the gods. You've no right to it. They were wrong to even show it to you."

Pia frowned in confusion. She thought this was a simple conspiracy that would unravel once he knew she was on to them.

"Rational Light is the exclusive domain of the deserving peerage and others who honor and respect the ancient codes of conduct." Eden-Sonnet's face grew red. "It's the perfect method for achieving one's goals and ambitions. It works where nothing else will. Consider Anton Petrova, an honorable Russian of substantial influence. He snuck into the country twice—at considerable risk—to spend time in the spiritual enlargement chamber. He's done remarkable things and plans a third trip soon."

He wiped his brow with a handkerchief. "You can see the problem we—the worthy—have with the Morpheus admitting the likes of you. Americans have no boundaries, no honor system. With people at your level running around doing things like snatching Vermeer from me, inevitably followed by some other insufferable fool snatching it from you, and then a footman snatching it from them. Why, the whole system breaks down into a typical American morass. Everyone ends up with the same power. The global elite will become what passes for upper class in America: a bunch of little tasteless, tiresome tyrants like you."

She looked down at him. They faced off in silence for a long time. She checked for the tells of liars. His face and gaze were steady. His pupils remained constant. He refrained from hand gestures. He sounded as if he believed the whole thing. How could he? He was a sensible, educated man. No one capable of coherent thought would ever believe in black magic or Rational Light. Yet Eden-Sonnet was convinced Rational Light worked as advertised. Was he that good an actor? Or was he brainwashed?

Eden-Sonnet picked up a service bell and rang it. "We must maintain the ranks at our level or, good heavens, the Americans will eventually invade the House of Lords."

Four black-clad men with automatic rifles materialized in the room. One of them wore a diamond earring.

He leveled his rifle and put a round in her chest.

CHAPTER 51

EVEN THOUGH THE LIQUID ARMOR did its job, the surprise combined with the impact of a supersonic projectile knocked her crashing into a chair behind her. Her chest reverberated with shockwaves of pain while her lungs struggled for air. Voices in the room shouted and screamed. She could hear Tania talking in a calm, practiced voice while suppressing a good deal of anxiety under her breath. That meant the ear-canal comm link was still working. It could only be seen with an otoscope.

Tania's words weren't a top priority. She knew what Tania was asking.

Pia rolled quickly to all fours and tried to stand. A rifle barrel met her cheek. She froze.

As much to Tania as the man with the gun, she said, "What, you want my hands on my head?"

The man jerked his head toward Eden-Sonnet.

"Not in the house, you fool!" Eden-Sonnet shouted. "Take her outside. Hey! Don't you point that thing at me."

The Lord quivered with a shocked-white face in the center of the room, a rifle pressed into his back.

In the comm link, Tania said, "Do you want us to breach now?"

"Wait a minute," Pia said. "What are you doing? Where are the others? What have you done with Bethany and Rain?"

Mr. Bling stepped into her personal space, his diamond glittering. He grinned and backhanded her bandaged cheek.

Pia saw it coming and dodged half the impact. She let him connect to make him feel he'd made his point, preventing a second slap.

"What are you doing, Kieran?" Albert's voice came from behind her.

"Lord Eden-Sonnet, how could you? What is this?"

"They arrived this afternoon," Eden-Sonnet said to Albert. "I had no choice, but they weren't supposed—"

A rifle butt slammed into his round belly, sending him to the floor. One of the men pulled him back to his feet and pressed a finger to his lips. Eden-Sonnet got the message.

While Pia watched the exchange, one of the men pulled her wrists behind her back and slapped on metal handcuffs. A black bag went over her head. Shackles around her ankles. The bag felt like a large pillowcase, extra cloth piled around her neck. Very little light penetrated the cloth.

To warn Tania, she said, "Hey, I can't see."

She was rewarded with a rifle butt to her midriff.

Tania responded, "Hoods are not in the plan, Pia. Do you want us now?"

"I'm fine." She braced for another rifle butt but didn't get one. "I'm fine. Where are the others?"

"I don't like it," Tania said. "But we're standing by outside the perimeter. It'll take us five minutes to cross the property, so don't be pulling one of your Wonder Woman stunts."

A hand gave her a rough push. Another gave her a tug. She followed the unspoken instructions and started walking. Ahead of her, she heard another set of chains dragging across Eden-Sonnet's floors. It had a short stride, indicating the waddle peculiar to her host.

An athlete who relished movement, Pia hated the shackles and hood. Her heart rate accelerated from the growing sense of imminent danger. She stumbled into a lamp. Two hands grabbed her before she fell and pulled her upright.

She hadn't expected Eden-Sonnet to be taken prisoner. She'd expected him to give orders. Was she wrong about Eden-Sonnet, or was this staged? And where was Albert?

The sound of the footsteps in front of her changed, from solid floors to what she guessed were stairs. A hand stopped her, then inched her forward. She felt carefully for the first riser. When she understood the tread width, her guide picked up the pace. They were efficient and purposeful. A pre-planned exercise.

She smelled musty dampness. A basement. The sensation of other people nearby.

A woman's voice said, "Who's there? Who's—"

Whump. A rifle butt silenced her.

"Bethany?" Pia risked.

"Ms. Sabel?"

This time they both got slammed. *Whump. Whump.*

Pia doubled over. The ache in her gut was mitigated by her body armor. Bethany had none. She couldn't imagine how much pain her employee endured. The sound of gasping echoed in a small space.

"Rain?" she asked.

"Here," he replied.

They both paid for their words. *Whump. Whump.*

Nothing pissed her off more than being under someone else's control. She expected to be taken prisoner, that was part of the plan, but not blindfolded and shackled. Losing control of her athletic advantages put them all in grave danger. She needed to get the hood off fast.

Someone turned her and pushed her forward again. Now four pairs of chained feet shuffled single file. She was second in line. From the sound of it, Eden-Sonnet first. Rain and Bethany behind her. A hundred short, restricted steps across a cracked cement floor. A clumped collapse of clothing and soft body tissue thumped on the floor. Someone had fallen. Whoever it was said nothing. They were helped to their feet and the hobbling resumed.

"Sounds like you've found them," Tania said. "We're coming in now. If you want us to hold off, cough real hard."

Pia considered the options. Whatever Mr. Bling had planned was coming soon. She saw no option for a heroic escape. No wonder-woman moments. She made no sound.

"Alright then," Tania said, "gonna take five minutes to cross the farm here. Hang on until then."

A door creaked open. Cold night air whirled around her feet. Grass. A slope. From her research, Pia recalled that Eden-Sonnet's house sat on a gentle incline, the basement partially open at the back. From there, his property ran down three hundred yards to a lake a mile long. A wooden dock stretched deep into the lake.

They stumbled on the uneven ground. Pia found a gopher hole the hard way. Unseen hands picked her up. Bethany's voice cried out and thumped on the ground. Pia was shoved forward.

Their abductors marched them to the dock as shouts came from the front of the main house.

"Carry on, gentlemen." A harsh voice with a Scottish accent commanded.

Mr. Bling, she presumed. No doubt a reaction to seeing concerns in his men. It's easy to get tough guys to do tough jobs under the cover of darkness. But when the long arm of the law takes a swipe, discipline breaks down quickly. Every man for himself.

Someone pushed her.

Ahead of her, footsteps landed on wooden planks. The group shuffled onto the dock. Hands pushed her over a distance longer than she expected. They stopped. The planks creaked. Eden-Sonnet whimpered. Bethany and Rain stayed silent. Water lapped against the hull of a small boat.

"He'll sink the damn thing," someone said.

"Take him first, then come back for the others." That from the commanding voice.

Eden-Sonnet's quivering voice shouted, "No, you mustn't do—"

They hit him in the gut again. He moaned.

An outboard motor burbled to life and took the boat from the dock. It went a good distance across the lake.

She felt the contagious fear radiating from the others. The black-out hood created an ominous sensation of helplessness. Combined with the removed location from the house, the only conclusion one could draw was that an imminent death awaited them. The lake was a handy disposal site. The boat would have weights in it to carry their bodies to the bottom. Divers might find them, but little evidence would remain to identify their killers.

Pia didn't see any option. She had to do something. Wooden planks creaked near her as a guard shifted his weight.

Across the water, a gunshot cracked the silence. A splash followed. The boat motor rose in volume as it headed back for the next victim.

Tania's voice in the comm link: "What was that?"

"We're at the boat dock, back of—"

A rifle slammed into her again, giving her the exact position of the man wielding it. Pia bent her knees and, squatting low, leaned toward the rifleman and jumped upward. As she hoped, her shoulder connected with a body. He fell sideways into the lake.

She staggered and regained her balance just in time to stop herself from following her victim overboard. She leaned back into the person behind her. "Bite in front of you until you get my hood, then pull back."

The form felt male, possibly Rain. He did what she asked. His teeth grazed the side of her head until he found enough cloth to grip. He also got some of her ear, but let it go and re-bit the cloth before yanking backward. She dropped down. The hood came off.

Orienting herself quickly, she located two men on a boat coming toward them. The man she'd knocked into the water tried to swim to the pier, weighed down by his body armor and weapons. He was the biggest threat.

His large hand reached a pylon and pulled hard.

Shackled, Pia couldn't kick his head. She dropped to the planks, positioned her butt at the edge and kicked both shackled feet hard into his face. He fell backward with a gurgle of inhaled water.

Her hooded companions started shrieking, confused in their blindness about who was in the water.

Pia looked around quickly for the fourth man, the one with the diamond earring. Nowhere to be seen.

Flashlights flickered from the back of the house. Tania and her agents on their way.

The men in the boat saw the lights and turned the boat, arcing away into the dark. Every man for himself.

Pia pulled her feet up, trying to step through the cuffs on her wrists. Flex cuffs have more give in the middle and would have allowed her to push her feet through, but the metal ones were too tight. Instead of getting stuck, she gave up and scrambled to her feet. Mr. Bling had to be around somewhere. She peered into the darkness as the man thrashing in the water made his way back to the dock.

Torn between the imminent threat of the drowning man and the ominous threat of the missing Mr. Bling, she made one more quick survey of the area for the leader.

Nothing.

When her scrutiny returned to the man in the water, she found herself looking down the muzzle of his rifle. Too late to replay her earlier kicking trick. She dove sideways, knocking Bethany to the boards as the man fired a three-round burst.

Nothing struck her. She knew he'd reacquire her as a target, so she rolled onto her back and popped up to her feet. She saw the barrel track her and dove to the planks again as another three bullets buzzed her ears.

A pistol fired from shore. To Pia's ear, it sounded like a Glock—hopefully Tania's.

A flashlight beam swept over the dock. The man in the water fell back and submerged, his head bloody and lifeless.

The beam of light continued sweeping the area as second and third beams joined.

"You good, Pia?" Tania's voice called from the bank.

"Yes, thank you," she said. "One more shooter unaccounted for. Mr. Bling."

Benton ran onto the dock. He helped Pia to her feet and almost hugged her. "When we heard the shot, we feared the worst."

"Didn't know you cared."

"Of course. You owe me a career." He guided her turn. "Let me get those cuffs."

As Benton worked the lock, he called over his shoulder to Tania, "That was a damn fine shot, ma'am.'"

"Thank you," Tania replied. "Had to do it. He was about to mess with my meal ticket."

Benton worked on Bethany while Pia removed the young woman's hood.

With her arms free, Bethany gave Pia a silent and shivering hug. Pia held her as long as she needed. Bethany sniffled, stood up straight, and gave her a nod when she was ready to move on.

When she removed the last hood, she found a clean-cut young man with wide eyes.

She frowned and said, "Who the hell are you?"

"Rain Meyer," he said before getting her joke. "Yeah, cleaned up. Hey, were they going to kill us? They were, weren't they? They killed Lord Eden-Sonnet. Holy shit. Did they dump him in the lake? Was that the splash? Did we just survive getting murdered? But we made it. Thanks to you. Wow. We almost got killed. Holy shit. I've got to admit, I've never been so scared in my life."

"That's your adrenaline talking," Pia said.

Benton worked on Rain's cuffs. He said, "Right. Hanging around her is dangerous."

Pia shrugged at Rain. "You get used to it."

CHAPTER 52

BEDFORDSHIRE'S CHIEF INSPECTOR SUSAN BARNETT took detailed notes during her interrogations. Without a warrant or credible sign of imminent threat, her department had not gone along on the initial operation. They remained on the road until called. Only Sabel agents had swarmed the premises. In their statements, Pia and her team went over the details patiently and professionally. Bedfordshire's finest patiently and professionally listened. With Benton's help, the two teams lined up the evidence to corroborate the narrative.

Then a new man showed up. He pushed through a clump of constables and tapped Benton. He glanced at Pia, then did a second glance at her black eye and bandage before facing Benton.

He said, "Superintendent Martin, Eastern Region ROCU."

Benton shook his hand. "NCA then?"

"Right."

"You just got here?" Pia asked. "Where the hell have you been? Where're your people?"

"And you must be the American I've heard tell about." He didn't offer her a hand to shake.

"Pia Sabel. I'm the American who bothered to rescue four kidnap victims when NCA wouldn't."

"That was a headquarters decision. I'm here now and will assess the situation. I understand from Bedfordshire that Lord Eden-Sonnet has passed. They'll have the lake cleared in the morning." He pointed at the dead gunman lying on the shore. "They have determined this poor chap brought about his own demise by firing on—"

"Do you actually do anything, Martin?" Pia asked. "Ten hours ago, we explained to you all about the organized crime operation that carried out Chuck's assassination. That falls under your watch, doesn't it? I heard ROCU stands for Regional Organized Crime Unit. Why were my people storming the gates alone?"

"I beg your pardon," Superintendent Martin said. "We know all about you and your MI5 connections, Ms. Sabel. If this is a design of yours to force the NCA to hire on Sabel Industries in some—"

Benton saw Pia about to explode and pulled the man's sleeve. "I'm the liaison here. Have you met Ms. Sabel's VP of Protection, Tania Cooper? She's a helluva shot and quite an interrogator as well. Ms. Cooper led the rescue operation with astonishing efficacy. She helped out the RMPs in the war, as well. She's quite a remarkable woman, really." Benton pointed to a nearby tree. "I'll fill you in. Let's have a chat just there, shall we?"

As the two men moved a good distance away, Martin glowered over his shoulder at Pia.

Tania handed her a paper cup. "Locals are nice though. Barnett brought tea."

Pia took the cup and wondered if Eden-Sonnet would've survived had the NCA not been in a territorial spat with MI5 over her company's services. Internecine squabbles happened all the time, throughout the world, in every bureaucracy. How many people died because of middle-management egos?

She tasted the tea. "Hmmm. Pleasant and soothing. Maybe this stuff does serve a purpose after all."

Albert walked nearby flanked by a constable.

"Where have you been?" Pia called out. "Why didn't they drag you out to the dock with us?"

"Why don't you ask them?" he shouted back. "Oh. I see. You've gone and lost them and in your tiny mind that's my fault."

The constable tugged Albert's sleeve and pointed toward the chief inspector. They marched on.

Turning back to Pia, Tania said, "Tanner called. Liam's in-laws are taking him to a car rental place."

Pia frowned. "He's renting a car in Glasgow? To go where? Why?"

"Help us—or cover his tracks." Tania shrugged. "I don't know what to think about him."

"But you know what to think about Abby."

"Well, something's going down at Abby's. Maybe she's scared of Mr. Bling. Or do you believe she had a 'bug man' all up in her greenhouse and she don't know?"

Pia sipped her tea as she thought about that. Bethany waved goodbye to a constable who'd been reviewing her statement and wandered near the lake edge. Pia said, "Would Bethany know anything?"

Tania watched their rescued executive. "If she did, it wouldn't be much, but worth a shot. I'll check. You go make your call, and we'll compare notes in a minute."

Pia watched Tania walk away while wondering what call she was supposed to make. Then it came to her. She dialed Liam.

"Aye, and what do you want then?" he asked.

Pia felt her confidence slip. Who was she talking to, the charming Scot—or a man who bashed his wife's face in? A mastermind who killed Krueger and Vermeer, then came to her bed? Or the man who hoped to sell her his company to spare his employees the indignity of unemployment?

She sucked it up and said, "Why are you in Glasgow?"

"What's it matter to you?" He heaved his words with an angry breath. "You think I'm guilty of … I don't even know what all. What do you care where I am or where I'm going?"

"I tried to reach you at the hospital. I want to know if you're OK."

"Well I'm not, am I? Got shot this morning. Put a bloody bullet through my arm."

"I'm sorry. I should've cancelled the mission when I found out how vicious they are."

"And what good would that've done after you found out someone murdered my wife? You think I did that. I saw it on your face."

There was no point denying it. She could only change the subject. "What's in Glasgow?"

"Before the shooting started, I was going to claim her remains and bring her home. Seemed like the decent thing to do. Scotland Yard told me not to leave the country, so I've had to leave the arrangements to her parents now, thanks to you."

"I'll help," Pia said. "I'll have my people contact her family and cover all the arrangements and expenses. Where are you going now?"

"I'm going to prove myself innocent, since you've convicted me."

"You need protection. My people are—"

"Aye, right," he said. "You'll have your people keep an eye on me. Find out where I'm going and what I'm doing. I'll tell you right off: I'm going to the Morpheus to get this all sorted. I don't need your people reporting back about everything I do."

"Don't go there. The killers are out there. They're still dangerous and they still have a contract out on you. You need my agents to keep you safe."

"That's how it is, is it?" he asked. "I say no and that makes me look guilty as hell. I say yes and I can't go to the loo without a man holding my dick for me. What good is that? How do I have a conversation with this Rohan fella if I've got one of your men standing over my shoulder? Ach, bloody hell. I'm starting to sound guilty to myself now."

"These people just executed Lord Eden-Sonnet. You need protection. If you don't want my people, hire someone else. G4S is one of our competitors. They have offices in Glasgow. Hire them and I'll pay for it."

"And they'll not tell you anything? That wanker from Manifest Morals was right about your kind. Corrupt, the lot of you. Always suspecting people of taking something from you. Well, you had me fooled, Pia Sabel. Aye, I did know who you were in that coffeeshop. I felt something real and honest. I thought you felt it too. Now I see you're too paranoid about all that stuff you own to know when someone's having a wee flirt. Well, don't worry, I'm not taking anything from you."

"You're taking *you* from me …" She trailed off when she realized the line was dead.

Superintendent Martin marched towards her with Benton trotting alongside. Benton appeared to be making a last-ditch effort to change the man's mind about his conclusions. Martin wasn't having it.

Tania came toward her on a different angle. Martin arrived first.

NCA's man in Bedford said, "We've been over the incident report and you're damn lucky the local constabulary isn't keen on taking you in for interference."

"Are you serious?" Pia's voice betrayed her anger. "They'd have killed all of us—"

"There's no evidence of organized crime here. Your man Benton has explained your theory involving the Morpheus Institute. Where is the connection, we wonder? We don't see one. No evidence tying them—or anyone else—to this unfortunate murder. We will monitor the situation but are leaving this matter to Chief Inspector Barnett. She's doing a brilliant job."

"You didn't notice the dead man had expensive body armor and carried an illegal automatic weapon? Where do you think a gangster-for-hire got that?"

"I am hereby ordering you to stay clear of the Morpheus Institute. You are not to mess about with British institutions or businesses in any manner. And—before you say anything—I am keenly aware of your connections at the highest levels of MI5 and MI6. Having a permit to brandish deadly weapons is not an investigator's license. Do you understand my orders?"

Pia gritted her teeth while doing her best to maintain a mildly pleasant expression. "I have an appointment at the Morpheus tomorrow afternoon. Do I have your permission to keep it? I paid £5 million to have my chakra repaired, or whatever they do, and I understand there are no refunds for cancellations. Or is the NCA prepared to cover my expenses?"

"The NCA won't be covering any expenses." Martin folded his hands behind his back and pursed his lips. "Well. If it's an appointment already made, I suppose that would be alright. Otherwise, I'm going to take your word for it that you'll keep your nose out of this affair. This is official police business. Good evening, Ms. Sabel."

Superintendent Martin strode away in the dark.

Pia looked at Benton and waited for an explanation.

Benton lifted his hands in the air, palms up. "What can I say? He's put himself and the Eastern ROCU in the perfect bureaucratic position. If

Barnett finds the killers and they turn out to be organized in any fashion, he can step in and take over. If they don't and the whole thing turns ugly, meaning they can't find who murdered a local lord, he can claim it was a simple murder. Nothing to do with him. Now he's going to bed to get a good night's sleep."

Pia marveled at Martin's middle-management efficiency. A credit to his caste.

Tania said, "Tanner used that old 'hey buddy, do me a favor, my job's on the line' routine. It worked. Liam's riding with them. Bethany doesn't know anything about Abby. Her relationship hasn't gotten beyond hot sex yet."

"Let's leave them a little privacy in that regard." Pia started up the hill.

"Girl, you can't get squeamish if you're gonna investigate." Tania kept up with Pia's long strides. "You're gonna need details to corroborate their stories. I mean, did Bethany really have her first multi? If they both say the same—"

"First what? Oh! Never mind. I get it. You've got them covered, that's all I need to know."

"Where are you going?" Benton asked. He still stood where they'd last spoken.

Pia stopped and faced him. "Every place Martin told me not to."

CHAPTER 53

PIA DROVE BACK TO LONDON alone to do some thinking. Despite having stayed in the correct lane the whole way, all she could think about was Liam. Did he hate her? Seemed like it. Was he the mastermind she was looking for? Could she trust herself to think rationally?

Benton and Tania followed, hoping to dislodge something from their passenger, Albert Tindall. No luck, Tania reported on arrival. He'd refused to speak. They had decided to deal with him in the morning and spent the drive chatting about their careers instead. Bethany and Rain came to London in one of the three other Sabel Security cars. A Sabel jet collected Dame Millie and Abby for their own safety. Given the events of the evening, neither complained. Especially when they found Sabel agents roaming Pia's floor in the Lanesborough. Nor did they complain about their rooms in the suite.

Pia did a wake-up run hours before dawn that took her down the Thames, across Tower Bridge and back, around the City of London, circling Saint Paul's Cathedral, before going back to the hotel the long way. Plenty of time for thinking. She came up with several good ideas about how to unmask the mastermind.

She wanted someone to challenge her ideas, so she waited until sunrise at five. Then waited another hour and a half. Then she went into Tania's room. "Tania, guess what? I have—Oh. Sorry. I, uh … it'll wait until breakfast."

Pia backed out as Tania raised a scowl over Benton's chest.

"Sorry," Pia whispered one more time.

Closing the door behind her, she did more thinking before a reminder popped up about her interview with Wayne Walker. She considered cancelling it until she realized she could use it as leverage with Albert Tindall. She wondered if Walker were any good at interviews. Not that it would matter. She could do interviews in her sleep. They'd been a staple in her life since her freshman year in high school.

Finally, Tania and Benton staggered out, dressed but still sleepy. Before they could discuss Pia's ideas, the Tindalls arrived, then Rain Meyer a minute later. They assembled in the dining room, where the morning butler took their orders and served Pia's coffee.

Abby and Bethany opted to stay in their room, trying to keep a good distance from Tania. Pia couldn't blame them. Those questions could wait.

Albert and Dame Millie sat as still and pale as ghosts. Rain studied the décor as if convinced he'd sold his soul to the devil. Even Pia thought the opulence exceeded the let-them-eat-cake threshold.

Tania and Benton sat opposite each other sharing a nervous glance every few seconds. No one knows how to behave the morning after. Not even uber-confident Tania.

Benton made a show of setting his phone to record and setting it in the center of the table. "This may not be an official setting, but my questions are part of an official investigation, Albert. Do you understand?"

"I've nothing to say."

Pia said, "You get paid a commission if I keep my appointment with Wayne Walker, right? We're set for this morning. What happens if I cancel it?"

"Blackmail, is it?" he asked. "You would resort to that. I'll tell you what I can."

"We want our solicitor," Dame Millie said.

"If you drag an attorney in," Pia said, "the questions will be asked in a police station. The press will have pictures of you coming and going. Someone in the station will leak your statements because someone always does. Your involvement in Chuck's death will become common knowledge. The police may or may not provide protective custody from Mr. Bling. Answer questions here, and I guarantee you protection and anonymity—up to a point."

Dame Millie folded her hands in her lap and lowered her chin.

Down the table, Rain's jaw dropped.

"You can call it corruption," Pia said to him, "or you can call it effective. Do you have a better idea?"

Rain thought it over and gave a shrug of approval.

After establishing everyone present for the recording, Benton said, "Albert, who were the men who killed Lord Eden-Sonnet?"

"They put a bag over my head. I didn't see any of them."

"Before they put a bag over your head, did you recognize any of them?"

"No."

Pia put a hand on Benton's wrist, silently asking permission to speak. He gave her a subtle nod. She said, "Albert, what is Kieran's last name?"

Albert's gaze snapped to her so quickly she thought he might break his neck.

Benton eyed her suspiciously while thumbing through his notes. When he found the reference in her statement he smiled as if to say, *I missed it.* He faced Albert again.

She said, "You called him Kieran before they put the sack on your head."

Albert folded his arms and stared at the table.

Dame Millie sent a pleading glance to Pia. They feared Kieran—Mr. Bling—no matter how well-intentioned her offer to protect them. Benton caught Pia's gaze, telling her he understood the problem. Something they would have to work out some other way.

The staff flowed in on silent feet, serving each guest their order with flawless precision. Salmon and blinis for both Tindalls, avocado toast for Rain, a double veggie and bacon omelet for Pia, and eggs Benedict for Benton and Tania.

As forks and knives scraped fine china, Benton resumed his questions. "Who is this Geoffrey Skilling who collects large sums of money from the Morpheus Institute's guests?"

"I don't know anything about that. No one's ever mentioned money to me. When I was a client, they charged a fee, £500 for a month's sessions. I understand they've a benefactor now. Funded by donations instead of fees."

"Have they told you anything about the benefactor?"

"No. Only that there's no fee for people at a certain level."

"You've made some introductions before Ms. Sabel. Who were they?"

"Eden-Sonnet, Kusumawati, Duval, Petrova, Santos, and Krueger."

Benton and Tania shared a knowing glance with Pia: the names from Chloe's list.

Benton said, "They must have asked you to make other introductions, perhaps people you've not yet brought to them."

Albert recited a list of names that sounded like Europe's elite class.

"What is the extent of your introduction? At what point do you hand off prospective customers to the Rohans?"

"Once they attend their first session, I'm done."

Pia leaned forward and asked, "You haven't been paid for introducing me?"

"Not as yet, no." Albert refused to face her.

"My session is later this afternoon. When will you be paid?"

"After you leave. It's a wire transfer."

"And how much am I worth to you?" Pia asked.

Albert took his time wiping his lips with his napkin. "Fifty thousand."

Benton whistled. Rain nearly fell off his chair.

Calmly, Benton asked, "Did it occur to you that was a good deal of money for an introduction?"

"Not at all," Albert said smugly. "In mergers and the like, the right introduction at the right time can earn you millions. I complained about the sparse arrangements but to no avail."

Rain was apoplectic.

Benton continued, "Did you happen to notice the extraordinarily fortunate events that befell your guests shortly after their sessions at the Morpheus? I'm referring to buying companies at half-price or seeing competitors collapse in bankruptcy."

"Not really, no. People at their level always have the best luck. That's how they get to their level."

"Albert," Pia said softly, "am I going to survive my session this afternoon?"

"Why wouldn't you?" he asked with indignation. "You're one of their clients. Once you're done, Krueger will be a problem no longer."

Pia, Benton, and Tania shared quick glances. However the communications system among the conspirators worked, no one had updated Albert on Pia's change in victims. Yet Krueger was dead—ahead of schedule. A puzzle the three of them found confusing.

"But Krueger was one of your introductions," Benton said.

"It would seem he's fallen out of favor," Albert replied. "No one explained that to me. I've not been paid for introducing him even though he's been through."

Dame Millie rolled her eyes to the heavens and bit her lip.

"How long after I'm done will Krueger stop being a problem?" Pia asked.

"From what the satisfied customers tell me, their problems are resolved in twelve to twenty-four hours."

As soon as he'd spoken, Dame Millie slammed her fist across his chest. She sneered at him, "You bloody fool." To Benton, she said, "All appearances aside, we will make no further comment without our solicitor."

She snapped her fingers and, when the butler arrived, asked for fresh-squeezed orange juice as if it would be her last. Pia told the man to serve the Tindalls in to-go cups. They wouldn't be staying.

The meeting reminder for Walking with Walker pinged. It was the last thing to finish before returning to the Peak District and her Rational Light session at the Morpheus.

She wondered how much danger Liam would be in if she went through with her session at the Morpheus. His fate could end up like Abby's: only his death would prove his innocence.

Tania sensed her concern. "He's safe," she said. "Tanner and the other guy are with Liam now. He made them give up their phones, so we won't get any updates. But I put the fear of God into them earlier. He won't be doing anything bad. If he even takes a piss, one of our guys will hold his dick for him."

CHAPTER 54

Wayne Walker waited in the lobby, dressed in a long coat and sweater, reading his phone. He leapt to his feet when Pia approached and greeted her with a disarming smile. "Ah, Ms. Sabel, good to see you again. Enjoying London, are we?"

Pia exchanged pleasantries as she studied him. He didn't shake hands. He kept them behind his back. He spoke in a slow and careful voice. She didn't know much about English accents but had the impression he was hiding his. Putting on airs, perhaps? The Lanesborough could bring out the uncertain social status in anyone.

With gloved fingers, he fitted her with a lavalier mic and led her outside. They crossed into Hyde Park and made their way to a sparsely populated gravel footpath before beginning the interview.

Walker's first question: "How old were you when you first drank from the skull of an enemy?"

Recalling that he'd promised to ask this question when they first met, she calmly deadpanned, "Four."

His eyebrows rose. "Quite literally then? When you killed Leroy Johnson, the man who murdered your mother?"

Trying to rein in her shock, Pia faced him and studied the smirk on his pudgy face. She noted the mischievous twinkle in his blue eyes. Walker had done his homework and was proud of it.

"Don't be so surprised, Ms. Sabel," he said. "The police reports were released with your name redacted, but not Alan Sabel's. One has only to research a bit here and there to find it all. No one's done that before?"

"Plenty," she said with ice. "The others have had the decency to leave my childhood trauma out of the interview."

"All very well and good for the common 'casters, but my listeners want to know what drives the driven. They want to see the crucible in which you were forged. They want to feel the origins of your core philosophy." His gaze scoured hers. "You're scared to death of losing. Is that because you lost your parents at such a tender age?"

Pia repressed a growing urge to kick him in the balls.

But she remembered Abby telling her not to be an emotional holdout. Maybe it was time to talk openly about what she hoped to leave in therapy. Nothing makes it go away, they said. Talking about it dilutes the terror.

They passed a memorial to the dead of some long-forgotten battle. Several yards to their left, a mother and child attempted to launch a kite. Warm sunshine glinted off every blade of grass. Perhaps it was time for her to forget the dead and fly her own kite.

"You could make an argument for that scenario," she said. "Sounds a bit Freudian though, doesn't it?"

Walker smiled. They walked on. He left a silence for her to fill.

"Trauma like that fills every moment of your life," she said. "There are many ways to deal with that residual fear. You can let it consume you, leaving you unable to function. Or you can use it to drive you. I chose the latter."

"Is that what fuels your extraordinary willpower?"

"I've never made a conscious decision to do this or that because of what happened then or in later events. I've always sought to stay one step ahead of the bad guys."

"Obviously, you saw your football competition as bad guys. Do you feel the same way about your corporate rivals?"

"No to both," she said quickly. "I'm talking about people who destroy other human beings. Whether it's a corrupt politician or organized criminals, I bring them to justice. No one should have to suffer the loss of a loved one to violence."

He nodded as if this were a wise statement. "You keep your goals in front of you?"

"Exactly. Always know what you're after and head straight for it."

"And crush everything between you and the goal, is that it?" The mischievous gleam returned in his eyes.

Sensing he was digging for a sensational headline, she said, "Crush the destructive elements that oppress people."

"Is that why you came to England, to free the oppressed from their inevitable destruction?"

"A friend of mine was murdered. I came to find her killers."

"Are you close to revealing them?"

"Not as close as I'd like, but closer than they realize."

"You intend to dominate the police investigation, then?" His words were delivered playfully, almost a tease, as if urging her to utter another ill-advised statement that would scroll across social media for a week.

"We have offered them every assistance they were willing to take. Unfortunately, the NCA were not in sync with us in time to save Lord Eden-Sonnet last night. But we hope to get ahead of the killers soon."

"Excuse me." Walker's face turned white. "What happened to Lord Eden-Sonnet?"

"He was murdered by the same man who killed Chloe England."

She watched Walker dissolve in shock and surprise. She hadn't expected him to be so fond of obscure lords, but he seemed genuinely shaken. The English saw their extended royalty as an inviolable institution. Even upstart podcasters.

"Do you plan to murder these killers?" he asked.

"What?"

"You've been in the news several times after rather controversial shootouts with criminals. Conveniently for you, the authorities always pronounce it some form of self-defense, but you popped them just the same. And then there's the less-than-public slayings, like Viktor Popov. Everyone knows you murdered him in cold blood. You're a serial killer. How do you get off acting high and mighty about who killed Chloe England?"

The urge to kick the arrogant bastard returned with a vengeance. She took a deep breath and said, "If you have a shred of evidence to back up your bullshit, tell it to the authorities. Since you haven't done that, it's obvious you're peddling lies."

Walker looked as if she had kicked him. He seethed for a minute before pulling himself together. "You're on the verge of catching Lord Eden-Sonnet's murderers then?"

Pia glanced at the time. Barely enough to get out of London and up to the Morpheus for her appointment. She thought about what lay ahead and how to determine who was the mastermind behind the whole operation. One thing was for sure: she didn't have time for this interview. She said, "This has been nice, Wayne. But duty calls—I must be going. I've a question for you, though. Albert Tindall told me he gets a commission from lining up your interviews. Is he good at it?"

"Are you applying for the job?" Walker leaned in with a grin, his affable side having recovered. "You have remarkable contacts."

"I'm asking if he's as connected as he claims. I might need his services. Would you recommend him?"

"Depends," he said. "He knows people and they like him. He's like the rich kid who hangs around the club all day. Everyone knows him and likes him enough, so why not do him a good turn? He got me in front of society people and executives—like you. Has his limits, though. Tried to outsource his work once."

Pia's brain kept working on who the mastermind might be while Wayne Walker waited for a reaction with his standard smug look. Dr. Harrison had warned her that avoiding the tragedy of her childhood clouded her thinking. And Wayne had brought it all back. Chasing Chloe's killer was an excuse not to deal with her past. Strangely enough, it worked out as a form of circular therapy, each topic informing the other. Sometimes taking a step back from the problem helped focus on it. And diving into her past helped her see who killed Chloe England.

Everything clicked into place. At their first meeting, Eden-Sonnet had said, "Isn't that grand." Now she knew what he meant. The clues had been there all along.

What had been a distant bluff through thick fog at the beginning, and had become clearer as she discovered different aspects, now came into sharp relief. She knew who stood astride the bluff and who guarded the approaches. A theory formed in her mind about how the killer operated and why the poison used was untraceable. Benton had told her criminals became overconfident when they got away with their crimes. All she needed was to prove it. Evidence. And for that, she knew where to look.

It was time to go. She backed up a step. Looking for a polite way to wrap up the interview, she said, "You keep Albert busy and the Morpheus Institute uses him too. That speaks well of him."

"The who? Oh, that place up in the Peak District. They hire him on a bit, do they? I wouldn't know about them at all. Are you off then? This is all I get?" He looked annoyed.

"Actually, you mentioned you had dirt on Liam Pickford. What is it?"

"If I tell you, do I get another ten minutes?"

"If it's something my extensive research hasn't turned up."

"His wife cleaned out his company bank account and ran off with an Iranian." His grin returned.

"Knew that," Pia said. "She was killed in Croatia."

She didn't know about the woman draining the company of cash, though. That gave Liam motive and explained his desperation to sell the company.

Wayne's grin grew. "He did it, I'll wager."

"What kind of dirt do you have on the Tindalls?"

"What? Nothing." His demeanor reversed again. "Like I said, Albert's a fine chap for some purposes. Don't know much about her."

"This has been enlightening," she said. "Thank you, but I must run."

"Alright then." He reached for her mic with a cleaning wipe in his gloved hand.

Pia backed up three steps and pulled the mic off herself. She tossed it to him from ten feet away. "Thanks."

She turned and ran back to the hotel.

Behind her, he called out, "I didn't think you meant 'run' literally."

CHAPTER 55

SABEL ONE ROARED ITS WAY northward to Manchester while Pia searched for another ebook on the Chocó tribes of South America. The last two included little about the pre-Columbian life of the obscure indigenous peoples. Apparently, the Spanish worked them to death and spread disease among the rest, without ever bothering to document their way of life. Finally, she found a book on the Embera which led her to another on the Wounaan peoples. She skimmed through it before finding what she needed to know. There were no examples or diagrams. She memorized the important part by muttering to herself, "It all makes sense now. The fear of death. Desperation."

Her next research project was the Walking with Walker podcast. The man had an impressive list of interviews with business leaders. His questions to her had been upsetting. From the sensationalized descriptions on his episodes, it appeared to be his claim to fame. What had he said? His listeners wanted to see the crucible in which you were forged. It was the one thing most CEOs always loved to talk about: themselves. Pia's PR manager had told her he had lots of listeners but few subscribers. What did that mean? She researched the podcast on Chartable.com to see how Walker ranked. Fairly low in subscriptions, regular listeners that formed the basis for advertising revenue. Yet many of the episodes had tens of thousands of listeners. That indicated success. She checked the podcast site again to see how long he'd been doing it. The list of interviews was extensive, several years. And the list of interviewees was revealing and impressive. It took her a moment to understand what that meant. When it came to her, she said out loud, "Damn."

Bianca texted her an update, "Croatia has no record of Liam Pickford entering the country through passport control at any time. I've attached the contact info for the detective on the case."

Knowing Croatia's extensive and porous coastline was the reason for the equivocation about passport control, she dialed the detective. His accent was so bad she wasn't sure she understood him, but she got the gist of where his investigation was headed. She thanked him and clicked off.

Rain Meyer stood nervously in the aisle. She sensed he had something to say and motioned him forward. He shook his head. That got the attention of both Benton and Tania sitting next to her at a table for four. The two of them had been snuggling like otters and she welcomed the break. Pia excused herself and led Rain to a grouping of chairs farther forward.

"What is it?" she asked.

"A dilemma," he said as he took his seat. He grimaced. "I've done something that could be considered corrupt."

Pia wanted to laugh and make a joke about losing his moral virginity. She took pity on him. "And you want me to absolve you? You called me part of the corruption."

"Yeah," he tucked his hands between his knees. "I'm starting to see how that happens."

"OK, what did you do?"

"You know I hacked Eden-Sonnet's email. And I stopped when you sent word to keep out of it because they'd catch me. Well, he's dead, he has no heirs, and no one's minding the store. So, curiosity got to me and I dove back in."

"And?" She sensed his conflict about hacking emails of the dead. It was not so long ago that she too considered morality to be a black-and-white proposition. Over the years, she'd made a few similar bargains. It was sad to see him wrestle with that inevitable choice. And at the same time, reassuring. At least he cared.

"Most hackers look at inboxes, whereas I prefer sent files." He hung his head in shame. "People delete everything, but they never delete the reply. Those are the important ones. There wasn't much incriminating in there. Either he was careful, or maybe he used a different account. So, I searched for obvious stuff like Morpheus, Rohan, Tindall, and so on. That's when I found an email where he replied to Albert Tindall." Rain glanced over his shoulder at the back of the plane, where the Tindalls sat. "Albert asked Eden-Sonnet if he had any employees who could make calls for him. Helping him set up appointments."

Rain glanced around again, then looked up at Pia. "Eden-Sonnet recommended Bella Davis—three weeks before she died."

Pia couldn't help but look past Rain at the Tindalls. They whispered to each other in the back row. Walker had told her Albert had outsourced part of his work. She wanted to go back there and beat the truth out of them. Had they masterminded the whole thing? They knew a lot more than they were saying.

Pia replayed their first meeting in her head. They had picked her up at Manchester airport and taken her to meet Benton. The Tindalls had been keen on knowing Chloe's message to Pia. Had she told them Chloe was relaying Bella Davis's final statement? No. Their interest indicated they knew something was wrong. They quickly defended the Morpheus and threw her off the subject. What was that about? She should ask them. Or not.

Pia's disastrous interrogation of Liam stung before she could think of her next step. She had two expert interrogators onboard. She would leave it to them since she already knew more than the Tindalls. She needed Tania at the Morpheus. And that meant she would have to trust the Brit.

Pia noticed Rain studying her. She said, "And you met Bella Davis online? What, in Reddit forums?"

"Yeah, in the Plutocracy and Conspiracy subreddits."

"And on these forums she mentioned she knew Albert? Had conversations about the Morpheus?"

"She said her boss told her over drinks. Never said who he was, but after reading the email from Eden-Sonnet, it's gotta be him, right?"

"Maybe." She thought for a second. "By any chance, were those forums the same place you read rumors about me?"

Rain sheepishly turned to the window. "Uh. Yeah."

"Well, let's hope Davis was closer to the truth than the people posting about me. So, let's talk about how to use Bella's information. First: illegally obtained evidence is admissible in English courts only when the police and prosecutors didn't do it or sanction it. If you agree to the downside, we'll tell Benton."

"Agree to what downside?"

"Hacking is illegal. He could charge you with a crime."

"Would he do that?"

"Doubt it, but it's possible." Pia shrugged. "Want to take your chances?"

Rain looked over his shoulder at Benton. "I'll risk it."

They joined Benton and Tania. Pia alluded to the emails without explaining the details in case she had the admissibility wrong.

Benton was more circumspect about the revelation than she expected.

"I'll need to come across that information in the course of investigation," he said. "To keep everything airtight, Rain, you'll need to be questioned about your time at Eden-Sonnet's office. And you'll need a solicitor."

Seeing the concern on Rain's face, Pia said, "I'll provide counsel for him."

"We'll take the Tindalls in at the same time." Benton stroked his chin and thought. "Best be done downtown, keep everyone off their guard. Let the Tindalls sweat while they wait for representation." He smiled to himself. "They'll have a devil of a time trying to guess what Rain Meyer has on them."

"You gotta get on that right away," Tania said. She shouldered into him.

"But you're going to the Morpheus," Benton said. "I want to be there."

"They're not going to let you in," Tania said. "You don't have jurisdiction and the NCA chose to sit this one out. You go to work on the Tindalls and we'll work on the Morpheus. We'll be fine. What damage can a couple doctors do?"

CHAPTER 56

PIA RESISTED THE URGE TO speed. Which was tough because her McLaren hugged the gently rolling hills of Snake Pass in the Peak District like a race car. A carpet of green rolled out across the valley around them. The sun lit up patches of flowers when it found a break in the clouds.

"What about a truth serum?" Pia asked.

"Why would they give you a truth serum?" Tania asked.

"To find out where the victim is, so they can kill him."

"Truth serums are not whatcha call reliable. No, they gotta be working on something that works every time. They need to show up in court and say, 'We did the same for all of them. Never touched nobody. We clean as Santa Claus.'"

"You mean, Santa the serial-burglar? Yeah. You must be right about hypnosis then."

"Don't worry, I got you. Ain't nobody gonna hypnotize you on my watch. And you're not gonna go hypno-crazy and kill Liam. Now if they got hypno-something that works, maybe I'll bring Benton on down here."

"Why? I thought that was going pretty well."

"Y'know how it is with men. If everything's going fine, there must be something wrong."

"Have we heard anything from Tanner and the other guy with Liam?"

"Phones are still off."

Pia's gut twisted up again as she thought about Liam. He was like Schrodinger's cat. Until they knew either way, he was simultaneously guilty and not.

The Morpheus Institute appeared in the distance. Its white walls caught the last rays of sunshine as the clouds conspired to blot out the light.

They pulled into an eerily quiet campus, parked, and walked in. A notebook lay on the floor next to the reception stand. Only a torn page remained.

"Liam told you he was coming here," Tania said. "Is this his work?"

"Why would he tear up a reservation book?"

"Destroying evidence."

Pia called out, "Anyone home?"

They walked through the doorless halls, waving at the security cameras. No one responded. They came to the terrace overlooking the lily pond.

On his knees at the patio's edge, Edward Rohan stretched his hand to a lounge chair sticking halfway out of the water. Two pillows floated among the lilies.

"Dr. Rohan?" Pia said.

He snapped around, his face red with exertion and surprise. "Oh. Oh. Uh." He gave up on the chair and scrambled to his feet. His left hand swept his hair into place while his right extended to shake. "Ms. Sabel, so good to see you again. You bring a, um … well, an enchanting presence wherever you go."

The sleeves of his designer shirt were rolled past the elbows. His linen pants were muddy at the knees. Yet his bright blue eyes held hers with a steady gaze. Then his charming smile suddenly switched on and stretched wide.

The clouds completed their coup of the sun. Gloom closed in with a hint of deeper darkness to follow.

"Let me help," Pia said. She knelt and grabbed the chair leg.

"Oh, don't bother." Edward tried to sound casual. "It's nothing really."

Pia yanked it up and tossed it behind her. The waterlogged fabric splashed gallons of pond water onto the deck. The three of them stared at it for a moment as if it might spring to life.

"Tornado?" Pia offered.

"Unpleasant visitor," Edward said. He let out a wistful sigh. "Some people refuse to believe in Rational Light regardless of how much evidence one provides." He brushed himself off and said, "No matter. You're here and nothing could brighten a day better than your, um, presence. Yes. Well. Let's get your introduction session started, shall we?"

He looked around nervously.

"How about here?" Pia pointed to a group of undisturbed furniture near the back wall.

"Yes, indeed." He motioned to them as if it had been his idea. "Have a seat. I'll just fetch us some tea."

He shot out of the enclosed space like an impala bounding from a cheetah.

"Wonder what happened to their security," Tania said. "Ima have a look around."

Sybil entered the space and did the left-right dance with Tania until Tania put a hand on the woman's shoulder and pushed around her.

Sybil's brightly colored pantsuit flapped at the bottom where a ragged section appeared to have been ripped away. "Welcome, Pia. Your presence is always enchanting. I am in awe of how you stand unbowed regardless of the beatings you suffer—"

"Virtually the same words you said last time."

"Ah. Well, it's true." She produced an uneasy grin and held Pia's gaze. "No need to be cynical about it. Now then, have a seat and Edward will be right back. Your friend can't be roaming the halls like that. She'll have to wait—"

"Someone busted in here, chased off your security, and tossed the place. She'll roam anywhere she damn well pleases, and you'll welcome her scrutiny, Sybil, because she's going to keep you safe as well."

Sybil started to protest but quickly saw the advantage of Tania's protection. She said, "Perhaps that's for the best."

Edward returned with a tea service and set it on a small table between the chairs. He'd also found his uber-confidence in the kitchen next to the china. He smiled with an invitation to join him.

Pia blocked Sybil's exit. "Want to tell me what happened?"

Sybil and Edward Rohan put their doctorates together in wordless communication that ended with a nearly imperceptible shrug from Edward.

Sybil took a breath and faced Pia. "A disturbed man came here after hearing unfounded rumors that his name had been bandied about unfairly in our halls. We tried to convince him otherwise. He became unreasonable and turned violent. Then he left. You're right, he scared off the security people. I'll have a word with their supervisor shortly."

Pia waited in case there was more. Sybil averted her eyes, then glanced back to see if Pia believed her.

Sybil said, "If you'll excuse me, I have a few things to attend to. Edward will explain your journey in detail now."

It suddenly occurred to Pia the danger Liam was in. She tapped out a text to both Liam and Tanner. It read, "If you see Wayne Walker, do not let him touch you."

She hoped someone would turn a phone back on before anything bad happened.

Pia took her seat. Edward showed her a sealed box of chamomile mint tea from Vahdam Tea Company. The brand was the latest in conscientious firms favored by the trendy. The flavor was known as the most soothing. The ritual of displaying the sealed box meant the Rohans' other customers were as suspicious as Pia. Executives at her level lived and breathed *Stearne's Law.*

She helped herself to tea and poured water from their shared kettle. She settled into her comfy chair and Edward began his spiel.

Having been through pre-game speeches by internationally renowned coaches thousands of times, Pia showed him an attentive, fascinated face while she tuned him out. He went on about stars, fate, history, and alchemy, and she thought about the events that had led her here. Now that she had a calming tea and a monotonous male baritone to help her meditate, one big flag came up. Why did they kill Krueger? She hadn't contracted them. Had he been on Chloe's list as a victim all along? No. He'd been far too conceited on the call with her, as if he expected her to die. And he'd choked when she mentioned the Morpheus, which meant he knew them. Albert said he'd been for a session.

She tuned back into Edward's bafflegab monologue.

"Our bodies are gardens, our minds the gardeners," Edward said. "Your intellect is the most powerful device in the universe."

Yeah. Coach Guardiola used that same line in one of the World Cup halftimes. A variation on a Shakespeare verse, if she recalled correctly. She tuned him out again.

The Rohans had been ransacked and their security staff scattered by a single visitor. She knew who it was; should she confront them about it? No. She should wait until Tania figured out the Rohans' method.

Edward had a visual presentation showing on a flat screen. Graphics described sleep in excessive detail. Pseudoscience buzzwords flowed out to a hypnotic beat: slow-wave sleep, prolactin production, skeletal muscle activity, rapid eye movement, parasympathetic activity, homeostatic response, and Stage 1 NREM sleep. Accurate information as far as she knew. Then they got into the sketchy area of dark matter and Rational Light. All of it sounded reasonably scientific.

He ended the presentation and rose. His next speech was all about training the mind to separate from the body and find Rational Light. He explained how to walk in dark matter and assured her that with his guidance in the spiritual enlargement chamber, she could easily make this journey.

They both glanced across the lily pond that had gone black as the dark clouds closed in. The air smelled of rain.

He motioned to the exit, where a curved wall led to a private cove.

She disrobed and climbed onto a pre-warmed massage table. Sandalwood permeated the air. He smoothed fragrant oils over every square inch of her skin and worked them in. He was an expert masseur; that much was clear. As the massage progressed, the scent in the room changed to lavender. Edward murmured deep vowel sounds as he worked. It occurred to Pia that it was one of the best massages she'd ever had, and—at £5 million—the most expensive. But she leaned into it because, why not?

After a while, his sounds became more melodic and slightly more distinct. They were long, stretched-out words like *conquer, dominate, excelsior, pinnacle, unique, leader,* and *destiny.* The last one caught her ear and almost made her sit up to ask questions. She calmed herself and relaxed. The scent changed to frankincense.

He gave her a robe and they crossed the empty hall to the control room. Tania sat on the long desk watching over Sybil, who tried hard to not look intimidated.

Edward ushered Pia into the chamber. She showered to remove all traces of oils. Still nude, she climbed into the spiritual enlargement chamber and slid into the skin-temperature salt water. Immediately, she felt the comforting sensation of buoyant weightlessness. The top of the chamber lowered hydraulically to seal with a satisfying and reassuring whoosh of air.

The absolute darkness was oddly pacifying. There was no scent, only warm humidity. There were no sounds, no light, no feeling. The demarcation on her skin where water met air was difficult to gauge. It took a couple blinks to tell if her eyes were open or closed. She felt a warm vibration which she couldn't discern. It was something like a pulse or a wave. Was it the ominous sound of silence or Edward's resonant humming? Her heartbeat? Whatever it was echoed in her bones as if she'd reached a state of supernatural harmony. *Om.*

In spite of her reservations and skepticism, for the first time in her life, she felt peace.

After a long time, Pia remembered that she was supposed to meditate and focus on confronting her spiritual stress by traveling through dark matter. According to Edward, at some point, she would see Rational Light and follow it to where she needed to go. Recalling the monitors in the control room, it occurred to her they could read her brain activity and wouldn't release their magic—or whatever it was they did—until she'd reached a certain state. She wondered if they could monitor her brain at a distance the way they took her temperature. She had to assume that was how it worked these days.

She closed her eyes, placed her faith in Tania, and focused on taking down the mastermind of the operation.

Time became fluid, her senses melted, and the hum echoed in her bones. Her mind let go of all the body's distractions from sight, sound, taste, smell, and touch. She could see the mastermind in her head.

Masterminds. Plural, she realized. Brains and brawn, she labeled them. One she'd already identified. The other was a revelation. They were struggling for control. Who was the other man?

CHAPTER 57

SUDDENLY PIA REALIZED THE VIBRATION in her body wasn't keeping a steady beat, it intensified. Different voices were coming into her chamber, disturbing her meditation. Then she heard a distinct clank. The hollow sound of a gas cylinder banged on the hard surface of the control room desk.

Tania's voice was in the middle of saying, "… cause I unplugged your secret sauce, motherfucker. What is this? See that tank over there? That's got the yellow diamond on it says 'oxy 2' for medical-grade oxygen. This little can ain't got no stickers on it. So tell me what's in it before I get real mad like my grandma used to."

Sybil's voice said, "Please calm yourself, sister—"

"Don't pretend your ancestors clapped on beat," Tania said. "We ain't sisters."

Pia realized the hum had been Edward's voice coming from the desk mic to the tiny speakers in the chamber. He'd been humming empowering words again. Hypnosis comes in many forms.

"I can explain that," Edward said. "It's a special formula to enhance—"

"The hell it is. This is a psycho-suggestive mixture combined with a psychedelic. What is it, ketamine and LSD? Don't be shaking your head like that. I do my research. In 2015, Dr. Carhart-Harris at Imperial College in London came up with the concept that people are susceptible to suggestion under the influence of psychedelics. When I was in the MPs, we had bulletins about the Taliban using methods like this to produce more suicide bombers. Their methods could trigger spiritual or mystical experiences while the subject remained open to suggestion.

That's what you're doing here, ain't it?"

Tania smacked the table hard. Pia visualized the Rohans cringing.

"It's a special mixture of harmless—" Edward's voice.

"I asked what's in it. Don't be lying to me. I don't like that."

"You're right," Sybil said. "It's a cocktail of propanolol, scopolamine ... and dimethyltryptamine, DMT, a short-duration psychedelic. But only to enhance—"

"Yeah. I got your enhanced right here. Get her out of the damn tank."

And Pia wanted out. She pushed on the chamber's lid. Locked down tight. Total darkness. The only sound funneled to her from the control room. She was not in control of her surroundings. That made her feel vulnerable. For the first time in her life, she felt the panic of claustrophobia.

CRASH.

The sound of splintering wood, the crashing of large objects, and a scream came through the chamber's speakers.

Sybil Rohan cried, "Who are you?"

More crashing. Grunts and shouts of pain from Edward.

"Easy there, Kieran," Tania said. "Sybil, get out of my line of—"

A bang and crash. Tania started to swear but was cut off by another loud noise.

Edward shrieked, "My leg! Help! No, no, no!"

Silence. Then a gunshot. A male voice grunted in pain.

Tania: "Next one's in the head, mutha—"

Another bang followed by Sybil screaming in fear and pain. Feet pounded out of the room.

Sybil and Edward cried in pain. Tania's voice was gone.

The chamber's top began to rise. Light seeped in. It stung Pia's eyes. She glimpsed her surroundings, closed her eyes, and scrambled out. Another glimpse earned her a robe. She slipped into it and ran to the control room.

Edward lay on the floor, his leg pumping blood from a compound fracture. Sybil cradled her shattered arm with the other. The exterior door had been kicked in. Splinters covered the entry. No one else in the room.

Pia looked for her 9 mil. Her clothes were back in the spa area. With a barefoot running start, she jumped the splinters scattered in the entryway and ran for the lobby.

Rounding a curved wall at speed, she saw a figure in the dark that was too big to be Tania. She jumped on him. Sliding her forearm around his neck, she drove her knee into his kidney and rode him to the ground. She locked and tightened the headlock against his windpipe for maximum choking effect. Police had banned the hold for the many deaths it caused—and both Pia and her victim knew it.

But her adversary was no novice. He didn't fight for air. He didn't grab at her arm. Instead, he tucked his knees under and flipped them both head over heels with shocking strength.

He was not an amateur fighter. He was much better, stronger, and heavier than she. He could kill her with his bare hands if he wanted to. This time, she might have made a mistake.

Pia slammed to the floor on her back with him on top. His weight crushed her lungs. Bolts of pain shot through her chest. He used the disorientation to pull her fingers away from her already dislodged grip. As he did, he tried to twist and break her hand. Just as the pain was beginning to register, she gave up her hold and pushed off. Rolling out from underneath him, she slammed an elbow to his kidneys.

She jumped to her feet and aimed a kick at his head.

He rolled away. She barely caught herself before falling over.

To Pia's surprise, he held a cricket bat in one hand. He swung it at her head. A tactical mistake. While it's a game winner if you connect, the head is a small and mobile target. When his arm sailed over her ducked head, she launched into his swinging shoulder and struck upward, slamming her forehead into his chin. He stumbled backward. Unfortunately, it left her off balance. She spun away from him and danced three steps to find her feet.

He launched into her with his forearm heading for her nose. Reacting as fast as she could, she bent her knees. His arm grazed the side of her head, but his body weight toppled her. Her butt hit the floor hard, sending a zap of pain up her tailbone.

Rolling on her curving back, she shoved her feet into his groin and launched him sideways. He landed, rolled, and leapt to his feet. They stared at each other for a second, sizing each other up. Her robe swung open. The distraction might have saved her life.

Pain locked her spine in place. He didn't know it, but she couldn't move. Her remarkable skill was the only thing holding him back. He wasn't sure what damage she could do. She sensed he was assessing if she had a weapon behind her back.

Around a wall or two, a man's voice shouted something.

Her adversary heard the call and sprinted away. Zaps of pain in her back kept her from giving chase for a few seconds. Finally, her agony subsided.

Another pistol shot came from the lobby. Pia straightened up, toughed out her aches, and ran the corridors toward the sounds.

"Damn it," Tania said from a shooting stance. "They're gone. And they slashed your tires."

"Who?"

"Mr. Bling and his buddy."

CHAPTER 58

Examining the bullet holes in the reception stand, Derbyshire Chief Constable Sumithra Swann said, "These people still don't like you very much."

"Funny," Pia said.

The Morpheus was so rural, she'd had time to stabilize the Rohans and get dressed before the authorities arrived.

She and Sumithra watched Benton's small convoy arrive from Manchester in a steady rain. The GMP contingent parked among the county's scattered police cars already overflowing the parking area. The McLaren repair crew had just enough time to squeeze out before the cops closed the lane.

Benton bounded out of his car, followed by several constables, Rain Meyer, and both Tindalls. Three men in suits came last, holding umbrellas. The lawyers, Pia figured. PC McDonald took a shovel from the trunk of one of the cars and began digging out the front tire where it had sunk in the mud.

Tania and Benton hugged tightly as if one of them had survived a life-threatening shootout. Dame Millie and Albert focused on Pia. Rain glanced around, looking left out and nervous. The solicitors looked like they'd been on the clock for the long drive and didn't mind a bit if it went late into the night. Easy billable hours.

Sumithra introduced herself and led the way to the largest meeting area at the Morpheus: the patio overlooking the lily pond. Her people scrounged up chairs from other areas until everyone could sit.

"The Rohans chose to make no comments before being taken to casualty," Sumithra began. "We've taken the statements of Ms. Sabel and Ms. Cooper and find them supported by the evidence. They were attacked and acted out of self-defense."

Rain and Pia exchanged a quick glance in which he conceded the police might be reporting the incident correctly and not due to corruption or influence by Pia. She gave him a smile.

Sumithra continued with more details for Benton's benefit. She concluded with an appeal. "As you are the liaison to the NCA in this matter, Derbyshire would appreciate support. The perpetrators are on the loose and we have a large county to cover."

"You're looking for air and ground resources?" Benton asked, tossing a glance at the rain. "In the interest of transparency, I must warn you I've been liaison for less than forty-eight hours. I'll put in a request to Superintendent Martin for manpower to—"

"Martin?"

"You know him?"

"Enough to know we're going it alone. Alright, Derbyshire people, listen up. Let's set up a grid—"

"You don't think he'll be motivated?" Benton asked.

"The only way to motivate that bloody fool is to shoot him in the leg." She waved her people out of the area. "We'll start with the mud tracks leading east on A57."

Addressing the backs of the exiting constables, Benton said quietly, "We should wait for Martin anyway."

"Why?" Pia asked.

He craned over his shoulder. "Because this is police business—and don't start squirming your way into it again. We have to do this by the book so we can get convictions."

"Convict who?"

"This lot, for starters." Benton pointed at the Tindalls sitting on a loveseat nearby. They stared at the floor. Their solicitor stood next to them, shaking his head in warning at Benton.

"For what, willful ignorance?" Pia asked.

"For being the masterminds," Benton said. "They had Anectine, SUX and plenty of financial motive."

"Sorry," Tania said. "While Pia was walking with Walker, I did some online research. Turns out Scoline, Anectine, SUX—whatever you wanna call it—is the stuff of spy novels. It was untraceable back in the 60's but science done caught up since then. When I found that out, I asked the coroner in San Diego to run a test for it. Krueger didn't die from SUX. The injection mark was from an EpiPen. When he was dying, he thought it was from his peanut allergy. As much as I'd like to arrest them, the only charge we could make stick is 'World Class Assholes.'"

Benton turned to Pia. "Alright then, what's your theory?"

"Albert must've been scared to death when he heard about Chloe's murder. He doesn't know who did any of it, but he's had his suspicions for a while. Too many of the people he introduced had problems solved in 'twelve to twenty-four hours.' When his list ran dry, he hired Bella Davis to find leads for him. Rain found out he'd spilled his concerns to Davis over a few drinks. The mastermind heard about Davis's rants on conspiracy sites. Same places Rain Meyer heard about it. Someone with the GMP sent Chloe to check out her story. Albert should've reported his worries, but he was never sure and didn't want to know more. He never even told Millie."

Dame Millie nearly fell out of her chair with newfound gratitude for someone believing in her. Then she turned a hateful glare at her husband for bringing shame to her home.

"All true," Albert squeaked out. "What she said, it's all true."

"We're leaving then," the Tindalls' solicitor said.

"They're still facing obstruction charges," Benton said. He faced Albert. "Are you going to tell us Kieran's surname?"

The solicitor put his hand on Albert's shoulder and said, "That's our last bargaining chip with the Crown. No comment."

"You sure about these two?" Benton asked Tania.

"Albert's too stupid to mastermind this and Millie's too full of herself." Tania leaned into Dame Millie's line of sight. "Millie, a colored woman from the hood is vouching for you. Remember that."

The Tindalls stared at the floor and made no argument. Rain stroked his chin with utter amazement written on his face. He studied the Tindalls and decided she was right. Benton did the same.

Waving at the solicitor, Benton said, "Get them out of my sight."

They rose and left.

"What about Liam?" Benton asked Pia.

Pia took a deep breath. "I spoke to the detective investigating his wife's murder. She had been running around with a wealthy Iranian. He left Croatia two days before her murder. However, the Iranian's wife arrived the day of the murder. They're focusing on her."

"What about all this?" Benton waved at the building around him. "Was he involved in this operation?"

"I know who the mastermind is. It isn't Liam. Unfortunately, he turned off his phone, so I can't call him. He's running around with two of my agents desperately trying to prove his innocence. He came here half an hour before we arrived, tore up the place looking for their customer records, and left. We found the receptionist's appointment book on the floor. He didn't find anything to clear his name because the Rohans never kept any records. With what customers paid, they didn't need to. That's why they don't have computers. No trace, nothing to subpoena. If I could reach Liam, I'd let him know he's no longer a suspect."

"Why couldn't it have been him?"

"Because Wayne Walker is the killer."

A moment of silence passed while everyone thought through her conclusion.

"What about Abby?" Tania asked. "Are you glossing that one over?"

"I eliminated her financial motive a couple hours ago," Benton said. "She's been approved for a restoration grant from the government. That doesn't mean she's not involved. It only means we haven't established a motive. Same thing for Eric Stone. He sold a William Blake painting that had been in his family for two hundred years and made a pretty penny. They both have explanations for their financial affairs. But what's all this about Walker?"

Pia said, "Lots of things came together for me to figure that out. First time I met him, Walker bragged about the people he interviewed. That stuck out in my mind. Then, Eden-Sonnet asked me if I had an appointment set with Walker. When I told him I did, he said, 'Isn't that grand.' That also stuck in my mind. During the interview, I realized Chuck meant Walker would kill me and thus it was grand that his problem was solved. Benton, you said criminals become arrogant, and when he interviewed me, I realized he was extraordinarily arrogant. But then I asked him about Albert, and he said Albert had gotten him in front of society people and executives. Early on, Tania said we were looking for someone who 'flows like water through high society.' Walker was flowing across continents and executive offices like water. That's when I cut the interview short and did my research.

"When I checked his site," Pia said, "he had interviewed virtually all the victims on Chloe's list. He left it out there as if he were bragging, Breach, Yang, Vermeer, the rest. His podcast gave him access to any giant ego. Some were customers and others victims. And some, like Krueger, went full circle. What tipped his hand was his interest in how close I was to catching the killers, the fact that he wore a coat and gloves on a warm, sunny day, and he tried to touch me with a cleaning wipe. But the biggest kicker of—"

"What's wrong with a cleaning wipe?" Benton asked.

"That's how the Russians deliver Novichok. We ruled that chemical out, but he's using something just as lethal."

"But how did you know the wipe was deadly?" he asked.

"Any successful person will tell you, there's always a bit of luck involved. At the time, I was in a hurry. My impatience paid off. Later, when I researched the Wounaan peoples, I realized I'd just escaped death."

"The who?" Tania asked.

"Wait," Rain said. "What was the kicker about Walker?"

"He had a lot of listeners but doesn't have many subscribers. I knew Albert made commissions from his introductions, so I skipped that step and agreed to the interview as a favor. I should've known it was him earlier because my PR lady told me he had listeners but no subscribers. That means the employees of every CEO interviewed listened because it was their boss, but they didn't subscribe. Advertising revenue comes from subscribers, people who tune in each week. He wasn't making money."

The others exchanged confused glances.

"He lives in Mayfair," Pia offered. When they still looked confused, she added, "How does he pay Albert £10,000 to arrange an interview if no one advertises on his podcasts? They're financed by ads. If you don't have subscribers, you don't have money to pay big bucks for appointment makers like Albert."

The rain came down harder, pounding on the lily pads beyond the cover of the overhang. Everyone stared absently as they raked through their thoughts.

Rain canted his head and asked, "What's a podcast got to do with walking through your dreams to kill your enemies?"

"Nothing and everything," Tania said. Her face glowed as she began to understand how it worked. "The Morpheus is a front. Three years ago, their little sleep center was doing OK, but not raking in the cash, even at £500 each. It was too remote as a retreat and had too much competition in the big cities. Then Wayne Walker comes along and says, 'In my interviews, rich people tell me that dreaming about killing their adversaries keep them awake at night. They'd like to kill them but don't want to get caught. You Rohans put together a good story, slip them a psycho-suggestive cocktail that makes them think they did it themselves, and I'll make their dreams come true. Rich narcissists will think they've found the solution to all their problems.' And the Rohans bought into that idea right off."

"But they're doctors," Benton said. "They could make a good living in any big city. Why would they take the risk?"

"They were uncertain about their social standing," Pia said. "Look at this place. Built by a Saudi billionaire who was jailed by the Crown Prince and they got it cheap as caretakers. Only they didn't have the income for maintenance. The maintenance on a property like this is almost as expensive as the property. They had a wonderful lifestyle and a beautiful facility, all they needed was a bigger income and they would be living the life. It's an age-old motivator from spies to swindlers: prestige. They wanted the Tindalls' royal connections, remember? They were after *Dame* Millie's stature."

"What about Eden-Sonnet?" Rain asked.

"When I went there," Pia said, "I was sure he was the mastermind. But when he broke down, I realized he was just another narcissist wanting the world to worship him. When they killed him, I understood the nature of these guys. Walker, the Rohans, and Skilling are educated people. Not muscle. That's why they needed Kieran, Mr. Bling. He had access to a few former Paras who'd hit hard times and could get things done that Walker couldn't. When Eden-Sonnet met with me, I had him cold with blackmail. He was my bitch. That drove him to complain about me to Walker. Walker sent Mr. Bling to Claigeann Cottage. When they lost that fight, Eden-Sonnet whined louder, which sealed his fate. Criminals don't tolerate the weak in their midst. They had to take him out."

"From what I found in his emails," Rain said, "Lord Eden-Sonnet was their first customer. Why would they kill him?"

"I'm working on that part," Pia said. "Walker was leaving when we were arriving at Eden-Sonnet's. At the time, I thought Walker had just given the orders to eliminate all the loose ends. Yet, the next morning, he was shocked to learn Eden-Sonnet was dead. There's a power struggle going on between Walker, the mastermind, and Skilling, the financial guy."

"Why did they kill Krueger?" Tania asked. "You didn't hire them for that one."

"He never pays his bills," Pia said. "When I met with Skilling, I told him, 'Everyone knows he never pays his bills,' and Skilling looked like he'd seen a ghost. I knew then that Krueger had done what he always does—he stiffed them. He engaged them, told them he'd wire the money, and talked his way through. Albert told us he'd taken the treatment but later fell out of favor. Sybil knew about his op-ed before it was published. He'd written it thinking it would force their hand. Unlike most people he's stiffed, he knew they wouldn't sue him. Walker didn't like that."

"How did the money work?" Benton asked. He jotted notes with his old-fashioned fountain pen.

"That was the part that helped them get away with it for so long. Hiding the money in a sketchy, unregulated financial instrument obscured the whole operation. Skilling'll be the hardest one to find. We've already scoured facial recognition and passport entries and came up empty. Skilling, whatever his real name is, takes my money and places it in escrow. The only reason it's legal is because he's the only one using a merger-default swap and none of his customers are going to complain to the SEC or the British FCA. He took Eden-Sonnet's money, shuffled it around some shell companies, and siphoned off a million to Walker for his role. He then shuffled it around a few more shell companies before landing another million in an anonymous account that donated to the Morpheus."

"Bloody brilliant," Benton said. "That leaves Skilling with three million. He must be the mastermind."

"Yes and no," Pia said. "When I asked about the Rohans, Skilling told me, 'I've never met them. I've never been there. I've never spoken to them.' I believe him because he said it in a way that, if he were being recorded, it could be proved in court. Which indicates he's not the one doing the communications. They have a firewall Walker set up to avoid prosecution. His mistake was making it too solid because he had no way of knowing how much Skilling was charging. When you ask them, I'll bet Walker and the Rohans think Skilling is getting three million per customer and they're all splitting it equally."

"Now that's corrupt," Rain said.

"No honor among thieves," Pia replied.

Benton thought out loud. "Plausible deniability for each of them. Skilling says, 'I had no idea they were killing people, I'm just a financial guy who sponsors podcasts and makes charitable contributions to a sleep center.' Then the Rohans will say, 'We had no idea they were killing people; we just help them get sleep.' So where does Walker come in? What's his way out?"

"He uses a slow-moving poison that gives him time to leave town. He's delivering it through a cleaning wipe when he removes the microphone from the victim. Medical examiners test for an array of standard drugs and poisons, but this one looks like a natural cause, so they don't look too hard. Because their victims are all over the world, there is no pattern. When you bring him in, he's going to produce a brand name sanitizing wipe and you'll have nothing."

There was a long silence while everyone stared at Pia, waiting for the last answer.

She tossed her hands up and said, "I'm not sure what the drug is, but I know where he keeps it—at Abby's greenhouse."

CHAPTER 59

The rain came down with a vengeance as Pia aimed her McLaren down Eric Stone's lane. Tania called and she picked it up on Bluetooth.

"Do you have PC McDonald?" Tania asked.

"I don't have anyone," Pia said. "PC Who?"

"That constable who tried to kill me but now has seen the light. You were supposed to bring him."

"That guy? Last I saw, he was digging a car out of the mud."

"Well, then, slow down and let Jeff and me get to Abby's first. I'm security, remember? Until Sumithra finds Mr. Bling and his sidekick, I clear strange buildings before you go in."

Gritting her teeth, Pia pulled to the side and waited. Tania was right though. Sumithra and her crew had followed Mr. Bling's tracks to the east, Sonse End was west of the Morpheus, but there were at least two more Paras on the loose since Eden-Sonnet's killing.

A few seconds later, a car came up from the greenhouse and passed her. As it went by, she could just make out Bethany driving. Either it was the rain-streaked windows or Bethany had makeup streaming down her cheeks.

After what seemed an age, Benton's car appeared through the trees and came up behind her. He passed her like a turtle at full gallop. She fell in behind and followed them past Eric Stone's aging mansion. There was one light on. She thought he waved from the window, only it wasn't quite a wave. It was hard to tell in the rain. She waved back. They pulled into the parking area behind the greenhouse. She waited in her car while Tania and Benton went inside.

She listened to patter on the roof of her car until she couldn't take it any longer—about twelve seconds—and went in after them.

Abby opened the door for her. "Lotta nerve showing up here, Sabel. Haven't you done enough damage?"

"I need a shovel."

"You turned Bethany against me. She thinks I'm bloody guilty, thanks to you."

"Shovel." Pia pushed around her and checked the work area until she spotted tools. She grabbed one.

"Just cause you're rich doesn't mean you can barge in here and take my stuff. Oi! Sabel! Come back here. I'm talking to you."

Pia went back outside and crossed the gravel parking area. Wiping rain out of her eyes, she made her way to the mound of milky-brown clay. Abby caught up as she drove the shovel in deep. Pia turned over the load and dug in for another spade full.

"Did you hear me? Bethany walked out on me."

"This is the mystery dirt from Colombia, right? The shipments you keep getting that you didn't order?"

"Yeah, what of it?"

Pia dug more, sticking the shovel in, turning over dirt and staring at the pile, then repeating the action again and again.

Abby watched her. "What are you doing?"

"Trying to prove you—" Pia cranked over another chunk of dirt "—innocent."

"What the hell are you two doing out in the rain?" Tania called from inside the greenhouse door.

Pia and Abby had spent most of their lives playing in rain, snow, heat, and wind because soccer never stops. They didn't understand Tania's question. They ignored her. Pia turned over another spade.

"What are you looking for?" Abby asked.

"That." Pia pointed to a large, puffy black plastic bag the size of a couch pillow peeking from the mud. She yanked it out and headed for the greenhouse.

"Drugs?" Abby followed her.

"Not exactly."

Tania and Benton met them at the door and made way as Pia marched through.

She laid the bag on the workbench and said to Abby, "If I'm right, this is full of bugs. We'll need to contain them."

"What kind of bugs? Flying, crawling, tunneling?"

"Beetles."

Abby pulled a large sheet of plastic from a roller and pushed it under the bags.

Pia opened the outer bag, releasing a noticeable amount of air from inside. She pulled a cloth pouch from the outer wrapper and laid it on the table. Opening the inner bag as little as possible, she peeked inside, then aimed the opening for Abby to see.

"You're right, beetles," Abby said. "Funny looking ones, too."

"From Colombia," Pia said. "We need to search that section of your greenhouse with a fine-toothed comb."

Abby resealed the bags and sealed the outer bag with duct tape.

"What are we looking for?" Tania asked.

"I'm not sure, but I guarantee when you find it, you'll know it. It'll look like a Stone Age ritual in progress. Something that invokes the fear of death. Whatever you do, don't touch it."

Abby handed out flashlights and warned them not to damage the plants. She led them to the acre of Colombian rain forest. Above them, moveable glass panes were open, letting in the English rain. Below them, the Colombian mud was slick. A lightning bolt streaked across the sky. Thunder rattled the windows.

"It's not going to be ghosts, is it?" Abby asked looking up.

"Not exactly."

They started from opposite corners of the Utría section and worked their way to the center. They carefully stepped around trees and through bushes, pushing the broad leaves aside. When they were halfway in, Tania screamed.

"Think I found something," Tania called out after taking a deep breath.

They worked their way toward her, arriving at the same time. She pointed to a small, golden frog impaled on a two-foot stick. Beneath it lay a pie pan.

"Oh the poor bugger," Abby said. "Who'd do a thing like that?"

"What is it?" Benton asked.

Pia squatted and examined the scene. "That is what the predecessors of the Wounaan tribes of Pacific Colombia did to make poison darts. In captivity, the *Phyllobates terribilis*, the poison dart frog, doesn't produce poison. The theory is that they don't eat the same beetles as in the wild. Wayne Walker paid for the extra shipments of Colombian soil in which someone stashed the beetles native to the area. His 'bug man,' Mr. Bling, came in and fed the beetles to the frogs."

Benton looked at Abby. "I'm placing you under—"

"She didn't have any part of it," Pia said.

"Right here under her nose, and you think she didn't know?"

"Four acres, she's only here forty hours a week, leaving it unattended and unlocked for over a hundred hours a week. Mr. Bling had full access anytime he wanted. Plus, Abby is a prankster, and in all her thousands of pranks, none of them were dangerous. Yet she tossed this frog at me a few days ago. If she'd known they were feeding it beetles, she'd never have done such a thing."

"But it didn't poison you."

"Because the frog only excretes the poison when under stress," Pia said. "That's why they impaled it on the stick. When the ritual invokes the frog's fear of death, it produces the poison as a final act of desperation. It's an alkaloid toxin called batrachotoxin. Extremely rare. Walker diluted it, soaked wet wipes with it, then smeared it on his victim's skin. When we ask the coroners for Breach, Yang, Krueger, and Vermeer to test for it, that's what they'll find. It has a direct effect on the peripheral nervous system and kills by blocking the nerve signal transmission to the muscles—the most important of which is the heart. Boom. Heart attack. Exactly what Bella Davis died of."

Abby stared at her with her mouth hanging open. "How d'you know all that then?"

"Wikipedia."

"Right, that's going to be evidence." Benton began taking pictures. "Back away and don't touch anything. Can we close the window above to preserve everything?"

Lightning flashed as bright as daylight and seconds later thunder shook the building.

"The plants need lots of water, but I've a tarp," Abby said. She started for her work area.

She stopped a few steps away and tapped Pia's shoulder. "Thanks for believing in me, Sabel."

"You're a good woman, Abby. I never doubted you for a minute."

"You mean it?" Abby raised a brow and nudged her. "Got your eye on me, do you? Have I got a shot then?"

"You know, you're worse than any guy I've run across," Pia laughed. "Get the tarp."

"I get away with it cause I'm so cute."

Pia's expression changed suddenly. She lunged at her friend, knocking her down, and landing on top.

Abby was about to say something salacious when the shot rang out.

CHAPTER 60

BEHIND THEM TANIA OOFFED.

Pia rolled off Abby and reached for her pistol. Abby crawled under a bush and drew her knees to her chin as a second shot banged through the rain.

Pia took a quick check of Tania while trying to locate the shooter. Tania was on the ground, trying to stand. A direct hit in the body armor.

Pia tracked around a tree, eyes wide, pistol steady in front of her. The late afternoon storm combined with the rain forest canopy made it dark as night. The open windows concentrated run-off every two feet. Visibility was an arm's length with another six to eight feet every now and then. That's what saved Pia: the shooter couldn't see her any better than she could see him.

Pia assessed the situation quickly. She was up against a professional who'd already taken down her bodyguard. Tania would be up in seconds, but Pia had to take this guy out before he did any more damage. She mentally reviewed her Close Quarters Battle—CQB—training sessions where they'd attached a glass of water on the iron sights of her pistol. Bending her knees and walking heel-toe, heel-toe, she had to move from target to target without spilling any water or making any noise. Once they thought she could keep the pistol level, they repeated the training, having her fire at pop-up targets while moving from one place to another. Motion keeps you alive in CQB.

Pia heel-toed carefully around the tree to where she expected to see the shooter.

Moving leaves revealed his direction. Her adversary was heading toward Tania and Benton. Tactically, that was good. It meant Abby was safe and they would have him in a crossfire. Provided he wasn't moving branches to trap her in an ambush. He was a veteran and would do that. She followed into the brush carefully, heel-toe, heel-toe.

Lightning struck again. Followed by thunder.

In the flash she saw motion, this time to the left. He should've gone straight. He was circling her the same way she was circling him. Which left one option: reverse direction. She regretted not having entered the greenhouse with the comm link going. As soon as she felt safe, she would fish out her earbud and check the comm channel. She found a place where the branches were far enough apart that she could circle around with her pistol still in front of her.

She heard mud sucking a boot, to her left and back ten feet. He was one move ahead of her.

Pia tucked and summersaulted to the right as three bullets ripped through the leaves over her head. Her roll slammed her into a knee-high tree root. Pain ricocheted up her back. Twisting around, she popped up and aimed into the darkness. Her heart rate felt like a hummingbird's, her adrenaline-strained muscles verged on spasms.

She saw nothing.

She retrieved her earbud and mashed it in left-handed.

Tania was already on. She said, "Bout time, sister. I'm flanking those last shots, south side. Try not to shoot me."

Pia answered, "Mm-hm," as quietly as possible. She figured he would be close enough to hear her if she spoke. Then she checked her position. She was not a combat veteran like Tania, the sun was blotted out, a rainforest canopy covered her—which way was south? Visually retracing her steps from the front, she calculated her position as northwest of the shooter. Perfect.

She listened for movement. Rustling. Exactly where she estimated, just north of his last position. She moved silently, as her people had trained her. One step at a time, no slipping, no tripping on uneven terrain. She saw a silhouette for a fleeting second. It was facing to her right and moved away from her.

She slid in behind him and took hold of a sapling in her line of sight. When she yanked it back, she held her fire. He was gone. Which could only mean one thing. She jumped to her left as his bullets shredded the sapling.

Rolling on her butt, she sat up and fired at a shadow.

"See him, girlfriend," Tania said. "Keep down."

Tania fired from 90 degrees away.

"Shite," a male voice said.

The diamond flashed one sparkle in the darkness. Pia took aim, but he vanished. She rose, carefully sweeping an arc of possible hiding places. Then she heard feet pounding and branches slapping.

This time, the sudden burst of lightning made her jump. The thunder made her shiver.

Pia made it to the aisle in time to see Mr. Bling rounding the bend for the loading dock. He disappeared behind the stone building that served as Abby's office. Tania came out of the brush next to her and fired through trees at where he might have gone. They heard no howl of pain. Tania took the outside of the aisle and Pia took the near side. They cautiously approached Abby's work area and cleared it.

Benton joined them. He said, "I've called this in. Reinforcements are on their way, but we're twenty minutes from Sumithra's people. They went east on A57 and we're west on Edale Road."

Right then, Mr. Bling darted out of Abby's office, crossed the space in front of them, and bolted out the back door.

Benton took off after him. Tania grabbed at Benton. Her fingers slid off the back of his jacket. She fell and yelled, "No! Benton! Don't go—"

It was too late. The rifle crack shattered the dark as he left the building.

CHAPTER 61

"IT'S A TRICK!" TANIA WAS still yelling her warning when Benton hit the ground. She shrieked her pain and anguish into the night. Then she ran out after him.

Pia bent one knee and leaned around the door frame. She fired suppressing fire at the roof and windows of the upper floor while Tania dragged Benton back. When her last round left the pistol, she stepped out to help. Grabbing Benton's jacket, she pulled him inside just as three more shots buzzed by them.

Tania checked him over quickly. She found a neat entry wound on his right pectoral, inches from the heart. She looked at Pia, tears in her eyes, and nodded. They had to turn him over to see the exit wound. Pia grabbed a chunk of jacket and Tania counted to three. They rolled him on his side. Tania examined the damage and held up her thumb and forefinger, showing Pia the bullet had ripped out two inches of flesh on his back. Sniper rounds tumble on impact, shredding everything inside and making a larger hole on the way out. Maximum destruction. He needed medical attention quickly.

Lightning lit up the dark and thunder crashed through her bones. A shadow caught Pia's eye on her right. She aimed her pistol, despite the slide being open.

"It's me. Don't shoot." Abby poked her head around a stack of burlap.

Pia holstered her weapon. "First aid kit?"

Abby ran into her office and returned with a large tin box. It held everything needed for a horticulture accident. Pruning shears can cause serious injuries. There was plenty of gauze and tape. Nothing for massive bleeding, though. And no plasma. Because the Army gives all soldiers basic triage training, Tania would lead the effort.

Benton groaned. "Sorry. Didn't think …"

"Don't talk. Just stay with me." Tania smiled at him, then sniffled back her tears and took a long deep breath.

"I've done a course on first aid," Abby said. "Nothing like this, but I can help."

Glass shattered and shards rained down a few feet away. Then another glass panel exploded. Unable to see them through the rain and smeared glass, the sniper was firing a pattern to dislodge them.

Abby spasmed and screamed.

"Do you have any solid walls?" Pia asked Abby. "Brick or concrete?"

"The office." Abby's voice wavered so much Pia looked her over for injuries. Nothing physical.

Right behind her, the former outhouse made of stone stood silently immovable under the greenhouse glass. A stone refuge from the sniper just yards from the loading dock.

She squeezed her friend's arm and said, "It's going to be OK. We just need to keep it together."

Abby nodded while trembling. "How do you live like this?"

"Think of the alternative," Pia said. Her words didn't help as much as she hoped. She needed to address Abby's inner athlete, a cliche that connected with her lifelong training. "We have to win in our heads before we can win on the pitch."

"Yeah, right," Abby said. It took a couple seconds to register but the message came through. "OK. OK. I'm with you." Abby looked up and held Pia's gaze. She took a deep breath. "Let's get him in there."

Pia picked up Benton and carried him into the office. The desk wasn't big enough to put him on. Abby pushed some boxes and a file cabinet aside to make a space on the floor. They laid him out as flat and comfortable as possible.

Pia could only watch. She had no training and no idea what to do next.

Tania went to work. She opened a package of small sterile scissors and used them to cut away Benton's shirt. Pia pulled him forward, bending him at the waist. Tania and Abby worked quickly to place as much gauze as they could under the exit wound.

"I'm sorry, I should never …" Benton ran out of breath. "It burns."

"We need to get his feet up," Tania said. "Prevent shock. Slow it anyway."

She looked around for something.

Abby pulled the chair from the desk and rolled it up. She set his legs on it while Tania looked at the entry wound. She cut bandages and taped the gauze down. Then she applied pressure. Looking at Pia, she said, "Take his pulse."

Pia took his wrist but felt nothing. She looked at Tania.

Abby grabbed the wrist and said, "Got it. Give me sixty seconds, Sabel. Wait. I'm not feeling it. Right weak, I'm afraid."

Tania pressed fingers to his neck. Then put her ear to his chest. "Damn. This is … what's it called? Shit. He's turning blue."

"What's that mean?" Pia asked. "What do we do?"

Tania stared at his face. "Give me a minute."

Benton looked like a man in a vacuum, struggling for air. His mouth gaped open.

Pia said, "I don't think he has a minute."

"Shut up and let me think." Tania bit her knuckle. "It's not like I dress battlefield wounds every day, y'know."

Pia sat as still as possible and willed her friend to remember the procedure.

"Air got in the chest cavity. His lung's collapsing. It's putting pressure on the other one. Every breath he takes makes it worse. Tension pneumothorax, that's what it's called. And that means I need to …" Tania frowned while thinking.

When it came to her, her face changed. Her confidence returned.

"I need a pen," Tania said and snapped her fingers. She picked up the scissors and felt Benton's ribs. "A pen, damn it."

Abby handed her a Sharpie.

"Not this! A pen. Like a ball point with the ink part removed."

"These are the only sodding pens I've got. We only write on waterproof stem tags."

Tania looked expectantly at Pia. Pia hadn't used a pen in years, everything she did was phone messaging. She remembered Benton's fountain pen and rifled through his jacket pocket until she found it. She held it out.

Tania frowned at it. "No, a pen. I need a hollow tube."

"Like a tracheotomy?" Abby asked.

"Exactly."

"How about a straw?" She pulled a recyclable aluminum straw from a glass on her desk.

"Yeah, that. Clean that out and bring it here. Hold it right next to me." Tania opened the scissor to use one side as a scalpel.

Outside the office, another glass panel shattered and crashed to the greenhouse floor.

Abby recoiled and then poured alcohol from the kit over the straw.

Tania made an incision at the top of one rib. Air pushed out. She grabbed the straw from Abby and slammed it into the hole. Air whistled out of Benton's chest cavity. He inhaled like a swimmer coming up from the deep.

Tania sat back on her heels. "Whew. Here, Abby, tape this straw in place. I don't want it going in deeper, making it worse."

While Abby worked, Tania looked at Pia. In a whisper meant to shield Benton and Abby from the reality of the situation, she said, "He's got twenty, maybe thirty minutes. What do you think Mr. Bling has planned for us?"

"When his sniper has one of us down, he'll come in and mop up. He needs to destroy the evidence. The sniper will kill the first responders to keep anyone out of the area."

"True that. We gotta get that sniper."

Abby finished the bandages and positioned an ice pack on the bullet wound.

Benton's eyes were wide open. He asked, "Am I going to die?"

"If you have to ask that question," Tania said, "then yes. If you keep a positive mental attitude and trust in us, then no. Guess which attitude you better have."

"Right." He smiled weakly.

An explosion of lightning lit up their surroundings, the thunder instantly on top of them. They all flinched.

Tania checked her 9 mil and whispered to Pia. "Three left. You're empty. British cops don't carry guns. I don't suppose Abby has anything."

"I have an MP7 in the McLaren," Pia whispered. "One magazine for it and three 17-round magazines for the Glock."

Tania looked at the boss. "Tell me you've got a remote opener so I don't have to push a button inside the car. Twice the time exposed."

Pia nodded. "Remote."

Tania turned to Abby and Benton. "We're gonna step out for a minute. You take care of our boy here. Hey Benton, you with me? Just nod. That's good. You gonna be fine. Ambulance is on the way. Save your strength but stay with us."

"Step out?" Abby's voice quivered.

"Well, there's no smoking in here, right?" Tania gave her a big, bright, fake sparkling smile. "We gonna be right back, ten seconds. You got this, girl."

Tania and Pia walked out of the office.

"OK," Tania said. "Ima get the ammo and come back here."

"I'll go. I'm the faster runner."

"Sister, you got sixty-thousand people need you. Benton's the only one caring about me. Don't argue, just do what I tell you. Now, you take my 9 mil and cover me. Only three rounds left."

They both knew what that meant. The sniper would duck Pia's first two, then notice she was counting her rounds. At which point he'd make a withering comeback.

Tania edged to the door. The sniper took out another pane of glass, sending shards to the floor inches from them. Pia set up by the door frame. Tania waited. Pia peeked but saw only rain.

"The lights will blink when the hood releases. He'll see that. It's the only bag in the front compartment."

"On three then," Tania readied herself as another pane of glass blew out on the side. "Screw it, three."

Tania bolted before anyone could talk her out of it. Pia bent her knee and leaned around the jamb and fired one shot at the roof. She clicked her trunk release on the key fob. The lights blinked. She kept her eye on the roof the whole time.

The sniper put three rounds through the glass covering the McLaren's engine compartment. The alarm went off. One tire sank. He put three more into the cockpit, reasonably assuming someone was trying to drive away with the evidence.

Tania grabbed the bag and started back.

Pia had seen the sniper's muzzle flash. He was covered by the façade and set up behind a chimney. Huge field of fire for him, tiny target for her. She aimed carefully and fired.

So did he.

Tania went sprawling across the gravel just a few feet away.

CHAPTER 62

TANIA THREW THE BAG AT Pia, expecting her to pull out the rifle and shoot the sniper. That would take too long. He'd get Tania first.

Pia ran out, grabbed a fistful of Tania's jacket, and threw her into the greenhouse. Tania screamed in pain when she landed—a good sign. She'd survived.

Pia snatched the bag, then froze in place, then blasted forward again. As she expected, the sniper aimed at her run. His shot hit the dirt in front of her. Her stutter-step trick had saved her life. She was inside before his second bullet smashed a mulch bag just beyond her.

Abby was tugging Tania into the office. Pia picked her up and carried her around the corner to safety. They laid her out next to Benton.

"You don't just throw a girl ten feet," Tania complained. "I got me a bullet hole. Damn. Lemme see."

She sat up, wincing in pain as she moved. She ripped her pant leg to get a look at the wound. There was a finger-sized hole in her leg. She grabbed Pia's shirt and pulled her nose to nose. Through clenched teeth, she said, "Tourniquet and I'll be good. Just—" She breathed three times to handle the pain. "—don't go after them. They'll ambush you. Wait for the troops."

"They'll take out the first responders."

"Yeah, but more will come. Don't do it."

Lightning flashed and thunder rolled. No one noticed.

Pia and Tania stared into each other's eyes, communicating telepathically. Pia telling her how she could make it work: zig-zag to the kitchen door, run to the roof, shoot the sniper. Tania stating the opposite, expanding on the risks. And there were plenty. Pia was a world-class athlete who had started boxing at fifteen. She could hold her own in a street fight, hand-to-hand. She'd trained on operations with her security team many times. She'd been on several missions that had ended in firefights. She knew how to clear a room. But none of that made her a pro like Tania or Jacob. There would be a seasoned pro on the roof and a second seasoned pro—Mr. Bling—coming behind her. Either he'd finish off Abby and Benton, or he'd follow Pia into the building. She'd never cleared a dilapidated mansion against two heavily armed professionals. Alone.

Pia said, "Mr. Bling could finish off all four of us, and the sniper could still take out ten first responders. We aren't going to let that happen."

Tania glared at her.

Another pane of glass crashed to the greenhouse floor. Abby ducked despite the office having its own slate roof.

"Nothing you can say will stop me," Pia said. "I don't go, he's coming in here with a grenade and everything gets worse. I have to take out the sniper."

"Keep your earbud live and I'll tell you when the cavalry arrives," Tania said, shaking her head. She tightened her tourniquet. To Abby, she said, "Hand me some ibuprofen."

Abby shook out two tablets and held them out to her. Tania grabbed the pill bottle and gulped a mouthful, then chugged a bottle of water.

Abby looked on with new respect.

Pia unzipped her bag and pulled out the automatic rifle and magazines. The bag also had body armor and a fourth magazine. Better than she expected. But. No Sabel Visor to help with night vision. And no Sabel Darts, her non-lethal—and silent—weapon of choice. She donned the armor. Athleisure for women has few pockets, forcing her to tuck the extra 9 mil magazines into her waistband.

Abby stared at her with an open mouth. "You carry a machine gun and bulletproof vest in your boot? Sabel, you've got to consider changing your lifestyle."

Pia looked at Abby and jammed one of the two pistols in her concealed carry holster at the small of her back. She said, "It's an automatic rifle. There's a difference."

Abby shook her head in disbelief. With a shaky voice, she asked, "We can just hold up in here, eh? She's right, you don't need to go out there."

"That guy who was in here earlier didn't expect four of us, that's why he left. He knows his sniper took two out of commission. He's coming back to finish us off and take the evidence."

Abby looked sick. "You can stop him from here, though, right? You said it would be OK."

"Those guys intend to kill us," Pia said. "I intend to stop them. I can't guarantee who will win, but I've got to try or we're sitting ducks. I'm going to make a run to Eric's house. You're going to cover me with this rifle."

She held out the MP7. Abby's eyes went wide, her mouth fell open. Her head moved slowly from side to side.

Lightning cracked directly overhead while thunder shook the building and rattled their nerves.

"Sabel, I'm a horticulturist," Abby cried. "A botanist. A phytologist. I can't …"

"You can do this—because you're a winner." Pia squeezed her shoulder and gave her a grim stare. "You have that infinite positive mental attitude."

"I'm not a gunfighter. I can't kill people. I can't shoot a gun."

"I'm going out there. I have to cross the open space to the house. If you cover me, I have a chance at surviving the run. If you don't, I'll probably die ten yards from your door."

"Don't put this on me." Abby's eyes doubled in size. "I-I-I've never even pulled a trigger. I can't be responsible—"

"I'm the only one responsible for what I do. What I need from you will be easy. No experience required. I know you can do it because any woman who can summon the will to play international can do any damn thing she wants." Pia took a breath. "And because if you don't, he's coming in here to kill you." Pia grabbed Abby's shoulders. "Abby, this is what it feels like to be desperate."

"Jesus," Abby said slowly.

Two more glass panels blew out and slammed to the ground. Abby ducked.

When she looked up, she said, "I used to think you were the luckiest woman in the world cause you flew around in a jet and lived in a mansion. But this …" Abby bit her lip as her words trailed off. She sniffed and raised her chin. She took the rifle. "Hell, Sabel, you are the luckiest woman in the world—you've got me to cover for you. What do I do?"

Pia took her to the office door and showed her how to stand with her feet apart and bend one knee to lean around the doorjamb, presenting the smallest possible target. It was all about balance and stance. They practiced a couple times. Balance is second nature to athletes, so she picked it up quickly.

"I've set this to a three-round burst. Every time you pull the trigger, it will fire three times real fast. Don't hold it down. Pull, release. You get ten pulls, then you're out of ammo. This isn't a movie; you don't get endless refills. So, don't lose count. Got it?" She watched Abby nod. "Good. Now. It will kick you in the shoulder real hard. It will be noisy. It will be scary. Don't close your eyes and NEVER take your eyes off your target. Got it? Good. The barrel will rise. You hold it tight, like you were grabbing a player's shirt. It will still rise. It takes training to prevent that. We don't have time for training. If you have to shoot a man coming in the door, aim at his balls. The rise will hit him in the core and head. Got it? Good."

"Hey!" Tania said. "Don't be giving her the rifle. You're gonna need it."

"If she covers me with a pistol, the sniper will figure that out quick. I figure Mr. Bling is in the woods behind the compost heap. He'll walk in here if he thinks he's only up against a Glock."

Tania nodded. "Yeah. You're right. Sucks."

"Why?" Abby asked. "Why does that suck?"

"She means for me. Pistols are not terribly accurate due to the short barrel. Don't worry about that. Eric's kitchen door is about two hundred yards. Now, when I run, I'm going to do it like I'm driving against a defender, right? I'm going to juke this way, run that way, stop, and blast forward, to make him miss. When I make my first dodge, you're going to lean out, aim in the general direction of the chimney but below the roof line. Don't worry about aiming. Just get the barrel above my head. He won't know you're not an expert. He'll duck. That'll earn us both ten seconds. You count to eight, use that time to aim at the point where the roof meets the chimney, and fire another burst right there. With any luck, he'll be sticking his head around the corner. But we can't count on luck. Once you've pulled your trigger the second time, then count to four and do it again. Same routine. I don't expect you to hit him—that would take an expert. I expect you to scare him into thinking there's a pro down here and he's got to keep down. That'll give me enough time to get to the kitchen door. After the third burst, do not hang around. Three pulls, got it? No more. Then go back in the office, give the rifle to Tania."

"What if you fall or get … hurt?"

"After your third shot, you'll be down to twenty-one rounds. If I don't succeed, Tania's going to need all of those to keep Mr. Bling from killing the three of you. That means, do what I told you. Don't look at me. Don't worry about me. I'm one person—you've got to be responsible for three. Got it?"

Pia walked to the door. She scanned the woods. And the compost pile. And the Colombian dirt pile. She checked her shattered McLaren. She checked Benton's car. There was no sign of Mr. Bling. And that scared the hell out of her. She sensed Abby watching her closely. She did a mental inventory. Her back still hurt. Her ribs still hurt. Her cheek still hurt. In fact, everything hurt.

Abby was right—it was like playing France.

She gave herself one last chance to talk herself out of it. They could hide in the office until Sumithra's people showed. They had plenty of ammo for a last stand. As long as Mr. Bling didn't have grenades. Would a Para have a grenade? He was operating with handguns and automatic rifles in a country where they were banned a quarter century earlier. They'd used explosives at Claigeann Cottage. He most likely had grenades. She had to do this. She was desperate.

Only one thing gave her confidence: Abby wouldn't let her die.

She faced her friend who held the rifle in trembling fingers. "Ready?"

Abby nodded.

Pia took off running across open ground—and slipped.

CHAPTER 63

PIA'S FOOT WENT SIDEWAYS ON the soaking-wet grass. Ankle pain shot straight to her head. *Walk it off,* coaches always said—even when it was broken. There was no time to walk it off. She put a hand down, staggered, then pushed herself upright and kept running—because that's what champions do. The injuries covering her back and ribs tore at her every step. She ignored the agony and zigged and stopped and started and zagged.

The sniper put a round into the ground to her right. He was trying to predict her turns. If Chloe England couldn't predict her twists, this guy didn't stand a chance.

Lightning cracked the sky again. Abby fired her three-round burst before the thunder came. With the sound suppressor, Pia almost missed it. Chips of stone erupted from the top level. The horticulturist had done well.

Pia blasted forward and yanked her body right. The sniper's next round skimmed her left knee. She kicked up her speed another notch. Halfway.

Abby's second burst hit stone again. She hadn't raised the muzzle enough.

Pia cranked to the left, back to the right, slowed, sped up. The sniper held his fire. Either Abby's shots had him spooked or he was watching for a pattern.

Abby's third burst didn't hit stone. Which meant she'd buzzed the air next to the chimney. Perfect. The sniper would think twice before taking another shot. Maybe.

On the second floor, she saw a hunched figure in the window. She ran and stopped and looked left but turned right and ran. She was heading for the side door. The kitchen, Abby had told her. The figure on the second floor banged his forehead on the window. She looked up while running.

It was Eric, scared and pale. He was gagged. He was shaking his head.

Damn, that was the odd movement she saw on her way in. It made sense now. He had been trying to tell her Mr. Bling was in his house, one step ahead of Pia. Bling was a pro. He'd left muddy tracks leading away from Morpheus in the wrong direction, buying himself time to track the long way around to Sonse End. The only reason she beat him to the greenhouse was that he stopped to tie up Eric Stone.

A bullet shattered Eric's window. The report came from behind her. She turned left and right, planted a foot and zagged again. What was Eric trying to tell her this time? Another pistol shot came from behind her, making Eric's message clear.

She bolted for the front door, around the corner. It was an extra fifty yards on the side facing the driveway.

Mr. Bling had been hiding in the woods behind her, covering his sniper, waiting for her to reach the kitchen door. Most likely he'd locked it. That would have made her a stationary target for ten seconds. Eric just saved her life.

She rounded the corner, putting stone walls between her and Mr. Bling. She sensed him coming out of the woods to chase her down. She had to hope the front door was unlocked. Staying this close to the building gave her some protection from the sniper. He'd have to lean over the façade to get an angle on her, which would make him a target for Abby. She hoped he hadn't yet guessed Abby was an amateur who couldn't aim well.

Tania's voice came through her earbud. "Mr. Bling is going for the kitchen door."

Pia knew what that meant. She didn't have to waste time covering her back. She turned on the afterburners, sprinting for all she was worth in a straight line. It also brought up a question Pia had to ask. "How do you know?"

"I'm using Abby as a crutch. If I had a shot at that sniper, I was gonna take it. But it's no good. Can't hold steady enough."

On the far end of the house, Pia heard shooting. Mr. Bling had locked the kitchen door but didn't have the right key. He was blasting his way in.

Pia reached the front door and pushed it open carefully. She stood well back, clearing the angles before sliding in and looking around. There was no grand staircase leading up a level as she'd hoped. The home was built in the era when guests never left the ground floor. She would have to find the stairs quickly. A few rooms away, she heard Mr. Bling kick in the kitchen door with a splintering crash.

She stood in a reception hall with an unfinished floor. There was a light around a corner, giving her minimal visibility. To her right was the drawing room, the dining room on her left. Most likely a cross-building central hall lay in the middle of the structure. The stairs leading up would be on the far side of that hall. The kitchen would be down the hall to the left. Meaning, she'd have to cross in front of Mr. Bling, directly in his line of fire. Which is why he'd chosen that entry point.

Crossing that hall as fast as possible was her safest option. Maybe. If the stairs were where she expected, and the sniper had not come down to welcome her with bullets.

She was about to start running across the empty space when she heard boots pounding up a staircase. The noise came from the kitchen area. That meant there was a second staircase for servants. She bolted for the back hall, where the main family stairs should be and found them. It would be a footrace to the second floor. First one there would own the high ground.

Taking the steps two at a time, she turned the landing and jumped the last three to get in a shooting stance on the second floor. She was in a hallway that ran the length of the building. She checked left and right quickly, before refocusing on her right. That's where the servants' stairs should be. That end of the hall was completely dark. No light at all. She was standing in front of a large window. More light than she wanted came in from an outside light on the floor below.

She moved to a bedroom doorway. Using the jamb for cover, she exposed the thinnest sliver of herself possible, and surveyed the area. She listened.

Nothing but rain.

He was an expert. He would be as silent as she.

Lightning exploded across the meadow outside. It lit up two banks of windows. The ones on her side, and the ones behind him. For two heart beats, she saw his silhouette. She fired three rounds and listened, hoping to hear him gasping for air.

Nothing.

Then the thunder hit. Because of the noise, she couldn't tell if the pounding she heard was him moving through the five rooms between them or heading upstairs to the servants' floor. She would have to go through that level to get to the roof. She had to assume he now held the high ground. If she was right, she would never make it up the stairs alive.

A different sound came from the end of the hall. Muffled noise. Eric, gagged.

He'd tried to warn her earlier. She had to free him, get him to safety. Then she remembered he walked with a cane. He would never outrun the sniper.

Floorboards creaked overhead.

She had to help Eric. She ran down the hall to the last bedroom, then slowed, and heel-toed her way to the door. It stood partially open. She inched toward it. Her spine tingled. Fear hollowed her insides, making her breathing fast and shallow. The creepy feeling that Mr. Bling was sneaking up behind her made her swivel her head several times.

The servants' staircase was to her right at the end. Both an up and a down next to each other. They were both narrow. The sniper could be on his way down with Mr. Bling hiding below, waiting for her to commit to Eric's room. And cutting off her exit at the same time. A perfect trap.

CHAPTER 64

THE DOOR WAS OPEN A sliver. Light flowing from inside threatened to blind her to anyone hiding in the servant's stairwell. Approaching cautiously, she peered in without pushing the door. Only part of the right-hand side of the room was visible. A bookcase and part of a rug was all she could see. She would have to commit if she wanted to know who was in there.

She inched closer. Pushing the door slowly and clearing the space to the right, she widened her view with each step.

Her eyes checked all directions as she edged into Eric's room. It was extra-large and long, originally a library judging from the bookcases lining the walls. Three windows faced the front drive, two faced the greenhouse. Eric Stone lay on the floor, bound and gagged; an overturned chair next to him. Broken window glass surrounded him. Barefoot, he wore light, indoor clothes. The rain swept in the window, drenching him. He shivered.

Pia kept calm and slid in slowly, keeping her back pressed firmly to the wall. It was load-bearing stone, her best bet against surprises. She eased the door shut with her foot. Eric watched her. She assessed the room. His bed was in the middle, a bathroom door beyond it. From there, a sitting area. Basically, a studio apartment while he worked on renovations.

She whispered, "Anyone else in here?"

Eric shook his head.

She moved to him quickly and quietly. Pulling her tactical knife, she sliced through his bindings and brushed off the glass. She gave him a hand and pulled him to standing. A scratching noise made her spin with her 9 mil aimed at the doorway. She held steady; her pistol leveled at the dark.

Nothing.

"Thank you, love," he whispered. "There are two of them. Arrived shortly before you. One went to the roof. I heard the other one follow you up here just now. He's gone upstairs to wait for you. But there is another staircase on the other end. It will also take you to the roof. The floor on that level is torn up. He can't cross to your side, nor you to his. But he'll not know that."

More creaking overhead.

"Do you have extra shoes in here?" Pia asked in a whisper.

He looked at her funny. "A few. Why?"

"When I get to the far end, I'll whistle. You go to the stairs on this end, toss up one shoe at a time. Three should do it. When you hear those creaking floorboards coming toward you, get back in here quickly. Lock your door, go to your bathroom, lock that door, then get in the bathtub. Stay there until I come back."

He gave her another curious head tilt. "Bathtub?"

"Closest thing to bulletproofing."

He nodded, a tremble in his frame. "Indeed."

She started out of the room, clearing the hall to one side.

Headlights swept up the drive. One pair. It drove down the lane toward the green house.

The sniper's rifle banged away from the rooftop.

Pia ran to the window in time to see a car with a shattered windshield driving an evasive route. More bullets landed in its roof and blew out glass in the doors. The car stopped behind her McLaren. A figure popped out and crouched behind the front wheel. Safest place, using the engine block for cover.

"That's PC McDonald," Tania said over the comm link. "You got that sniper yet?"

"You're still out where you can see him?"

"Maybe."

"Get back in the office, put the leg up. I'll take care of the sniper."

She looked at Eric. Leaning on his cane, he had three shoes in the crook of his free arm, and a fateful look in his eye.

Waiting any longer would work to Mr. Bling's benefit. She knew the sniper was on the roof, distracted by the new arrival. That meant Mr. Bling waited for her at the top of the servant's stairs.

She crept silently down the hall toward the opposite end of the house, turning 180 degrees every few steps to check her back. The sensation that Mr. Bling's pistol was aiming at her head followed her every footfall. The staircase was right where Eric promised. She whistled before taking the stairs. Even using the sides of the treads, a few groaning boards worried her as she made her way up.

She didn't hear the shoes thud. But she thought she heard Eric's door close. It was hard to tell in the big house.

Just as she made it to the servant's floor, lightning flashed through all the windows, illuminating a hall the length of the building. For one brief instant, she saw Mr. Bling's silhouette. He was leaning forward, pistol aiming down. Presumably, waiting for her to come up the stairs on that side. The shoe trick had worked. She aimed in the dark. Before she squeezed the trigger, another lightning bolt lit up the far end. He was gone.

She rounded the bend and found the stairs to the roof across the hall. She turned the knob easily, but the door didn't budge when she pulled.

She pulled harder. Still trying to keep the noise level down. It grumbled a quarter inch.

Lightning struck again. He wasn't where she'd last seen him. Thunder shook the walls. As good a time as any. She tucked her pistol into her waistband and used both hands to yank the door open. It made a louder noise than she wanted. One that Mr. Bling would surely hear. More lightning lit her up.

That's when she saw him—swinging into a shooting stance and aiming at her.

CHAPTER 65

PIA DROPPED TO THE FLOOR, her pistol in front of her. Bullets buzzed overhead. She fired back, then rolled, and fired again, emptying her magazine. She rose and stepped into the cramped roof access stairs and swapped magazines. She leaned one eye around the jamb, looking back down the hall at Mr. Bling.

He held his fire. She couldn't hear any sound and couldn't see him without more lightning. If she took another shot in the dark and missed, her muzzle flash would give away her hiding place—and her last chance at surprising the sniper.

To keep Tania from misunderstanding her ruse, she muted her comm link before shouting, "I'm hit. I'm hit. Damn it."

She heard what she hoped for: his boots pounding down the hall. He hoped to take her out while she was down. She timed her steps on the stairs to match his running down the hall. Just as she reached the roof door, she heard him crash to the floorboards with a surprised shout.

Running through a dilapidated building in the dark. Bad idea. Whatever Eric meant by "torn up" had felled Mr. Bling for the moment. She weighed going after him to finish him off versus going for the sniper. Mr. Bling would have the advantage of hearing her coming. Which was bad for her. The sniper was seconds away from picking off a first responder. Making the sniper the greater threat. She'd deal with Mr. Bling on her way back.

She opened the door and stepped into the rain. She did her recon. The house was one huge rectangle, fifty feet by two hundred feet. The 15 degree zinc roof was hidden from the ground by a waist-high faux-balustrade façade on all sides. The roof peak ran the length of the building with hip roofs at each end. A narrow walkway ran the circumference where the roof line met the façade. The gutters and downspouts had been cleverly hidden within Sonse End's walls. Unfortunately, the poorly maintained system was hopelessly clogged. Pia was wading through knee-high water and leaves.

She sloshed through muck for ten feet before realizing it was a slow and noisy way to sneak up on someone. Tracking up the rain-slickened sheet-metal roof, she slipped and slid and scrambled to the ridge, grabbing it with both hands. Rain came down fast. Lightning flashed and thunder rolled. She lay against the surface to think. She had no traction. The only way to go would be run the two-inch wide rounded metal cap that formed the roof ridge. Speed would keep her upright. Like riding a bicycle. Maybe.

"McDonald says there's a van blocking Edale Road." Tania's voice in the comm link. "He had to go back and start over the long way."

"Shit, that means Sumithra's people are more than twenty minutes out."

"You got the sniper yet?" Tania asked. "He knocked out a cinderblock down here and he's working on another one. He's gonna bring the roof down soon."

"Get back in the office like I told you."

"And he's got McDonald zeroed in too." Tania paused. "No pressure."

"Give me a minute." Pia closed her eyes and visualized the run. If she slipped, he'd hear her hit the water. No slipping then. All the way, straight down the center, not too fast, just fast enough.

She pulled herself up to the center and straddled it. Dry, this would be easy. Wet, a nightmare.

Lightning lit up the roof. She could see the sniper. She could also see two chimneys she hadn't calculated into her run.

Headlights turned off the main road and drove toward the house. The vehicle passed the turnoff to the greenhouse and kept coming to Eric's front door. It disappeared beneath Pia's angle. The sniper did not fire at the car.

Police? Finally? No, they knew there were shots fired. They would arrive en masse with flashing lights.

Reinforcements for Mr. Bling? Where were the two Paras from Eden-Sonnet's?

Damn.

She pulled her feet under her and ran down the tightrope ridge. Reaching the first chimney, she swung around it while keeping her eye on the dark place where she'd last seen the sniper. She righted herself and pushed off the brickwork for her second leg.

The next chimney was older brick, and softer. A chunk gave way in her hand and banged down the zinc roofing. Carefully, she slipped around the edge and reassessed her position. The wind was in her face, the rain steady. A lightning rod ran up the brick to a point just over her head. She realized she was holding the copper grounding cable for support. She let go and kept one hand on the brick. Not much safer, but some.

Her adversary was a stationary shadow behind the kitchen chimney. The roof's hipped end came down to his feet. A monopod supported his rifle behind the façade. His head was canted toward her. He'd heard the brick give way.

Another flash of lightning left her exposed, standing on the razor's edge of the roof, one hand on the chimney, the other to her side for balance. She froze in place, knowing movement would draw his attention. Although that might not be a bad thing. If he saw her, she would look like a demon about to descend on him with her jacket flapping behind her like black wings.

A cricket bat lay at his feet. The same guy she'd tangled with at the Morpheus. His peripheral vision didn't find her. He turned back to his rifle scope and sighted a juicy target. Pia could tell because he breathed in, wriggled his shoulders, and exhaled before lining his eye to the scope. He was about to kill someone.

Tania still stood in the loading dock.

In her experience, the most effective attack was always a surprise attack. She planned her run and estimated three seconds to reach him. He could pull the trigger in one. She brought her pistol up and aimed with one hand while steadying herself on the chimney with the other. It would be pure luck to hit him in unarmored flesh through the rain. Balancing on the ridge, she let go of the brick and aimed with both hands at his head. She fired.

A tuft of fabric waved. She'd hit his hoodie, not his skull.

And lost her balance. She windmilled to stay upright.

He turned around, the rifle and monopod acting like an extension of his arm. He pulled the trigger.

His bullet singed her ponytail as she fell sideways and slid down fast. She smashed into the façade at full force, knocking a chunk of stone loose. Her foot went over the edge. A rush of water poured through the opening, nearly taking her with it. More chunks of stone façade fell and crashed on the terrace three stories below. At eight pounds per gallon, it was like having someone hand you an eighty-pound weight and give you a push. Her butt slid toward the opening. Her feet kicked nothing but air. The power of hundreds of gallons tried to sweep past her, pushing her toward the edge.

Slamming her Glock in her teeth, she stuck her arms out to the stonework and levered herself back. The water kept coming, half a ton of it. She threw herself into the channel to her right and grabbed a piece of stone. She stuck her foot in the broken place. Water poured over and around her.

That's when she saw the shadow coming. A big hulk of a man in the dark, his rifle raised and looking for the best target, the barrel aiming over her head. His side of the break was shorter than hers. It might've emptied. He didn't seem to be struggling as much as she. Dressed in black, against a black gutter, lying in a stream of leaves in the dark, she had an advantage. He couldn't see her.

Moving slowly to minimize her visibility, she pulled the pistol out of her mouth with her left hand and aimed. She had practiced left-handed at the shooting range and knew it wasn't her best option. She checked her aim again.

He hadn't spotted her but sensed her presence. He lowered his rifle and stepped forward, heel-toe, heel-toe. He was nearly on top of her.

With her free foot, she kicked his knee as hard as she could.

He howled in pain and twisted. Losing his balance, he spun to the stone and grabbed for something.

Pia pulled both her legs back and pounded him hard in the hip. He fell sideways, spun, and tumbled into the empty space of the broken façade. When he realized his fate, he windmilled and screamed. His shriek trailed his body to the stone surface of the North Portico.

She scrambled to her feet and looked over the edge. Falling three or four stories is rarely fatal but always traumatic. An outdoor light illuminated him. A compound leg fracture and a broken arm. A pool of blood grew near his knee.

"What happened? What was that? Pia! Speak to me." It was Tania's voice on the comm link.

"As Abby would say, I've got the sniper sorted."

Below her, a man stepped out on the North Portico and checked the injured man. A vaguely familiar form, she saw only his back. He turned to look at the place the sniper had fallen from. Pia pulled back quickly. It wasn't Mr. Bling. It wasn't a uniformed constable. Was the most recent arrival one of the missing Paras from Eden-Sonnet's? How many reinforcements did Mr. Bling have? And where was Mr. Bling? Behind her?

CHAPTER 66

PIA RAN BACK TO HER secret roof access and came quietly down to the servant's floor. She cleared the door and the hall as best she could in the dark. She made her way down the hall to where she'd last seen Mr. Bling.

A step before she fell in, a lightning bolt exposed the bad part of the hall. Near the middle were exposed joists and gaping holes that could swallow a leg. Piles of lumber, both rotted and new, were stacked on the other side. One knee-high stack of new floorboards had been scattered. Probably what saved her from Mr. Bling's charge.

Something bumped nearby. Something on the same floor with her but not in the hallway. She crouched with her back to the outside wall. She looked left and right. Trying to see in the dark. Waiting for lightning. Hoping to hear Mr. Bling give himself away. Which would be exactly what he was doing: listening for her. For all she knew, he was an arm's length from her. Tingles ran up her spine.

Desperation had driven her to win in the past. Would it work against a man trained to outwit desperation?

She reached out with her pistol to the left. Nothing. She stretched to the right. Nothing.

Rain pelted the windows. Wind rattled the trees. The house was solid. Nothing moved.

Footsteps. Below. Coming up the main staircase from the ground floor to the second. The man she'd seen outside? She replayed the brief glimpse in her mind. Who was he? Not a cop.

"Pia, PC McDonald made it to us." Tania's voice scared her enough to let out a small gasp. "He says someone's working their way through the cars in a clearing operation. They're not police."

Pia heard movement down the hall toward Eric's end. She rose to a shooting stance and aimed into the dark. She considered shooting wildly and hoping for the best. If she didn't hit anything, her muzzle flash would give away her position. That idea was high-risk.

She willed herself to see into that dark corner where there were no windows. She tried again.

Nothing.

Her back tingled. She twisted around. Nothing behind her but that creepy sensation. Mr. Bling was somewhere nearby. She could feel it.

Something dropped behind her at the far end. Pia wheeled back and fired. At the same time, she saw a string running the length of the floor. It had moved. Mr. Bling had tricked her into looking the wrong way. He was behind her. With no time to turn around, she leaned right.

A bullet buzzed her earlobe. She bent her knee, jumped to the left, and slammed into the wall as another bullet zipped by her head. Dropping, rolling, and spinning, she ended up prone on the floor. The third bullet came closer than the first two, right over her butt and between her feet. Mr. Bling was moving. She leveled her pistol and almost pulled the trigger.

Before she did, she heard someone take three big, heavy steps and body slam into the shooter. Presumably, a friendly ally. She held her fire and scrambled to her feet. A fight broke out between two men in front of her. She could see only shadows and forms. One of them had to be Mr. Bling. Who was the other?

She aimed her pistol at both of them and yelled, "Freeze!"

Neither man followed her instruction. They were in a frantic fight to the death.

The lightning bolt she'd been waiting for arrived. In the four flashes, she saw Mr. Bling up against the wall with a forearm crushing his windpipe.

The owner of that forearm—Liam Pickford.

She ran up and shoved her pistol under Mr. Bling's jaw. "Thank you, Liam."

Both men stopped struggling.

She slammed her knee into Mr. Bling's balls to pacify him while she came up with a plan. She asked, "Do you have a belt?"

"Aye," Liam said.

"Wrap it around his wrists and cinch it hard."

She leaned close to Mr. Bling's face. "Kieran, I'm going to give you a choice. First option, I blow your brains out on the wall here. There's been enough shots fired that they'll give me a pass for self-defense."

She left a long silence.

"Oh aye?" Kieran said in an accent almost identical to Liam's. "What's the other option then?"

"You cooperate and get maybe five years."

"Yer aff yer heid."

Pia tried to translate Scottish to English and thought it meant, *you're off your head.*

"Listen to her," Liam said angrily. "She's a crabbit lass who's already done for your mate. You've got two seconds, not more."

"She can't. She's with the plod."

"Wrong," Pia and Liam said in unison.

"They're not fond of her," Liam said. "But they won't ask her too many questions either."

"Pull him back from the wall," Pia said. "The blood splatter will give it away if he's too close."

"Hang on." Kieran swallowed hard. "Whatcha want to know?"

"Why are you trying to kill me? I'm the customer."

"No idea. Cobra offered £200,000 for your lot and destroy the frogs. We're to get another £200,000 for taking care of Viper."

"Who are Cobra and Viper?"

"Cobra's the stockbroker ya met in Camden Town. Viper's the guy who used to call the jobs. I reckon he ran out of luck with Cobra."

"What are their real names?"

"Didnea ask. Knowing that would be a death sentence, yeah?"

She worked out his codenames to mean Skilling was Cobra and Walker was Viper. She asked, "How many more men do you have?"

"Just the two of us. You got the others arrested in London."

"There were two more of your boys at Eden-Sonnets. Where are they?"

"Bastards. They didn't answer the call tonight, or we'd be having this conversation the other way round, with you at the end of my pistol."

Pia checked the belt around his wrists. It was tight. She backed away from Kieran, pulling Liam with her, while still holding her pistol hard against Kieran's neck.

She gave Liam a big kiss. "Thank you. You saved my life."

"Oh? Does this mean I'm not a suspect anymore?"

"Not anymore. I've been trying to call you all afternoon." She pulled back from him. "Where are Tanner and the other guy?"

"We thought the house was empty, so they went to check out the greenhouse." He grinned. "But then a man crashed to the ground. When I looked up, I saw a flash of ponytail. There's only one lass in Britain who'd be tossing men from the roof."

CHAPTER 67

LIAM DRAGGED KIERAN WHILE PIA held her pistol to his head. Mr. Bling had too many tricks up his sleeve for her to relax. The lightning had moved north and taken most of the rain with it. A fine, refreshing mist still fell. When emergency lights appeared through the surrounding hedges, she tugged Kieran's leash and stopped.

She said, "Did you guys kill Krueger because he wouldn't pay?"

He sneered at her.

"We've got you cold on enough crimes to wreck your life as it is. I'm just asking out of professional curiosity." She pushed in close to his face. "You tried to kill me three times and I won every time. I'd like to know if you were just some idiot they pulled off the street, or a professional. A pro would know things, even if they kept him in the dark. So tell me, did you guys kill Krueger because he wouldn't pay?"

"Wouldnae tell me if that was the case. Viper was right pissed at the Morpheus for letting him have a go at the machine, though."

Pia considered the timing. Viper/Walker and the Rohans couldn't have clear lines of communication or the firewall between them would be easy to crack. When the three-way system finally revealed that Krueger hadn't paid, Walker took him out.

"Why did you guys attack us at Claigeann Cottage?" she asked.

"At that plod's funeral, Viper saw them Morpheus people talking to you. Then they sent word they'd bring you in. Viper called me right after. Worked up something awful." Kieran snickered. "He thought you'd crack them before they cracked you. He didnae have time for his usual methods, so he hired us on."

Ten Derbyshire police cars arrived, and constables started piling out.

"Viper and Cobra had a falling out after your attack at the cottage."

"Aye, Cobra was not happy about that. Thought it made too much noise."

"Why did you kill Eden-Sonnet?"

Kieran said, "That's when Cobra stepped in. Thought Viper had exposed us all. Cobra expected Eden-Sonnet to go clyping to the plods—"

"Talking to the cops," Liam translated.

"—while you and your people were getting a wee bit nosy."

"Walker, aka Viper, was there, at Eden-Sonnet's place. Why?"

"Tried talking us out of it. He and Cobra were having a row about it. I do what they pay me for. And Cobra's the one with the money."

That made sense to Pia; mercenaries always went to the highest bidder. She asked, "Tindall told us you were in it from the beginning, is that right?"

"Aye." Kieran looked her over suspiciously. "When they need me."

Pia had the picture now. Albert started out making appointments for the podcast, but Walker didn't want to be connected to the Morpheus operation once he branched out. He used Kieran to draft Albert for that part of the operation, and that allowed him to keep Albert in the dark.

She asked, "I still don't understand why Skilling—I mean, Cobra—wanted to kill Viper."

"I donnae know, but I reckon he's clearing out. Getting done with loose ends. Him with all the money."

That made sense too. Pia knew that meant the last piece of this puzzle, the one guy they hadn't yet identified, was skipping town.

Chief Constable Sumithra Swann joined them.

"Heard there was another gunfight," she said. "People really don't like you much, do they?"

"Here's the man who killed Chloe England," Pia said. "I don't need his admiration."

Sumithra nodded her approval while three of her people began the process of arresting Mr. Bling.

An ambulance drove by them on the grass, going around the scattered shot-up cars. Abby had the loading dock open and they backed into it.

Pia and Liam headed for the greenhouse. She put her arm around him and squeezed. He reciprocated. She stopped and pulled him into a long kiss. It felt good to feel him close. To feel his arms encircle her. To see his smile. Those green eyes.

When they broke it off, he said, "It's a wee bit easier to kiss you when you're not holding a gun to a man's head whilst I do it. Are ye alright, then?"

He pulled back, still holding her arms, and looked her over. He tilted his head wistfully. "Aye, no bad looking, bruises and all."

She pulled him back and said, "I didn't mean to piss you off, you know."

"I shouldnae have reacted so harshly. I'm sorry. My first time being accused of murder and all."

"Yes, it's a hard thing to handle. It was necessary, though. We have to eliminate all possibilities to be certain—"

"Your man Tanner said, 'You're innocent until proven guilty but everybody's a suspect.' That's a right paranoid way to operate. I'll not say I like it."

Pia almost recited *Stearne's Law: Paranoia is the result of acute situational awareness. Everyone really is trying to kill you.* But decided against it. Liam was not in a good mood about her trust issues.

She changed the subject. She asked, "What does crabbit mean?"

"A what?" He glanced at her as they walked through the jumble of bullet-riddled cars.

"You said I was a crabbit lass."

"Oh, what I told that fella?" They stopped next to the McLaren. "Uh … well. It means a bit bad-tempered. Sorry. Just wanted him to cooperate."

"Fits her, though," Abby said as she jogged to them. "You made it, Sabel." Abby smashed into Pia and wrapped her arms around her. Tears slipped from her eyes as she looked up. "You lived through it. I was scared for you. I thought that bastard was going to get us all. But we made it! We're alive!"

"Surviving is a rush, right?" Pia said.

Abby pushed back a step. "Like winning a championship."

In that moment, they understood each other. Abby had her figured out. Out of the game and missing the adoration of screaming fans, Pia survived on danger for that self-affirming high. Not that she'd ever admit it to Dr. Harrison. Abby looked horrified and amazed at the same time. Mostly horrified.

For a moment, Pia felt like a drug addict who'd been exposed. It wasn't too far from the truth, as she thought about it. She was addicted to adrenaline. Unable to look at her friends, she swept chunks of safety glass from the McLaren's engine compartment.

"You drove that all the way up from London?" Liam asked.

"An agent drove it for her," Abby said. "She took the jet. That's how her kind do things."

"Aye, might be time for another French Revolution," Liam laughed.

Pia said, "I was going to raffle it off for the Chloe England Foundation."

"Shame for the Foundation," Liam said.

"I'll have the factory send another." Pia sighed.

"Just don't drive the new one," Abby laughed. "Everything you touch gets used for target practice."

Pia gave Abby a hug. "Thanks for keeping that sniper cowed behind the chimney. With a little training, you'd make a great agent."

"Oh no," Abby backed away with her hands up. "I'm sticking with horticulture. Until you came along, it was right boring. Boring's not so bad now that I've seen the option."

Liam nosed at three figures coming out of the greenhouse. "Who's this one? What's his role in this?"

Tanner and the guy whose name Pia never learned marched Wayne Walker toward them.

"All of it," Pia said. "He dreamed up the whole thing only to have his financial guy turn on him. Typical of capitalist corporations. No matter how things are going, there's always a palace intrigue."

"If history's any gauge, it happens a wee bit in monarchies too."

A group of constables met them. Pia held a hand up to the PCs, asking for a moment. She faced Walker and asked, "You were hiding in the bushes like a fan watching a game this whole time?" When he didn't answer, she asked, "What was it like cowering in the cold, hoping your man—who lost to me twice already—would win the title fight?"

He looked her over with disdain. "No comment."

"Pretty diabolical plan you put together. How many people did you kill?"

"No comment."

"Ever hear of Andrew Grove?"

"No."

"He wrote a book called, *Only the Paranoid Survive.* You should've paid attention, cause your finance guy turned on you. Skilling stole your money and your mercenaries. He paid Kieran £200,000 to kill you."

"No comment." He sounded petulant.

"It'll be a sign of cooperation if you give us his name. I know it isn't Skilling."

"No. Comment."

"Maybe you're under the mistaken impression he still has my £5 million. News flash: Bethany, my financial expert, traced every penny through every bank. We have all the accounts flagged. Even in Luxembourg. Even yours."

"Did you say £5 million?"

Pia nodded and took pride in watching the color drain from his face. She took only a few seconds before letting the PCs have their man.

Out of the dark came a figure with a purposeful and confident stride. He approached Pia and demanded, "Where is DI Jeff Benton?"

"Just in time, Superintendent Martin," she said. "The shooting is over. Benton is clinging to life in the back of that ambulance. For an update on the organized crime syndicate Benton took down—without your help— you're better off talking to Chief Constable Swann. She's that way."

Pia pointed. Martin looked at her suspiciously as if she were making fun of him. He looked up the hill, where the Derbyshire Police had set up an operations center with lights and a tent. He looked back at the greenhouse, its many shattered panes, and the EMTs working inside. His gaze moved to the destroyed cars, and the torn metal and glass scattered around them. He faced Pia again. "Well. Ms. Swann seems to have things well in hand."

He walked in the direction of the Derbyshire ops tent, giving it wide berth, and headed back to his car.

Inside the greenhouse, two EMTs and PC McDonald rolled a gurney out of the office with Tania on top. She whacked at one of them. "Stop, I need to talk to this lady."

She turned to Pia. "Did you get anything out of Walker?"

"Just a moment to relish the smug taste of victory. Nothing about Skilling."

"Me either. Did you—"

"Bloody hell, Cooper," Abby said. "You've got a hole in your leg. Let them take you to casualty. Don't muck about chatting all night."

Tania stared at her for a long, silent moment. Then turned to Pia. "Tell Chef to send me her recipe for popovers. Ima whip me up some and take them to Benton. He's going to be OK, they said. It'll take a while to graft new bones for his ribcage, but he's going to live."

"Did they give her some of that funny medicine?" Abby asked PC McDonald. When he shook his head, she said, "Shouldn't you be on your way then?"

"Oh, I see how it is with you, Stokes," Tania said. "This is a whites-only greenhouse. Fine, I think it stinks like dead frog in here anyway. C'mon McD, get me outta here. Now that you're one of the good guys, you can ride with me."

They pushed her into the ambulance. PC McDonald hopped in back with Benton and Tania. The techs closed the doors and drove away.

"She didn't mean it, did she?" Abby asked. "She was having me on about that racist thing, right?"

"She likes you enough to joke about it."

"Oh good," Abby said. "I mean there's some painful truth in that. The Royal U's horticulture department is all white and all female. I'm the whole department."

Bethany came running in, straight to Abby. "Are you all right? I heard on the radio. Are you hurt?"

Abby wrapped her up in a hug. "Hurt all over. But you can kiss it and make it better."

"Speaking of which." Liam pulled Pia in. "You've got a new scrape just there. Does it hurt?"

"A little."

He kissed her laceration.

"Um, there's another one right here."

CHAPTER 68

LIKE MOST GOVERNMENT OFFICES, THE hearing room at NCA's headquarters in London was efficiently depressing and drab. The sheetrock walls were adorned with nothing more than a thin coat of battleship gray. The drop-panel ceiling and the heavily tinted windows didn't help. The drone of the official hearing matched its surroundings for dullness. Pia gave her statement and answered all questions asked of her, including a few pointed ones from Superintendent Martin. She listened as Tania gave her testimony, followed by Bethany. She began to lose interest when Bedfordshire's Chief Inspector Susan Barnett testified about the death of Eden-Sonnet.

For a while she leaned against Liam, savoring his scent, and reminiscing about their last few days and nights together. They'd learned a good deal about each other. He was a great dancer. Everywhere they'd gone, she savored the jealous looks of the other women. She'd won the best catch. They continued to share plates of food without a hitch. They'd both grown up with Pussycat Dolls, Shakira, and Rihanna. She even sang *Shut Up and Drive* while pushing him into the bedroom. Which is where they'd spent most of the last few days. She'd been incredibly happy. Everything about them fit together.

Except.

Something had bothered him at breakfast, which she chalked up to concern about his testimony. He'd never been grilled by national police. After her in-depth questioning, he'd seemed edgier still. She patted his arm and told him she would step outside to enjoy the beautiful sunny day for a few moments. He would be called before long and couldn't leave. Her real purpose in leaving: she thought he'd be more relaxed about his statements if she wasn't there.

When she stepped out, Abby and Bethany were deep in conversation. A tough one from the look of it. She left them alone.

Tanner and the man she still hadn't met stood on either side of her while she sat on the cement steps to soak up some sun in her silk sundress. She thought about Chloe England and how the world would be a sadder place without her. She thought about Benton. The NCA had an offer waiting for him when he recovered. He wasn't sure if he'd take it. She thought about Tania and how she refused to use crutches after Eric Stone gave her one of his grandfather's silver-handled canes. Tania had taken to smacking the servants at the Lanesborough with it. Pia might have to confiscate it. She thought about Wayne Walker and how his arrogance had set off her paranoia alarms the first time she'd met him. Perhaps she should lean into her suspicions more often. She thought about how Abby had recommended a lifestyle change after seeing her portable armory. Maybe that was a better plan than ramping up her distrust.

She tilted her face to the sun and closed her eyes. After all, Jonelle had figured out how to turn the McKenna disaster into a hot prospect and ended up closing the deal. She ran the company better than the great Alan Sabel had. Pia could leave everything in the Major's capable hands and retire to a remote tropical island with Liam. It would not be hard to gaze into those green eyes for eternity.

Bethany walked away quickly. Abby stood silently where they'd been talking, toeing the sidewalk. She took a deep breath and exhaled slowly. After a second, she sensed Pia watching her.

Pia waved her over. "Pull up a stretch of concrete and sit with me."

Abby dropped next to Pia and wrapped one arm around Pia's shoulder, the other around her waist, and nuzzled her cheek to Pia's breast.

Abby said, "You know I'm madly in love with you, Sabel."

Pia leaned her cheek to the crown of Abby's head. "You've mentioned it a couple times."

Abby raised her cherubic face to Pia as her auburn hair fell away from her big brown eyes. "Story of my life, y'know, crushing on straight girls."

"Didn't go well with Bethany?" Pia asked.

Abby sat up straight and together they turned to study the subject of her question. Bethany stood at the corner, twenty yards away, staring at her Uber app.

"She's conflicted." Abby sighed.

"I thought she broke up with you back at the greenhouse and came back only out of concern."

"Couldn't stay away, that one." Abby looked at the sun. "Today, she felt like everyone was looking at us funny in the hearing. For someone like her, someone like me is an attraction she doesn't want to be attracted to. Afraid to be ..."

Abby drew a slow, thoughtful breath. For a moment, Pia thought her friend was fighting back a tear. Abby looked away from her and wiped her eyes on her shoulder. She sniffled a couple times, took another deeper, confident breath, and smiled until her cheerfulness returned. She said, "Not everyone's cut out to be gay. It's not as easy as I make it look."

"Her loss."

Abby looked up as Liam stepped outside. He took a seat on the other side of Pia. Abby squirmed nervously until Pia touched her hand—stay.

Liam gave off nervous energy. She had thought he was wound up about his deposition; now she wasn't so sure. A sense of foreboding overcame her. She slid her hand in his and gave a reassuring squeeze. He didn't squeeze back.

"I've given it a good deal of thought," he began. He paused too long. "I meant what I said when we first met. I felt our meeting was destiny. You felt it too. The more I got to know you, the stronger I felt that connection. I thought you felt it too. Then I learned about your violent side. It doesn't bother me in the least, dating a lass who carries a gun and gets into a fight now and again. I worry about you, I cannae deny that. I don't mind worrying a wee bit more. But the thing I cannae get over—"

Pia's heart stopped beating.

He turned his face skyward while choosing his words.

He met her gaze again. "—that you didnae trust me."

A thousand things to say flooded into her head. All of them true and reasonable. But all of them sounded weak and clingy. She refused to let any of them out of her mouth.

He let go of her hand and rose. With deep remorse in his eyes, he waited a moment for her to say something.

Those thousand things to say screamed in her head. But she was frozen. Nothing could open her mouth. The Pia who never hesitated to kick a man off a roof couldn't say a word to save her relationship. Abby thought she was brave? Not where love was concerned. Her body refused to move. Her heart refused to beat.

"Lang may yer lum reek," he said.

An old Scottish saying that she knew meant, *long may your chimney smoke*, or, may you live long and prosper. Her heart still wouldn't beat.

Liam gave her a melancholy nod, turned and walked away. He pulled his phone to order an Uber.

"Losing's so hard for you, you can't summon the humility to beg?" Abby asked.

Pia sensed the truth in that assessment. She thought she'd won him. She took it for granted and glossed everything over. Now she was losing him and found herself paralyzed.

"He wants you to chase him down and apologize," Abby said. "Is he worth it?"

Pia heard the word *yes* escape her lips in a whisper.

"Don't make me say it out loud. I'm not going to tell you to go after him and beg his forgiveness. Because you know that's what you need to do."

Something strange occurred to Pia. She looked at Abby. "Who are you talking to, you or me?"

Abby looked shocked, then turned to see Bethany standing on the corner, still waiting for her cab.

Abby turned back to her and sighed. "Shite, Sabel, you're right. But I'm scared. What if I beg and it doesn't work?"

"We can do this, Stokes," Pia said. "We're world class athletes. We don't give up. We play hard. We win. And we're desperate."

Abby smiled. "Betcha I can win mine back before you win yours."

They both bolted off the steps. In unison they called out to their respective lovers, "Wait!"

CHAPTER 69

PIA SAT ON THE EDGE of the bed with a pistol in one hand and a handful of passports in the other. The W Barcelona had a terrific view of the beach. But she wasn't looking at it. She was flipping through the passports one-handed. Which was awkward, but she managed.

The man at the other end of the Glock blinked awake. Twisting in the sheets, he became aware something was wrong. His eyes crossed when he discovered the barrel. He gasped in shock and horror and refocused on the woman at the other end.

"Hakan Tosun. Is that a real name?" she asked as she waved a Turkish passport at him. "Do you even speak Turkish?"

"A bit. Who are you?" He tried to sit up, but she pushed the pistol into his nose.

"You don't remember me?" She fake-smiled before going to the next passport. "David Janko, another British passport. That makes three so far."

"Pia Sabel?" the man asked.

"Oh good. I would've been hurt if I was just another face in the crowd." She flipped through another one. "Antoine Legget. Sounds French but it's your fourth British passport. Does he look French to you, Liam?"

She glanced over her shoulder. Liam held a phone in camera mode as he leaned against the window.

"Not at all," he said. "I do wish you'd not wave that gun about. You don't want another accident like those other fellas."

The man in the bed swallowed hard.

She nudged his face with the muzzle. "Don't worry. One of them survived."

Liam coughed and said, "You've got a text from Abby Stokes, says, 'Admit it, Sabel, I won—and you know it.' What's that about?"

Pia felt herself blush. "Just text back, 'It was a tie.'"

"What are you two competing about this time, and why do I have a feeling I'm involved?"

"Let it go. Remember, you're livestreaming." She turned back to her victim.

"What d'you want?" the man in the bed asked. His voice trembled.

"She wants her bloody £20 million since I'm quite well and alive," Liam said.

The man's eyes swiveled back and forth between them three times before he figured it out. He was still sleepy, she guessed. He said, "You're Liam Pickford."

"Say, you're pretty good at this." Pia patted his cheek with the barrel. "Since you didn't kill him, I bought his company and had to pay full price. I even hired him on for the transition. He's my Executive VP— with benefits."

The man looked sick.

"What's your real name?" Pia asked. She held up a passport. "I'm guessing it's this one: Tyler Morrell, Cardiff. Am I right?"

He nodded and blinked. "I'll get your money to you."

"Too late," she said. "I already took it. Along with all the rest in that account. See, the problem with you super-genius bean counters is you're lousy with security. Your keychain has the passwords to all the sites you visit because—like an idiot—you clicked 'remember me' on your browser for convenience. And that gave me access to sixteen bank accounts in seven countries."

He sat up quickly and shouted, "Bollocks! You're not allowed to transfer—"

"Oh, I didn't. You did. Facial recognition and everything. See, your phone and laptop doesn't care if you're awake." She tapped the pistol to his nose. Then tossed her head in the direction of several Cava bottles lying on the floor. "Did you get a good night's sleep?"

His eyes scanned the room more intently this time.

"We sent the hookers home," she said.

"Where's my money?" Tyler Morrell asked.

"In a victim's fund."

"Victim's what?"

"The rightful heirs of David Breach, Martin Vermeer, and all the others, even Krueger's wretched offspring, were thrilled to hear you'd decided to donate all your remaining profits as restitution. And the prosecutors around the world also liked the idea. But they said if you were looking for a plea bargain, it would be best to start talking, because Wayne Walker says the whole thing was all you."

"Bloody hell." Tyler Morrell licked his dry lips and wiped his face with his hand. He glanced at Liam. "What's he doing?"

"Livestreaming your confession. Say hello to the authorities from Hong Kong, New York, Vancouver, and so on. Leading the charge from his hospital room is Superintendent Jeff Benton, now with the NCA. Say hello to Mr. Benton, Tyler."

"How d'you find me?"

"I said, say hello to Mr. Benton, Tyler."

Tyler faced Liam's phone and waved weakly. "Hello, Mr. Benton." Back to Pia, he asked, "How d'you find me?"

"You can thank Bethany Palanski and Rain Meyer for that. Rain gave up his moral crusade for twenty-four *steady* paychecks a year from Sabel Capital. You know how it is. Everyone sells out to corporate corruption eventually. Anyway, it was their painstaking and detailed sleuthing that led us to your door. That and your sudden profligate spending from the main account. Once you paid Kieran to bump off Wayne Walker, you thought you were free and clear. With all these passports, I'd say you were close. Real close. You know where you went wrong?"

"No."

"You put me on the list." She smiled. "And you play *Galactic Multiplayer Dodgeball* on your phone. It's produced by Sabel Gaming."

Tyler Morrell fell back in bed and pulled the covers up.

"Don't be shy. The Guàrdia Urbana are coming up. You'll want to get dressed before they haul your ass to prison."

Pia stood and offered Morrell a hand. He refused it and trudged to the toilet. Liam followed him. He tried to close the door behind him.

"Oh aye?" Liam said and pushed the door open. "Can't have that now. You're on suicide watch."

Pia let the police in when they urgently pounded on the door. She showed them to the perpetrator and tugged Liam out of the way.

They went to the balcony and admired the view. Below them, an arc of golden sand stretched from the hotel to downtown Barcelona. Sailboats bobbed on the Mediterranean in the bright warm sun.

Liam leaned against the sliding glass door and stared at her.

"What?" she asked. "Is it my height? Am I too tall? Tell me the truth."

"A lass should be tall enough to hold her head up," he said grinning. "You seem to be doing alright in that regard. Besides, if you're too tall, where would that leave me?"

He moved in and swirled his arms around her waist.

She reciprocated, getting lost in his green eyes. They swayed with the warm breeze.

"Sorry," she said. "It's just … I get insecure once in a while."

"I'm sure Mr. Bling would disagree."

"Well." She turned around to face the sea. His arms kept her close. "Who cares what he thinks? That's not where my insecurities lie. It's people like … well, my employees, for example. I'm ten years younger than the company's average age. What do they think of me doing a high-wire act on a rainy roof in the Peak District instead of doing something sensible, like buying McDowell Aerospace?"

"You forget, Pia. I was by your side when you first walked back into Sabel Towers. The lobby was flooded with your people. They were calling your name, popping champagne, and throwing confetti. Aye, they were well pleased. And what did I get for my homecoming? A weegie nod from the blootered lot of them. And I saved their bloody jobs!"

"A what?" She laughed and enjoyed his cheek pressed against the side of her head.

"Weegie, Glaswegian. They were drunk."

"Oh."

"Still, I can't shake the feeling that some people think I don't belong."

"Who?" he asked.

"Well, Charles Williams for one. He's nice enough in person. And I realize he has a lot going—"

"The President of the United States?" Liam let go and stepped back. "I donnae know any of Scotland's MPs when we've no more population than Tennessee. And you're humble-bragging about what presidents think of you?"

She leaned into him, longing to feel his embrace again. He didn't disappoint. They stood still and gently rocked.

Then he pulled back and looked into her gray-green eyes. "Is this the paranoid social cognition problem you were telling me your Dr. Harrison was on about?"

"Fuck him," she said. "I don't care what anybody thinks."

The breeze curled around them like a warm winter blanket. Inside, the Spanish police were mopping up. Someone knocked on the glass and motioned it was time to go.

"You know, this is not a bad hotel," Pia said. "Jacob stayed at a suite on the twentieth floor here and said it was the finest place he'd ever seen."

"Jacob?" He stepped back again, focusing on her eyes.

"My bodyguard and good friend. Not a rival, so chill."

"Have I met Jacob?"

"Well, he's in the hospital at the mo—"

"Do you know anyone who's not in hospital?"

She put a couple fingers through his beltloops and pulled him to her. "You."

THANK YOU!

Thank you for choosing my book. I hope you enjoyed reading it as much as I enjoyed writing it. As an independent writer, I am dependent on word-of-mouth referrals and book reviews. If you liked this book, please tell everyone, and leave reviews all over the place. I will be eternally grateful.

When you do write a review, send me a link to it and I'll put you in the next drawing for an autographed book. I run at least three or four drawings a year.

If you can't get enough of Pia, Tania, Miguel and Jacob*, checkout the series at SeeleyJames.com/books. While you're there, join my newsletter to get discounts, drawings, fun, news, outtakes, and more about the Sabel Agents club on Facebook! Every week (or so, sometimes I'm lazy), I'll let you know about the book in progress, personal triumphs & tragedies, what I'm reading and other fun stuff. I even had one person write to me to say, "I don't like your books, but I love your newsletters." To which I replied, "Thanks, Mom." Yeah … whatcha gonna do?

I'd love to hear from you. Please write, message me on Facebook, let me know what you think.

*I like you already.

NOW THAT YOU'VE READ THIS BOOK, WHICH ONE SHOULD YOU READ NEXT?
HTTPS://SEELEYJAMES.COM/BOOKS

TRUTH IN FICTION

From time to time, I get emails inquiring about the validity of certain premises in the book. The nicer ones ask things like "are you making this up?" There are a few others who simply ask, "What's wrong with you?" To address the former and other commonly asked questions:

1) **Does it really take X hours to travel from A to B?** Yes! Probably. There is an actual timeline involved when I write books. I painstakingly chart each chapter on a spreadsheet and enter times and dates, including travel times. Why? Because I once read a book by a famous author who had a helicopter fly 2,000 miles across Central Asia in two hours. If you're wondering what's wrong with that, it's 10x faster and 10x farther than a chopper can fly. I didn't want to make that mistake myself (not that anyone bothered to call the famous author on it), so I've kept track ever since.

2) **Can a suicide plant really kill you?** Yes! And no. If someone were to bludgeon you to death with it, yes. But its poison is not as deadly as I let on in the book. I hate giving good ideas to bad people, so I intentionally mislead certain aspects. However, the poison frog is indeed deadly. In that case, a good deal of knowledge on how to harvest the poison (without dying) was lost to eternity by the Spanish Conquistadors, so there's little chance of that going wrong. (But if I should die mysteriously, you can rest assured that my wife figured it out.)

3) **Are these places real**? Yes! Some are, some have fictional additions, and others should be. Before I start writing, I look up candidate sites and pick a few. As I write, the place I picked may be lacking a patio or a third floor (or a second roof-access door). I take the liberty of adding those as needed. Real places are used fictitiously, but, because they exist and you might go there one day, I try to keep them accurately portrayed. The Lanesborough Hotel really is ridiculously, French-Revolution-Inspiringly opulent …

although, if they wanted to spot me a week in the Royal Suite, I wouldn't turn them down.

4) **Have you been to these places**? Yes! In my dreams, mostly. I've always wanted to visit the Peak District, but never got there on my UK itineraries, so the second-best option is to write about it. Same for many places in my books. Others, such as the Mayan ruins of the Yucatan, I've visited and researched extensively. Of my friends who own private jets I constantly ask things like, "Wouldn't you love to help me research hiding places in the sewer systems of Brest, Belarus?" So far, no love.

5) **Can you prove any of this? Like Psychotherapeutic Suggestibility?** Yes! Maybe. Terrorists have used psychedelics to help radicalize suicide bombers for years. Psychologists have been working on these dark matters for decades (the CIA *claims* they stopped). I also contact experts in many topics. In this book, Tania executed a tension pneumothorax operation thanks to the brilliant tutelage of Dr. Louis Kirby. In a previous book, the functions and limitations of LIDAR were kicked around by several professors at the University of San Diego (where they have a massive system for visualizing such things).

For more information, **including links** to some of the research (I often forget to collect some stuff in my OneNote files) visit my blog post replicating this page. There you will find a link to my OneNote research where you'll see everything but the timeline (which would be a spoiler).

Thanks for listening, you're now my favorite reader!

ACKNOWLEDGMENTS

My heartfelt thanks to the people who, without hesitation or concern for bodily injury, gave their time and attention to make *THE MORPHEUS DECISION* the greatest book ever written by a human. (That's my opinion, deal with it.) Without the insightful contributions of these few selfless, hardworking writers, the story would teeter on the verge of putting you to sleep better than the Morpheus Institute. I am forever in debt to these brave souls:

- **Extraordinary Editor and Idea man:** Lance Charnes, author of the highly acclaimed *Doha 12, SOUTH,* not to mention the DeWitt Agency series: *THE COLLLECTION, STEALING GHOSTS, CHASING CLAY* and, if you like ass-kicking heroines: *ZRADA.* I highly recommend his exciting novels, visit http://wombatgroup.com
- **Medical Advisor and Character Diviner:** Dr. Louis Kirby, famed neurologist and author of *SHADOW OF EDEN.* http://louiskirby.com Without his help ratcheting up the tension, the ending would've been a snooze fest and saving Benton would've gone horribly wrong.
- **Scene and Character Advisor:** Shannon Humphrey, social justice and science fiction author of *SKIN TRIALS* and *BLOOD REPUBLIC* series. Without Shannon's excellent ideas, Tania would've been a cardboard character. Thanks to her, several scenes are now more visceral and insightful. Visit her site at https://www.shannonhumphrey.com/
- **Amazing Editor:** Mary Maddox, horror and dark fantasy novelist, and author of the *DAEMON WORLD* series and the fantastic thrillers: *DARK ROOM* and *HOMETOWN BOYS.* http://marymaddox.com
- **Story Editor:** Chris Montooth, junior at USC's Marshall School of Business, is responsible for helping develop the Liam Pickford character arc, transforming him from a simple love-interest to a

conflicted mirror of Pia's personal problems. Excellent work from a young man with a bright future.

And my additional thanks to the beta readers who aided and abetted my endeavors. No amount of proofreading, professional or amateur, can match their diligence in finding the niggling little malapropisms, mondegreens, spoonerisms, homophones, and other typos: Rick Tara, Michael Davis, Marigene Maki, Fritzi Redgrave, Lovelace Cook, and Serena Montague. But don't blame them for my bad grammar. It's intentionally bad. (That's the story I'm telling this year.)

A special thanks to my wife whose support, despite being a tad reluctant, has gone above and beyond the call of duty. Last but not least, my children, Nicole, Amelia, and Christopher, ranging from age twenty-one to forty-eight, who have kept my imagination fresh and full of ideas.

ABOUT THE AUTHOR

His near-death experiences range from talking a jealous husband into putting the gun down to spinning out on an icy freeway in heavy traffic without touching anything. His resume ranges from washing dishes to global technology management. His personal life stretches from homeless at 17, adopting a 3-year-old at 19, getting married at 37, fathering his last child at 43, hiking the Grand Canyon Rim-to-Rim several times a year, and taking the occasional nap.

His writing career ranges from humble beginnings with short stories in The Battered Suitcase, to being awarded a Medallion from the Book Readers Appreciation Group. Seeley is best known for his Sabel Security series of thrillers featuring athlete and heiress Pia Sabel and her bodyguard, unhinged veteran Jacob Stearne. One of them kicks ass and the other talks to the wrong god.

His love of creativity began at an early age, growing up at Frank Lloyd Wright's School of Architecture in Arizona and Wisconsin. He carried his imagination first into a successful career in sales and marketing, and then to his real love: fiction.

For more books featuring Pia Sabel and Jacob Stearne, visit: SeeleyJames.com.

www.ingramcontent.com/pod-product-compliance
Lightning Source LLC
Chambersburg PA
CBHW030829110726
47900CB00006B/1802